PARTIALS

DAN WELLS

HarperCollins *Children's Books*

First published in hardback in the USA by HarperCollins*Publishers* Inc in 2012
First published in Great Britain by HarperCollins *Children's Books* in 2012
HarperCollins *Children's Books* is a division of HarperCollins*Publishers* Ltd,
77-85 Fulham Palace Road, Hammersmith, London, W6 8JB.

The HarperCollins website address is: www.harpercollins.co.uk

1

ISBN 978-0-00-746522-4

Dan Wells asserts the moral right to be identified as the author of the work.

Printed and bound in England by Clays Ltd, St Ives plc

Wells, Dan, 1977 –

Partials

YA

1943096

This book is dedicated to the rule breakers,

the troublemakers, and the revolutionaries.

Sometimes the hand that feeds you needs a good bite.

PART 1

CHAPTER ONE

Newborn #485GA18M died on June 30, 2076, at 6:07 in the morning. She was three days old. The average lifespan of a human child, in the time since the Break, was fifty-six hours.

They didn't even name them anymore.

Kira Walker looked on helplessly while Dr. Skousen examined the tiny body. The nurses—half of them pregnant as well—recorded the details of its life and death, faceless in bodysuits and gas masks. The mother wailed despondently from the hallway, muffled by the glass. Ariel McAdams, barely eighteen years old. The mother of a corpse.

"Core temperature ninety-nine degrees at birth," said a nurse, scrolling through the thermometer readout. Her voice was tinny through the mask; Kira didn't know her name. Another nurse carefully transcribed the numbers on a sheet of yellow paper. "Ninety-eight degrees at two days," the nurse continued. "Ninety-nine at four o'clock this morning. One-oh-nine point five at time of death." They moved softly through the room, pale green shadows in a land of the dead.

"Just let me hold her," cried Ariel. Her voice cracked and broke. "Just let me hold her."

The nurses ignored her. This was the third birth this week, and the third death; it was more important to record the death, to learn from it—to prevent, if not the next one, then the one after that, or the hundredth, or the thousandth. To find a way, somehow, to help a human child survive.

"Heart rate?" asked another nurse.

I can't do this anymore, thought Kira. *I'm here to be a nurse, not an undertaker—*

"Heart rate?" asked the nurse again, her voice insistent. It was Nurse Hardy, the head of maternity.

Kira snapped back to attention; monitoring the heart was her job. "Heart rate steady until four this morning, spiking from 107 to 133 beats per minute. Heart rate at five o'clock was 149. Heart rate at six was 154. Heart rate at six-oh-six was . . . 72."

Ariel wailed again.

"My figures confirm," said another nurse. Nurse Hardy wrote the numbers down but scowled at Kira.

"You need to stay focused," she said gruffly. "There are a lot of medical interns who would give their right eye for your spot here."

Kira nodded. "Yes, ma'am."

In the center of the room Dr. Skousen stood, handed the dead infant to a nurse, and pulled off his gas mask. His eyes looked as dead as the child. "I think that's all we can learn for now. Get this cleaned up, and prepare full blood work." He walked out, and all around Kira the nurses continued their flurry of action, wrapping the baby for burial, scrubbing down the equipment, sopping up the blood. The mother cried, forgotten and alone—Ariel had been inseminated artificially, and there was no husband or boyfriend to comfort her. Kira obediently gathered the records for storage and analysis, but she couldn't stop looking at the sobbing girl beyond the glass.

"Keep your head in the game, intern," said Nurse Hardy. She pulled off her mask as well, her hair plastered with sweat to her forehead. Kira looked at her mutely. Nurse Hardy stared back, then raised her eyebrow. "What does the spike in temperature tell us?"

"That the virus tipped over the saturation point," said Kira, reciting from memory. "It replicated itself enough to overwhelm her respiratory system, and the heart started overreaching to try to compensate."

Nurse Hardy nodded, and Kira noticed for the first time that her eyes were raw and bloodshot. "One of these days the researchers will find a pattern in this data and use it to synthesize a cure. The only way they're going to do that is if we . . . ?" She paused, waiting, and Kira filled in the rest.

"Track the course of the disease through every child the best we can, and learn from our mistakes."

"Finding a cure is going to depend on the data in your hands." Nurse Hardy pointed at Kira's papers. "Fail to record it, and this child died for nothing."

Kira nodded again, numbly straightening the papers in her manila folder.

The head nurse turned away, but Kira tapped her on the shoulder; when she turned back, Kira didn't dare to look her in the eye. "Excuse me, ma'am, but if the doctor's done with the body, could Ariel hold it? Just for a minute?"

Nurse Hardy sighed, weariness cracking through her grim, professional facade. "Look, Kira," she said. "I know how quickly you breezed through the training program. You clearly have an aptitude for virology and RM analysis, but technical skills are only half the job. You need to be ready, emotionally, or the maternity ward will eat you alive. You've been with us for three weeks—this is your tenth dead child. It's my nine hundred eighty-second." She paused, her silence dragging on longer than Kira expected. "You've just got to learn to move on."

Kira looked toward Ariel, crying and beating on the thick glass window. "I know you've lost a lot of them, ma'am." Kira swallowed. "But this is Ariel's first."

Nurse Hardy stared at Kira for a long time, a distant shadow in her eyes. Finally she turned. "Sandy?"

Another young nurse, who was carrying the tiny body to the door, looked up.

"Unwrap the baby," said Nurse Hardy. "Her mother is going to hold her."

Kira finished her paperwork about an hour later, just in time for the town hall meeting with the Senate. Marcus met her in the lobby with a kiss, and she tried to put the long night's tension behind her. Marcus smiled, and she smiled back weakly. Life was always easier with him around.

They left the hospital, and Kira blinked at the sudden burst of natural sunlight on her exhausted eyes. The hospital was like a bastion of technology in the center of the city, so different from the ruined houses and overgrown streets it may as well have been a spaceship. The worst of the mess had been cleaned up, of course, but the signs of the Break were still everywhere, even eleven years later: abandoned cars had become stands for fish and vegetables; front lawns had become gardens and chicken runs. A world that had been so civilized—the old world, the world from before the Break—was now a borrowed ruin for a culture one step up from the Stone Age. The solar panels that powered the hospital were a luxury most of East Meadow could only dream of.

Kira kicked a rock in the road. "I don't think I can do this anymore."

"You want a rickshaw?" asked Marcus. "The coliseum's not that far."

"I don't mean walk," said Kira, "I mean this—the hospital, the infants. My life." She remembered the eyes of the nurses, pale and bloodshot and tired—so very tired. "Do you know how many babies I've watched die?" she asked softly. "Personally watched, right there, right in front of me."

Marcus took her hand. "It's not your fault."

"Does it matter whose fault it is?" asked Kira. "They're just as dead."

"No one has saved a child since the Break," said Marcus, "no one. You're a three-week intern in there. You can't beat yourself up for not doing something even the doctors and researchers haven't been able to do."

Kira stopped, staring at him; he couldn't be serious. "Are you trying to make me feel better?" she asked. "Because telling me it's impossible to save a baby's life is a really stupid way of doing it."

"You know that's not what I mean," said Marcus. "I'm just saying it's not you, personally. RM killed those children, not Kira Walker."

Kira glanced out across the widening turnpike. "That's one way of looking at it."

The crowd was getting heavier now as they approached the coliseum; they might even fill it, which they hadn't done in months. Not since the Senate passed the latest amendment to the Hope Act, dropping the pregnancy age to eighteen. Kira felt a sudden knot in her stomach and grimaced. "What do you think the 'emergency meeting' is about?"

"Knowing the Senate, something boring. We'll get a seat by the door so we can slip out if Kessler goes off on another tirade."

"You don't think it'll be important?" asked Kira.

"It will at least be self-important," said Marcus. "You can always rely on the Senate for that." He smiled at her, saw how serious she was, and frowned. "If I had to guess, I'd say they're going to talk about the Voice. The word in the lab this morning was that they attacked another farm this week."

Kira looked at the sidewalk, studiously avoiding his eyes. "You don't think they're going to lower the pregnancy age again?"

"So soon?" asked Marcus. "It hasn't even been nine months yet—I don't think they'd drop it again before the eighteen-year-olds even come to term."

"They would," Kira said, still looking down. "They would, because the Hope Act is the only way they know how to deal with the problem. They think if we have enough babies, one of them's bound to be resistant, but it isn't working, and it hasn't worked for eleven years, and getting a bunch of teenagers pregnant is not going to change that." She let go of Marcus's hand. "It's the same thing in the hospital: They take care of the moms, they keep everything sterile, they record all the data, and the infants are still dying. We know exactly how they're dying—we know so much about how they're dying it makes me sick just to think about it—but we know absolutely nothing about how to save them. We get a bunch of new girls pregnant, and all we're going to have are more dead babies and more notebooks full of the same exact statistics for how those babies died." She felt her face grow hot, tears coming behind her eyes. Some of the other people were looking at her as they passed on the road; many of the women were pregnant, and Kira was certain some of them had heard her. She swallowed and hugged herself tightly, angry and embarrassed.

Marcus stepped closer and put his arm around her shoulder. "You're right," he whispered. "You're absolutely right."

She leaned into him. "Thank you."

Someone shouted through the crowd. "Kira!"

Kira looked up, wiping her eyes with the back of her hand. Madison was weaving through the press of people, waving excitedly. Kira couldn't help but smile. Madison was a couple years older, but they'd grown up together, practically sisters in the makeshift family they'd formed after the Break. She raised one hand and waved back.

"Mads!"

Madison reached them and hugged Kira excitedly. Her new husband, Haru, followed a few steps behind. Kira didn't know him well; he'd been in the Defense Grid when he and Madison met, and only transferred into civilian duty when they'd gotten married a few months ago. He shook her hand and nodded solemnly to Marcus. Kira wondered again how Madison could fall for someone so serious, but she supposed everyone was serious compared to Marcus.

"It's good to see you," said Haru.

"You can see me?" asked Marcus, patting himself in sudden shock. "The potion must have worn off! That's the last time I give my lunch to a talking squirrel."

Madison laughed, and Haru raised his eyebrow, confused. Kira watched him, waiting, until his lack of humor was so funny she couldn't help herself and burst into laughter as well.

"How are you guys doing?" asked Madison.

"Surviving," said Kira. "Barely."

Madison grimaced. "Rough night in maternity?"

"Ariel had her baby."

Madison went pale, and her eyes drooped in genuine sadness. Kira could see how much it hurt her, now that she was almost eighteen. Madison wasn't pregnant yet, but it was only a matter of time. "I'm so sorry. I'll follow you back after the meeting to say hi to her, and see if there's anything I can do."

"That's a good idea," said Kira, "but you'll have to do it without me—we have a salvage run today."

"But you were up all night!" Madison protested. "They can't make you do a salvage run."

"I'll grab a nap before leaving," said Kira, "but I need to go— I've been falling apart at work, and I could use the change of pace. Plus I need to prove to Skousen that I can handle it. If the Defense Grid wants a medic on their salvage run, I'll be the best damn medic they've ever seen."

"They're lucky to have you," said Madison, hugging her again. "Is Jayden going?"

Kira nodded. "He's the sergeant in charge."

Madison smiled. "Give him a hug for me." Jayden and Madison were siblings—not adopted siblings, actual birth siblings, the only direct genetic relatives left in the world. They were proof, some said, that RM immunity could be inherited, which only made it more frustrating that so far none of the newborns had done it. More likely, Kira thought, Madison and Jayden were an anomaly that might never be repeated.

Jayden was also, as Kira often informed Madison, one of the more attractive human beings left on the planet. Kira glanced impishly at Marcus. "Just a hug? I could pass along a kiss or two."

Marcus looked awkwardly at Haru. "So. Any idea what the meeting's gonna be about?"

Kira and Madison laughed, and Kira sighed happily. Madison always made her feel better.

"They're closing the school," said Haru. "The youngest kids on the island are turning fourteen, and there are practically more teachers now than students. I'm guessing they're going to graduate everyone into trade programs early, and send the teachers somewhere they can be more useful."

"You think?" asked Kira.

Haru shrugged. "It's what I'd do."

"They're probably going to yak about the Partials again," said Madison. "The Senate can never shut up about those things."

"Can you blame them?" asked Haru. "They killed everyone on Earth."

"Present company excepted," said Marcus.

"I'm not saying they *weren't* dangerous," said Madison, "but it's been eleven years since anyone has seen one. Life goes on. Besides, we've clearly got bigger problems now. I'm guessing they're going to talk about the Voice."

"We'll find out soon enough, I guess," said Kira, nodding toward the north; the coliseum was just visible beyond the trees. The Senate had its own building, of course, in an actual town hall, but "town hall" meetings like this one, where the entire city was asked to attend, were held in the coliseum. They rarely filled it, but the adults said it used to fill up all the time, back in the old days when they'd used it for sports. Before the Break.

Kira had only been five years old in the Break; most things about the old world she couldn't even remember, and she didn't trust half the things she could. She remembered her father, his dark face and his messy black hair and his thick-framed glasses pushed up on the bridge of his nose. They had lived in a split-level house—she was fairly certain it was yellow—and when she turned three she had a birthday party. She didn't have any friends her age, so there were no little kids, but most of her father's friends were there. She remembered she'd had a big toy box full of stuffed animals, and she'd wanted to show it to everyone, so she'd puffed and strained and pushed it down the hall; it seemed like a half an hour or more in her mind, but she knew it couldn't have been that long in real life. When she'd finally reached the living room and shouted for everyone to look, her father had laughed and chided her and taken the whole thing back to her bedroom. All her effort, gone in seconds. The memory didn't bother her; she never thought of her father as mean or unjust. It was simply a memory, one of the few she had of her life in the old world.

The crowd was heavy now, pressing together as they passed through the trees around the coliseum. Kira held tight to Marcus with one hand and Madison with the other, Haru trailing off the back like the end of a human chain. They wove a path through the mass of people and found a row of empty seats—near a door, like Marcus wanted. Kira knew he was right: If Senator Kessler got off on another rant, or if Senator Lefou got talking about shipping schedules or whatever boring thing he was on about this month, they'd need an easy way to slip out. Mandatory attendance was one thing, but once the important stuff was over, they wouldn't be the only ones leaving early.

As the senators filed onto the dais in the center of the floor, Kira shifted uncomfortably in her seat, wondering if Haru would be right. There were twenty senators in all, and Kira recognized just about all of them, though she didn't know all their names. One of the men, though, was new: tall, dark, powerfully built. He stood like a military officer, but his suit was simple and civilian. He whispered something to Dr. Skousen, the Senate representative from the hospital, then slipped away into the crowd.

"Good morning." The voice boomed through the massive stadium, echoing through the speakers and off the ceiling. The center of the coliseum lit up with a giant holo-image of Senator Hobb. There were twenty senators, but they always let Hobb take the lead in town hall meetings, delivering the opening remarks and most of the announcements. He was definitely the most charming.

"This town hall meeting will now come to order," Senator Hobb continued. "We're very glad to see you all here; it's important that you take part in your government, and these town hall meetings are the best way for everyone to stay connected. At this time we'd like to offer special thanks to the Long Island Defense Grid, specifically Sergeant Stewart and his team, for hand-cranking the generators all night here in the coliseum. As we have pledged to you, these meetings have never and will never draw electricity away from the community." There was a light smattering of applause, and Hobb smiled kindly while he waited for it to die down. "We'll start with our first order of business. Ms. Rimas, if you'd please join me on the stand?"

"It's the schools," said Kira.

"I told you," said Haru.

Ms. Rimas was the head of the East Meadow school system, which had dwindled over time to a single school for which she now served as principal. Kira listened with her hand on her mouth as the old woman spoke proudly of the work her teachers had done, the success their system had shown over the years, and the great things accomplished by the graduating students. It was a send-off, a triumphant look back at their hard work and dedication, but Kira couldn't help feeling sick about the whole thing. No matter how they spun it, no matter how much they tried to focus on the positives, the ugly truth was that there simply weren't any children anymore. They were closing the school because they had run out of students. The teachers had done their job, but the doctors hadn't.

The youngest human being on the planet, as far as anyone knew, would be fourteen years old in a month. It was possible that there were survivors on other continents, but no one had ever been able to make contact with them, and over time the refugees on Long Island had come to believe that they were alone. That their youngest was the world's youngest. His name was Saladin. When they brought him onstage, Kira couldn't hold back her tears.

Marcus put his arm around her, and they listened to the string of heartfelt speeches and congratulations. The youngest students were being accelerated into trade programs, just as Haru had predicted. Ten were accepted into the pre-medic program Kira had just completed; in another year or two they would begin interning at the hospital just like she was. Would anything be different then? Would infants still be dying? Would the nurses still be watching them die and recording their stats and wrapping them for burial? When would it all end?

As each teacher stood to say good-bye and wish their students well, the coliseum grew quieter, almost reverent. Kira knew they were thinking the same thing she was. The closing of the schools was like the closing of the past, the final acknowledgment that the world was ending. Forty thousand people left in the world, and no children. And no way to ever make more.

The last teacher spoke softly, tearfully bidding her students good-bye. The teachers were joining trade schools as well, moving on to new jobs and new lives. This final teacher was joining Saladin in the Animal Commission, training horses and dogs and hawks. Kira smiled at that. If Saladin had to grow up, at least he could still play with a dog.

The last teacher sat down, and Senator Hobb rose and walked to the microphone, standing calmly in the spotlight. His image filled the coliseum, solemn and troubled. He paused a moment, gathering his thoughts, then looked up at the audience with clear blue eyes.

"This didn't have to be."

The crowd murmured, a rustle of movement rippling through the stadium as people muttered and glanced at their companions. Kira saw Marcus look at her; she grabbed his hand tightly in her own and kept her eyes glued on Senator Hobb.

"The school didn't have to close," he said softly. "There are barely twenty school-age children in East Meadow, but across the whole island there are more. Far more. There's a farm in Jamesport with ten children almost as young as Saladin—I've seen them myself. I've held their hands. I've begged them to come in, to come here where it's safe, where the Defense Grid can better protect them, but they wouldn't. The people with them, their adopted parents, wouldn't let them. And just one week after I left, a mere two days ago, the so-called Voice of the People attacked that farm." He paused, composing himself. "We've sent soldiers to recover what we can, but I fear the worst."

Senator Hobb's hologram surveyed the coliseum closely, piercing them with his earnest stare. "Eleven years ago the Partials tried to destroy us, and they did a pretty damn good job. We built them to be stronger than us, faster than us, to fight for us, in the Isolation War. They won that war handily, and when they turned against us five years later it didn't take them long to wipe us off the face of the earth, especially after they released RM. Those of us who survived came to this island with nothing—broken, fragmented, lost in despair—but we survived. We rebuilt. We set up a defensive perimeter. We found food and shelter, we created energy and government and civilization.

When we discovered that RM would not stop killing children, we passed the Hope Act to maximize our chance of giving birth to a new generation of humans with RM resistance. Thanks to the act and our tireless medical force, we grow closer to realizing that dream every day."

Senator Hobb nodded to Dr. Skousen, sitting beside him on the dais, then looked back up. His eyes were shadowed and solemn. "But along the way, something happened. Some of us decided to break off. Some of us forgot about the enemy that still lurks on the mainland, watching us and waiting, and they forgot about the enemy that fills the air around us, that fills our very blood, killing our children like it killed so many of our families and friends. Because some of us have now decided that the civilization we built to protect ourselves is somehow the enemy. We're still fighting for what is ours, only now, we're fighting with one another. Since the passing of the Hope Act two years ago, the Voice, these gangsters, these armed thugs in the mocking guise of revolutionaries, have been burning our farms, pillaging our stores, killing their own flesh and blood—their own brothers and sisters and mothers and fathers and, God help us, their own children. Because that is what we are: We are a family, and we cannot afford to fight one another. And whatever their motivations are, whatever they claim to stand for, the Voice—let's just call them what they are: barbarians—are simply trying to finish the job the Partials started. And we are not going to let them." His voice was hard, a force of pure determination. "We are one nation, one people, one will." He paused. "Or at least we should be. I wish I had better news, but the Defense Grid found a Voice strike team raiding a supply depot last night—do you want to know where? Can you guess?"

A few people in the crowd shouted out guesses, mostly outlying farms and fishing villages, but the giant holo-image shook its head sadly. Kira looked below to the man himself, a tiny figure in a worn brown suit made almost white by the spotlight. He turned slowly, shaking his head as the crowd called out locations from all across the island. He stopped turning and pointed at the floor.

"Here," he said. "Actually, just over there, south of the turnpike, in the old Kellenberg High School. The attack was small, and we managed to contain it without much bloodshed, so you may not have even known about it, but still, they were right there. How many of you live near there?" He raised his hand, nodding at the others in the crowd who raised theirs as well. "Yes," he said, "you live right there, I live right there, that is the heart of our community. The Voice isn't just out in the forest anymore, they're here, in East Meadow, in our own neighborhood. They want to tear us apart from the inside, but we are not going to let them!

"The Voice objects to the Hope Act," he continued. "They call it tyranny, they call it fascism, they call it control. You call it our only chance. You want to give humanity a future; they want to live in the present, and to kill anyone who tries to stop them. Is that freedom? If there's anything we've learned in the last eleven years, my friends, it is that freedom is a responsibility to be earned, not a license for recklessness and anarchy. If someday, despite our strongest efforts and our deepest determination, we finally fall, let it be because our enemies finally beat us, not because we beat ourselves."

Kira listened quietly, sobered by the speech. She didn't relish the thought of getting pregnant so quickly—she had fewer than two years left before she came of age—but she knew the Senate was right. The future was the most important thing, certainly more important than one girl's hesitation to take the next step.

Senator Hobb's voice was soft, grim, resolute. "The Voice disagrees with the Hope Act, and they've decided to express their disagreement through murder and theft and terrorism. They're allowed to disagree; it's their methods that are the issue. There was another group, not so long ago, who used the same methods—a group who didn't like the way things were and decided to rebel. They were called Partials. The difference is that the Partials were unthinking, unfeeling, inhuman killers. They kill because that's what we built them to do. The Voices are human and, in some ways, that makes them even more dangerous."

The crowd murmured. Senator Hobb glanced down, cleared his throat, and continued.

"There are some things more important than ourselves—more important than the limits of the present, and the whims of the now. There is a future to build and protect. And if we're going to make that future a reality, we have to stop fighting among ourselves. We have to end dissent wherever we find it. We have to trust one another again. This is not about the Senate and the city, this is not about the city and the farms, this is not about any little group or faction. This is about us. The entire human race, united as one. There are people out there who want to tear that apart, but we are not going to let them!"

The crowd roared again, and this time Kira joined them. Yet even as she shouted in chorus, she couldn't shake a sudden sense of fear, like icy fingers in the back of her mind.

CHAPTER TWO

"**Y**ou're late, Walker."

Kira didn't speed up, watching Jayden's face as she walked casually to the wagon. He looked so much like Madison.

"What?" she asked. "Don't soldiers have to attend mandatory town hall meetings anymore?"

"And thank you very much for the attitude," said Jayden, leaning his rifle against his shoulder. "It is a pleasure to have both you and your delightful wit with us on this run."

Kira mimed a gun with her forefinger, silently shooting him in the face. "Where are we going this time?"

"A little town called Asharoken." He helped her up into the back of the metal wagon, already full of ten more soldiers and two portable generators; that meant she was probably going to field-test some old equipment to see if it was worth bringing back. There were two other civilians as well, a man and a woman, probably here to use the second generator on some equipment of their own.

Jayden leaned on the edge of the wagon. "I swear, this island has the weirdest town names I've ever heard."

"You guys are loaded for bear," said Kira, looking at the soldiers' heavy rifles. They were always armed when they left the city—even Kira had an assault rifle slung over her shoulder—but today they looked like a war party. One of the soldiers was even carrying a long tube she recognized as a rocket launcher. Kira found an empty seat and tucked her bag and medical kit behind her feet. "Expecting bandits?"

"North Shore," said Jayden, and Kira blanched. The North Shore was essentially unsettled, and thus prime Voice territory.

"Valencio, you're late!" shouted Jayden, and Kira looked up with a smile.

"Hey, Marcus."

"Long time no see." Marcus grinned broadly and vaulted into the wagon. "Sorry I'm late, Jayden. I had a meeting that got a little heavier than I planned. Very hot and sweaty by the end. You were a major topic of conversation, though, in between bouts of passionate—"

"Just skip to the part where it's my mother," said Jayden, "and then I'll do the part where I tell you to go to hell, and then we can maybe get on with our jobs like we're supposed to."

"Your mother died of RM eleven years ago," said Marcus, his face a mask of pretend shock. "You were, what, six? That would be incredibly crass of me."

"And your mother's already in hell," said Jayden, "so I'm sure you'll be seeing her soon. We should probably just drop the whole thing. Bastard."

Kira frowned at the insult, but Marcus only smirked, looking at the other people in the wagon. "Ten soldiers, huh? What's the run?"

"North Shore," said Kira.

Marcus whistled. "And here I was worried we wouldn't get to do anything fun. I guess we've pretty much picked everything else clean by now, though, huh?" He looked across the truck to the two other civilians. "You'll have to forgive me, I don't recognize either of you."

"Andrew Turner," said the man, reaching out his hand. He was older, late forties, with the beginning of a sunburn through his thinning hair. "Electrician."

"Nice to meet you," said Marcus, shaking his hand.

The woman smiled and waved. "Gianna Cantrell. I'm in computer science." She was older as well, but younger than Turner. Kira guessed maybe thirty-five—old enough to have been in computer science well before the Break. Kira glanced at her stomach, a reflex she wasn't even aware of until she'd done it, but of course the woman wasn't pregnant. Salvage runs were too dangerous to risk a child; she must have been between cycles.

"Interesting mix," said Marcus. He looked at Jayden. "What's the deal with this place?"

"Grunt salvage went through a few days ago," said Jayden. "They logged a clinic, a pharmacy, and a 'weather station,' whatever that means. So now I get to go all the way back out there on a bunny run. You can imagine my joy." He walked to the front of the wagon and climbed up beside the driver, a young woman Kira had seen a few times before—still a year or two below the pregnancy age, which made her fit for active duty. "All right, Yoon, giddyup."

The girl flicked the reins and clucked at the four-horse team—the Defense Grid had a few electric cars, but none strong enough to haul a load this heavy with any degree of efficiency. Energy was precious, and horses were cheap, so all the best electric motors had been commandeered for other purposes. The wagon lurched into motion, and Kira put her arm behind Marcus to grip the side of the wagon. Marcus pressed in closer.

"Hey, babe."

"Hey."

Andrew Turner looked at them. "Bunny run?"

"That's just slang for a salvage run, with specialists like you guys instead of the normal grunts." Kira glanced at the man's growing sunburn. "You've never been on one?"

"I did a lot of salvage in the early days, like everyone, but after a year or so I was assigned to solar panels full-time."

"Bunny runs are easy," said Marcus. "North Shore's kind of spooky, but we'll be fine." He glanced around and smiled. "Road conditions aren't great outside of the settlement, though, so enjoy the smooth ride while you can."

They drove for a while in silence, the wind whipping through the open wagon and tossing Kira's ponytail straight toward Marcus. She leaned forward, aiming the frenzied hair squarely at his face and laughing as he spluttered and brushed it away. He started to tickle her and she backed away in a rush, slamming into the soldier beside her. He smiled at her awkwardly—a boy about her age, obviously pleased to have a girl practically sitting in his lap, but he didn't say anything about it. She scooted back into place, trying not to laugh.

The soldier next to Kira barked an order. "Last marker. Eyes up!" The soldiers in the truck bed straightened a little, held their weapons a little closer, and watched the passing buildings with hawk-like intensity.

Kira turned, watching the vast, empty city roll past—it looked empty, and it probably was, but you could never be too careful. The markers showed the edge of the East Meadow settlement, and the edge of the region their military could reasonably patrol, but it was hardly the edge of the actual urban area. The old-world city stretched out for miles in every direction, almost coast to coast on the island. Most of the survivors lived in East Meadow, or in the military base to the west, but there were looters, drifters, bandits, and worse sprinkled all around the island. The Voice had become the biggest fear, but they were far from the only one.

Even outside of East Meadow, the road here was well traveled and fairly open; there was garbage, of course, and dirt and leaves and the random debris of nature, but regular traffic kept the asphalt relatively clear of plants, and only rarely did the wagon bump over a major rut or pothole. The realm beyond the curbs was another story: Eleven years of disuse had left the city derelict, the houses crumbling, the sidewalks cracked and buckled by burgeoning tree roots, rampant weeds, and vast masses of kudzu that coated everything like a carpet. There were no lawns anymore, no yards, no glass in any of the windows. Even most of the side streets, less traveled than the main roadway, were crisscrossed with lines of green, Mother Nature slowly reclaiming everything the old world had stolen.

Kira liked it, in a way. Nobody told nature what to do.

They rode in silence a while longer; then one of the soldiers pointed to the north and hollered.

"Pack rat!"

Kira twisted in her seat, scanning the city, then caught a flash of movement in the corner of her eye—a school bus, the sides hung heavy with odds and ends and the top piled high with boxes and crates and sacks and furniture, all precariously strapped down with hundreds of yards of rope. A man stood beside it, siphoning gas from the tank of a parked car; two teens, Kira guessed maybe fifteen and seventeen years old, stood next to him.

"Dude," said Marcus, "he's still using gas."

"Maybe he's found a way to filter it," said Gianna, peering at the bus with interest. "A lot of the outer communities do—still destroys the engines, but it's not like we're running out of those anytime soon."

"They should just move into town," said Turner. "He could have a real house, we could hook him up with electricity and security and . . . well, everything."

"Everything but mobility," said Gianna. "And anonymity, and freedom—"

"What do you mean, 'freedom'?" asked the soldier sitting next to Kira. His name tag said BROWN. "We have freedom—what he has is anarchy."

"Safety, then," said Gianna.

Private Brown hefted his rifle. "What do you call this?"

"Large communities were the first to fall in the Partial rebellion," said Gianna. "Population centers make easy targets, and if the Partials, wherever they are, develop a new strain of RM that overcomes our immunity, guns aren't going to do any good

23

against it. A place like East Meadow would be the worst possible place you could be."

"Well, you're welcome," said Brown. "I'm glad all my life-risking is so appreciated."

"I'm not saying you're not appreciated," said Gianna. "I'm just saying . . . well, I just said what I'm saying. Obviously I chose to live in East Meadow, I'm just pointing out why he maybe didn't."

"He's probably a Voicer," growled another soldier. "Raising those kids to be spies or assassins or hell only knows what else."

Private Brown cussed him out, and Kira turned away, ignoring them and feeling the wind on her face. She'd heard enough of these arguments to last a lifetime. It was a hot day, but the wind made it pleasant enough, and she always enjoyed the chance to snuggle up to Marcus. She thought about her night, and her morning, and the dead child and everything else. *What was it my father used to say?* she thought. *"I am stronger than my trials."*

I am stronger than my trials.

CHAPTER THREE

It was hours later when they reached Asharoken, and the sky was already beginning to dim. Kira hoped they could finish the salvage quickly and camp somewhere farther from the shore. Asharoken was more of a neighborhood than a town, connected to the rest of the island by an unbroken mass of houses and roads and buildings, but Kira could instantly see why the grunt runs had avoided it for so long—it was a narrow isthmus of land stretching north from the island, the sound on one side and a bay on the other. One shore made people nervous enough; two was almost too much to handle.

The wagon stopped in front of a small veterinary clinic, and Marcus groaned.

"You didn't say it was a dog clinic, Jayden—what are we going to find here?"

Jayden jumped down from the wagon. "If I knew that, I would have picked it up myself when I was here two days ago. Grunts tagged meds and an X-ray machine; go do your thing."

Marcus hopped down to the street, and both he and Jayden held up a hand to help Kira. In a fit of mischief she took both hands, and smiled inwardly as they helped her down with sullen scowls.

"Sparks, Brown, you go in first," Jayden barked, and half the soldiers began to pour out of the truck, hauling one of the generators with them. "Patterson, you and your team secure the area, keep it secure, and escort the medics to the next site. It looks like someone's been through here since yesterday, and I don't want any surprises."

"Someone's been here?" asked Kira. "How can you tell?"

"Eyes and brains and a shiny new haircut," said Jayden. "It's probably just a pack rat, but I'm not taking chances on the effing North Shore. If you find something good in there, honeybunnies, prep it for transport and we'll pick it up on our way back. I'm taking my team north to site three—Patterson, I want blips every fifteen minutes." He climbed into the back of the wagon and called out to the driver, "Let's move."

The wagon lurched into motion and headed north. Kira slung her medkit over her shoulder and looked around; Asharoken was buried in kudzu, like most of these little cities, but the Long Island Sound was lapping gently at the shore, and the sky was clear and calm. "Pretty town."

"Eyes up," said Patterson. The other soldiers fanned out, slowly building a perimeter around the clinic while Sparks and Brown approached the broken building with assault rifles raised to their eye line. Kira was fascinated by the way they moved, their entire bodies turning and raising and lowering to keep that eye line as solid as a rock—it almost looked like the gun was on invisible rails, while the soldier moved freely around it. The front wall of the clinic had been mostly glass, now shattered and overgrown with kudzu, but a central pillar of concrete had been marked with the bright orange glyph of a salvage crew. Kira had done enough runs to recognize most of the glyphs, but this was the one she knew best: "partially catalogued, return with medics." Sparks and Brown covered each other seamlessly as they entered, picking their way through the rubble and vegetation. Patterson climbed carefully to the roof, keeping to the edges where the footing was firm, and kept watch from elevation.

While they secured the building, Kira and Marcus tested out the generator. It was a heavy frame with two wheels on one end; the bottom held a massive battery and a hand crank, while the top held a small solar panel and coil after coil of cords and plugs. Medics came on every salvage run to keep the workers safe, but when the grunts tagged a piece of medical equipment, they brought these generators so the medics could plug it in, test it, and see if it was worth bringing back. The island was cluttered enough as it was, there was no sense filling East Meadow with salvaged junk they couldn't even use.

The street was full of parked cars, the paint rusted, the tires flat, and the windows broken by years of neglect and exposure to the elements. One of them held a skeleton, grinning horribly in the driver's seat—an RM victim who'd tried to go somewhere, tried to drive away from the end of the world. Kira wondered where he'd been trying to go. He hadn't made it out of his driveway.

A full two minutes later, Brown opened the door again and waved them in. "All clear, but watch your step. Looks like some wild dogs are using this place as a den."

Marcus smirked. "Loyal little fellas. Must have really loved their vet."

Kira nodded. "Let's fire it up."

Marcus tilted the generator back on its wheels and slowly walked it in, but Kira noticed Brown had pulled up his mask, and she paused to prep her own: a folded cloth bandanna that she dabbed with five tiny drops of menthol. Any bodies left behind would have rotted years ago, like the skeleton in the car, but a pack of dogs would have brought in more carrion of their own, not to mention musk and urine and feces and who knew what else. Kira tied the bandanna around her nose and mouth, and walked in to see Marcus gagging and searching his pockets for his own mask.

"You should pay better attention," she said smoothly, walking past him to the back room. "All I smell is the brisk scent of mint."

The med room was well stocked and didn't look like it had been hit yet—though someone had obviously been rifling through it recently, leaving prints and scuffs in the thick layer of dust. *Probably the grunts,* she thought, *though I've never seen a grunt run actually sort through the meds before.*

Kira started organizing the counter space, designating one area to keep and one to destroy. Salvage training was the first thing the interns learned: which meds could last, and for how long, and which were too far gone to be safe. Bringing expired medication back to East Meadow was even worse than bringing back broken machines, not because they took up space but because they were dangerous. The medics were the caretakers of the entire human race; the last thing they needed was for someone to take the wrong pills—or worse yet, for a vast stockpile of discarded medication to get into the water table. It was safer and easier to sort it out here; they'd even learned how to deal with animal meds, for exactly this kind of scenario—a dog antibiotic was still, at the end of the day, an antibiotic, and without extensive manufacturing facilities, the islanders had to take what they could get. Kira was already sorting the cupboards efficiently when Marcus staggered in, his mask finally in place.

"This place smells like a crypt."

"It is a crypt."

"And the animals are not the worst part," he said, "though I swear there must be a whole dog civilization in here to have this kind of stink." He opened another cupboard and started tossing medicines into Kira's piles, knowing exactly which was which without even looking. "No," he said, "the worst part is the dust. Whatever else we collect from this place, I'm taking a pound of it home in my lungs."

"It will build character," said Kira, laughing as she tried to impersonate Nurse Hardy. "I've been on nine million-billion salvage runs, intern, and you just have to learn to deal with it. Breathing corpse dust is good for you—it activates the kidneys."

"Salvage isn't just good for you," said Marcus, launching into a dead-on impersonation of Senator Hobb, "it's essential for the very survival of all mankind. Think of the part you'll play in the glorious new page of history!"

Kira laughed out loud—Hobb was always talking about the "new page of history." Like all they had to do was keep writing, and the book would never end.

"Future generations will look back with awe at the giants who saved our race," continued Marcus, "who threw down the Partials and cured RM once and for all. Who saved the lives of countless infants, and . . ." His rant died off, the room feeling suddenly uncomfortable, and they worked in silence. After a while Marcus spoke again.

"I think they're getting more nervous than they let on," he said. He paused. "They didn't mention it in the meeting, but they really are talking about lowering the pregnancy age again."

Kira stopped, her hand in the air, and shot him a quick look. "You're serious?"

Marcus nodded. "I saw Isolde on my way home to change. She says there's a new movement in the Senate pushing for statistics over study—they say we don't need to look for a cure, we just need to have enough children to hit the immunity percentage."

Kira turned to face him. "We've already hit the immunity percentage. point-oh-four percent means one out of every twenty-five hundred kids will be immune, and we've passed that twice now."

"I know it's stupid," said Marcus, "but even the doctors are getting behind it—more babies helps them either way. More opportunities to study."

Kira turned back to her cupboard. "Another drop would take it to seventeen. Isolde is seventeen—what's she going to do? She's not ready to be pregnant."

"They'll find a donor—"

"This isn't a dating service," said Kira harshly, cutting him off, "it's a breeding program. For all we know, they put fertility drugs in the water supply—in fact, I wouldn't be surprised if they did." She took the boxes from the cupboard angrily, slamming them down in the keep pile or throwing them full force in the trash. "Forget love, forget freedom, forget *choice*, just get yourself knocked up and save the damn world already."

"It's not seventeen," said Marcus softly. He paused, staring at the wall, and Kira felt her stomach twist into a knot as she anticipated what he was going to say. "Isolde says there's a referendum in the Senate to drop the pregnancy age to sixteen."

Kira froze, too sick to speak. The pregnancy age wasn't a restriction, it was a rule: All women of a certain age were required, by law, to get pregnant as soon as possible, and to be pregnant as frequently as possible.

I've known this was coming for two years, Kira thought, *ever since they enacted the thing. Two years to prepare myself, to psych myself up, but still—I thought I had two more. They keep dropping it. There's no way I'm ready for this.*

"It's stupid," said Marcus. "It's stupid and unfair and I know—I can only imagine how it feels. I think it's a terrible idea, and I hope it dies as quickly as possible."

"Thank you."

"But what if it doesn't?"

Kira coughed, squeezing her eyes shut. "Don't start this now, Marcus."

"I'm just saying that we should . . . think about it," he said quickly, "*if* the law goes into effect. If you don't make your own choice, they'll just—"

"I said not right now," said Kira. "This is not the time, this is not the place, this is not anything approaching the circumstances in which I want to have this conversation."

"I'm not just talking about sex," said Marcus. "I'm talking about marriage." He took a step toward her, paused, and looked at the ceiling. "We've been planning this since we were thirteen, Kira—we were going to intern together, work at the hospital together, and get married—this was your plan too—"

"Well, it's not my plan anymore," she said quickly. "I'm not ready to make these kinds of choices, okay? I'm not ready now, I sure as hell wasn't ready at thirteen." She turned to the cupboard, swore softly, and turned again to the door, walking out. "I need some air."

Outside she pulled off her mask, sucking in long, deep breaths. *The worst part is, I can totally see their point.*

The trees to the north lit up suddenly with a brilliant orange, followed a second later by a deafening roar. Kira felt the shock wave pass through her, twisting her gut. She'd barely had time to process the sight and sound of the explosion when her hearing returned and she heard the soldiers shouting.

CHAPTER FOUR

Private Brown rushed toward Kira, grabbing her in a full tackle and dropping her to the ground beside a parked car. "Stay down!"

"What's going on?"

"Just stay down!" Brown pulled out his radio and thumbed the call button. "Sergeant, this is Shaylon. Are you taking fire, over!"

The radio crackled; nothing but white noise.

"Someone's shooting at us?" asked Kira.

"If I knew that, I wouldn't be asking Jayden," said Brown, and thumbed the radio again. "Sergeant, do you read? What's your situation?"

The radio buzzed emptily, Kira and Brown staring at it desperately—an explosion could be an accident, or the Voice, or even Partials, for all they knew. Was this an attack? An invasion? The radio said nothing; then abruptly Jayden's voice tore out of it in a ragged burst of static.

"Site three was rigged to blow! Five men trapped inside—get

33

the medics up here ASAP!"

Brown whirled toward the clinic, rising to his feet in one smooth motion. "Casualties at site three!" Kira started running before he even turned back—she could see the smoke rising up from the site, not more than a mile down the road. Brown fell into step behind her, his rifle held tightly in front as he pelted full speed down the road. Kira felt for her medical bag, whispered a silent thank-you to whatever had kept it on her shoulder, and lowered her head for a sprint. Brown barely kept up with her.

She saw Jayden first, standing on the cab of an overgrown truck with a pair of binoculars, scanning the full circle of the horizon. Next was the wagon, the left front wheel blown off and at least two of the horses down, the others whinnying in terror. Last of all she saw the building—a smoking ruin between two other structures, like a tower of wooden blocks thrown down by an angry child. One of the soldiers was dragging another by the hands, pulling him clear of the wreckage. Kira dropped next to the fallen man, one hand on his wrist to check his pulse while the other probed his chest and neck for injuries.

"I'm fine," the soldier coughed. "Get the civvies."

Kira nodded and sprang back to her feet, staring at the shattered house in shock—where should she even start? She grabbed the standing soldier and pulled him away from the fallen one.

"Where are the others?"

"The basement," he said, pointing down. "This corner."

"Then help me get in there."

"The building was two stories tall—they're completely buried."

"Then help me get in there," she insisted again, pulling him toward the house. Kira was already picking her way through the rubble when Marcus arrived, still out of breath.

"Holy . . . crap."

Kira delved deeper into the ruin. "Mr. Turner!" she called. "Ms. Cantrell! Can either of you hear me?" She and the soldier froze, listening, and Kira pointed to the floor on her left. "Down there."

They knelt down, flipping aside a wide piece of ruined flooring. She paused, and heard it again—a faint flutter, like a gasp or a muffled cough. She pointed at a section of brick and the soldier helped her move it, handing up bricks to Marcus and Sparks and the other soldiers, all scrabbling at the wreckage to clear it away. Kira shouted again and heard a feeble answer.

"Right here," said a voice. Kira recognized the feminine timbre, knew it was Gianna, and hefted up a piece of fallen furniture. The soldiers pulled it up and out of the hole, and underneath, Gianna grunted in pain. "Thank the gods."

Kira slithered farther into the hole to help her. "Are you still pinned?"

"I don't think so," said Gianna. Kira grabbed her hand firmly, bracing herself on another section of overturned floor. She lost her grip, slid down, and felt a strong hand grab hers from behind.

"I've got you," said Kira, "and they've got me. Keep coming." Slowly Gianna pulled herself free of the broken wood and bricks, and Kira hauled her up inch by inch. When Gianna was high enough, the strong hand on Kira's pulled them both to the top of the pile, and Kira turned to see Jayden straining with the effort.

"Thanks," said Kira.

He nodded. "Help me find the other one."

Kira turned back to the hole. "Mr. Turner! Can you hear me?"

"He was next to me when the bomb went off," Gianna panted. "He can't be very far."

Kira scrambled back down the hole, still calling his name. "Mr. Turner! Andrew!" She paused, listening closely, and bent down as far as she could. *Nothing.* She leaned back, examining the wreckage, trying to guess where he might have ended up.

"Behind that stone," said Gianna, pointing past her to a large, flat rock standing upright in the rubble. "There was a fireplace in the basement, like a big chimney, all done in stone instead of brick. Probably the oldest part of the house."

"We'll never be able to move it," said Marcus. Kira slithered down next to it, leaning in close.

"Andrew Turner!" shouted Marcus, but Kira shushed him.

"Quiet, I'm going to try something."

The dust settled, and the air was still. Kira opened her medkit and pulled out the stethoscope—one of the digital models with sound amplification. She thumbed the switch, silently praying that the battery hadn't degraded, and pressed the scope to the rubble.

Pom, pom, pom, pom . . .

"It's his heartbeat," Kira called out. "He's right under the fallen chimney."

"Those stones are propping up half the house," said Marcus. "We're not moving them."

"As long as his heart's beating, we are," said Jayden. "Out of the way, Walker." He slid down next to Kira and called for help from the others. "Yoon, get me rope, and tie the other end to one of the horses." A moment later the soldier dropped a stiff nylon cord in between them, and Jayden huffed, reaching out to loop the rope around the rock. Kira pressed the scope to the stone again.

Pom, pom, pom.

"I can still hear the heartbeat." She turned, looking for beams of wood. "Marcus is right, though—if we move this now, the whole first floor will come down on him. Here, brace it with this." She pulled on a long joist, still attached to shards of wooden flooring, and Jayden shoved it into place, propping up the rubble.

"All set." Jayden called out orders to the wagon driver. "Take her forward, Yoon! More . . . more . . . okay, the line's taut, now just an inch at a time."

The rope stretched tight; Kira couldn't see the stone move, but she could hear it scraping loudly against the stone floor below. "It's working!" she shouted.

Jayden called more orders to Yoon. "Keep going—nice and slow, that's perfect. Now ready on the line." The stone dislodged from its hole, and Jayden grunted as he helped shove it to the side.

Kira turned to the open hole, eyeing the makeshift support beam nervously, when a shape in the darkness stopped her cold. She hadn't seen it before—it had been behind the stone.

It was a human leg, severed just above the knee.

"No," she murmured. She reached forward cautiously, probing the jagged edge where the bone had broken. *Crushed,* she thought, feeling the damage. *The chimney fell and snapped his leg right off. How can he still be alive?* She pressed her scope against the next stone.

Pom, pom, pom.

"Bloody hell," said Jayden, crouching behind her, "is that his leg?"

"It means we're close."

"It means he's dead," said Jayden. "That chimney would have pulverized him."

"I told you I can hear his heartbeat," Kira hissed. "Give me the rope."

The rubble shifted, and Kira closed her mouth and eyes tightly against a hail of rocks and dust. The rafter above her groaned, and she heard shouts of alarm from the soldiers above.

"Get her out of there!" called Marcus.

"He's right," said Jayden. "This is coming down around us any second. One dead man isn't worth losing a medic."

"I'm telling you, he's alive."

"Get out," Jayden snapped. "If we can't dig him out of here, we definitely can't dig you out."

"This is a human life," said Kira. "We don't have any of those to spare right now."

"Get out!"

Kira gritted her teeth and inched forward; Jayden swore behind her, reaching for her feet, but she kicked him away.

Pom, pom, pom.

She felt the next stone in front of her, testing for handholds, probing its stability. *I think I can move this one*, she thought. *He's got to be right on the other side of it, and then they'll see. I know he's alive.*

"Hey, Mr. Turner," she shouted, "can you hear me? I'm coming to get you—we're not leaving you behind." She braced herself on the basement floor, praying she didn't dislodge anything vital, and pushed on the largest stone, feeling it rotate slightly against a stiff, off-center axis. She pushed again, straining at the weight, then shoved the stone to the side. There was another shape in the darkness, too twisted for her to recognize the outline. She thumbed the scope again, reaching forward desperately.

Dit, dit, dit, dit . . .

Wait, thought Kira, *that's not right*, and then her fingers brushed against slick, wet flesh. She caught a piece of fabric between two fingers and pulled it closer, hearing the *dit* grow louder in the tiny cavern. She felt the bloody limb with both hands, refusing to believe it; she inched back toward the light and held it up, confirming it with her eyes.

"It's his arm," she said softly. "He's gone."

Jayden stared. "And the heartbeat?"

She held up the arm, the wrist glinting metallically. *Dit, dit, dit.* "His wristwatch." She felt drained and lifeless. "He's gone."

Jayden pulled the arm away from her, steadying her with his hand. "Let's get out of here."

"We have to take him back," said Kira.

"This was not an accident," said Jayden. "Someone came through here and set this bomb—someone who knew we were coming. They're probably still nearby."

Kira frowned. "Why would someone blow up a weather station?"

"It was a radio," said Gianna. "We didn't see it all before it blew, but I know that much for certain. This was the biggest communications hub I've ever seen."

"Voice," said Kira.

Jayden's voice was low and grim. "And after that noise, they definitely know we're here."

CHAPTER FIVE

Jayden gathered the survivors in the shadow of the smoking wagon. "There's no way we're getting home in this thing, which puts us at least two days out from civilization. Our radio's been destroyed as well. We're on our own."

"We'll have to rig a stretcher for Private Lanier," said Marcus. "He has a compound fracture in his shin. I've set it as best I can, but he's not walking anywhere."

Kira scanned the trees and ruins around them, tensing at every movement. She'd been in the hospital once when the Voice attacked; she'd seen the wounded soldiers they brought in, moaning and screaming in pain as the triage medics wheeled them into surgery. It still shocked her to think that any human would harm another one.

"Build a stretcher," said Jayden. "We have two horses left: Patterson and Yoon will ride ahead and send backup as soon as they can reach the Defense Grid perimeter. The rest of us follow on foot."

"It's nearly thirty miles," said Yoon, "and the horses are already tired. They can't do it in one shot."

"They can go for at least another hour," said Jayden. "You'll run out of light by then anyway. Go as far as you can, then let the horses rest till first light."

"We don't have to go all the way back to East Meadow," said Gianna. "There's a farm community west of here, and several more to the east. They're a whole lot closer than thirty miles, and Lanier can get help sooner."

"Our map was in the side of the wagon that blew up," said Jayden. "I'm not in the mood to just wander around the island looking for rednecks."

"They're not rednecks," said Gianna. "Most of them have more education than you do—"

"Their amazing educations aren't much good to us without a map to find them," said Kira. Why was Gianna arguing at a time like this? "East Meadow's our best bet—we can follow major roads the whole way."

"Lanier's not going to make it back," said Gianna, "not with that fracture. The farms have hospitals just like we do."

"Not 'just like we do,'" said Kira, "and no, Lanier's not going to die on the road. Do you have some kind of medical background you forgot to mention?"

"Anyone can see—"

"Anyone can see that he's bad," said Marcus, speaking calmly, "but we've splinted it, we've wrapped it, and I can drug him so hard he'll think he's flying home on a magical gumdrop rainbow. You could get high on his farts."

"Patterson and Yoon, go south to East Meadow," said Jayden

firmly. "The rest of us follow with the same goal, but"—he looked at Gianna—"if we run across a farm or an outpost or anything like that, we can try to commandeer another wagon."

"You don't have the authority to commandeer a wagon," Gianna snapped.

"And you don't have the authority to disobey my orders," said Jayden. "This is a military operation, in a state of emergency, and I will take you home the way I think is best if I have to drug you as much as Lanier to do it. Am I clear?"

"Is this what we have to look forward to?" asked Gianna. "Is this our brave new world when you plague babies grow up and start running things?"

Jayden didn't waver. "I asked you if I was clear."

"Perfectly," said Gianna. "Let's get back to paradise."

Jayden stood up and the group dispersed, gathering their equipment and preparing for the journey. Kira took Jayden's arm and pulled him back.

"We can't just leave them," she said. "The dead horses, sure, but there's three dead people in that house. How are we going to get them home?"

"We can come back for them."

"I counted six feral house cats walking past us just during your little planning meeting, and that clinic you had us in was home to a pretty big pack of dogs. If we leave three bodies here, there won't be anything left to come back to."

Jayden's eyes were cold. "What do you want me to do, Walker? We can't carry them, and we don't have time to bury them. We'll come back in force to investigate the site and recover the generators, but right now ten live people are more important than three dead ones."

"Ten minutes," said Kira. "We can spare that."

"You think you can bury them in ten minutes?"

"They're half-buried already."

Kira watched him consider, then shrug and nod. "You've got a point. I'll help."

In addition to Andrew Turner, the explosion had killed two soldiers, and their bodies were laid out carefully by the house. A man and a woman—a boy and girl, really, probably no more than sixteen years old each. The girl might have been even younger, but Kira couldn't tell. She stood over them solemnly, wondering who they had been: what they had done for fun, who they had lived with, how they had come to be here. She didn't even know their names. Jayden took the girl by the arms, Kira grabbed her legs, and they picked their way carefully through the ruins. The deepest hole was the one they'd dug trying to save Turner, and they lowered the girl's body down into it as gently as they could, pushing her back into the recess behind the chimney stones. By now some of the other soldiers had finished their tasks and came to help, carefully carrying the boy and sliding his body into the hole as well. Kira watched numbly as Jayden and Private Brown destabilized the last remaining wall and knocked it over onto the hole, covering the bodies.

Kira felt her heart break as the wall came down. This wasn't enough—it was good to bury them, but they deserved more. She tried to speak, but the lazy clouds of dust from the rubble were too much to look at, and she couldn't speak.

Marcus watched her, his eyes aching and tender. He looked at Jayden. "We should say something."

Jayden shrugged. "Good-bye?"

"Okay," said Marcus, stepping forward. "I guess I can do it. Anyone know what god they worshipped?"

"Not a very good one," muttered Gianna.

"Maija was a Christian," said Sparks. "I'm not sure what kind. Rob was Buddhist. I have no idea about the civvie."

Marcus looked around for more clarification, but nobody knew any more. "Not the easiest mix to work with," said Marcus. "How about this, then. I think I can remember some of the old poetry they taught us in school." He straightened up, fixing his eyes in the distance, and the soldiers dropped their heads. Kira kept her eyes on the pile of fallen bricks, dust still hovering over it.

"'Death be not proud,'" said Marcus, "'though some have called thee mighty and dreadful.'" He paused, thinking. "I'm totally butchering this. 'Thou art slave to fate, chance, kings, and desperate men, but thou canst . . . not kill me. One short sleep and then we wake eternally, and death shall be no more.'"

Jayden glanced at Marcus. "You think they're going to wake up? Just like that?"

"It's just an old poem," said Marcus.

"Wherever they're waking up," said Jayden, "it's getting pretty damn crowded." He turned and stalked back to the wagon.

Kira held Marcus's hand and watched as the dust settled slowly on the fallen bricks.

The rain pooled in the mud, filling the fat rubber tire tracks with jumping drops of water. Kira pulled her hood forward, trying again to shield her eyes, but as the storm grew fiercer it almost felt as if the rain was pouring in from all sides, leaping up from the puddles and seeping down through every seam in her clothing.

Jayden stopped again, halting the line with a raised fist. The tire tracks hadn't come from Asharoken and the rigged bomb, but any presence could be dangerous out here in the wild. This part of the island had been wealthier than most, back in the day, so instead of close-packed houses and overgrown lawns, they walked through dense, dripping forest, dotted here and there with a lonely mansion looming out of the darkness. Kira cocked her head to the side, listening, hoping to catch a trace of whatever tiny noise Jayden kept sensing through the downpour; she could see Marcus doing the same. She heard the rain, the splashes, the squelch of mud as someone shifted their weight in the street. Jayden dropped his fist and pointed forward, and the group started walking again.

"I think he's just making it up," whispered Marcus. "He just likes making that little fist signal thingy and watching us all obey him."

"I've never been this wet in my life," said Kira. "Even immersed in a bathtub I swear I was dryer than I am now."

"Look on the bright side," said Marcus.

Kira waited.

"This is the point," she said, "at which you would tradition-ally suggest a bright side."

"I've never been a real traditional guy," said Marcus. "Besides, I'm not saying I know a bright side, I just think this would be a great time to look at one."

Jayden raised his fist, and the group stopped walking.

"Jayden just heard a bright side," whispered Marcus. "There's an uplifting metaphor creeping through those bushes."

Kira snorted, and Jayden turned to glare at them. He turned back, flicked his fingers toward the side of the road, and walked toward a break in the trees.

Kira followed, surprised; even she could tell that the tracks continued straight ahead through the saplings on the ruined road. The trees on either side were dark and ominous—what did Jayden hear in them?

The group picked their way carefully through a narrow gap that used to be a driveway, now cracked and broken by a decade of weeds. A large house loomed dark ahead, nearly as black as the night around it. Marcus crept forward to reach her, walking quietly beside her in a crouch. Kira leaned toward him to ask a question, then stopped abruptly as a flash of color caught her eye: orange light in the window, a tiny gleam here and gone in an instant. *Fire.* She froze in place, grabbing Marcus's arm and pulling his ear up to her lips.

"There's someone in there."

Kira gripped her shotgun tightly, hoping it hadn't grown so wet in the storm that it wouldn't fire properly. Even with five armed soldiers around them, she felt exposed. She lowered her body slowly to a crouch, pulling Marcus with her. Jayden stopped abruptly, raising his rifle to his cheek, and a voice called out from the darkened house.

"That's far enough."

The voice was thin and raw, a wraith in the darkness. Rain drummed on Kira's hood and back; she readied the safety on the rifle—a tiny button that turned it from a thick plastic club into a magic wand of death. Point and click, and watch the target explode. Water seeped down her collar, into her eyes, through the fabric of her gloves.

"My name is Jayden Van Rijn," said Jayden, "sergeant second class, Long Island Defense Grid." He kept his rifle trained on the same invisible target; he must have seen the man before he spoke. Kira still couldn't see anything. "Identify yourself."

"I'm nobody you need to have a problem with," said the voice. "And nobody who has a problem with you."

"Identify yourself," Jayden repeated.

Kira imagined the trees around them full of Voices—men in dark shadows, formless under rain ponchos, gripping their weapons as tightly as Kira was gripping hers. It was pitch-black under the trees, the moon and stars lost behind a thick layer of storm clouds. If anyone started shooting, she wondered if she'd even dare to shoot back—how could she tell which shapes in the darkness were enemies, and which were friends?

"They might not be from the Voice," Marcus whispered. His voice was nearly inaudible, his lips practically touching her ear. "They could be merchants, drifters, even farmers. Just stay low."

"You have a very pretty name," said the voice in the darkness. "You can take it with you when you go."

"We're on our way to East Meadow," said Jayden, "just making sure the area's safe before we make camp. How many you got in there?"

The voice laughed hoarsely. "That's a mighty dumb piece of intel for me to give you, not knowing your intentions. What if you're Voices?"

"We're from the Defense Grid," said Jayden. "I told you already."

"Wouldn't be the first time someone lied to me."

Kira heard a noise in the trees—a rustle of leaves, a snap that could have been a twig or a cocking gun. She sank lower to the ground, hoping it was one of their own people.

"There's ten of us," said Jayden. "The Voice is a lot more subtle than that . . . like maybe one old man hiding out in a ruined house."

"I suppose you've got a point there," said the man. "Doesn't seem likely we're going to trust each other either way." The voice paused, silent. Rain beat down through the leaves. After a moment the voice returned. "The name's Owen Tovar. I'm on my way to East Meadow myself, though, as it happens, and I could use the good word with the border guard. If you don't mind sharing the place with Dolly and me, you're welcome to come on in." Kira heard nothing, then the sound of a door swinging open. Jayden hesitated, just a heartbeat, then lowered his rifle to his hip.

"Thanks for the offer."

CHAPTER SIX

O wen Tovar turned out to be a tall man, thin and weathered, waiting just inside the door with a black plastic shotgun propped up on his shoulder. He smiled at Kira and Gianna.

"If that moron had told me you had women with you, I'd have let you in a lot sooner."

Marcus stepped in front of Kira protectively, but Tovar chuckled and clapped him on the arm. "Nothing unseemly, son, just good manners. Soldiers I can take or leave, but I'm afraid my mama trained me a little too well to leave a lady outside in a storm like this." He shut the door behind the last soldier and pushed his way through the group toward the dark interior of the house. "I gotta say, whichever one of you found me in here is a better tracker than most. You're wasting your talents in the Grid." He opened another door to reveal a brightly lit room—an old living room, maybe, with no exterior windows and a cheery orange fire in a stonework fireplace. The room was tightly packed with old couches and blankets, and a small wooden cart sat against a set of closed double doors on the far side. Kira turned to the right as she walked in, sizing up the area, and jumped back in surprise when she found herself nose to nose with a camel.

"Say hello, Dolly."

The camel groaned, and Tovar chuckled. "Don't be rude, folks, answer back."

Marcus smiled and bowed to the camel. "Pleased to meet you, Dolly. Mr. Tovar failed to mention how lovely his companion was."

"I don't know if every camel's as ornery as she is," said Tovar, "but we get along more or less. I figure she must have escaped from a zoo or something; I found her a few years back, just wanderin' around." He ushered the group through the doorway and closed it behind them. "I went through a lot of trouble to keep this fire invisible from outside," he explained. "Chimney still works, too, so with a storm like this to hide the smoke, you can't even tell I'm here."

"We followed the tracks," said Marcus, pulling off his coat.

"The tracks don't lead here," said Tovar. "At least not directly."

"I heard you," said Jayden, a small smile creeping through the corner of his mouth. "Dolly needs a few lessons in stealth."

Tovar shook his head. "She wanted more sugar. Figures you folks'd be passin' by for the two seconds she decides to argue the point. Most folks—meanin' those folks nosy enough to be lookin'—never find this place at all. They just follow my tracks down around the next house, back through the woods, and then give up when they hit the creek. Turns out the bridge is fallen down, if you'll believe it, and the planks I use to get across are pretty well hidden on the wrong side."

"You're a drifter," said Jayden.

"I'm a salesman. That makes me a target for all kinds of unsavories, but that doesn't mean I have to be a target of opportunity." He moved a pile of blankets from the couch nearest the fire. "Best seats to the ladies, naturally. This place is pretty cozy with just me in it, but we're going to get downright neighborly with this many people trying to sleep."

Kira watched the man as he sorted out the blankets, squeezing between the dusty couches to arrange sleeping space for ten people and a donkey. *Is he a part of the Voice?* There was no way to tell, not unless he tried to blow them up.

The drifter handed a blanket to Brown, who stared at him suspiciously before yanking it gruffly from his hands. Tovar smiled and stepped back.

"This is going to be an awful long night if we keep not trusting each other. You really think I'm a Voice?"

Brown said nothing, and Tovar turned to Gianna. "How about you?" He turned again, stopping in front of Jayden and opening his arms. "What about you, do you think I'm a Voice? Is risking my own life and sharing my dry blankets all part of some larger plan to destroy the last human civilization?"

"I think you're ex-military," said Kira, inching closer to the fire.

Tovar cocked his head to the side. "What makes you say that?"

"Some of the words you use," said Kira, "like 'intel' and 'target of opportunity.' The way you stowed your gun when we came in. The way you and Jayden are standing with absolutely identical postures right now."

Jayden and Tovar looked at each other, then at themselves:

feet shoulder-width apart, back straight, arms folded loosely behind them. They moved away from each other awkwardly, shifting their weight and shaking out their wrists.

"Being ex-military doesn't mean he's not in the Voice," said Brown. "A lot of them are soldiers, too."

"If being a soldier is proof of guilt," said Tovar, "seven out of ten people in this room are looking awfully guilty."

"So tell us about yourself," said Marcus, settling into a couch. "If I'm going to spend the whole night waiting for you guys to stop flirting and shoot each other, I want to at least be entertained."

"Owen Tovar," he repeated with a bow, "born and raised in Macon, Georgia. I played varsity football for two years, graduated, joined the marines, and blew off four of my toes in the war—this would be the Iranian war, not the Isolation War, the one with the Chinese that you kids are probably thinking of, the one we sent the Partials to fight for us. Though I suppose most of you are what, late teens? Two or three years old when that war ended, five or six when the whole world ended a few years later? No, when I say 'war,' you're probably thinking of the Partial War, things bein' what they are, but I hate to break it to you that that wasn't no kind of war at all, just some fightin' and some dyin' and some 'that's all she wrote.' War, see, is when two sides fight, maybe not evenly, but at least they both get a few swings in. What we call the Partial War was mankind gettin' mugged in an alley."

"I remember the Isolation War," said Gianna. "We're not all plague babies here."

"Not my place to speculate on a lady's age," said Tovar, sitting down by the fire. He looked relaxed, but Kira noticed that he was still in quick, easy reach of his shotgun. Jayden sat across from him, but most of the soldiers stayed standing. Kira sat by Marcus, pulling his arm over her shoulders. He was warm and reassuring.

"Doesn't matter which war it was, I guess," said Tovar. "I lost four toes, left the marines on medical leave, and went home to Georgia to play hockey."

"They couldn't have played hockey in Georgia," said Sparks. "That was one of the southern ones, right? Georgia? Hockey was an ice sport."

"Hockey was ice-skating," said Jayden, nodding, "and there's no way you could do that in Georgia. Especially with no toes."

Tovar smiled. "This is where you plague babies start to show your ignorance." He turned to Gianna. "You remember ice rinks?"

A small grin crept into her face. "I do."

"An ice rink," said Tovar, "was a giant room, like a whole basketball court, inside of a refrigerator. Just imagine—a whole building so cold the ice stays frozen. And then you fill it up with people, hundreds of people sometimes—we were only the minor leagues—and they'd all start cheering and yelling and getting worked up, and that room would heat up like this one is now, all those bodies packed in there like logs in a fire, and that giant refrigerator would keep chugging away and cooling it down and that ice would stay so frozen that all they had to do was spray it with water between periods, and a few minutes later it was as smooth and as flat as a Tiger Sharks cheerleader." He grinned maliciously. "I beg your pardon. Old rivalries."

"That is the dumbest thing I've ever heard," said Sparks. "You could power a whole city for a year with the kind of electricity you're talking about."

"A little place like East Meadow, sure," said Tovar, "you could power that town on a good-size corporate air conditioner. For the old cities, and the old ways, even a tiny little place like Macon could swallow East Meadow whole, and with all those hundreds of thousands of people driving cars and watching movies and surfing the Internet eighty-seven hours a day, we still had enough juice left over to run an ice rink in the state of Georgia—one of the hot ones, like you said, where we didn't have no business freezing anything at all."

"I still don't believe it," muttered Sparks.

"We're talking about minor league hockey in Macon, Georgia," said Tovar. "I didn't rightly believe it myself. You know what we called the team? If you're not believing anything else, you're sure not gonna believe me on this one: We called our team the Macon Whoopee." He cackled with laughter. "That sounds like the biggest lie yet, but it's true, the Macon Whoopee." He slapped his knee; several of the soldiers were laughing, and even Kira couldn't help but chuckle. "We were a minor league team that didn't feed into any majors, in a town that loved just about every sport but ours. We were going nowhere and we knew it, so why not have fun? In the forties, when I was playing, we were officially the most violent team in the country, and that means probably the whole world, and by the way, that's why I could skate with no toes. A figure skater, a speed skater, an NHL forward, sure, you need your toes for control, but all that finesse takes a backseat when all you're trying to do is slam somebody into a wall and break all his teeth."

"Hockey," mused Marcus. "The sport of kings."

Tovar paused, his eyes focused on a distant memory. "Sometimes I think that's what I miss most about the old days. The old times. We had so much of just about everything, we could waste it all on stupid junk that nobody needed. 'The Golden Age of Man.'" His smile returned, wry and sour. "Pride cometh, as they say, before the fall."

Jayden nodded, smiling faintly. "I can't say as that story makes me trust you any more than I did, but it does make me like you."

Tovar nodded back. "Very kind of you, under the circumstances." He pulled a flask from his back pocket, took a drink, and offered it to Jayden. The soldier took a swig and passed it back.

"I must admit," said Marcus, "that as a medic I am still waiting to get to the good part of this story."

Tovar looked surprised. "Excuse me?"

Marcus grinned. "The toes, man, bring out the toes!"

The soldiers cheered, and Tovar smirked. "You asked for it." He leaned down and started to unlace his boot. "Every biotech in North America offered gene treatments to regrow them for me, wounded veteran and all, but I figured a war wound was a war wound, and I had no business pretending I didn't have one. Now: The proprietor of this freak show recommends that all women and children avert their eyes before the coming horror, but as that includes pretty much all of you, I imagine he's going to be disappointed." He wiggled out of his boot, peeled back his sock from his pale, hairy leg, and whipped it away from his toe with a flourish. "Behold!"

The whole room gasped, half in shock and half in laughter, and Kira found herself smiling and grimacing at the same time. Tovar's foot was a lump of scar tissue and calluses, the four smaller toes burned or blown away and the big toe, the last one remaining, curled awkwardly to the side. The toenail was gone, and the whole foot was stark white.

"That is disgusting," said Kira, forcing each word through bursts of laughter. "How did you say you did that again?"

"I was a specialist in the Marine Corps," said Tovar, wiggling his deformed toe. "Demolitions."

The feeling in the room changed so suddenly Kira swore she could feel it: an icy chill in the air, a spray of cold water droplets as the soldiers swung their guns into place in a furious blur. Even sitting down, Tovar lost his balance and staggered back, fumbling with his sock and nearly falling off the couch as he pressed himself away from the guns.

"What the—what'd I do?"

"You have ten seconds to tell us where you've been in the last forty-eight hours," said Jayden, sighting down his rifle, "or we start shooting you just in case."

"What are you talking about?" screamed Tovar.

"Nine," said Jayden fiercely. "Eight."

"Hold on," said Kira, holding out her hands to try to calm everybody down. "Give him time to think."

"Seven," said Jayden.

"I don't know what you're talking about!" said Tovar.

Kira leaned forward desperately. "Just calm down," she said firmly. "He doesn't even know what you're talking about."

"Don't do anything stupid, Kira."

Kira turned to Tovar. "It's because you said you were in demolitions. We've had kind of a bad day, explosively speaking, and all they want to know is if you have been—"

"Not another word, Kira, or he'll know exactly what to deny."

Kira kept her eyes locked on Tovar's. "Just tell us where else you've been."

"I was in Smithtown yesterday," said Tovar. "Came straight here from there. They've got a farm there on an old golf course. I was selling them guns."

"Guns?"

"What, do you think I sell puppies? I'm a marine, I sell what I know, and out here without your Long Island Defense Grid to watch over them, people need guns. Most of these old houses have a gun safe in the basement, so I . . . blast them open and sell the guns."

"You're not sounding any less guilty right now," said Jayden.

Tovar's voice was thick and desperate. "As hard as it is to believe with ten-odd guns pointed at me, not everyone on the island has one. Not everyone on the island has a Defense Grid patrol ready to leap into action every time somebody looks suspicious. Out here, people know there's a war coming, between East Meadow and the Voice, and people need to be able to help themselves. I just make sure they have the tools to do it."

"He's lying," said a soldier.

"You don't know that," said Kira. "You can't shoot someone on a hunch."

"Did somebody try to blow you guys up?" asked Tovar.

"See?" cried the soldier, stepping forward. "He knows!"

"Stand down," said Jayden. "Do not shoot without my order."

Kira swallowed. "It doesn't take a genius to look at the last few minutes of this conversation and guess that someone tried to blow us up. If he knew about the bomb, he wouldn't have told us he was a demolitionist in the first place, would he?" She turned to Tovar. "Have you ever been to Asharoken?"

He shook his head. "That can't possibly be the name of a real place."

"You say you sell guns and ammunition," said Jayden. "Do you sell explosives, too?"

"I'd be an idiot if I did," said Tovar. "Anyone who'd buy them would either be after the same stuff I am, or planning something worse—like whatever happened to you guys. I keep all my explosives secret."

"Where?" demanded Jayden.

"Some in the cart, some in little caches around the island."

Gianna leaped away from the cart. "I've been leaning on a bomb?"

"It's stable," said Tovar, standing up. The soldiers retrained their guns on him, but he held up his hands in a show of innocence. "They're perfectly stable, okay?" He shuffled to the cart, limping in one heavy boot and one bare foot. "It's a water gel—it's completely inert until you activate it, and even then it needs a detonator."

"Where do you find explosives out here?" asked Jayden, still following him with his rifle. "I thought the military gathered up all that kind of stuff years ago."

"They got the weaponized stuff, yeah," said Tovar, "but this is used commercially all the time." He pulled back the heavy canvas tarp on his wagon and pointed to a white plastic package, like a ration bag of water. "I got this at a construction site; the activation powder's on the other side of the cart. And I swear I haven't sold any of it to anyone."

Kira looked back at Jayden. "If this is a lie," she said, "it's the most convoluted, well-acted lie in the history of the world. We're all headed back to East Meadow anyway, so let's just put down the guns and let them deal with it. If they decide he's guilty, then they can put him in jail, but I won't let you kill him here."

"That is the second worst idea I've ever heard," said Tovar, "but since the first worst is you shooting me in the face, I'm all for it."

Jayden stared at Kira, his eyes burning into hers like smoking coals. After an eternity of waiting, he lowered his gun. "Fine. But if he tries anything between now and then, I don't wait for your approval: He's a Voice, and he dies."

CHAPTER SEVEN

Kira slept fitfully, listening to Marcus and the others as they shifted and snored and muttered in the darkness. The camel made odd, semihuman moans all through the night, and the house creaked in the rain. Even the mice, ubiquitous in every home she could remember, seemed louder and more bothersome than usual as they skittered through the floor and walls. Rats, maybe, or something bigger.

Through it all, she couldn't stop thinking about Tovar's words. Was there really a war coming? Was the Voice really that desperate—or that organized? The Senate seemed to paint them as half-wild terrorists, raiding and running and killing indiscriminately, but then, she supposed, the Senate would want to paint them that way. If there were actually enough of them to mount a serious front, and start a real war, then they were a bigger threat than she had ever imagined.

RM would slowly strangle humanity, one death at a time, with no new generations to replace it. A war, on the other hand, could snuff it out in weeks.

Kira pressed herself deeper into the couch, willing herself to fall asleep.

In the morning she was tired and stiff.

Tovar led them out the back of the house and through his maze of safeguards: over a temporary bridge, through another house's weathered patio, and back to the road nearly half a mile down. The rain had stopped, and Dolly pulled the cart swiftly, so they kept a good pace. Kira tried to force herself not to look behind, not to focus on the hundred phantom Voices she imagined behind every tree and broken car. They had to stay visible, in case the Defense Grid backup came looking for them, but that visibility made Kira feel vulnerable and exposed. Even Jayden seemed anxious. They broke for lunch when the sun was high overhead, and Kira drank the last of her water while she watched the rows of ruined houses. Nothing moved. She rubbed her aching feet and checked Lanier on his stretcher; he was unconscious, and his temperature was dangerously elevated.

"How is he?" asked Gianna.

"Not good," Kira sighed. "We're running low on Nalox, and now I think he's got an infection." She rummaged in her medkit for antibiotics and began prepping a small shot.

"Is it good that he's asleep like that?"

"Well, it's not awesome," said Kira, "but it's not bad. The painkiller we're using is designed for battlefield use; you can give him way too much and not worry about killing him. Our battlefield cleansers, on the other hand, don't seem to be doing their job." She stuck him with the antibiotic and injected the full dose.

"If we don't get picked up by reinforcements pretty soon, he's in big trouble."

Kira heard a distant whistle and looked up suddenly; Jayden had heard it too. "The scouts," he said. "They've seen someone." They pulled everyone back into a nearby house, the windows broken out and the interior filled with enough windblown soil to support new plant growth; kudzu already covered the couch. Kira crouched in the corner behind a sagging upright piano, Lanier trembling fitfully behind her. Marcus caught her eye and forced a smile.

She heard another whistle, a series of short bursts she recognized as "the people I warned you about are friendly." She started to stand, but Jayden motioned her back down.

"Doesn't hurt to make sure," he whispered.

A minute later a wagon rolled past, a long, armored trailer pulled by six stamping horses. Jayden whistled loudly— "friendlies coming out, don't shoot"—and trooped outside. Kira and Marcus carried Lanier onto the porch, where they were met by another team of medics. Kira gave them a full update on his condition, and the newly arrived soldiers handed out water and protein bars as they helped everyone into the wagon.

Tovar led Dolly out from behind the house, grimacing unhappily. "Do they shoot me now, or when they get home?"

"Ideally they don't shoot you at all," said Kira.

Jayden saluted the leader of the new soldiers; Kira didn't recognize his rank insignia. "Thanks for the pickup."

The other soldier saluted him back. "We didn't expect to find you for a few more hours; you're making good time."

"This trader's been a big help," said Jayden, nodding to Tovar.

"Carried most of our gear in his wagon." He took a drink of water and wiped his mouth with the back of his hand. "We haven't seen anybody else, so if anybody followed us, they decided not to mess with an armed Grid patrol."

"Damn Voice," said the soldier. "We have outriders looking for whatever they can find—your explosion out there stirred up a lot of trouble back home. We're going to stop at Dogwood for a debrief."

The wagon turned and carried them back, the driver lashing the six-horse team into a pretty good gallop. The sun on the armored shell was hot, baking the inside, and Kira felt herself drifting away; she woke up with her head in Marcus's lap, sitting up abruptly as the wagon jerked to a stop. Dogwood turned out to be an old power station, a guardhouse on the edge of the settled East Meadow area. There was a high chain fence all around it, and another soldier opened the gate for them as they approached. Kira saw more soldiers on the perimeter.

"We can walk from here," said Kira, but the lead soldier in the wagon shook his head.

"Mkele wants to debrief all of you, not just the trader."

Debrief, thought Kira. *Military-speak for "interrogate politely."* "Who's Mkele?"

"Intelligence," said the soldier. "Command's getting pretty freaked out by your news. I think they're just hoping you'll know something important." He helped them down from the wagon and led them into the old power station building. A young man in full combat armor took Kira to a small room and left her there, closing the door behind him.

She heard the lock click shut.

The room was small and unadorned, though she could see from the discolored linoleum that several pieces of furniture had been recently removed. Rough outlines of desks and bookshelves covered the floor like a ghostly office, an afterimage of an older time. There was no table, but there were two chairs in the far corner.

She sat and waited, planning out her conversation, scripting both sides and sounding effortlessly brilliant, but the wait grew longer, and her subtle barbs about being held unfairly for questioning turned to angry rants about unlawful imprisonment. Eventually she got bored and stopped altogether.

There was a clock on the wall, the old circular kind with little black sticks, and she wondered for the umpteenth time in her life how they worked. She had a similar clock in her house, prettier than this one—whoever had lived there before her, before the Break, had had a thing for glass. Apparently the hands would move if you powered them, but digital clocks used less energy, so they were all she'd ever seen.

Well, all she could remember. Had her father ever had a round clock with sticks? It was stupid that she didn't even know what this type of clock was called—there was no good reason for something so ubiquitous to just disappear from human vocabulary. And yet try as she might, she couldn't remember ever seeing one that worked, or learning how to read them, or hearing what they were called. They were a relic of a dead culture.

The big stick was pointing at the ten, and the little stick was halfway between the two and the three. *Ten oh two and . . . a half?* She shrugged. *This clock ran out of juice at exactly ten oh two and half. Or whatever it said.* She stood up to examine it. *It must be bolted to the wall, or it would have fallen off by now.*

The door opened and a man walked in—Kira recognized him as the mysterious man from the town hall meeting. He was perhaps forty years old. His skin was even darker than her own—mostly African descent, she guessed, as opposed to her mostly Indian.

"Good evening, Ms. Walker." He shut the door behind him and extended his hand; Kira stood and shook it.

"It's about time."

"I am deeply sorry for the wait. My name is Mr. Mkele." He gestured to Kira's chair, pulled the other a few feet away, and sat down. "Please, sit."

"You have no right to hold me in here—"

"I apologize if you got that impression," said Mkele. "We are not holding you here, it was simply my desire to keep you safe while you waited. Did they bring you food?"

"They haven't brought me anything."

"They were supposed to bring you food. Again, I apologize."

Kira eyed him carefully, her anger at being locked in the room for so long turning slowly into suspicion. "Why 'Mr.'?" she asked. "Don't you have a rank?"

"I'm not in the military, Ms. Walker."

"You're in a military installation."

"So are you."

Kira kept her face rigid, trying not to frown. Something about this man irked her. He'd done nothing but speak to her calmly, a model of manners and courtesy, and yet . . . she couldn't put her finger on it. She glanced at the chair he had offered, but stayed standing and folded her arms. "You say you locked me in here to keep me safe. What from?"

The man raised his eyebrow. "That's an interesting question from someone who just got back from no-man's-land. My understanding is that someone tried to blow you up not two days ago."

"Not me personally, but yeah."

"My official title, Ms. Walker, is head of intelligence—not for the military but for the entire island, which in practice means I'm the head of intelligence for the entire human race. My job today is to ensure that there is still a human race tomorrow, and I do that by knowing things. Consider, if you will, the things we know now." He held up his hand, counting on his fingers. "One: Someone, potentially the Voice or, heaven help us, the Partials, has enacted another successful assault on East Meadow forces. Two: That someone is highly proficient with explosives and perhaps radio technology. Three: That person has killed a minimum of three people. Now. Given the ominous nature of these few, small things we do know, I think you'll agree that the massive number of things we don't know is, to put it mildly, incredibly troubling."

"Well, yeah," said Kira, nodding, "of course. But I'm not in no-man's-land anymore—I'm in a military base. That's got to be, like, the safest place on the island."

Mkele watched her calmly. "Have you ever seen a Partial, Miss Walker?"

"In person? No. I was only five during the war, and no one's seen any since then."

"How can you be sure?"

Kira frowned. "What do you mean? No one's seen one in years, they're . . . well, I'm alive, for one thing, so apparently none of them have seen me either."

"Let us assume," said Mr. Mkele, "just for the moment, that whatever the Partials are planning is larger in scope than the murder of one teenage girl."

"You don't have to be insulting about it."

"Again, I apologize."

"So is that really what this is about?" Kira asked, with more than a hint of exasperation. "Partials? Really? Don't we have more important threats to deal with?"

"If a Partial were planning something big," he said, ignoring her question, "some insidious attack on us or our resources or any other aspect of our lives, the most effective way would be to infiltrate us directly. They look exactly like us; they could walk among us without any fear of discovery. You're a medic; you should know this as well as anyone."

Kira frowned. "The Partials are gone, Mr. Mkele—they backed us up onto this island and then disappeared. No one has seen one anywhere—not here, not on the border, not anywhere."

Mkele flashed a small, mocking smile. "The innocent complacence of a plague baby. You say you were five when the Partials rebelled; the world you see is the only world you've ever known. How much of the rebellion do you remember, Ms. Walker? How much of the old world? Do you know what even one Partial is capable of, much less an entire battalion?"

"We have bigger problems than the Partials," said Kira again, trying not to lose her cool. It felt like the same old attitude she got at the hospital—from every adult, really, a stubborn, brutal insistance on dealing with yesterday's problems instead of today's. "The Partials destroyed the world, I know, but that was eleven years ago, and then they disappeared, and meanwhile RM is continuing to kill our children, tensions are rising because of the Hope Act, the Voice are out there raiding farms and stealing supplies, and I don't think—"

"The Voice," said Mkele, "look even more human than the Partials."

"What's your point?"

"This is the point, Ms. Walker. The Partials may indeed be gone, but they hardly need stage an outright attack on the island if tensions between the settlement and the Voice progress any further. RM is performing a more insidious function than even the Partials devised: our inability to produce healthy children and the measures we've subsequently taken to try to deal with it—"

"You mean the Hope Act."

"Among other things, yes . . . they are tearing the island apart. I have a hard time believing that what happened to your team yesterday didn't have something to do with this, and unless there is overwhelming evidence to the contrary, I'm going to assume that it was part of a plan to destabilize the human civilization and thus to hasten our extinction."

"You are an incredibly paranoid person."

Mkele tilted his head to the side. "I've been charged, as I said, with the safety of the human race. It's my job to be paranoid."

Kira's patience was wearing thin.

"Fine, then—let's get this over with. What do you want to know?"

"Tell me about the veterinary clinic."

"What?"

"The clinic you and Marcus Valencio were assigned to salvage—tell me what you saw there."

"I thought you wanted to know about the bomb."

"I have already spoken to other witnesses who were present both before and during the explosion, and their information trumps yours in that area. The clinic, on the other hand, you experienced directly. Tell me about it."

"It was a clinic," said Kira, searching for something interesting to say. "It was the same as every clinic we salvage—old, smelly, falling apart. There was a pack of dogs living in it, and, um . . . what else do you want to know?"

"Did you see any dogs when you were there?"

"No, why? Is that important?"

"I have no idea," said Mkele, "though it does seem odd that a pack of wild dogs would fail to defend their home against a group of invaders."

"I guess so," said Kira. "Maybe the salvage group that went through a few days earlier scared them all off."

"It's possible."

"Um, what else . . . ," said Kira. "We started on the meds, and then the bomb went off after just a few minutes, so we didn't get a chance to test the X-ray machine."

"So you saw the front exterior, the foyer, and the medicine storage."

Kira nodded. "Yeah."

"Did you see anything out of the ordinary?"

"Nothing comes to mind. Except . . ." She paused, remembering the marks in the dust. "Now that you mention it, the pill bottles had all been messed with before we got there."

"Messed with?"

"Moved," said Kira, "like someone had gone through them or something. Like they were looking for something."

"How recently?"

"Not very long. There were smudges and tracks and marks all through the dust, both up in the cupboard and down on the counter."

"It could have been, as you suggested with the dogs, the grunt salvage crew that went through before you."

"I guess," said Kira, "but I've never seen any of the grunt crews go through the meds like that."

Mr. Mkele pursed his lips, thinking. "Do any of the drugs you found there have recreational uses?"

"You think one of the grunts was trying to get high?"

"It is one of many possibilities, yes."

Kira closed her eyes, racking her brain to remember the names of the medicines. "I'm not sure—it's all kind of rote at this point, you know? You know which ones last and which ones don't, and you toss them in the piles without really thinking about it. But these vet clinics always have painkillers, stuff like Rimadyl, and a big enough dose of almost any painkiller will get you high. It might also kill you, though, unless you use the military nanoparticle stuff that obviously wouldn't be in a veterinary clinic. Aside from that, though . . ." She paused, thinking. If she were a Voice, living in the wilderness and getting into fights with the Defense Grid, she'd have bigger concerns than recreational painkillers. She started to see where Mkele was coming from, and thought about the clinic as a military target. "Clinics like that have a lot of meds a group of rebels might find really useful," she said. "Antibiotics, antiparasitics, flea powders and shampoos—there's any number of things a band of forest raiders could make good use of."

"Interesting," said Mkele. "You'll have to forgive my ignorance on the subject of veterinary clinics, but do you think there's any way to find a record of their inventory? It might be possible to determine, within a small margin of error, exactly what might have been present, missing, or tampered with."

"I doubt they have anything on paper," said Kira, "but the clinic had a computer system. You could hook it up to a generator and hope they stored their inventory on the hard drive. If they stored it on an exterior network, you're probably out of luck." They used computers in the hospital, thanks to the solar panels, but the old world had used them for everything, all linked together in a worldwide network Kira couldn't even fathom. It had collapsed along with the power grid, and everything on it had been lost forever.

"We'll do that," said Mkele, nodding. "Is there anything else you think might help us?"

Kira shrugged. "If I remember anything, I'll be sure to let you know."

"Thank you very much for your time," said Mkele, gesturing to the door. "You're free to go."

CHAPTER EIGHT

Private Brown drove Kira home in a small wagon, and she sat in the back holding tightly to Marcus's hand. Jayden and his soldiers were staying for more debriefing. She didn't see Gianna or Tovar.

It was nearing twilight, and the rocking of the wagon was putting Marcus to sleep. Kira watched as his head drooped, nodding, then jerked up as he came awake, then slowly dropped again. Over and over. The horse's hoofbeats echoed dully off the empty houses, but as they drew closer to the populated area, Kira saw the familiar signs of human activity: painted houses, mowed lawns, roofs that were still standing. East Meadow. Kira watched closely for the gleam of reflected light, and smiled when she saw it: glass windows. Everywhere else on the island the windows had been shattered by cats and birds and weather and the uneven shifting as wooden walls rotted around them. Not here. Here the windows were protected and cared for, and most were still as clean and clear as a piece of solid sky. Out in the wilderness there were thieves and the Voice and the dying carcass of an entire world.

Here, there were glass windows.

"Wake up, sleepyhead," said Kira, bumping Marcus's ear with her shoulder. "We're almost home."

"I didn't order sushi."

"What?"

Marcus opened his eyes warily. "What did I say?"

"Nothing I have to smack you for. You're lucky you were dreaming about food instead of girls."

"I'm male," said Marcus, rubbing his eyes. "It was a fifty-fifty shot."

"Our overnight vacation turned into two days, a Voice attack, and a military debrief," said Kira. "You think we'll get in trouble for missing work today at the hospital?"

"The Defense Grid must have told them what was going on," said Marcus, stretching the kinks from his neck. "I figure if we even try to go in for the rest of the day, they'll send us home with ration packs of chicken soup."

Kira laughed. "That sounds like an excellent reason not to go in."

Marcus grinned and looked at the sun. "Not much daylight left, anyway. And if they'd send us home from the day shift, there's no way they'd let us work the night."

"Then it's settled," said Kira, shifting her weight on the hard floor of the wagon. "I'm going to head home, get cleaned up, and fall asleep. I might wake up for the party this weekend, but I'm not making any promises."

"I wouldn't miss that party for the world," said Marcus.

"Xochi's gonna make a chicken—a real, live chicken. Though I suppose it won't be live for long. I'll even pluck the scabby thing myself."

"You think her mother will be there?"

"Senator Kessler?" asked Marcus, his jaw falling open in disbelief. "Xochi owns a gun now—Kessler won't get anywhere near the place."

Kira laughed and nodded. She hoped Xochi wouldn't actually shoot her adopted mother—but she couldn't be sure.

"Just bring something to share this time," said Kira, turning back to Marcus and tapping him pointedly in the chest. "I'm not covering for you like last time."

"That was a one-time thing," said Marcus, laughing, "and it wasn't last time, it was four times ago, and I've covered your share way more than that."

"I'm just saying," said Kira, poking him again in the chest, "I don't want my good-for-nothing, freeloader boyfriend to make me look bad in front of everybody. Again." She poked him one last time, glared at him playfully, then poked him again for good measure.

"Do you poke all the boys, or am I special?"

She leaned closer. "It's just you." She kissed him on the cheek. "Until somebody better comes along."

Marcus put his hand on the back of her head and pulled her in for another kiss, on the mouth this time, slow and soft and perfect. Kira pressed herself closer, feeling his body against hers, thinking about what he'd said at the clinic. Was it time? Was she ready?

"Guys," said Brown, "I'm like two feet away."

Kira pulled back, embarrassed. "Sorry."

"I'm not," said Marcus. "Totally worth it."

"You said the blue house, right?" Brown pointed ahead to the row of houses, and Kira recognized her street.

"Yeah, the blue one's mine."

Brown nodded. "Is Romeo getting off with you?"

"I would," said Marcus, "but Nandita wouldn't let me in anyway. I'm just two streets over, if you can do it."

"Not a problem." The young soldier slowed the wagon and pulled the horse to a stop. Kira gave Marcus a final peck on the cheek and hopped off.

"There's Nandita," said Marcus, straightening up and pointing. Kira turned and saw her working busily in her garden. Marcus lowered his voice. "See if she's got some herbs for the chicken."

"Rosemary, I assume," said Kira, and Marcus nodded with a grin. "Anything else?"

"Whatever she can spare," said Marcus. "Everything in your garden is awesome."

"You got it," said Kira. "Thanks, Brown."

The soldier smiled. "Call me Shaylon."

"Easy, tiger," said Marcus. "She's spoken for."

The wagon pulled away, and Kira shouldered her pack and walked toward her house. Kira shared her home with several other girls and their "nanny," Nandita, though after eleven years she seemed more like a grandmother than anything else. Between the Partial War and RM, no family had survived intact: Every surviving wife became a widow; every child an orphan. Those few humans who'd been immune to the virus had banded together for protection, gathering here on Long Island because it was a developed, defensible position with good access to fish and arable land. The children had been divided among the adults, and Nandita had happily laid claim to four of them: Kira, Madison, Ariel, and Isolde. Ariel had moved nearly three years ago, on her sixteenth birthday, and Madison had moved in with Haru when they got married. Ariel had hardly spoken to any of them again, but Kira loved them all like sisters.

Nandita was working in the garden, and Kira could smell the exotic mix of aromatic herbs: rosemary, nutmeg, anise, cilantro, basil, marjoram. . . . Kira helped in the garden every summer, and she still couldn't keep track.

"Does Marcus want rosemary on the chicken this Friday?" asked Nandita. The old woman straightened up from the garden, brushing soil from her hands. She spoke quickly, almost impassively, but Kira could tell from her eyes that she had been worried sick the entire time Kira had been gone.

Kira smiled.

"Did you hear him?"

"I didn't need to hear him," said Nandita. "That boy has a one-track mind." She grunted and stood up, picking up a basket of fresh leaves and sprigs and berries. Even while gardening, she was wearing a sari. "The market was good today. Help me inside."

Kira shouldered her pack and her medkit, following the old woman up the porch steps and in through the doors; Xochi's music was blaring upstairs, and Kira smiled. She'd have to go talk to her when she was done helping Nandita.

Nandita loved all her girls, but she'd always had a soft spot for Kira. Maybe because she was the youngest, or maybe because she was so precocious; Kira remembered helping Nandita in the market as a child, calling out fearlessly to passing adults and ordering them sternly to buy a sprig of mint. Nandita called her the Little Explosion.

Sometimes Kira felt guilty that she had so many memories of Nandita, and none of her real mother. Her father she knew, but her mother . . . It was okay. She had Nandita.

"Did anything exciting happen while I was gone?"

"My Little Explosion almost died in a big one," said Nandita, pushing the door open. The previous owners—the Martels, according to the papers and photos and scrapbooks they had found inside—had died with the doors locked, and the early survivors had been forced to break them open to get inside and clean up the bodies. Nandita had replaced the door four times over the years, as one or the other of the girls had forgotten their keys after a long night out. Replacing the door, she said, was preferable to leaving it unlocked. It wasn't like the island was short on unused doors. Kira dropped her pack inside and followed Nandita into the kitchen.

"You have grown up well," said Nandita, turning in the kitchen doorway and regarding Kira with a smile. "You will make a good wife."

"Um, yay?"

The woman walked to the counter and set down the basket, opening the cupboards to look for bowls. "You do not want to be a wife? You are not going to marry Marcus?"

Kira opened a cupboard and handed Nandita a ceramic bowl. "I . . . haven't really thought about it."

Nandita stopped moving, turned, and stared at Kira. Kira squirmed uncomfortably, waiting for her to look away, then finally sighed and threw up her hands. "Okay, so I've thought about it, but I haven't decided anything. I don't know what I want."

"You want to be happy," said Nandita, reaching past Kira to the open cupboard and pulling out the entire stack of dishes. "That's what everybody wants. You just don't know what will make you happy."

Kira grimaced. "Is that weird?"

Nandita shook her head kindly. "Happiness is the most natural thing in the world when you have it, and the slowest, strangest, most impossible thing when you don't." She set out the dishes and started sorting through the herbs, separating them into groups and tearing off leaves and branches for the bowls. The scent of crushed mint filled the kitchen. "It's like learning a foreign language: You can think about the words all you want, but you'll never be able to speak it until you suck up your courage and say them out loud."

"What if you say them and they're wrong?"

"Then you've probably just asked the waiter for a bowl of library elephants," said Nandita, "or whatever the metaphorical equivalent of that would be. I can't carry these analogies very far, I get mixed up."

"Too bad," said Kira, picking up a handful of rosemary and breaking off pale green twigs for the bowl. "I was hoping you'd just keep going: happiness, love, the whole . . . purpose of life, I guess."

"Whose life?"

"What do you mean?"

"Each life has a different purpose, and some people can find their purpose more easily than others. The key," she said, turning to Kira and gesturing firmly with a sprig of cilantro, "the most important thing you can ever know, is that whatever your purpose is, that's not your only choice."

"Huh?"

"No matter why you're here, no matter why any of us are here, you're never tied down to fate. You're never locked in. You make your own choices, Kira, and you can't let anyone ever take that away from you."

"Okay," said Kira. "That's not really where I was expecting this conversation to go."

"That's because I make my own choices, too," said Nandita, picking up her basket. She still had nearly half the herbs unsorted. "I'm taking these to the neighbors; Armand is sick. You go and get cleaned up—I want my house to smell like basil, not teenage armpits."

"Done," said Kira, and ran upstairs. The music was louder up here, the usual assortment of screeching, booming, yelling music that Xochi always chose when she was alone. Kira smiled, then smelled herself, grimaced, and went straight to the shower.

On the very small list of benefits to the end of the world, at or very near the top, was clothes. Long Island had once held nearly eight million people, with the shopping malls and department stores and fashion meccas necessary to clothe them all. The Break had reduced that population to a tiny fraction, and obliterated the economic system in the process, leaving all those clothes pretty much free for the taking. It was horrible, Kira knew, and the survivors lived their lives in a brutal mix of hard work and desperation and fear. But they were very well dressed.

Many of the clothes on the island were too shabby to wear—too moldy, or too moth-eaten, or too faded from exposure—but a lot of them were still good, even today. "Shopping" was as simple as combing through an empty store or neighborhood, finding something that fit, and giving it a good wash to get rid of the bugs and the smell. Storage rooms and warehouses were the best. There the clothes were sealed in boxes instead of loose to the world, and Kira had spent many of her weekends with her friends, picking through ruined strip malls in search of a Twenty-Two or a Threadless or some little boutique that no one else had found yet. Nandita's girls had an entire room filled with every kind of outfit they could imagine, from baggy sweats to slinky dresses and everything in between. Kira chose something that showed off her legs—might as well have some fun after two days of near-death experience—and went to say hi to Xochi.

Xochi Kessler had moved into their house soon after Madison left it; Xochi had just turned sixteen and couldn't wait to escape from her "mother." She'd brought with her four banks of solar panels—her adopted mother was rich, if nothing else—enough to run lights, an electric stove, even a toaster if she wanted it, but instead every ounce of juice those panels brought in went straight to Xochi's music system. Music was practically Xochi's life. Kira had met her years ago while shopping, Kira for clothes and Xochi for digital music players. They were palm-size tablets of metal and plastic and glass, on which their former owners had stored hour after hour of every kind of music imaginable. Xochi had collected nearly a hundred of them.

Xochi waved as Kira stepped into the doorway. "Give it up for Kira, mighty hero of the infamous Asharoken salvage run! You are rocking those shorts, girl."

Kira grinned and waved back. "When one has legs like mine," she said airily, twirling on one foot, "one has a responsibility to display them. For the little people."

"Is that an Irish joke?" asked Xochi, frowning in mock solemnity. "I certainly hope so." Senator Erin Kessler was a proud Irish woman, and thus Xochi had been adopted and raised in an aggressively Irish home. Her actual heritage was more southwestern, Mexican or even Aztec, but that hadn't stopped the senator from forceful cultural indoctrination. When Xochi got mad, she even slipped into an Irish brogue. Kira thought it was hilarious.

"I don't mean leprechauns, I mean commoners," said Kira. "It was a peasant joke, but I guess it's not funny unless you imagine that I'm actually a princess."

"I'm totally a princess," said Xochi, "and I dare anyone to prove otherwise."

"Princess of what?" asked Xochi. "Lincoln Avenue?"

"My parents were the rulers of a vast, exotic empire," said Xochi, waving her fingers mysteriously. "Or at least, since nobody knows who they were, they might as well have been."

"What are you planning for the party this Friday?" Nandita was a good cook, but Xochi was an excellent one, and always provided the food for special occasions.

"Roast chicken, fried potatoes, and doughnuts if I can get the flour for them. Sweet rice is good, but for the love of all that's holy, I want some effing chocolate."

"Chocolate doughnuts?" asked Kira, whistling appreciatively.

"Who died and made you senator?"

"Unfortunately, not my mother," said Xochi. She jumped up, heading for the door. "I found a guy in the market yesterday who swore he had some wheat flour. Want to come?"

"These legs aren't doing the little people any good locked up in here," said Kira, standing with a flourish. "The people need to see their princesses."

It was Friday. Rebuilding Day.

Time for a party.

There were no births on Friday, and no fevered babies to monitor, so Kira came home exhausted but ready to enjoy herself without feeling guilty. She bathed, brushed out her hair, and chose a bright-colored outfit from her "flirty" section: a silk shirt with Chinese embroidery, a pair of high-heeled sandals, and a pair of jeans just short enough that she paused to worry about the weather. It was summer, but a cold one, and another rainstorm could really make her wish she'd gone with something heavier. She mulled over the decision, comparing the jeans with a longer pair, and finally decided to go with the shorts. They looked better with the shirt, and better on her, and she needed the boost. She could risk cold legs to feel like a normal person again for a while. They probably wouldn't go outside anyway.

"Hurry up," said Xochi, rapping on Kira's bedroom door. She was dressed in all black, including lipstick and eyeliner, with an incongruously colorful apron tied around her waist. "Madison and Haru are already here, and some dude named Marcus—tall, goofy-looking, easy to push around. You'd like him."

"I can see why your royal parents got rid of you," said Kira with a playful sneer. "You can be a delightfully snotty person when you put your mind to it."

"My wit is like your legs," said Xochi. "It would be selfish of me to keep it hidden." Kira followed her to the kitchen and waved to Nandita, busily washing dishes in the sink. Xochi pulled a bowl of sliced potatoes from the counter, drizzled them with olive oil, and sprinkled Nandita's rosemary liberally over the top, stirring the concoction with her hands. "Nandita, these herbs smell great."

"Thank you, scary one," said Nandita. It was their private joke: Nandita's entire wardrobe was brightly colored saris, and she simply couldn't understand Xochi's preference for black.

"Your kitchen smells great," said Kira, taking a deep whiff, "but I'm going to tear myself away and find Marcus."

"Give him a kiss for me," said Xochi.

"Tongue?"

"Not too much. I don't want to seem easy."

Kira walked down the hall, breathing deeply as another wave of mouthwatering smells washed over her. Say what you will about Xochi's mom, she taught that girl how to cook.

The hall was lit with gasoline lamps, all hooded and filtered to catch the smell. Kira could hear the hum of voices from the living room, and the hiss and crackle of fire from the wood-burning stove in the kitchen. *This is what the farmers eat like all the time,* she thought. *Almost makes me want to try the life.*

Almost.

She followed the voices to the living room. Marcus and Haru were deep in discussion on the couch, while Madison reclined nearby on an easy chair. The stereo was in this room, and the sound filled the room like a storm cloud.

Madison smiled. "Hey."

"Hey, Mads. What's up?"

Madison smirked and darted her eyes toward Marcus and Haru. "Just relaxing while your noble boyfriend takes the brunt of my husband's righteous fury. He's really on one today."

Kira nodded. Haru was an intense talker.

"Of course it's about freedom," Haru was saying, "it's about preserving freedom through law." His eyes were fierce, and Marcus looked pale but determined under his glare. "Any society needs a certain amount of law: Too much gives you tyranny, but too little gives you chaos."

"Kira!" said Marcus, practically leaping out of his chair when he saw her. He crossed and gave her a hug, coming away with her hand clasped tightly in his own. He looked her up and down, pointedly not looking at Haru. "You look great."

"Thanks," said Kira. She led him to a couch and sat down, looking across at Haru. "Hey, good to see you." She really didn't want him to start up again on whatever he was ranting about, but she couldn't just refuse to acknowledge him.

"You as well," said Haru. "I'm glad to hear you both survived your adventure on the shore."

Kira raised an eyebrow. "You've heard?"

"Everybody's heard," said Madison. "I suppose we all have more exciting things to talk about than a mysterious radio installation rigged with a massive bomb that killed three people, but you know how it is. Sometimes we talk about boring stuff, too."

"It was the Voice," said Haru. "That woman who was with you, Gianna or whatever, was one of them."

Kira laughed. "What? She was in the middle of it—I pulled her out of the rubble myself. Or are you saying she blew herself up? On purpose? Or is she just a really lousy terrorist?"

"Maybe she was trying to protect whatever was there from being found," said Haru.

"She never came back," said Marcus softly.

Kira looked at him in surprise, then at Haru. She shook her head. "She came back with us."

"To the Dogwood station," said Marcus, nodding. Kira could see the sadness in his eyes—sadness mixed with confusion, and a hint of fear. "No one's seen her after that."

Kira shook her head; this was crazy. "Gianna was not a Voice. She didn't like Jayden very much, but he was throwing his weight around a little more than necessary—nobody would have liked him much." She glanced at Madison. "No offense."

"None taken."

"She's the one who identified that thing as a radio," said Haru, "and the only person who could argue with her died in the explosion. For all we know, the other guy figured out that it was an active Voice base of operations and this Gianna woman triggered the bomb to shut him up. She's the only one who lived."

Kira laughed out loud, then felt guilty and tried to stifle it. "I'm sorry, but that's . . . incredibly paranoid. You're almost as bad as the guy who debriefed us the other day."

"Paranoid or not," said Haru, "obviously the Defense Grid agrees or they wouldn't have kept her in custody."

Xochi stepped into the room and leaned against the doorway. "You're talking about that computer scientist from the salvage run?"

Kira threw up her hands, eyes wide. "Does everyone know about this but me?"

"You spend fifteen hours a day in the hospital," said Madison. "The Voice could kidnap the Senate and you wouldn't know about it."

"The Defense Grid shouldn't be able to hold people like that," said Xochi. "They should have public arrests and public trials, not people who disappear for no reason."

"It's not for no reason," said Haru. "She's a terrorist. That's a pretty good reason."

"You don't know that she's a terrorist," said Xochi, "or have you been rehired into the Defense Grid with top-level clearance and just forgot to tell us about it?"

Haru glared at her. "Do you have a problem with the Defense Grid doing their job?"

"I have a problem with 'making people disappear' suddenly being a part of their job. When did that happen?"

"Their job is to protect us, and they do it the way they think is best. If you don't trust them, why are you still here?"

"Maybe I believe in solving problems instead of running away from them."

"Maybe?"

This is getting too heated, thought Kira, but just as she was about to step in and stop the argument, Marcus spoke up and did it for her.

"I think that's enough on this topic," he said. "Everybody just calm down." He looked at Xochi. "Is there anything I can do to help with the food?"

"We're just about done," said Xochi, casting a last, withering look at Haru. "You can help me bring it in."

They walked back down the hall, and Kira took a slow breath. She wanted to blame Haru for the fight—and he was certainly a big part of why the argument had become a fight in the first place—but she knew it wasn't all his fault. Tensions were high all through East Meadow, probably all across the island, and everyone was on edge. Had Gianna really been part of the Voice? Had the government really just made her disappear?

It had been easier, in some ways, when Kira was a kid, and the Partials were the big bad guy. Everything terrible that had happened could be explained, and while the explanation might be scary, at least it was simple. Darkness was clearly divided from light. These days . . . Kira had no idea who the enemy was, or who you could blame, or who you could trust. If Gianna was a Voice, then you couldn't trust your neighbors, and if she wasn't a Voice, then you couldn't trust your government. Kira didn't like either possibility.

Haru stood up, still scowling. "I'm going outside; I need some air." He walked away, and Kira heard the back door click open and closed.

Madison smiled sadly. "Sorry about him," she said. "He's under a lot of stress."

"Rough week at work?" asked Kira. Haru worked in construction. Not building things, because everything they could ever need had already been built by the old world. In East Meadow the construction department maintained the buildings currently in use and analyzed new ones the Senate thought the community might need. They spent a lot of time on salvage runs, studying old buildings' stability before the crews went

87

through and stripped out anything useful. Haru had shown a knack for excavation, so they'd transferred him over from the Defense Grid, but he apparently hadn't been happy about it. Kira knew that every time something went wrong on his job, it left him surly for days. She'd wondered on more than one occasion if Haru's transfer had been a veiled dismissal for some conflict or infraction.

To Kira's surprise, Madison shook her head. "His job's been fine," she said softly, "it's . . ." She stopped, staring at the floor, then looked up at Kira intently. "Come here." Her voice was soft but excited, here eyes suddenly alive with energy. Kira narrowed her eyes, wondering what could make Madison so happy and Haru so edgy. She slid across the couch while Madison looked over her shoulder, and suddenly it hit her; she felt the emotional weight like a punch in the gut. She looked at Madison with wide eyes, her breath caught in her throat.

"No . . ."

Madison turned back, her smile stretching from ear to ear. "I'm pregnant."

Kira shook her head, still trying to take a deep breath. "No, Mads, no—"

"Yes," said Madison, "I'm positive. I've been sick for weeks, too sick to even eat sometimes, and then ravenous thirty minutes later for something totally weird. I've been craving dirt, Kira, like dirt from our garden. Is that the craziest thing?"

"We don't get certain minerals in our diets here," Kira whispered. "Pregnant cravings are your body's way of telling you what nutrients it needs. Dirt's not that uncommon with our diet."

"I'm going to go into the hospital in a few days to get tested for real," said Madison, "but I wanted to tell you first."

"No," said Kira again, shaking her head. This couldn't be happening—she knew that it could, that it was in fact very likely, but at the same time she knew that no, this was Madison, this was the closest thing to a sister, to a family, that Kira had left. "Do you have any idea what it's like?" she asked. "The pain? The danger? Women die in childbirth; even with all our equipment and experience at the hospital it still happens, and then even if you live, your baby won't. We haven't cured RM yet—you're going to live with this for a few more months, and go through all that pain and terror and blood and everything else, and then it's going to die." Kira felt herself tearing up, felt a hot wetness welling up in her eyes and spilling coldly down her face. She imagined Madison where Ariel had been, wide-eyed and screaming, banging on the glass as her daughter squirmed and wailed and died. "Haru is right to be upset," she said, wiping her face with her fingers. "This is too much for you, you don't need this."

"Yes, I do," said Madison softly.

"It's a stupid law," said Kira, raising her voice angrily before glancing nervously toward the hallway and lowering it again. "You don't have to go through with this. Give me more time— fake sterility or something, it happens, just don't—"

"It's already done," said Madison. Her smile was the sweet, beatific smile Kira had seen on a dozen other mothers, and it broke her heart. Madison put her hand on Kira's. "I didn't do this for the Hope Act, and I didn't do this for the Senate, I did it for me."

Kira shook her head, tears still rolling down her face.

"I want this," said Madison. "I was born to be a mother—it's in my genes, it's right here in the center of who I am." She clutched at her chest and blinked back a few tears of her own. "I know that it scares you, and I know it scares Haru. It scares me too, it scares me to death, but it's the right thing to do. Even if it only lasts for a few days—even if it only lasts for a few hours."

"Oh, Madison." Kira leaned forward, clasping her friend in an embrace. She felt terrified and guilty, knowing she was right but ashamed of herself for dumping on Madison like that. Of course Madison knew the risks; everyone on the island knew them. Madison wasn't running away from them, she was meeting them head-on.

Kira pulled back, wiping her eyes again.

"One of these days we *will* have a survivor," she said. "It's inevitable. A child will live. It might be yours."

Marcus walked in with a broad wooden tray and stopped at the sight of them hugging and crying. "Is everything okay?"

"I'll tell you later," said Kira, pulling back from Madison and wiping her eyes again. Her cheeks felt raw from the constant scrubbing.

"Okay," he said slowly, setting the tray on the low central table. Xochi had covered it with a whole roast chicken, crusted with herbs and dripping with juices, and a heaping pile of pan-fried potatoes. Xochi followed next with a tray of vegetables—all fresh in honor of the holiday—and Nandita came last with a tray of chocolate-covered doughnuts. Kira's mouth watered; she couldn't remember the last time she'd had anything so good. It might have been a full year ago on the last Rebuilding Day.

Marcus stooped in front of Kira. "Do you need anything?

Can I get you a drink or whatever?"

Kira shook her head. "I'm fine, but could you get Mads some water?"

"I'll get some for you, too." He slid his hand gently across her shoulder, then walked back to the kitchen.

Xochi looked at Madison, then at Kira. She said nothing, but turned to the stereo. "I think we need something a little more laid-back." The music hub was a small panel on a shelf along the wall, connected wirelessly to a series of speakers around the room. The center of the panel held a small dock for a digital music player, which Xochi unplugged and dropped into a basket. "Any requests?"

Madison smiled. "Laid-back sounds nice."

"Use Athena," said Kira, standing up to help. "I always like Athena." She and Xochi sifted through the basket—a wide wicker thing filled with slim silver bricks. Most of them were monogrammed: TO CATELYN, FROM DADDY. TO CHRISTOPH: HAPPY BIRTHDAY. Even the ones without monograms bore some kind of identifying mark: a plastic cover with a picture or pattern; an image etched into the back; a small charm dangling from the corner. They were more than receptacles for music, they were records of a personality—an actual person, their likes and dislikes, their tastes and inner thoughts reflected in their playlists. Xochi had spent years scavenging the players from the rubble, and she and Kira would lie on the floor for hours on end, listening to each player and imagining what its owner must have been like. TO KATHERINE ON HER GRADUATION was full of country music, cheerful and twangy and wearing its heart on its sleeve. JIMMY OLSEN listened to everything, from ancient chants to orchestral symphonies to thrashing rock and metal. Kira found her favorite almost at the bottom, ATHENA, MY ANGEL, and plugged it into the dock. A few seconds later the first song started, soft and driving at once, a subtle wall of electronic waves and dissonant guitars and intimate, throaty vocals. It was calming and comfortable and sad all at once, and it fit Kira's mood perfectly. She closed her eyes and smiled. "I think I would have liked Athena. Whoever she was."

Marcus returned with the water, and a moment later Haru came in from the back porch. His face was solemn, but he seemed calmer, and he nodded politely to Xochi. "This smells delicious. Thank you for making it."

"My pleasure."

Kira glanced quickly around. "Are we waiting for anyone?"

Madison shook her head. "I tried to talk to Ariel, but she's still not talking to me. And Isolde's going to be late, and said to start without her—there's something big at the Senate, and Hobb's keeping her longer."

"Lucky girl," said Xochi. She passed out plates and forks, and they paused before digging into the food.

"Happy Rebuilding Day," said Marcus. He raised his glass of water, and the others did the same; the glasses were perfectly matched, crystal goblets salvaged from a huge estate outside of town, and the water inside was boiled and fresh, tinged slightly yellow from the chemicals in Nandita's purifier.

"The old world ended," said Madison, intoning the familiar words, "but the new one is only beginning."

"We will never forget the past," said Haru, "and we will never forsake the future."

Xochi raised her chin, holding her head high. "Life comes from death, and weakness teaches us strength."

"Nothing can defeat us," said Kira. "We can do anything." She paused, then added softly, "We will do everything."

They drank, and for a moment all was silent but the music, soft and haunting in the background. Kira swallowed the water in slow gulps, sloshing it thoughtfully in her mouth, tasting the chemical tang. She rarely even noticed it anymore, but it was there, sharp and bitter. She thought about Madison and Haru, and about their baby, perfect and innocent and doomed. She thought about Gianna, and Mkele, and the explosion and the Voice and the Senate and everything else, the entire world, the future and the past. *I'm not going to let it die*, she thought, and looked at Madison's belly, still firm and flat and unchanged. *I'm going to save you, no matter what it takes.*

We will do everything.

CHAPTER NINE

"I need a sample of your blood," said Kira.

Marcus raised an eyebrow. "I didn't know we'd reached that stage of our relationship."

She ripped up a tuft of grass and threw it at him. "It's for work, genius." They were on Kira's front lawn, enjoying a rare instance when they both had the same day off. They'd helped Nandita with the herb garden for a few hours, and their hands were rough and fragrant. "I'm going to cure RM."

Marcus laughed. "I wondered when someone would finally get around to that. It's been on my to-do list for ages, but you know how things are: Life gets so busy, and saving the human race is such an inconvenience—"

"I'm serious," said Kira. "I can't just watch children die anymore. I can't just stand there and take notes while Madison's baby dies. I'm not going to do it. It's been weeks since she told us, and I've been racking my brain for anything I can do to help, and I think I finally have a workable starting point."

"All right, then," said Marcus, sitting up in the grass. His face was more serious now. "You know that I think you're brilliant, and you got better grades in virology than . . . anyone. Ever. How do you expect to suddenly solve the biggest medical mystery in history? I mean, there's an entire research team at the hospital that's been trying to figure out RM for a decade, and now a medical intern is going to step in and just . . . cure it? Just like that?"

Kira nodded; it really did sound stupid when he said it like that. She glanced over at Nandita, wondering what her opinion would be on the matter, but the old woman was still working in the garden, completely unaware. Kira turned back to Marcus. "I know it sounds like the most arrogant thing in the whole world, but I—" She paused and took a breath, looking him squarely in the eyes. He was watching, waiting; he was taking her seriously. She put her hand on his. "I know I can help, at the very least. There has to be something that's been overlooked. I joined maternity because I thought that was the nerve center, you know? I thought that was the whole point, the place where it all happened. But now that I've been there and I've seen what they're doing, I know it's not going to work.

"If I can put together something concrete for Skousen, I bet I can transfer to research full-time—it'll take another month or two, but I can do it."

"That's a good move for you," said Marcus. "It'll be good for them, too—coming from maternity like that, you'll have a different perspective from the others. And I know there's an opening, because we got a transfer from research into surgery last month."

"That's exactly what I mean," said Kira, "a new perspective. The maternity team, the research team, everybody's been

95

studying the infants exclusively. But we don't need to look for a cure, we need to look for immunity. We're resistant to the symptoms, so there has to be something in us that fends off the virus. The only ones who aren't immune are the babies, and yet that's where we keep looking."

"That's why you need my blood," said Marcus.

Kira nodded, rubbing her fingers over the back of his hand. That was why she loved Marcus: He was funny when she needed to laugh, and serious when she needed to talk. He understood her, plain and simple.

She plucked a blade of grass and slowly peeled it until nothing remained but the soft yellow core. She studied it a moment, then threw it at Marcus; it traveled only a few inches before it caught the air, stopped, and fluttered in erratic circles straight back into her lap.

"Nice shot," grinned Marcus. He looked up over her shoulder. "Isolde's coming."

Kira turned and smiled, waving at her "sister." Isolde was tall and pale and golden-haired—the lone light-skinned outlier in Nandita's makeshift foster home. Isolde waved back, grinning, though Kira could see that the smile was forced and tired. Marcus scooted over as she approached, making room beside them on the grass, but Isolde shook her head politely.

"Thanks, but this is my best suit." She dropped her briefcase and stood next to them wearily, arms folded, staring straight ahead.

"Rough day in the Senate?" Kira asked.

"Is there ever a smooth one?" Isolde glanced around, looking for something to sit on, then sighed and sat down on her briefcase, cross-legged to keep her pale gray pants out of the grass. Kira studied her in concern—Isolde could barely even mention her job without swooning over Senator Hobb. If she wasn't doing that, she must really be exhausted. Isolde stared blankly, then roused herself to look at Kira and Marcus. "Hey, neither of you do much traveling outside of the city, right?"

"Not really," said Kira. She looked at Marcus, who shook his head. "When they call us on salvage runs, I guess, but never really on our own. Why?"

"Because they just voted to institute border checks," said Isolde. "The Voice hit a watchtower last week—knocked the whole thing down and took off with the soldiers who were manning it. Combine that with the raid on the old school depot and you've got at least one cell of the Voice working right here in East Meadow, maybe more." She shrugged. "That's a little too close to home. The Senate figures the best way to root them out are searches and examinations every time somebody enters or leaves the city."

"The perimeter of the city is huge," said Kira. "There's no way they can patrol the entire thing."

"That doesn't mean they shouldn't try, though," said Marcus. "It's better than nothing—"

"Please don't," said Isolde, rubbing her temples. "I've heard these same arguments a hundred different times today, and I don't need to hear them again. The vote is done, the checks are official, let's stop arguing about it."

"How did Senator Hobb vote?" asked Kira. Isolde was his personal assistant. She opened one eye, peered wearily at Kira, then opened the other and crossed her arms.

"If you must know, he voted for," said Isolde. "He wasn't in favor of sacrificing personal rights to privacy, but he didn't want to stand in the way of stopping another attack." She shrugged. "I don't think he's right, but I don't have any better suggestions. If the Voice have started kidnapping people now, who knows what they'll do next?"

"What are the Voice trying to accomplish?" asked Kira. "That's what I can't figure out. They don't need supplies—food and clothes are free for the taking all over the island—and yet they keep raiding East Meadow and the farms. They're not winning support for their cause, they're just making everyone angry and jumpy and . . . I don't get it. The watchtower attack by itself probably took weeks to plan and pull off, and for what? They didn't get any supplies, they didn't make any statements, they got maybe two or three clips of ammunition each from the soldiers they kidnapped—they didn't get anything."

"They got two soldiers," said Marcus. "Maybe it was a staged battle to hide a defection."

Isolde shook her head. "As near as we can tell—or at least the current best guess in the Senate—is that they're trying to destabilize the government. If they hit enough targets, rouse enough rabble, and shake enough beehives, pretty soon the people in East Meadow are going to get pissed off. That'll make them harder to control, which will make things harder for the Senate, which will give the Voice a prime chance to swoop in and attempt a coup."

"Ouch," said Marcus.

"Back up," said Kira. "Did you say it's harder for the Senate to 'control' us?"

Isolde grimaced. "That's not what I meant, that's just the first word that came out—"

"But that's the sentiment, right?"

Isolde closed her eyes, trying to think, and Kira felt guilty for pushing her. She didn't deserve this, and yet Kira's ire was up. She wanted to know. "Well?"

"Well, come on, Kira, you know what the Senate does." Isolde shrugged weakly. "The Senate 'governs,' and there's a lot of control inherent in that. It's not like they're controlling our minds or anything, they're just . . . keeping the peace. Making sure people do their jobs. That sort of thing."

Kira heard hoofbeats and looked behind her; two mounted soldiers were clomping toward them down the street. Their house was near the edge of the settled city, so patrols weren't exactly rare, but this was an odd time of day for one. Kira felt nervous and comforted at the same time.

Until they started angling toward her.

"Marcus," said Kira softly. He seemed to sense the worry in her voice and sat up immediately.

"What is it?" He saw the horses and frowned. "Why are they coming here?"

"I don't know. You recognize them?"

"The uniforms aren't standard," said Isolde. "They're not regular Defense Grid."

Marcus stared at them, brow furrowed in concern. "Who else wears uniforms? They actually look kinda like Mkele's guys." He shook his head, looking back and forth at the two soldiers: one about their age, one in what looked like his forties. "I don't recognize them; I don't think they've been stationed in East Meadow."

"Anything we can do for you?" Kira called out, but the

soldiers rode past her toward Nandita. The old woman sat up from her digging, watching as they stopped in the yard.

"Nandita Merchant?" asked the younger soldier.

"Yes," she said calmly. "No relation."

"What?"

"Ms. Merchant," said the older soldier, shaking his head and urging his horse forward, "we've been informed that you make frequent trips outside the boundaries of East Meadow. Is that correct?"

"Is that a problem?" she asked.

"I didn't say it was a problem," said the soldier. "Is it true?"

"She collects herbs," said Kira, standing and walking toward them. "You see this amazing garden? She collects these from all over the island."

"I can answer my own questions, Kira," said Nandita. Kira closed her mouth tightly, feeling nervous.

The lead soldier gripped the reins loosely, using his knees to keep the horse steady. It was nervous too. The man looked at Nandita firmly. "You collect herbs?"

"I collect them out there and I grow them in here," said Nandita, "and in a hothouse in the backyard. I sell them in the market, they're the best around."

The soldier nodded. "Where do you typically travel on these excursions?"

"That's none of your business," said Kira. The news from Isolde had made her angry, and she was in the mood to yell at someone. "You think you can just barge into someone's front yard and ask anything you want? What if she went somewhere you don't like—are you going to arrest her?"

"Nobody is talking about arrest," said the soldier. "We're just asking questions. Calm down."

"Just asking questions," said Kira. "Well, what if she refuses to answer?"

"Kira . . . ," said Nandita.

"In case you didn't notice," said the older soldier, angling his horse toward Kira, "we're in a lot of trouble right now. We're fighting for our lives against a hidden enemy that wants to destroy our city, and the only weapon we have against that enemy is information. We think your grandmother might have some information we can use to help us stay alive. Now if that offends whatever weirdball ideals you've cooked up for yourself, I'm sorry. Consider for a moment that soldiers acquiring the information they need to protect you is more important than five extra minutes of digging a hole in the ground."

"You arrogant jackass—"

"I travel all over," said Nandita, stepping in front of Kira. "Out by the farms when I have a ride, nearby when I don't. I can't walk as far as I used to, but there are plenty of untended gardens even here in East Meadow, just waiting for someone who knows her botany."

"We need specific locations," said the younger soldier. "Is there a reason you're not providing that information?"

The older soldier sighed. "She's a scavenger," he said. "They don't go to specific locations, they just wander." He looked back at Nandita. "Could you tell me who you tend to get a ride with, on the occasions you're able to do so?"

"Traders," said Nandita, "sometimes farmers going home from market day." She gave the man a look as hard as steel.

"Even drifters now and then, if they look trustworthy."

The soldier returned her glare. "And what does a trustworthy drifter look like?"

"I saw one last week who looked more or less like you," she said. "Different shirt, of course, but the same eyes, the same gun, the same self-importance. There's a lot of you around these days." She glanced at the younger soldier. "He had a kid with him, too."

"You need to check your attitude," said the younger soldier.

"And you need to check yours," said the older man sharply, and gestured at Kira. "You're as bad as she is." Kira bit her tongue, eager to yell at the soldier some more, but acknowledging that it would only make things worse. He turned back to Nandita. "That's pretty much all the questions we have for you, ma'am. Just doing our jobs, following up on some information. Sorry to be a burden."

"No harm done," said Nandita, her demeanor still hard as a rock.

"I'm glad to hear it," said the soldier. "Now if you'll excuse me . . ." He pulled the reins and turned the horse, then stopped suddenly and turned back again. "I'm sorry, this isn't official, just my own curiosity: How did you happen to come to live out here, so close to the edge?"

"I'm not sure I follow you," said Nandita.

"It's just that most folks try to live as close to the city center as they can. This neighborhood is mostly just kids, new married couples who chose their house recently enough that none of the center homes were left. You must have chosen ten years ago, like most of the rest of us, but you're way out here. Just curious."

Nandita studied him. "If you're asking as a curious neighbor instead of a soldier, I think I ought to know your name."

"Sergeant Jamison, ma'am. Alex."

"My house in the center had water damage, Alex," said Nandita. "Something got into my foundation and froze a few winters ago, and when it thawed out in the spring, my back wall practically fell in on itself. My girls and I needed a new place, and this one had a plastic hothouse in the backyard. It was the best choice available."

"I suppose it was," said the soldier. "Thanks for your help." He turned again, and the young soldier turned with him, and they rode away back down the street.

Kira watched them go, her stomach tied in knots. "What was that about?"

"The Secret Service," said Nandita. "They have them at the market now, watching the traders."

"They're just trying to do their jobs," said Isolde. "You didn't have to jump down their throats."

"They didn't have to jump down Nandita's," said Kira, and looked back at Isolde. "This is exactly what I was talking about—just because someone's in charge of something doesn't mean they're in charge of everything. They can't just order us around."

"They're the government," said Marcus. "Ordering people around is their job, and frankly, I think talking to people who travel a lot is a good way to get information. They weren't trying to antagonize anybody—though I admit that the younger one was kind of being a blowhole about it."

"Everyone on this island is too paranoid," said Nandita. "They assumed the worst about me, but Kira assumed the worst about them." She looked at Kira sharply. "Your attitude was completely uncalled for, and if you don't change it, it's going to get you in a lot more trouble than you know how to deal with."

"I'm sorry," said Kira, but then she shook her head and blurted out, "If they want me to be calm, they should let me sit on my own front lawn without being interrogated. How about that?"

Nandita looked at her, then turned to watch the horses disappear around the far corner of the street. "It's only going to get worse," she said. "Every new border patrol, every new amendment to the Hope Act, it's all only going to make the people angry." She glanced at Isolde. "If the Voice are trying to foment a rebellion, they're doing a brilliant job."

Kira felt a sudden flush of embarrassment; Nandita had been listening to their entire conversation.

"So what happens now?" asked Marcus. "You run off and join the Voice?"

"I run off and cure RM," said Kira. "No more RM, no more Hope Act. And I'm starting with an experiment. We've got a decade's worth of data on how the virus works in the infants it infects, but I haven't seen one study on how it works within those of us who are immune. It's time to change that."

Isolde turned to her quizzically. "How?"

"I'm going to take a blood sample from my loving, helpful, noncomplaining boyfriend," said Kira, "and I'm going to inject the RM into it."

Marcus whistled. "Your boyfriend sounds dreamy."

Nandita gave Marcus an appraising look, then stooped to pick up her gardening tools. "She could do better."

CHAPTER TEN

"Ow!"

"Hold still, you big baby." Kira pulled the pin away from Marcus's fingertip and placed a narrow glass tube against the wound. It filled quickly, and she pulled it away and filled another one. She capped them both, set them in a tray, and pressed a small ball of cotton against his finger. "All done."

"I don't know how you do it," said Marcus, "but my fingertip feels almost as good as if you'd pricked it correctly on the first try. I bow to your skills."

"I'm a natural," said Kira. "Move the cotton." He lifted the cotton ball, and Kira clamped down with a bandage, wrapping it tightly around his finger. "You are now officially the oldest person I have ever drawn blood from in the maternity clinic. Now, just take two of these and you'll feel better in no time." She leaned in and gave him two quick kisses.

"Mmmm," said Marcus, grabbing her by the waist, "how many of those did you say to take?"

"Just two," said Kira, "but I suppose it couldn't hurt to take more." She leaned in again, licking her lips, but he stopped her with his hand.

"No," he said firmly, "as a medic I just don't feel comfortable with it. Medication is nothing to play around with—what if I overdose?" He pushed her gently away. "What if I become addicted?"

Kira pushed back toward him. "You are such a geek."

"What if I build up a tolerance?" he asked, his face a rictus of mock horror. "Two now and two later and suddenly two won't be enough—I'll need four or eight or twenty just to take the edge off! Do you think I can handle that many kisses?"

Kira moved in again, turning on her most sultry voice. "I think you could find a way."

He froze, watching her come closer, their faces almost touching, then stopped her at the last moment with a finger on her lips. "You know, the best way to prevent an overdose is to vary the active ingredient. That blond nurse at the south clinic is great at drawing blood; I could get two from you, two from her."

Kira snarled playfully, grabbing his collar. "Oh no, you don't."

"Medically speaking, it would be perfectly safe," said Marcus. "I could even get two from you and two from her at the same time. I might get a little dizzy, but—ow!"

"I still have the finger poker," said Kira, pressing the sharp pin against his side just hard enough to let him know it was there. "You are a one-phlebotomist man, Marcus Valencio. You got that?"

"I got it," said Marcus. "Speaking of which, I think my meds are wearing off."

"No more today," she said, pushing him back to his chair and picking up the tubes of blood. "It's time to find out what kind of man you really are." She took his blood to a medicomp in the corner, switched it on, and started preparing a sample while it booted up. Marcus followed, handing her glass slides and plastic pipettes and other little tools exactly when she needed them. She liked working with Marcus; it reminded her of the easy, unspoken rhythm they had sorting medicine on salvage runs.

She finished the slide, popped it into the medicomp bay, and slid her fingers across the screen; the computer detected the blood and offered the basic information.

"Type O positive," said Marcus, reading over her shoulder, "good cholesterol, good glucose; hmm, a very high hotness count, that's interesting."

"Yes," Kira murmured, fingers flying across the screen, "but look at all those arrogance particles." Marcus started to protest, and she laughed, tapping out instructions for a deeper scan. An option popped up for a "Full Blood Analysis," and she tapped yes; she'd never asked for this much information before, and apparently there was a simple "everything on the menu" option. It made her wonder how life had been different in the old world, when computers were used for every aspect of life, and not just in the hospitals where they could generate enough electricity to use them.

Mere seconds later the computer offered a list of various electrolytes and glucose molecules and other little bits in the blood; it would take longer for a full analysis, calculating what, for example, the glucose density suggested about his liver health, but the computer would update those details as it went. The next set of notes to appear were genetic modifications; they had been so common before the Break that almost everyone on the island had at least a few. Marcus had the genetic markers for in vitro gene correction, meaning his parents had scrubbed his DNA for congenital diseases before he was even born. He had another marker in his red blood cells, signifying some sort of bone marrow modification, but neither Kira nor the computer could tell exactly what it was without a full bone sample. It didn't matter either way; Skousen and the other researchers had already examined the gene mods as a possible source of RM immunity, but it was a dead end—if anything, it seemed to make the subjects more vulnerable to the virus, not less. Kira moved on and started taking 3-D photos of the blood, examining individual portions of it for anomalies, when the computer chirped a small alert, and a glowing blue rhombus appeared in the corner of the screen. She frowned, glancing at Marcus, but he only shrugged and shook his head. She looked back at the screen and tapped the alert.

A new section expanded across the screen, one brief sentence with a handful of pictures attached: *27 Instances of RM Virus.*

"What?" Kira whispered. The number blinked, updating to twenty-eight. She tapped one of the pictures, and it flew up into a corner of the screen, enlarging to a 3-D representation of RM. It was a rough, fat sphere, highlighted in yellow to stand out from the background image. It looked putrid and menacing.

The number in the alert continued to grow: *33 Instances. 38. 47. 60.*

"This virus is everywhere," said Kira, flicking through the images almost as fast as they popped up. She'd seen the structure of the virus before, of course, as part of her early medical studies, but never like this. Never so much of it, and never in a live human. "This can't be right."

"I'm not sick, obviously," said Marcus.

Kira frowned, and studied one of the images more closely. The virus loomed over the other data like a predator, vast and insatiable. "It's not telling me this is abnormal," said Kira, "it's just telling me it's there. Someone told the computer how to recognize the virus, but didn't tell it the virus was a cause for concern. How common is it?" She looked back at the alert and saw a small link to the database. She tapped it, and a new box appeared, a long, thin rectangle down the full right side of the screen. When she expanded it, she found it was a list of similar references. She sifted through it with her finger, pulling up page after page of links. She clicked one, and found another patient's file, their blood filled with RM. She looked at another and another, all the same. She almost didn't dare to say it out loud.

"We're all carriers," she said. "Every single survivor has it in us, all the time. Even if we're resistant to it, we can still pass it along. That's why the babies die—that's why it gets them so fast. Even in an airtight room." She looked up at Marcus. "We can never get away from it." She sifted through the images of the virus, trying to remember everything she'd learned about how it spread and functioned. Part of RM's danger was that it didn't behave like a normal blood-borne virus—it lived in the blood, yes, but it lived in every other part of the body as well; it could be passed through blood, saliva, sex, and even the air. Kira pored over the images, looking at the structure of the virus, looking for anything that would key her in to the secret. It was a big virus, big enough to contain every function of a very complex system—though they still didn't know exactly what that system was.

Marcus rubbed his eyes, dragging his hands slowly down his face.

"It's what I told you before—the top minds left in the world have been studying RM for eleven years. They've looked at everything."

"But there has to be something else," said Kira, flipping furiously through the list.

"Live studies, dead studies, blood scrubbers, dialysis, breath masks. There are even animal studies in here. Kira, they've studied literally everything they could possibly get their hands on."

She kept flipping through study after study, variable after variable. And as she reached the end of the list, something dawned on her.

There was one test subject not included anywhere in the database. A subject no one had seen in eleven years.

Kira paused, staring at the screen, feeling dirty and uncomfortable as the virus stared darkly back.

If they wanted to understand that virus, why not go to the source? If they wanted to see what true immunity looked like, why not look at the subjects who were truly immune?

If they really wanted to cure RM, what better way than by studying a Partial?

CHAPTER ELEVEN

"**C**ome in," said Dr. Skousen. Kira opened his door slowly, her heart in her throat. She'd spent a week going through the current research with Marcus, convincing herself of the need to come to Skousen, and several days more planning exactly what she'd say and how she'd say it. Would it work? Would he agree, or would he laugh her out of his office? Would he get mad and throw her out of the hospital completely? Skousen's office was bright, lit by both the wide glass windows and a brilliant white lamp on his desk. Electric light always surprised her, no matter how many times she saw it. It was an extravagance few people could afford. Did those people realize how casually they used it in the hospital?

"Thank you for seeing me, Doctor," said Kira, closing the door behind her and walking crisply to the desk. She'd put on her most professional-looking outfit: a red blouse, a coffee-colored skirt with matching jacket, and even a pair of heels. She usually hated heels—they were ridiculously impractical, both for her job and for post-Break life in general—but Skousen had grown up in the old world, and she knew he would appreciate them. She needed him to see her as an adult, as an intelligent, mature person, and she'd use every advantage she could get. She held out her hand, and Skousen shook it firmly; his hands were old, the skin wrinkled and papery, but his grip was still strong.

"Please," he said, gesturing to a chair, "have a seat. It's Walker, right?"

Kira nodded, sitting straight-backed on the edge of the chair. "Yes, sir."

"I was impressed with your paper."

Kira's eyes widened in surprise. "You read it?"

Skousen nodded. "Very few interns attempt to publish research papers; it caught my attention." He smiled. "Imagine my surprise when it turned out to be not only well researched but wholly original. Your conclusions on the structure of RM were flawed, but innovative. You show a lot of promise as a researcher."

"Thank you," said Kira, feeling a surge of warmth flow through her body. *This might actually work.* "That's what I came to talk to you about: more research."

Skousen leaned back in his chair, his eyes focused on her; he wasn't enthusiastic, but he was listening. Kira plunged ahead.

"Consider this: The Hope Act is really just a streamlined version of the same thing we've been doing for eleven years—have as many newborns as possible—and in eleven years it hasn't yielded a single viable success. We're throwing mud at a wall to see what sticks, and eleven years is long past time to say that more mud is not the answer. We need to start throwing something else."

Skousen stared back, stone-faced. "What do you suggest?"

"I want to transfer from maternity to research."

"Done," he said. "I was going to suggest that anyway. What else?"

Kira took a deep breath. "I think we need to seriously consider the benefits of opening a program for the study of Partial physiology."

"What do you mean by that?"

"For lack of a better way to put it, sir, I think we should organize a team to cross onto the mainland and obtain a Partial for study."

Dr. Skousen was silent. Kira waited, watching him, not even daring to breathe. She heard the hum of the electric bulb, a stringent buzz just at the threshold of her awareness.

Skousen's voice was low and hard. "I thought you were taking this seriously."

"I've never been more serious in my life."

"Your life is not a very large sample size."

"This is about extinction," said Kira. "You said so yourself. Our one and only plan at this point is to put on gas masks and isolate the mothers and keep good notes on how the babies die. And yes, against all odds we've managed to glean some useful information from those notes, but I'm not willing to hang my species' future on a long-shot version of what was already a long shot to begin with. The Partials are immune: They engineered a virus perfectly designed to kill human beings, but they're immune to it."

"That's because they're not human," said Skousen.

"But they have human DNA," said Kira, "at least in part. The virus should affect them just as much as it does us. But it doesn't, and that means their immunity was engineered, and *that* means we can decipher it and use it."

Skousen shook his head. "You're insane."

"We're trying to solve the puzzle of RM immunity by looking at infants who are not immune—the answer is simply not there, no matter how many more subjects we test. If we want to learn about immunity, we have to look at Partials. We have no records left of how they were built, what went into constructing their genetic code, nothing. There must be answers there. It's worth a shot, at the very least."

"They're not going to just hand themselves over for study."

"So we take one," said Kira.

"Crossing the line could start another Partial War."

"If it does, we might die tomorrow," Kira shot back, "but if we don't cure RM, we die every day for the next fifty years—or sooner, if the Voice starts a civil war. And if we don't find an answer for RM soon, it's going to happen."

"I'm not having this conversation with a plague baby," snarled Skousen. "You weren't old enough to know what was happening when the Partials turned on us. You didn't watch a small group of these things take out an entire military brigade. You weren't watching when everyone you knew wasted away and vomited blood and boiled alive in their own fevers."

"I lost my father—"

"We all lost our fathers!" yelled Skousen. Kira paled at the sound of it, leaned away from the mad look in his eyes. "I lost my father, my mother, my wife, my children, my friends, neighbors, patients, colleagues, students. I was in a hospital at the time; I watched it fill up and spill over until there weren't even enough survivors to carry away the corpses. I watched my entire world eat itself alive, Walker, while you were playing with your dolls. So don't tell me I'm not doing enough to save the human race, and don't you dare tell me we can risk another Partial War." His face was livid, his hands shaking with anger.

Kira swallowed her response, not daring to speak; anything she said now would only make it worse. She dropped her head, averting her eyes again, fighting the urge to simply get up and walk out. She wouldn't do it—he was angry and she was probably fired, but she knew she was right. If he wanted her out, he'd damn well have to do it himself. She raised her head and looked him straight in the eyes, ready for her sentence. She was done here, but she wasn't giving up. She hoped he couldn't see her tremble.

"You will report to the research department tomorrow morning," he said. "I'll let Nurse Hardy know you've been transferred."

CHAPTER TWELVE

Kira watched her friends as they laughed and joked in Nandita's living room. It was late, and the room was dimly lit with candles; the juice stored up in Xochi's solar panels was dedicated, as always, to the music player. Tonight's selection was CONGRATULATIONS KEVAN, one of Xochi's favorites: drill and bass, violent electronic music. Even turned down, it made Kira's blood pump faster.

Nandita had already gone to sleep, which was good. Kira was about to ask her friends to commit treason, and it wouldn't be fair to drag Nandita into the middle of it.

She couldn't stop thinking about what Skousen had said— about what it had been like to live through the Break. She couldn't blame him for feeling so strongly about it, because everyone felt that way, but it hadn't been until that moment when Kira realized just how differently it had affected people. Skousen would have been in a hospital when the virus was released; he would have watched it fill up in hours, spilling into the halls and out into the parking lot, consuming the world in a plague-borne storm. His own family members died in his arms. Kira, on the other hand, had been alone: Her nanny had died quietly in the bathroom, and her father had simply . . . never come home. She'd waited for a few days, until all the food she knew how to make was gone from the house, and then she'd wandered out to ask for more. The neighborhood was empty; the world itself seemed empty. If not for a passing army caravan, retreating desperately from the war front, she might not have survived at all.

Skousen remembered a world falling apart. Kira remembered a world pulling together to save itself. That was the difference. That was why Skousen and the Senate were too afraid to do what it took to solve this. If it was going to get done, it would have to be the plague babies who did it.

Haru was already talking—passionately, of course, since that seemed to be his only way of doing anything. He was always the center of any conversation he joined, not through charisma so much as sheer determination. "What you're not realizing," he said, "is that the Senate doesn't care. You can talk about being robbed of your childhood, you can talk about inefficient science, but that's all beside the point for them." The rumor mill was working overtime, insisting that the Senate was going to lower the pregnancy age again, and Haru had taken Isolde's refusal to comment as a tacit confession that the rumor was true. "They've decided that the best way to beat RM is to drown it in statistics, and that means they'll lower the pregnancy age as far as they think they can get away with. Lowering the pregnancy age from eighteen to sixteen gives them what, five thousand new mothers? Five thousand new babies every ten to twelve months? It doesn't matter if it's effective or not, it's the best and quickest advancement of their chosen strategy. It's inevitable."

"You don't know that," said Isolde, but Haru shook his head.

"We all know it," he said. "It's the only way this government knows how to make decisions."

"Then maybe we need a new government," said Xochi.

"Don't start this again," said Jayden, but Xochi was almost impossible to stop when she got going.

"When's the last time we actually elected someone?" she said. "When's the last time we voted at all? Sixteen-year-olds aren't even allowed to vote, and now they're making a decision that affects us directly and we have no say in it? How is that fair?"

"What does fairness have to do with it?" asked Haru. "Take a good, hard look at the world, Xochi, it's a pretty unfair place."

"The world, yes," said Xochi. "That doesn't mean we have to mimic it. I'd like to think humans have a stronger sense of justice than the random forces of nature do."

Kira watched Xochi's face as she talked, looking for . . . she wasn't sure. Xochi was different these days, more fiery than usual. The others probably hadn't even noticed—Xochi was always fiery—but Kira knew her better than anyone. Something had changed. Would that change make her more likely to help, or less?

"The Hope Act was enacted before any of us could vote," said Madison, "but I still would have had to get pregnant when I turned eighteen if I wasn't already. That's just the way it works." It was still early in her pregnancy, but she was already starting to swell. She patted her belly often, almost reflexively; Kira had noticed other pregnant women do the same. There was a bond there, a tangible link, even now when the fetus was barely recognizable as human. The thought of it broke Kira's heart.

Madison was sure to support her plan—it was her child, after all. She had the most to gain and the most to lose. Haru probably would as well, for the same reason, but you could never tell with him. She'd seen him argue against his own interests more than once. His opinions were stronger than his needs. As for Jayden, well, he was a mystery. He wouldn't want to lose his niece or nephew, Kira knew, but at the same time he was fiercely loyal to the Defense Grid. He wouldn't react well when Kira asked him to commit treason.

"What you're talking about is treason," said Jayden, staring coldly at Xochi, and Kira smiled. Good old predictable Jayden. "Replacing a senator is one thing—they retire and we elect a new one, it happens—but replacing the entire government is revolution. It's also suicide: Do you realize how vulnerable this city would be if the Senate weren't around to organize the Defense Grid and keep the peace? The Voice would blow it up in the first ten minutes."

"If the Senate's gone, the Voice have no reason to blow it up," Xochi countered. "That's their whole thing."

"Don't tell me you're a Voice now," said Jayden.

Xochi leaned forward. "If my alternatives are government by idiot or government by military, maybe government by rebel doesn't sound so bad."

"They're not rebels," growled Jayden, "they're terrorists."

Xochi would want to help, Kira knew, but she didn't know how much help her friend would actually be. She had no military training beyond the simple marksmanship classes they'd had in school, and her skills ran in surprisingly traditional directions: cooking, farming, sewing, and so on. She'd grown up on the farms, and that gave her some wilderness experience, but that was all. Isolde was even worse: She'd probably go along with it because that's who she was, a follower, but she wouldn't, and shouldn't, actually come with them. She might be able to help from behind the scenes, hiding their actions from the government and the Grid, but even that was a long shot. If Kira was going to pull this off, she needed dedicated people who could handle themselves in the field. Kira didn't really fit that description herself, for that matter, but at least she was a medic and had a bit more experience with weaponry from her salvage runs.

Which led her, at last, to Marcus. He was sitting next to Kira, relaxing on the couch and staring out the window at the last light of the setting sun, blissfully refusing to participate in Haru's argument. He wasn't a soldier, but he was a fair shot with a rifle and a gifted surgeon, especially in high-pressure situations. He'd been short-listed for the hospital's emergency room almost immediately. He'd keep her safe, he'd keep her sane. She patted his knee gently, bracing herself for what she was about to do, and sat up straight.

"I need to talk to you guys," she said.

"We know what you're going to say," said Haru. "You've got Marcus. Of course you don't have a problem with the Hope Act."

Kira shot an uncomfortable look at Marcus, then looked back at Haru and shook her head. "I'm actually not sure what I think, but that's not what I wanted to say. I want to talk about your baby."

Haru frowned and glanced at Madison, absently rubbing her belly. "What about it?"

"Can I be blunt?"

"Everyone else is," said Isolde.

"Okay then," said Kira. "Maddy's baby is going to die."

Haru and Jayden grumbled at the statement, but the look of hurt on Madison's face nearly broke Kira's heart. She fought back her tears and plunged ahead. "I'm sorry, I know it's harsh, but we have to be realistic. The Hope Act is stupid or evil or necessary or whatever you want to call it, but it doesn't really matter, because it's not going to save Maddy's baby. Maybe some other baby years from now, but not this one. Unless we do something."

Haru fixed her with a cold stare. "What did you have in mind?"

Kira swallowed and stared back, trying to look as certain and serious as he did. "I want us to capture a Partial."

Jayden frowned. "You mean an organized attack on the mainland?"

"Not East Meadow," said Kira, "not the Defense Grid. I tried talking to Skousen, and there's no way the Senate would ever go along with it. I'm talking about us, here, in this room. The Partials may be the key to curing RM, so I want us to go out, cross the sound, and catch one."

Her friends stared at her wordlessly, mouths open, the long-dead Kevan's music roaring angrily in the background. Madison was speechless, her eyes wide with disbelief; Isolde and Jayden furrowed their brows, probably certain she was crazy; Xochi tried to smile, perhaps wondering if it was a joke.

"Kira . . . ," said Marcus slowly.

"Hells *yeah*," said Haru. "That is what I'm talking about."

"You can't be serious," said Madison.

"Of course she's serious," said Haru. "It makes perfect sense. The Partials created the virus; they can tell us how to cure it. Under extreme duress, if necessary."

"I didn't mean we should interrogate one," said Kira. "There are a million of them; finding one with a working knowledge of viral biology is probably not likely. But we can study one. Marcus and I tried researching the immunity process using current data, but it's a dead end—not because the research team at the hospital isn't doing their job, but because they've been doing their job way too well for over a decade now. They've exhausted literally every other possibility. Our best shot—our only shot—is to analyze Partial physiology for something we might be able to adapt into an inoculation or a cure. And we have to do it soon, before this baby is born."

"Kira—" said Marcus again, but Jayden cut him off.

"You'll restart the war."

"Not if we do it small," said Haru, leaning forward eagerly. "A big invasion would be noticed, yes, but a small team might be able get across the line, grab one, and get out quietly. They wouldn't even know we were there."

"Except that one of their people would be gone," said Xochi.

"They're not people," Haru snapped, "they're machines— biological machines, but machines nonetheless. They don't care about one missing Partial any more than one gun cares about another. Worst-case scenario, some Partial commander notices a missing gun on the rack and just builds a new one to replace it."

"Can they build new ones?" asked Isolde.

"Who knows?" said Haru. "We know they can't reproduce, but who's to say they haven't found the Partial-making machines at ParaGen and gotten them working again? The point is, you can't think of them as people, because that's not even how they think of themselves. Stealing a Partial isn't kidnapping, it's . . . capturing equipment."

"We still get pretty upset when the Voice capture our equipment," said Madison.

"No," said Jayden, staring at the floor, "they're right." He looked up. "We can do this."

"Oh, not you too," said Madison.

Kira silently cheered—she didn't understand why Madison was so resistant, but it didn't matter if she'd won over Jayden. She caught his eyes and nodded, determined to keep his momentum going. "What are you thinking?"

"I know a few other guys in the Grid who'd help us," said Jayden. "Mostly scouts—we're not even certain where the Partials are, let alone how they're set up, so we'd need a small recon team that could cross over, watch for a lone scout or small patrol, then grab one and get back to the island without anyone noticing." He looked at Madison, then back at Kira. "It's not the safest plan in the world, but we could do it."

"I'm going," said Xochi.

"No, you're not," said Isolde, "and neither is anyone else."

Kira ignored them, keeping her eyes fixed on Jayden; she needed him to make this work. "Do you know a good place to cross the sound?"

"We shouldn't cross the sound," said Haru, shaking his head. "We watch our side like hawks, it's a good bet they watch their side too. If we want to cross the line, we do it through a place that's empty and isolated, where we know nobody's watching."

Jayden nodded. "Manhattan."

"Now I know you're all crazy," said Marcus, putting a hand on Kira's arm. "The reason nobody watches Manhattan is because it's filled with explosives—the bridges are rigged, the city on both sides is rigged, and for all we know the Partial border on the Harlem River is rigged on the north. One false move and the whole island'll blow up."

"Except that we know where our bombs are," said Jayden. "I can get access to all the old plans and records showing exactly where the safe routes are."

"There's safe routes?" asked Xochi.

"We'd have been stupid not to leave any," said Jayden. "They're small, and they're hard to find, but with the right maps we can find them all and slip right through."

"I want everyone to stop talking about this right now," said Madison. Her voice was stronger and darker than Kira had ever heard it. "No one is going to Manhattan, no one is going to pick their way through a minefield, and I guarantee you that no one is going to attack and capture a Partial. They're super-soldiers— they were created to win the Isolation War, they're not just going to roll over to a bunch of teenagers. They are monsters, and they are incredibly dangerous, and you are not taking my husband and my brother anywhere near them."

"We're doing this for you," said Haru.

"But I don't want you to," Madison insisted. Kira could see her eyes welling up with tears, her hand wrapped protectively around the small bulge in her belly. "If you want to protect my baby, don't leave her without a father."

"If I stay," said Haru softly, "our baby will have a father for about three days. Four if we're lucky. Kira's right—if we don't do something now, the baby will die, no question. But if I go, and if we can bring back a Partial, we might be able to save her."

Her, thought Kira. *They say it like they know, even though it's still too early to tell. This is a real person for them. Can't Madison see that this is the only way?*

Madison's voice cracked. "And if you die?"

"Then I trade my life for my child's," said Haru. "There's not a father on this island who wouldn't do the same."

"You've sold me," said Xochi, folding her arms. "I'm in."

"I'm not," said Isolde. "I'm with Mads on this one—it's dangerous, it's treasonous, and it's a one-in-a-million shot. It's not worth the risk."

"Of course it's worth it," said Kira. "Say that it's stupid, say that it's impossible, but never say that it's not worth it. We know full well that we might not be coming back alive, or successful, and I recognize that, and I wouldn't have suggested it if I wasn't ready to accept it. But Haru is right—trading any of us, even trading all of us, for the chance to start a new generation of humans is more than worth it. If we can actually pull this off and use a Partial to cure RM, we're not just saving Maddy's baby, we're saving thousands of babies, maybe millions of babies— every human baby ever born for the rest of time. We're saving our entire species."

Isolde was quiet. Madison was crying. She wiped her eyes and whispered, staring plaintively at Haru, "But why does it have to be you?"

"Because until we can prove it was the right move," said Haru, "this entire plan is illegal. The fewer people who know about it, the better. Jayden can grab a couple of more people as backup, but most of what we need is right here in this room, and that's our only chance of getting away with it."

"I still think you're insane," said Marcus. "Do you even have a plan? You're not just going to grab a Partial and push the 'cure RM' button—even assuming you catch one, do you have any idea what to do with him?"

Kira turned to face him, surprised to hear him argue against it. "What do you mean *you're* insane?" she asked. "I thought you agreed with us."

"I never said anything like that," said Marcus. "I think it's dangerous and unnecessary and stupid—"

"What about everything she just said about the future?" demanded Haru. "About the species? Don't you even care about that?"

"Of course I care," said Marcus, "but this isn't the way to do it. It's very noble to talk about giving your lives for a cause, and the future of mankind is a pretty great cause, I'll grant you that, but take ten seconds to be realistic about this and it all falls apart. No one has seen a Partial in eleven years—you don't know where they are, what they're doing, how to find them, how to capture one, what they're physically capable of, or anything else. And if by some ridiculous miracle you manage to capture one without getting massacred, what then? Are you going to waltz a Partial right into the middle of East Meadow and hope you don't get shot on sight?"

"We'll take one of the portable medicomps," said Kira, "and a generator to run it. We can do all the tests we need in the field."

"No, you can't," said Marcus, "because you'll be dead. You started this by being blunt, so here's some more bluntness for you: Everyone who goes on this idiotic adventure will die. There is no other outcome. And I will not allow you to kill yourself."

"How in the hell is that your decision?" Kira snapped. She felt her face suddenly hot, her blood boiling, her hands tingling with the sudden rush of blood and adrenaline and emotion. Who did he think he was? The room was hushed and uncomfortable, everyone staring at her outburst. Kira stood and walked away, not even daring to look at Marcus for fear that she'd yell at him again.

"This will take us at least a month, probably more, to put together," said Jayden quietly. "Haru has access to the maps through his construction contacts, and I can go talk to a couple of people I know will help us out. We'll say we're doing a salvage run, with personnel I select, and no one will think twice until we don't come back on time. By then it will be too late to stop us. But putting all of that paperwork in place, without raising suspicion, will take time."

"That's fine," said Kira. "We don't want to waste time, but we don't want to rush this either. If we're going to do it, we do it right."

"How are you going to request me?" asked Xochi. "I'm not certified for salvage missions."

"You're not coming," said Jayden.

"Like hell I'm not coming."

"You need to stay with Madison," said Haru. "Everyone does what they can, with the skills they have. Trying to take you into

Partial territory is asking for trouble; you'd be more of a hindrance than a help."

"Please stay with me," said Madison, holding a hand toward Xochi. Her eyes were wide and tear-filled, her face desperate and pleading. "I can't stand to lose everyone at once."

"If Xochi's no good out there, I'd be even worse," said Isolde. "But I can run interference with the Senate if they notice you're missing. Anything the Grid decides to do, though, is beyond my reach."

"That's good," said Haru, "but you'll need to do more. Your job is making sure that when we come back, the Senate will at least listen to what we have to say."

"I'm not going either," said Marcus. "And neither is Kira."

Kira whirled around, stalked to the couch, and yanked Marcus up by the arm. "Jayden, Haru, get started. Marcus and I are going outside to talk." She dragged him down the hall to the front door, banging it open violently. She shoved him down the steps and stormed after, planting herself firmly in front of his face. Her eyes were hot with tears. "What do you think you're doing in there?"

"I'm saving your life."

"It's my life, I can save it myself."

"Then do it. Do you really think you'll survive a trip out there? Do you really want to leave all this behind?"

"All what behind? Are you talking about us? Is that what this is about? I have to sit back and watch the whole world spiral down the drain because we might have to break up? You don't own me, Marcus—"

"I'm not saying I own you, obviously I'm not saying that. I

just don't understand why you're ready to throw everything away for this."

"Because it's the only way," said Kira. "Doesn't that even matter to you? Can't you see what's going on? We are tearing ourselves apart. If I go tomorrow I might die, yes, but if I stay, we *will* die, inevitably, and the whole human race with us, and I refuse to live with that."

"I love you, Kira."

"I love you too, but—"

"But nothing," said Marcus. "You don't have to save the world. You're a medic—not even a full medic yet, you're an intern. You have a gift for science, and you can do so much more here, in the hospital. Where it's safe. Let them go if they have to, but you stay." His voice faltered. "Stay with me."

Kira squeezed her eyes shut, willing him to understand. "Stay with you and what, Marcus?" She opened her eyes again, looking deeply into his. "You want to get married? You want to have a family? We can't do any of that until RM is cured. Whether or not they lower the required age, I will spend the rest of my life pregnant: Most of those women average one a year, and all the children die. Is that really what you want? We get married, we get pregnant, and twenty years from now we have twenty dead children? There is not enough room in my heart for that; there's not enough strength."

"Then we'll leave," said Marcus. "We'll go to one of the farms, or to a fishing village, or we'll join the Voice, I don't even care—anything to make you happy."

"The Voice and the Grid are going to tear the island apart if we don't find a cure, Marcus, we're not going to be safe anywhere."

She stared at him, trying to understand him. "Do you honestly think I could be happy in some tiny little village somewhere, ignoring everything while the world dies?" Her voice cracked. "Do you even know me at all?"

"It will never be cured, Kira." Marcus's voice was small and pained. He took a deep breath, setting his jaw firmly. "You're an idealist, you solve puzzles, and you look at something unsolvable and all you can see are the things nobody's done yet—the crazy, harebrained things that nobody has tried because they're crazy and harebrained. We have to face the truth: We have tried everything, we have looked everywhere, we have used every reasonable resource, and RM is still not cured because it is incurable. Dying across the river is not going to change that."

Kira shook her head, trying to find the words she wanted. How could he say something like that? How could he even dare to think it? "You don't . . ." She paused, crying, starting over. "How can you live like that?"

"It's the only way we have left, Kira."

"But how can you live without a future?"

He swallowed. "By living in the present. The world is already over, Kira. Maybe one day a baby will live, maybe not. It's not going to change anything. All we have left is each other, so let's enjoy it. Let's be together, like we've always said we'd be, and let's forget all this death and fear and everything else and just live. You want to leave the island, let's leave the island—let's go somewhere no one will find us, away from the Senate and the Voice and the Partials and everything else. But let's do it together."

Kira shook her head again, sobbing. "Do you really love me?"

"You know I love you."

"Then give me this one thing." She sniffed, wiping her face, and looked him squarely in the eyes. "Don't stop us." He started to protest, and she cut him off. "I can't live in the world you're talking about. I'm leaving tomorrow, and if I die, I die, but at least I'll die doing something. And if you love me, you won't tell anyone what we're doing, or where we're going, or how to stop us. Promise me."

Marcus said nothing, and Kira gripped his arms fiercely. "Please, Marcus, promise me."

His voice was slow and lifeless. "I promise you." He stepped back, pulling away from her grip. "Good-bye, Kira."

THREE YEARS LATER

PART 2

THREE MONTHS LATER

CHAPTER THIRTEEN

The wagon rolled out of town at 12:02, a small group armed for battle. Jayden had found an old salvage report for a southwestern location—a high school on the South Shore that no one had ever followed up on. Schools tended to have well-stocked nurses' stations, so requesting Kira had been easy; this particular school was also fairly old, which made it easy to request Haru: He'd test the place for stability, and Kira would look for meds. There was nothing out of the ordinary, and Jayden's superiors had rubber-stamped it without a second glance. The border patrol didn't even stop them, they just saw the uniforms and waved them through.

They reached the wilderness. Phase one was a success.

Kira and Marcus had fought again last night: his final attempt to talk her out of going. It drove Kira mad that he could be so obtuse—that he could misunderstand her so completely—and she was still fuming as she sat in the Grid wagon, trying to think of something else. She looked at the group they'd assembled.

Driving the wagon was the same girl they'd had on the last run, a small-framed girl named Yoon-Ji Bak. Next to her at the front of the wagon was Gabriel Vasicek, a battle-scarred mountain of a man who made the phrase "riding shotgun" sound pathetic—he was riding "chain-fed minigun," a giant metal monstrosity with at least eight barrels. Nobody who saw him wielding it was likely to give them trouble. In the back with Kira were Jayden, Haru, and two soldiers Jayden identified as Nick and Steve—Kira had no idea which was which, and chose to think of them as Skinny and Scruffy. They watched the empty houses roll past without comment.

Jayden laid out a map of the island. "We head south on Meadowbrook, west on Sunrise, and then south on Long Beach Boulevard to the edge of the island. We'll actually get pretty close to the school in the salvage report, just a few blocks away, so anyone who sees us and happens to get asked about it will report that we went exactly where we're supposed to."

Kira pointed at the map's south shore, a rough-edged maze of bays and inlets and narrow islands. "Your path takes us over a bridge—are we sure it's still up?"

"You're thinking of the wooden ones," said Haru. "These that we'll be using are steel, and even without maintenance, they can last a lot longer than eleven years."

"But why so far south?" asked Kira. "If somebody sees us near the school, hooray, we have a witness, but is that really likely enough to warrant going a day or more out of our way?"

"We have to head south anyway," said Jayden, tapping the western half of the map, "for two reasons. First is the airport, the block marked 'JFK'—it's big and solid and we don't use it for anything, which makes it practically the Voice capital of the island. Everyone who doesn't want to follow the rules ends up there sooner or later."

"Everyone but us," said Kira.

Jayden smirked. "It's also perfectly situated between East Meadow and the military base in Queens, which is our other big obstacle. If we travel too far north, we hit the Defense Grid, which is obviously out of the question; if we travel through the middle, we risk Voice raids out of JFK. But if we go all the way south, we avoid them both—we get pretty close to the airport, but our scouts say the Voice don't tend to patrol that far down." He gestured to Skinny and Scruffy; one of them nodded once, the other did nothing. "The shore has less loot to steal, and fewer people to rob, and a pretty straight shot here, to Brooklyn." He tapped the map again, then moved his finger south, to a place called Staten Island. "This is empty as far as we know, plus the Defense Grid collapsed this bridge, so there's no good way across. Obviously there's nothing south of us but ocean, which means ninety-nine percent of the military is up here, in Queens, where our land and their land are closest. All together, that means the route we've planned cuts deep to the south and far around everything we want to avoid."

Kira nodded, seeing their plan. "So we follow the southern coast, hope all these bridges still work, and then cut up behind the Defense Grid through"—she peered at the map labels—"Brooklyn."

"Exactly," said Haru, "and we cross on the Brooklyn Bridge."

Kira frowned, studying the map. "If this area is so undefended, why aren't we worried the Partials will sweep across it and kill us? The bombs you were talking about?"

"We've filled that area with every explosive we could find," said Jayden. "There are guard posts and watchtowers all through the area, and mines and traps all over both the city and the bridges. We can avoid them because we know where they are, but an army marching through would get blown up, bogged down, and sniped to death while our own forces march down to flank them."

"Aren't the Partials going to have the same defenses in . . . what is it called, the Bronx?"

"Possibly, if that's where they are, but I honestly don't think they even care. We're gnats to them: a few thousand humans against a million-plus Partials. They likely don't defend as well as we do, because they don't expect us to be stupid enough to attack."

Kira snorted. "I don't know if 'we're stupider than they think we are' is a really great attack strategy."

"Just trust us," said Jayden. "We know what we're doing. We can avoid our own mines—Nick and Steve here set half of them themselves—and we can find theirs before they get us. This will work."

Kira looked at Skinny and Scruffy again. One of them nodded, the same one as before. His companion again stayed silent. Kira pushed her hair from her face.

"We trust all these people? Nick, Steve, Gabe, Yoon?"

"Haru picked them," said Jayden. "He trusts them, so I have no reason not to. They know what we're doing and why, and they agree that it's worth the risk. I've met them before; they won't turn on us or rat us out, if that's what you're asking."

"Just curious," said Kira. She turned to Skinny. "What do you say? Why are you here?"

"I want a piece of a Partial."

"Great," said Kira. "Real upstanding motives." She looked at Scruffy. "How about you?"

Scruffy smiled, his eyes hidden behind jet-black glasses. "I just want to save the little babies."

"Awesome," said Kira. She looked at Jayden and opened her eyes wide. "Awesome."

"It's eleven miles to Long Beach," said Haru, "then we're going to push west as far as we can before dark. If you need some shut-eye, now's the time to get it. Vasicek, you got front?"

"Sir," said Gabe.

"I'll watch back for now. The rest of you rest up, it's going to be a long week."

"It's a double bridge," said Yoon, scanning ahead with binoculars. They had reached the small bridge to Long Beach on the southern shore of the island. "Steel and concrete, both sides look pretty good. Better than good, actually, they're almost clean—there's debris built up on the edges, but nothing in the center." She lowered the binoculars. "Those bridges get used, and regularly."

Kira peered ahead. "Voice?"

"Probably just a fishing community," said Jayden, "couple of makeshift family groups who use the bridge to sell fish in East Meadow. They're all over down here." He clicked his tongue and shrugged. "Doesn't mean they're not bandits when the opportunity presents itself."

"Then we make the opportunity as unappealing as possible," said Haru. "Vasicek!"

The giant man stirred and woke, moving from wagon-shaking snores to full alertness in a matter of seconds. "Sir?"

"Get back up front with that minigun; try to look scary."

Gabe shouldered the minigun and climbed forward, shaking the wagon perilously with every step.

"Why on earth is that called a minigun?" asked Kira. "It's bigger than I am—is it like calling a fat guy Tiny?"

"It's the same kind of gun they use on tanks," said Haru, "but small enough for infantry. When you call something mini, you gotta remember the scale of the original."

"So you're a walking tank," said Kira, whistling low as Gabe settled into the seat by Yoon. "Remind me not to call you Tiny."

"Move out," said Haru. Yoon whipped the horses, and the wagon lurched into motion. Kira watched the bridge as they approached it, her eyes flicking back and forth to the other buildings they were passing. The street here was wide, lined with parking lots and looted stores, and where it merged with another road, there were triangular patches of grass and trees springing up between the lanes. As they passed the last building on the corner, Kira whipped her head around to look down the other street, expecting an ambush at any minute, but all she saw were broken storefronts and rusted cars.

The wagon rumbled forward, the horses' hooves clattering on the broken asphalt. They reached the tip of the bridge, and Kira saw the narrow bay stretching out on either side, and then they were on it, out in the open, with hundreds of yards to cross without a tree or a building or any kind of cover. Kira had never felt so exposed. She'd grown up in the center of the island, surrounded by . . . stuff. By everything the old world had built and grown and left behind. It held its own dangers, but she'd learned to deal with them—holes to hide bandits or animals, walls to collapse on you if you weren't careful, metal spikes and shards of glass and a hundred other threats. She knew them, and she was used to them. To be out here, away from everything, with nothing to hide behind or shelter beneath or even lean against, she felt like the world was empty and alone.

The beach on the far side of the peninsula was, if possible, worse. Gray waves rolled against the shore, topped with white and whipped by a salty wind. Whereas the north shore looked across to the mainland, here the ocean simply continued, flat and featureless as far as Kira could see. She had often dreamed of the world beyond the island, the ruins and wonders, the danger and isolation. Here she saw the world as a great gray nothing—a broken wall, an empty beach, a dull wave slowly grinding it away to nothing. She saw a dead dog half-buried in the sand, brown with old blood and speckled white with maggots. She turned back to the road and kept her eyes from wandering.

If there were people on Long Beach they kept to themselves, and the wagon rumbled along without incident to another bridge on the western tip. Here they crossed back to the main island, circumventing a wide, marshy bay, and then turned west again through another empty city. This shore was much closer to the road than it appeared on the map, which heightened Kira's unease for reasons she couldn't explain. All the soldiers were awake now, alert in the fading light, and Jayden whispered at Kira's side.

"This is the closest we'll get to the airport—this urban strip heads straight up to it, just three or four miles."

"You think we'll see any bandits?"

"You got your rifle?"

Kira nodded, picking it up and checking the chamber. She took a deep breath, trying to calm her nerves. "Locked and loaded."

"Then you're ready, either way."

Kira swallowed and pointed the rifle out away from the wagon, holding it the way they'd taught her in school: left hand supporting the barrel, right hand on the grip, finger next to but not on the trigger. She thumbed off the safety and watched the buildings roll by—fancy town houses with tall, old-growth trees in the front yards, probably millions of dollars apiece before the Break. Now their windows and doors were broken, their yards had gone to seed, and rusted cars squatted in their driveways like giant, dead insects. They passed a stretch of trees, and a row of tall buildings beyond them—an old beach resort, probably half-flooded by now. She saw a glint of light in an upper-story window: an idle reflection from a shard of glass? Or a signal to someone hiding in the city?

The trees gave way to more buildings, the heart of the old town community, and Kira began to see signs of modern habitation: graffiti on the walls, tarps over broken roofs, boards nailed up across shattered windows. The front of an old bank had been hung with corrugated aluminum, and the cars in the parking lot had been pushed together to form a barricade. She couldn't tell how recently the work had been done, or if anyone was still there. Nothing moved, and no one spoke.

Two blocks later a loud clap echoed through the air, and Kira jumped in fright, clutching the gun. "Was that a shot?"

"Sounds like something fell," said Jayden, eyes peering carefully into every corner and shadow as they passed. "A sheet of plywood or something, I can't be sure."

"So we're not alone?"

"Oh, we're definitely not alone."

Kira scanned the windows along the road—old homes, condos, restaurants, and ice cream shops, all empty, all looted, all scarred by time and weather and human violence. Yoon kept the horses steady, whispering softly to calm their nerves. Gabe brandished his minigun like a talisman, half standing in his seat for better leverage. Skinny and Scruffy crouched low in the wagon, sighting odd places with their rifles that Kira would have never thought to look: a Dumpster by an alley, a billboard, a tipped delivery van lying dented on its side.

Footsteps echoed down the street, and Kira's heart tensed in her chest. She couldn't tell if they were running toward her or away. She strained her eyes and saw nothing.

"Could be Voices planning an ambush," said Jayden. "Could be fishermen thinking we're the Voice."

"You've got uniforms," said Haru. "They should know that we're safe."

Kira gripped her rifle tighter. "That also makes us a target for the Voice." She saw a flash of movement in an upper window and swung around quickly, training her gun on the enemy, finger moving fluidly to the trigger to fire the first shot.

It was a kid, maybe fourteen years old. As young as Saladin. His face was dirty, and his shirt was ragged and oversize. Kira gasped, breathing heavily, seeing the boy in her sights and feeling her finger on the trigger. She lowered her gun. "Nobody shoot him."

Jayden was already watching the boy in the window, who looked down at them stone-faced. The wagon rolled forward, and he disappeared from view. Kira turned and slumped against the inner wall of the wagon, dropping the rifle and covering her face.

The wagon rumbled on.

The peninsula was long, far longer than the last one. The sun began to set, and the buildings cast long shadows over the road. Kira watched as the stores turned to houses, the houses to apartments, and the apartments to forests of kudzu and narrow saplings. Just when Kira thought it was too dark to go on, Jayden called a halt and pointed to a run-down marina office. Skinny and Scruffy jumped out of the wagon and practically disappeared, melting into the shadows. Kira waited tensely, so nervous she even picked up the rifle again. She tried to speak, but Jayden hushed her with a motion of his hand. Minutes passed like hours, until a small light shone out from the windows of the marina. Jayden whistled softly, and Yoon flicked the horse's reins, guiding them toward the building. The front wall had been solid glass, a showroom for fishing boats, and the opening was wide enough to drive the whole wagon into shelter. Jayden jumped out, and Gabe dropped heavily to the floor, keeping his eyes on the street behind them.

"One door in the back," said Skinny, "and two windows too big to board up."

"Let's go," said Jayden, and they disappeared into the back rooms. Haru started untying the gear, and Kira hurried to help—blankets and food, extra ammunition, even explosives. She hadn't known about those. They handed them down to Yoon and Scruffy, and together they ferried it all into a back room with no other entrances. Last of all was the medical computer, a portable unit with its own generator, designed for fieldwork in undeveloped countries. Kira couldn't remember what the old world looked like—the old days, when she was a child, when the wasteland she lived in was still "developed." She thought about the maggots on the dog, crawling and eating and blind.

They tended to the horses, set a watch, and settled in for the night. Kira wrapped herself tightly in her blanket, not cold but still somehow freezing, teeth chattering in the darkness. Drifting through the air was a soft voice singing—Gabe, standing watch. His voice was low and sweet, surprising from such a large frame, and he sang an old song Kira's teacher had sung sometimes at the school, about losing a love and hiding from the memory. It made her think of Marcus, and the last thing they'd said to each other. She loved him, or she thought she did, or she thought she used to. And yet every time he talked about being together, she couldn't handle it.

Why can't I talk to him? About the things that really matter? And why can't he see that it's not enough to just give up and wait for the end? How can anyone even think that?

She covered her head with her blanket and listened to Gabe's melancholy singing. When she fell asleep, she dreamed of death—not just for her, not just for her species, but for every living thing she had ever known. The Earth was flat and wide and brown, a field of dirt as barren as the moon, a single road stretching into the endless distance. The last to fall were the buildings, distant and solemn, the gravestones for an entire world. Then they disappeared, and there was nothing left but nothing.

CHAPTER FOURTEEN

Jayden woke her early in the morning, and together they roused the others and set off through a thin gray mist. Haru was leading the horses this time, flicking the reins gently and clicking his tongue to urge them on. Yoon sat in the back with Kira, rolling her shoulders in slow circles to work out the kinks in her muscles. In the early light they could see the airport across a wide bay. Fog curled off the water.

They traveled through a few more miles of city before reaching the next bridge, the longest yet, stretching far across the bay to reconnect the peninsula with the main body of the island. They saw the bridge long before they reached it, and Kira hoped desperately that it was still intact. If they couldn't cross here, it would mean days lost from their journey.

Were people already looking for them? The salvage run was scheduled to go overnight, so no one should miss them yet—unless Marcus had told someone the truth about where they were going. She wanted to trust him, she couldn't think of a single reason not to, and yet he had refused to help. He had refused to come. She needed him with her more than she needed the rifle she was holding, and yet . . .

They stopped by a massive parking lot, acres across from one shore of the peninsula to the other. The bridge was blocked at the mouth; they crept forward to find a makeshift barricade of old cars, now long abandoned. Skinny and Scruffy stood watch while the rest of them heaved and pushed, hooking up the horses to clear a path through the wreckage. Kira forced herself to stand tall in the wagon as they crossed the bridge, the tallest thing for hundreds of yards in every direction. It terrified her. That was why she did it.

The far side was more open than the peninsula, full of fields and trees instead of abandoned buildings, and Kira breathed more easily with the airport far behind them. The openness lasted only a few miles before they plunged back into the city, following a wide avenue past shopping centers and close-pressed homes of wood and brick. Most of them were crumbling in on themselves, vine-covered ruins in a hungry jungle.

A cluster of cars in an intersection were charred and blackened by some ancient fire—an accident, maybe, or the central bonfire of some long-forgotten riot. This was a bigger city than East Meadow, denser and more populated than any of the places Kira had visited on salvage runs and other trips. The section of the island east of East Meadow had caught the RM virus with dignity, gathering their families and dying quietly in their homes. The outer boroughs of New York City, on the other hand, had fought back harshly, lashing out at themselves when there was no other enemy to fight, and the city showed it. Now it was empty.

Kira had grown up in the shadow of the Nassau hospital, the tallest building in East Meadow and, she had assumed, the tallest building in the world. The distant Manhattan skyline destroyed that illusion almost as soon as they got to Brooklyn. The road cut almost straight northwest, but Jayden pulled out a new map and guided Haru through corners and side streets, sometimes sticking to the main roads and sometimes taking long detours around them. After a few miles they halted by an overgrown cemetery and watered the horses in a pond, and while they drank, Yoon and Scruffy tied thick bundles of old T-shirts around the horses' hooves to muffle the sound. As Kira watched, a family of antelope crept out from the distant trees—beautifully striped, with delicate spiral horns. They nibbled on the green shoots growing up between the headstones, then sprang into motion in perfect unison, bolting away at desperate speed. A deep black blur followed close behind them.

"Panther," said Yoon.

Kira pulled her rifle closer. "Good to know."

"Panthers are supposed to be night hunters," said Yoon. "This doesn't fill me with confidence."

They climbed back into the wagon and continued moving, following the convoluted path on Jayden's handmade map. The buildings got larger as they approached Manhattan, and once in the late morning they paused in the shadow of a thirty-story apartment complex, waiting for nearly an hour while Jayden peered carefully around the corner. Skinny slipped into the building beside them, and Scruffy disappeared behind a line of cars. Kira leaned close to Haru.

"What are we doing?"

"There's a watchtower at the end of this road," Haru whispered. "Two men and a radio, watching the line for any Partial movement. There's no good way to avoid it, so we're waiting."

"Waiting for what?"

"They've got to pee eventually."

"Seriously?" Kira peeked around the corner cautiously, seeing nothing. "I can't spot anything."

"That's the point," said Haru, pulling her back. "We know where to look, so Jayden's got a bead on him. As soon as he moves, we move."

"And then we get seen by his partner," said Kira. "If this is as easy as you guys make it out to be, anyone could sneak across."

"We only make it look easy," said Jayden, lying behind a car with binoculars mounted on a tripod. "We're just too damn good at our jobs."

"Even the most dedicated watchman gets lax after a decade of never seeing anything," said Haru. "More than likely his partner's asleep from taking the night watch. Be patient, but be ready to blaze the instant we give the signal."

Kira sat down on the curb, looking up at the high buildings surrounding them. Every now and then she saw a feral house cat creep through the rubble, or watch her from a windowsill. Minutes seemed to last for hours, and in the bottom of the steel and plaster canyon, Kira couldn't tell how much time was truly passing. She started tossing bits of gravel into the street, trying to land them in the open window of a car across the way, but Gabe stilled her with a meaty hand.

"I know the watchmen can't see it, and they probably can't hear, but it's safer not to do that anyway."

Kira smiled sheepishly. "Yeah, sorry, that makes sense." She saw a flash of movement from the far side of the street and looked over to see Scruffy waving from behind a broken wall.

"How did he get over there?"

Jayden raised his hand. "Get ready."

Yoon grabbed the reins, and Kira jumped to her feet, swallowing anxiously. Jayden paused, his hand in the air, and suddenly dropped it.

"Go!"

Yoon flicked the reins and the horses leaped out, muffled feet thudding across the asphalt. Kira jogged along with the others, glancing up again at the watchtower, but still saw only empty buildings.

They reached the far side and pulled the wagon behind the wall of another building, and Jayden peeked back out with his binoculars. Scruffy emerged silently from the shadows.

"How did you get over here?" Kira asked.

He shrugged and climbed into the wagon.

"He's still not back yet," said Jayden, eyes glued to whatever he was watching. "And I don't hear any radio traffic. I think we're still secret." He ducked back behind the wall and stood up. "Let's go."

Skinny joined them a few blocks later, appearing out of nowhere and climbing into the wagon.

"He didn't see us," he said simply.

Jayden nodded. "Perfect."

They continued to dodge and weave through the buildings, keeping to low, narrow streets and using the map to avoid the Defense Grid watchmen. They stopped at a large stone courthouse, and Yoon began unhooking the horses.

"You can't see it from here," said Jayden, "but we're only a few blocks from the river. There are two bridges right next to each other, and a single watch post that covers both of them. We think we can sneak across, but we're leaving the horses and the wagon here."

Kira looked at the forested park across the street and imagined it full of more panthers, hiding in the shadows. "Is Yoon staying with them?"

Jayden shook his head. "I'd rather have an extra gun in Manhattan and risk walking home." He pointed up the steps to the courthouse. "We're going to put them in there and hope nothing happens."

The stairs were too steep, and the wagon too heavy, to risk pulling it up as well; they carried up the gear by hand and carefully walked the horses up the narrow granite steps. The courthouse windows were broken, of course, but the heavy doors were more or less intact. Yoon took Gabe and Kira to the park across the street, cutting armloads of tall grass with a thick, curved knife and carrying it back to the horses. They pushed the desks into a makeshift corral and blocked the doors closed with a set of heavy metal couches. It occurred to Kira that if they didn't make it back, the horses would be trapped inside forever. She shook the thought from her head.

The soldiers checked their weapons carefully, making sure the barrels were clear, the chambers were loaded, and the moving parts moved the way they were supposed to. Kira examined her rifle as closely as she could, studying pieces of the weapon she'd never even thought about before, realizing for the first time that her life literally depended on them. The chamber was fully loaded, plus she had more clips in her backpack, cinched tightly to her back, and two more in easy reach on her belt. Gabe revved his minigun, checking the rotation of the barrels, and shouldered a massive backpack full of ammo. Jayden slung his rifle over his shoulder and examined a pair of semiautomatic handguns on his hips. Skinny and Scruffy bore long-barreled rifles with thick sound and flash suppressors. Haru's gun was short and versatile with a collapsible stock; Yoon had a similar gun, plus the long, wicked knife strapped to her back.

Jayden clapped Kira on the back. "You ready?"

No, Kira thought, *I'm cold, and I'm hot, and I'm tired, and I'm terrified, and I've never been less ready for anything in my life.* She forced herself to smile.

"I'm ready. Let's go attack some super-soldiers."

The bridge started by the courthouse, and they were on it for nearly half a mile before they reached the water. As they neared the edge they dropped down to hands and knees, crawling below the rim of a waist-high wall, a tiny strip of concrete that would shield them from the sight of the invisible watchman on one of the buildings above. Skinny and Scruffy crawled ahead, marking traps and defusing trip wires for the rest of the group to pass through safely. Even with the marks, Kira sometimes couldn't see what each trap was supposed to be.

She imagined a vast Partial army hiding in the skyscrapers across the river, coincidentally—or not—choosing this exact moment to mount an attack. The traps were down; the door was open. Was she betraying humanity?

No. She was saving it. She clenched her jaw and kept crawling.

Brooklyn had surprised Kira by making tall buildings commonplace; Manhattan shocked her completely by making those giant buildings seem small. The island was a mountain of metal, stretching so high into the clouds it seemed to be literally scraping the sky. The base of the city was a carpet of green—parks and trees and strips of grass had long ago overrun their borders and stretched out into the streets, seeds finding cracks and roots finding weak spots until the asphalt had become warped and broken, and the roads had become a forest of new growth. Kudzu crept inexorably up the sides of buildings, coating the bottom stories in a layer of vines and leaves so thick the buildings themselves seemed to be growing out of the ground.

As their bridge reached the far side of the river and stretched out into the city, they finally stood up. Kira found herself at treetop level in a literal urban jungle. Birds nested in the vines and rain gutters, and feral cats prowled cautiously through the latticed framework of exposed offices hundreds of feet in the air. She heard a baying of hounds and, she was certain, the distant trumpeting of an elephant.

"They should call this Animalhattan," said Gabe, shooting Kira a quick smile. She grinned and nodded.

"Everybody stay down," said Jayden. "We know Brooklyn pretty well, but this is all new territory. We shouldn't see any Partials here, but it doesn't hurt to be careful." He pointed to a pale building just a block or two to the north. "That tower will give us the best vantage point over this section of the island; we'll go up, get the lay of the land, and move on from there. Stay close and try to keep quiet."

Kira crawled after the others as the bridge angled down and

curved through a stand of towering trees. Ground level was a whole new world—a schizophrenic blend of forest and junkyard where Kira had to be extra careful with her footing. The sheer mass of the skyscrapers around them resulted in more debris than usual—shards of glass and chunks of stonework, bits of plaster and crumbled drywall and untold reams of paper, some of it blowing free and some of it half-decomposed in a thick accumulation of dirt, leaves, and fungus. Long green tendrils wrapped around faded soda cans, wove through the spokes of rusted bicycles, and clung fiercely to the sides of old taxis and buses and road signs.

Kira and the soldiers followed the road carefully, picking their way between leafy cars and rusty trees and piles of unrecognizable rubble. When they reached the pale building, Gabe set watch at the bottom of the stairs, and the rest climbed as high as they dared before Haru grew worried about stability. Twelve stories proved to be enough—this part of the island was mostly government buildings and apartments instead of giant office buildings, giving them an unobstructed view of the terrain to the north.

"That strip of deeper green was probably a park," said Jayden, pointing northeast. "Looks like it goes at least ten blocks, and those trees will give us good cover."

"They'll also slow us down," said Haru. "We should pick a wide street and head straight up the middle." They debated for several minutes, while Yoon leaned out the neighboring window to coo at a pair of brightly colored birds. Kira studied the skyline, trying to drink in as much of the city as she could. Were there any landmarks she could use? Distinctive buildings she could find and remember if she ever got lost? As her eyes rolled over the cityscape, she saw a thin white line that seemed to be moving—a reflection, maybe, or . . . no. It was smoke. She pointed to it.

"There's a fire. Do you see it?"

Jayden and Haru stopped talking, following her finger with their eyes.

"Just beyond those three brown buildings, the ones sticking up."

"I see it," said Haru. "It's not a house fire, it's too small and controlled. I think it's a campfire."

"It's a chimney," said Jayden, peering through binoculars. "Someone's living there."

Kira frowned at the distant smoke. "Living or camping?"

"I didn't think there was anyone on the island," said Yoon. "Why would someone still be living here alone?"

"It might be a watch station," said Haru. "A Partial outpost."

"It's too low for a good watchtower," said Jayden. "It's just a small government building, maybe three stories at the most."

"A Partial camp, then," said Haru, "like Kira said. A patrol or something, stopped for the day."

"It doesn't have to be Partials," said Kira. "It might just be some weird old coot who didn't want to leave his home."

"There's no way anyone untrained could have made it this far without setting off an explosive," said Haru. "We should check it out; if it's Partials, we can set up an ambush and save days off our trip."

"And if it's just a refugee, we risk exposing ourselves unnecessarily," said Jayden. "Anyone crazy enough to survive out here is also paranoid enough to know we're coming, and to shoot first."

"You're the one being paranoid," said Haru.

"You're damn right I am," said Jayden. "If 'crazy hermit with a gun' doesn't scare you, how about 'Partial trap'? They might be setting this up just to lure us in and catch us."

"They don't even know we're here."

"We'll stay alive longer if we assume that they do," said Jayden. "I don't want to get near it."

"Noted and overridden," said Haru. "We go toward the smoke—but we'll go carefully. When we hit those three buildings Kira pointed out, we'll climb one for another look, and we'll send Nick and Steve around the sides to look for anything out of the ordinary."

"You're not in charge," said Jayden. "You're not even real military anymore."

"That's my wife and child back there dying," said Haru. "You can try to take command away from me, but I'm not going to make it easy."

"That's not how it works, Haru."

"The scouts are on my side," Haru hissed. Skinny and Scruffy shifted slightly, as if subtly reminding the others of their presence. "What do you have, a couple of girls? We're going to the smoke."

In a heartbeat the room turned cold and still, each person looking at the others, gauging their distance, watching their hands.

Jayden gritted his teeth, visibly swallowing his pride. "We'll have to use the radios to coordinate," he said. The tension in the room eased. "Channel thirty-five, with no real locations in case the Partials are listening in. We'll call the target building

Holly, and the three towers next to it Max; Partials are Fred and humans are Ethel, assuming they're wearing uniforms we can use to identify them. Anyone we can't identify is Lucy."

Jayden sketched out a quick map of the city, marking the smoke and any other landmarks he could find. The trip back down the stairs was tense, but nothing happened. Haru explained the plan to Gabe, and they set off through the city, climbing frequently on top of cars to get a clear view over the saplings that filled the street. Kira noted key buildings as they passed them, and stopped in surprise when she saw a lean black horse nibbling grass from a gutter. The horse looked back at her, whickered primly, and turned and trotted away down a side street. Yoon watched it go with almost wistful appreciation.

"You like horses?" asked Kira.

Yoon nodded. "Horses, dogs, cats, you name it. I had a pet penguin for years before I joined the Defense Grid."

"Why'd you join?" Kira asked. "Why not become a vet or a rancher or whatever?"

"Because my mom was a soldier," said Yoon, shrugging. "At least I'm pretty sure she was. I remember she had a uniform— navy, I think. It was blue. I have a picture somewhere." She paused a moment, then leaned in closely and whispered, "Keep your eyes open. We all knew Haru was a blowhole, but I never thought he'd challenge Jayden like that. And Nick and Steve are his guys, not ours."

"What about when we split up?" Kira whispered. "That will change the power structure."

"Nick and Steve are a lot more dangerous when you can't see

them," said Yoon. "Them leaving isn't going to set my mind at ease."

Kira watched Haru like a hawk all afternoon, but nothing happened. They reached the three apartment buildings—actually five, now that they had a better angle to see them—and Skinny and Scruffy split off on their flanking missions. Haru led the others to the northern building, and they picked their way carefully through the lobby and up the stairs. The building smelled strongly of rot, both plant and animal, and Kira pulled on her face mask to blot out the stench. They reached the top floor and quietly popped the lock on an apartment door. The family was still inside, leathery skin stretched tightly over old, dry skeletons. A swarm of rats scurried back into the walls, leaving a dead sparrow half-eaten on the floor. Jayden kicked it away and crept to the window.

The smoke was clearer now, a mere half mile away, rising up in a single windless pillar from a chimney in a small brick house. Jayden and Haru and Yoon all pulled out binoculars, and Gabe set up a watch in the hall behind them. Kira looked out the window—hundreds of houses and buildings, thousands of tiny black windows staring back like blind eyes. One of those eyes was looking for them—had it already seen them? Would they see it first? Which group of soldiers with binoculars would find the other, and what would happen then?

They watched and waited. A pair of rats crept out from the wall and pulled their sparrow under the couch. Kira grew restless and explored the apartment: one skeleton on the living room couch, one on the kitchen floor, two in the back bedroom. Their arms were draped over each other in a final embrace. Kira closed the door gently and walked back to the living room.

A radio crackled quietly. "Timmy calling Jimmy." The voice was distorted enough by static that Kira couldn't tell if it was Skinny or Scruffy.

Haru put his radio to his mouth. "This is Jimmy. Sitrep."

"I've got eyes on Holly, and I don't see anything. You want me to get closer?"

"Negative, Timmy. Maintain your position."

"Copy," said the voice on the radio. "No sign of Fred or Ethel, but Holly does appear to be inhabited: paths to the doorway, that kind of thing. Whoever's there has been there for a while."

"Copy, Timmy. Let me know if anything changes." Haru set down the radio and rubbed his eyes. "We'd better see something soon. I really don't want to sleep in this apartment."

Kira opened the cupboards, looking for canned food. She'd worked enough salvage runs that the habit was ingrained. "Jimmy and Timmy, huh? You guys have the manliest call signs ever."

"That's nothing," said Haru. "The other one is Kimmy."

As if on cue, the radio crackled softly. Kira pulled a trio of canned vegetables down from a cupboard over the fridge, and Haru picked up the phone.

"Kimmy calling Jimmy."

"This is Jimmy. Sitrep."

"The report from Timmy was false, repeat false. Fred is at Holly, I have them in my sights right now. Timmy is compromised."

"Radio silence," said Haru immediately, and set down the radio. "Bloody hell."

Jayden turned from the window, his brow furrowed in sudden worry. "That's not good."

Haru hit the table. "We do not have time for this!" He hit the table again.

Kira frowned. "They got . . . Timmy? Which one is he?"

"Steve," said Yoon.

"Skinny or Scruffy?"

Yoon hesitated a moment. "Skinny."

Kira swore. "You think he's dead?"

"We don't know that it's him," said Jayden. "The second call might have been a warning that the first was fake, but it's just as likely that the second was fake, trying to confuse us."

"If the second was fake," said Kira, "wouldn't the first have called us back to let us know?"

"I turned it off," said Haru. "If one of the scouts is compromised, they've already got the drop on us. The only reason to give up that info is to figure out where we are. They might have already traced the signal—I don't know what kind of tech they have."

"But both messages knew our code words," said Kira. "There's got to be some way that both scouts are still safe. Maybe they just didn't see the same thing—maybe they were looking at two different buildings."

"No." Haru shook his head. "They've worked together too long—they wouldn't accuse each other that plainly if they weren't completely sure. If the first call was real, the second can't be, and if the second call was real, obviously we have to believe that the first was lying."

"They couldn't have tortured anyone that fast," said Jayden, standing slowly. "There's no way they could have gotten the code words unless . . ." He paused. "What about . . . It couldn't be, that's insane."

"What are you talking about?" asked Haru.

"It's nothing," said Jayden. "I'm just being paranoid."

"That's a pretty healthy thing to be right now," said Kira.

Jayden swallowed, glanced at Haru, then looked back at Kira. "What if one of the scouts is a Partial?"

"That's not even—" said Kira, but stopped midsentence. She was about to say it wasn't possible, but what if it was?

"That's ridiculous," said Haru. "I've known both Nick and Steve for years."

"Since before the Break?" asked Jayden.

"Well, no," said Haru, "but still. There's no way."

"They look exactly like us," said Jayden. "Who's to say some of them haven't been living among us this whole time?"

Kira leaned back against the wall, her legs weak, feeling the sudden need for support. The ramifications were terrifying, but the logic . . . didn't hold up. "Why now?" she asked. "If they wanted us dead, they could have done it at any time—what do they gain by betraying us here, in the middle of nowhere?"

"I don't know," said Jayden harshly. "I'm just thinking out loud."

"Everybody calm down," said Haru. "They're not Partials."

"Voice, then," said Jayden. "They could be using a traitor in our own ranks to sabotage the mission."

"I vouched for both of them!" whispered Haru.

"That's exactly what I'm saying," said Jayden, and Kira saw that his hand was creeping near his pistol. She pressed herself back against the counter, caught between the two soldiers. Out in the hallway, Gabe turned to watch the exchange with a look of angry shock.

Haru saw the position of Jayden's hand, caught the tone of his voice, and stiffened immediately. "You bastard—"

"Wait," said Kira, "we don't have time for this—if one of us were a traitor, he could have betrayed everyone a lot more effectively a long time ago." She took a deep breath and stepped forward, blocking the line of fire between them. "There is a real enemy out there, whatever they end up being, and they know where we are. If one of the scouts was compromised, through torture or whatever else, he may have already told them we're in one of these apartment buildings—the only thing he didn't know was which one. That means they're closer than we think—"

Kira stopped and turned toward the hallway. Was that . . . ? She thought she'd heard something, but it was gone now. She made a move toward her gun.

A loud shot echoed through the hallway, and Gabe dropped like a side of beef. Kira yelped, staring at Gabe's fallen body in shock. Haru ran toward the door, stopping a few feet back to examine the body. He turned back and mimed with his hands: a explosion pointing one way, a gun, and then a strong point back in the other direction. The blood sprayed toward the left, Kira translated, which means the shooter was standing to the right. Haru pulled a grenade from his belt, pulled the pin, and tossed it toward the right. The building shook when it exploded, knocking dust from the walls.

"That'll buy us some time," he grunted, and picked up his rifle.

Kira fought to regain her composure, trying to force herself to react, and finally ran forward. Haru tried to pull her back, but she strained against him.

"I have to help him."

"He's dead."

Kira struggled to pull away. "I'm a medic, I can help him!"

"He's dead, Kira," said Haru fiercely. He whispered sharply in her ear, keeping his voice low while his hands held her back like iron bands. "Gabe's been shot and killed, and whoever shot him is still in that hallway, and the next person to stick her head out there is going to die with him."

"You have to let me help him!"

"There's nothing you can do for him," said Jayden softly. "Right now we've got to figure out how to survive the next five minutes."

Kira looked up and saw both Jayden and Yoon down on one knee, tucked into the corners of the room, rifles trained on the doorway. *Of course,* she thought, slowly regaining her composure, *the Partials took out Gabe because they're coming for us next.* She stopped pushing toward the door, and Haru slowly released her and raised his rifle, falling back into the cover of the hallway. She followed him, keeping her rifle up and her eyes trained on the open door.

"How much time do we have?"

"No idea," said Jayden, crossing to their hallway while Kira and Haru covered the door. Yoon followed. "Haru got that grenade out there pretty quick; they're going to be a little reticent to charge in."

"Which is the only reason we're still alive," said Yoon. "If this turns into a straight-up fight, we lose."

"There are no other exits," said Haru. "This is going to turn into a straight-up fight sooner or later."

"We could go out the window," said Yoon, "maybe get behind them."

"That's too exposed," said Jayden, "not to mention five floors up."

Kira cocked her head, listening. "They're coming again. Do you have any more grenades?"

Jayden frowned. "You can hear them?"

"You can't?"

Jayden shook his head, primed a grenade, and tossed it out the doorway blindly, past Gabe's motionless body and off to the right toward the Partials. The building shook, and Kira put a hand on the wall for stability.

"Couple more of those and there won't even be a floor for them to walk on," said Haru.

Jayden grinned and pulled out another grenade. "Not a bad idea."

"Wait," said Kira quickly, grabbing his arm. "Take out the hallway and all you do is postpone the attack."

"I know," said Jayden. "That's kind of the point."

She lowered her voice to the softest whisper she could make. "Do you have any other explosives?"

Jayden looked at her quizzically, and Haru stepped closer to listen. Yoon kept her gun on the doorway.

"Do you have any other explosives?" Kira repeated, as softly as she could.

Haru patted his backpack and whispered back. "C4."

Kira nodded. "If we take out the hallway, we'll still get attacked, but we won't know when or where it'll come from. But if we take out this living room, while the Partials are in it and we're not, we neutralize the threat."

"That could work," said Haru, "and honestly it might be our only chance against them, but this old building might not take it—it's mostly unreinforced masonry. Anything big enough to take out a team of Partials could take the whole building with them, or at least a few floors."

"A hole in the floor is a viable escape route," said Kira, "if we survive. It's that or a firefight, and I don't think the odds are in our favor."

Jayden nodded. "Let's do it."

CHAPTER FIFTEEN

The Partials were being cautious; by the time Kira heard them, they were already at the front door. A footstep, maybe, or a loud breath—she couldn't be sure what she'd heard, but she'd heard it. She waited, the silence stretching out to an eternity, then abruptly something clattered across the rubble in the doorway, followed by a loud bang like a gunshot. A flashbang grenade. The four of them stiffened, staying as silent as possible in the back room as heavy, booted feet ran into the kitchen beyond.

Jayden was lying on the floor by the closed doorway, holding one of Kira's medical tools: a small viewer with a narrow, flexible handle. It was designed for looking at noses and throats, but it worked just as well as a sort of tiny periscope—he'd curled it under the door and around the corner, giving him a perfect view of the rigged living room.

Kira heard a low mutter from the living room, and listened more closely. She couldn't be sure, but it sounded like *Which group is this?* There was no response.

Jayden raised his hand, preparing to give the signal, and Haru hovered his finger over the detonator. Kira stopped him, trying desperately to mime the phrase, *There's one more in the hallway.* She could hear its footsteps. Haru seemed to understand and nodded.

Jayden gave the signal and curled up behind the mattresses they'd piled against the wall. When nothing exploded, he turned in alarm; when he saw Haru waiting, he mouthed obscenities and gave the signal again.

Kira pointed at the hallway, miming as best she could, *There's one more.* She held up three fingers, stabbing the air emphatically. Jayden slowly, silently moved back to his looking device, then leaped up in surprise the instant he looked through it, lunging for Haru with wide, terrified eyes. The doorknob turned—one of the Partials was coming in—and Kira slammed her hand down on the detonator button.

The world roared.

The explosion shook the building, knocking frames from the walls and plaster from the ceiling. The wall shattered and flew toward them, and even with the mattresses it felt like being hit in the head with a hammer. In the same instant the entire room started sliding downward, the floor giving way with a sickening sense of vertigo. Kira clung to the empty bed frame, though it was sliding along with everything else. She heard another massive roar, saw an avalanche of wood and plaster thundering toward her, and let go of the bed to cover her head with both hands.

She felt herself buffeted from all directions, then enveloped by something rough and massive. The movement slowed, stopped, and as she slowly uncovered her head she saw other parts of the building still shifting—a shower of dirt and rubble, a falling refrigerator, a rug slipping slowly into a hole. The building's rooms and floors had become meaningless, smashed together in a three-dimensional chaos. Kira tried to move; she was buried to her waist in rubble. Her legs felt pinned by something huge and heavy.

She heard a cry from somewhere in the distance and shouted back, her throat dusty and her voice raw.

"Hello! Jayden!"

A hand rose up from the rubble in front of her, clad in the dark gray uniform and body armor she recognized from countless war-era photographs. It was a Partial.

Kira strained at her legs, unable to move, then looked for her rifle. It was nowhere—even her medkit was gone. The arm in the rubble moved slowly, tenaciously, searching by touch for something to hold. It found a jutting piece of rebar and gripped it tightly, straining at its own weight, and Kira saw the rubble begin to shift. The Partial was rising to the surface—

—and then a rat fell from the sky.

Kira flinched back in shock, her mind taking a second to process the object. The rat hit the ground, twisted to right itself, and hissed. Kira grabbed a piece of plaster from the pile that held her trapped and threw it at the rat, shooing it away. She heard more chittering above her and looked up to see a slanted ledge two feet above her head, the whole surface boiling with rats.

"No."

A couch behind the rats shifted suddenly, plunging six inches ahead. Two more rats fell toward her, one landing in her hair;

she knocked it away and dug furiously at the rubble around her. The Partial arm still strained, the debris slid and shifted, and slowly a helmet came into view. The thing's face was covered with a black visor, but she could hear it growl, low and guttural. Kira dug wildly, pulling in vain against the weight that pinned her legs. The couch above screeched harshly against the floor, bringing another shower of rats—three, five, she didn't bother to count them. The Partial lunged upward, and suddenly both arms were free. It shook itself to dislodge more rubble, knocking away broken bricks and shards of plaster.

Kira didn't have time to think—she reached up, grabbed the ledge, and pulled it down with all her strength. The rats tumbled down in a shower, covering her in fur and claws and writhing, wormlike tails. The Partial lunged forward, its hands like claws, and in that moment the couch gave way, plunging forward like a boulder, catching the Partial in the face and slamming it backward to the floor. Kira screamed as the couch ground the skin from her knuckles, screamed as she batted away the frantic swarm of rats. There were answering shouts in the distance, but she couldn't make them out. She strained again at her legs and felt them move, ever so slightly; the falling couch must have shifted whatever was pinning her. She pulled as hard as she could, then changed her focus and started pushing, flexing against the weight to push it even farther away. If the couch had dislodged it, she might be able to move it farther.

The couch moved again. The Partial underneath was still alive.

Kira grunted with effort, clenching her teeth and heaving against the rubble with all her strength. It shifted again, gravel running past her legs, and with a loud groan the entire floor beneath her seemed to disappear, sucking her down with a cry of terror. She fell ten or fifteen feet and landed in a coal-black pit, scrambling for footing as more debris rained down from above.

She heard an urgent whisper.

"Hello?"

"Yoon, is that you?"

"Kira! Help me move this dresser."

Kira's eyes adjusted slowly, and the pitch-black nothing became a dark gray outline of shapes and angles. The windows must have all been covered by rubble. She followed Yoon's voice, slipping and sliding across the rubble, and found her pinned beneath a heavy wooden dresser. She had a better angle of leverage than Yoon, and together the two girls shoved it aside. A loud thud sounded behind them, and Kira turned to see that the Partial from above had jumped down the hole after her. It landed easily, like a cat, and immediately stood. Kira ducked back, hoping its eyes would take longer to adjust than hers had, but it lunged forward with perfect accuracy and tackled her to the floor. She kicked and scratched, screaming for help, but the Partial had arms like iron; she felt its weight like a cage, its arms as solid as bars, and then suddenly it stiffened, its back arched. Yoon ripped her knife from the Partial's back, spun, and slashed again at its upraised throat. It fell to the side with a hissing gurgle and a spray of hot blood.

Yoon panted. "You are damn lucky he didn't know I was there."

"There's at least two more we haven't accounted for," said Kira, crawling to her feet. "We've got to find Jayden and Haru."

The building was more solid down here, two levels below the explosion, and they were able to move more easily. The first door they found was blocked by rubble, but they pried it open and explored quietly, listening for sounds. They found Jayden coming the other direction down the long central hallway; he still had both of his pistols, and gave one to Yoon.

"There doesn't seem to be much damage below," he said, "though the structure's getting weak on the west end. If Haru's still alive, he's above us."

Kira nodded, and they worked their way to a stairwell on the eastern, more stable half of the building. Two floors up they heard a faint voice and followed it all the way back to the far side. Light was shining through a wide hole where the outer wall had been blown away, and Haru was clinging to an exposed pipe, his elbow wrapped around it; his other hand clung to the backpack strap of a dangling, unconscious Partial.

"It's alive," said Haru through clenched teeth, obviously straining not to lose it. "I caught it just as the wall gave way."

"Then drop it," said Jayden, frowning as he struggled to identify a safe path toward Haru around the gaping hole in the floor. "We'll save you and get its arm or something down on the ground."

"Not a chance," said Haru. He grunted and adjusted his grip on the strap. "I want this thing alive, so I can beat the hell out of it back at home."

Kira shook her head. "We're not taking it home, we just need blood and tissue to study."

"We're taking it, and we're interrogating it. Our people don't even know where we are, and somehow the Partials were here, waiting for us? I want to know why they're here, I want to know what they're doing, and I want to know if our scouts are Partial agents."

"He's got a point," said Yoon. "Nick and Steve set half the traps in Brooklyn—if one of them's a Partial, our entire defense perimeter could be useless. And if the Partials are planning something, like an attack . . ." She trailed off.

Jayden frowned. "Kira, you still have your medkit?"

She shook her head. "Just the belt pouch; the main kit got lost in the rubble."

"Sedatives?"

Kira checked and nodded. "A painkiller that will do the same job, if we give it enough." She looked at the body swinging from Haru's arm. "And if its biology works the same as ours."

"I don't mean to be a burden," Haru grunted, "but this thing's a lot heavier than it looks." Jayden slowly picked his way around the periphery of the room to reach him. Kira studied the destruction, found a solid wall, and carefully climbed down to the next level. Yoon followed her, and together they grabbed the swinging Partial through the window and pulled it in. Jayden retrieved Haru, his arm hanging uselessly at his side.

Kira and Yoon laid the Partial down on a stable bit of floor. Kira pulled off the Partial's helmet and stopped, staring. She had expected them to look human—of course they looked human, that was the whole point—but even so, seeing one for the first time was . . . She couldn't put it into words.

A human face. A human mouth and nose. Human eyes staring blankly at the ceiling. A young man, handsome, with short, dark-brown hair and the beginning of a bruise on its jaw. The greatest enemy mankind had ever faced, the vicious monster that had ended the world.

It couldn't have been more than nineteen years old.

"It's weird, isn't it?" said Yoon. "All this talk about how they look like us, and then they just . . . look like us."

Kira nodded. "I don't know if that makes it less scary, or more."

Yoon drew the semiautomatic she got off Jayden and pointed it at the Partial. "Whatever you're going to do, do it fast."

Kira pulled out a bottle of Nalox.

"Best-case scenario, this keeps it down," she said, glancing at Yoon.

"Worst case it dies?"

"Worst case, it wakes up." Kira prepped the shot and held it over its neck. "We have no idea how these nanoparticles will react to its physiology. As far as I'm concerned, its death is very close to the 'best case' end of the scale."

She stabbed the needle into its neck, pushed in the plunger, and stowed the syringe. "It's done," she called out. Jayden was helping Haru climb down into the room. "But there're still one Partial we haven't accounted for."

Haru raised an eyebrow. "Not two?"

"Yoon killed one," said Kira, and Haru's eyes went wide. Kira laughed dryly. "I'm totally serious. Practically took its head off. Of course, that was after it got buried alive twice, caught a couch with its face, chased me through two stories of rubble, and almost killed me."

Jayden nodded. "And the explosion got the other one—I found enough pieces of it when I was upstairs that there's no way it's still a threat. Must have been right on top of the bomb when it blew. So we should be good."

They hefted the unconscious Partial between them and carried it carefully out of the building, through the multistory crater and down the stairs to the outer doors. Jayden stopped them.

"Wait—I spoke too soon," he said, scanning the overgrown apartment grounds. "There is at least one enemy unaccounted for: One or both of our scouts are still out there, and we still don't know whose side they're on. Plus, there could be more of these things that didn't assault the apartment."

Kira watched the grounds, saw the saplings waving in the breeze; they'd provide some cover, but it was essentially open ground. "We'll have to run for those buildings," she said, "but we can't move very fast with this deadweight between us."

Haru rubbed his left arm, the one he'd been hanging from, trying to force some feeling back into it. "Nothing to do but do it."

Jayden lifted the Partial, taking the full weight across his shoulders. "Sorry, ladies, I'm going to be selfish and keep the meat shield for myself. Now run!"

They dashed out through the vines and saplings, running full tilt for the next building. They reached it, rounded the corner, and kept running, between the cars and across the street to another building beyond. Just as Kira thought they were safe, a bullet ricocheted off the car beside her, inches from her head, and she ducked for cover.

"Don't stop running, Kira, move!" Jayden ran past with his load, and Kira took a deep breath and jumped back to her feet, expecting at any moment that a bullet would slam into her spine. Another bullet whipped past, several feet to the side. They reached the next road, a wide thoroughfare lined with high trees and battered storefronts. Yoon cut left and the group followed, using the cover to charge across the street and take shelter in a crumbling delicatessen.

"It's single shots, spaced out," said Jayden, gasping for breath. "That probably means it's not a group, just one sniper."

"Skinny or Scruffy," said Kira, "whichever one's the traitor. Nice going, Haru."

"We don't know if it's one of them," Haru snarled, but Kira could tell he had the same fears she did. Yoon was watching by the front windows, all but invisible behind a screen of overturned tables.

"We can't stay," said Kira.

"We'll head out the side window and down this little street," said Jayden. "We need to cut back and forth between the streets—the sniper's not as dangerous without a straight path and the time to line up a shot."

"The park you saw before is just a few blocks west," said Haru. "We can follow it most of the way back, and we won't lose time running back and forth."

"Agreed," said Jayden. "Let's go."

They slipped out the side, moving the captured Partial carefully over the broken glass. Yoon ran to catch up.

"I still don't see anything."

"What about the scout who didn't turn on us?" asked Kira, struggling to catch her breath as they ran. "Shouldn't we wait for him? Or try to find him?"

Haru shook his head. "If we can't trust one of them, we can't trust either of them."

"But we know one's innocent."

"And we don't know which," said Haru. "That makes them both suspects. There's the park; sprint to the trees and head left."

Another shot zipped by as they crossed to the thick forest, and Kira swore under her breath as she ducked behind a car. The others ran past her and she steeled her courage again, racing for the trees. The park turned out to be riddled with fences, keeping them out of the dense cover in the center, but the outskirts were still better than nothing, and they ran from tree to tree, always keeping something at their backs. Every few blocks a wide street cut through the trees, but the park kept going.

Jayden stopped by a cluster of taxis and lowered the Partial prisoner to the ground, wincing.

"Keep going," said Haru fiercely. "You can rest when you're dead." Jayden nodded and reached for the Partial, but Kira saw a drop of blood fall from his arm.

"Jayden, you're bleeding!"

"Keep going!" repeated Haru.

"He's been shot in the arm," said Kira, looking at Jayden's wound. "How long ago did this happen?"

"Just a few blocks." Jayden reached for the Partial.

"Haru can carry it," said Kira. "You just run. I'll bandage this when we get somewhere safe."

"My arm's practically broken," hissed Haru.

"Nut up and carry it," said Kira, shoving him toward the Partial. She took Jayden's semiautomatic and checked the chamber. "I'll take the rear, now run."

They took off again, Yoon leading the way through a maze of fences and trees and rusted cars. They passed a subway entrance, a dark stairway down underground, and Kira looked in as they ran past: It was flooded halfway up the stairs. *No cover there.* They kept to the park, and soon a thick steel tower rose up ahead of them.

"That's the bridge," said Jayden. "Take the first entrance you see."

Kira shook her head. "That's not the same bridge."

"Do you really care which bridge?" asked Jayden. "Just get off the damn island."

"But the traps," she insisted, glancing behind her as she ran. "The traps will still be in place on this one. It's too dangerous to cross."

A bullet flew by, and Jayden cursed. "We don't have a lot of options right now."

They burst out of the park and into a wide street. The bridge rose before them at an angle, up and southeast toward the river, and the four runners were now so tired that they staggered up the incline, panting with dry, scratched throats. A shot pinged off the cement barrier, and they collapsed behind it out of sight.

"I didn't see who it was," said Kira.

"Whoever it is," said Yoon, showing her pistol, "the Partial's effective range is a lot longer than ours. We can't outshoot it."

"You go on ahead," said Jayden, grabbing Yoon's gun. "Find the traps, defuse them or mark them or . . . whatever you can do. Haru and Kira will follow with the Partial. I'll guard the rear."

"She just said you can't outshoot it," said Kira. "Are you crazy?"

"I can't outshoot it at this range," said Jayden, and pointed back toward the base of the bridge. "I can outshoot it just fine from down there, if I get a drop on it. It has to come around that corner sooner or later if it wants to pursue us, so I'll hide behind one of the cars and wait."

"Then I'm waiting with you," said Kira. "I'm your medic, you idiot, I'm not leaving you behind with a bullet hole in your arm."

"Fine, just stay low."

Yoon crawled forward, and Haru followed, dragging the Partial behind him. Kira crept back down with Jayden and took position behind a fat truck tire. Jayden crouched by the next tire over, keeping an eye on the edge of the barrier below. The truck's driver, a weathered brown skeleton, stared forward blankly.

"Who do you think it's going to be?" asked Kira. "The Partial, I mean: Nick or Steve?"

"You mean Skinny or Scruffy?"

Kira laughed emptily. "It's not like they're hard to tell apart, I was just too embarrassed to ask which was which."

"I'll guess we'll see," said Jayden.

Kira looked up at the bridge, then whispered softly, "The watchmen will see us crossing the river."

"I know."

"We'll get reported, we'll get arrested, you'll probably get court-martialed. Our secret mission isn't going to stay secret." Kira watched him, but he said nothing. "I'm beginning to think this was kind of a stupid idea."

She saw a tiny smile at the corner of his mouth.

"Shut up, Walker," Jayden whispered. "We're trying to set an ambush here."

They waited, Jayden watching the edge of the barrier and Kira watching the rest of the road. As soon as the Partial appeared, they'd—

She heard a click.

"Drop it."

She looked up to see a Partial standing over them—not Skinny or Scruffy, a Partial soldier, likely one of the team they had encountered, black faceplate gleaming in the sun. Somehow it had gotten behind them. It gestured with its automatic rifle, and Jayden set down his pistol with a sigh. Kira set hers beside it.

"Don't make a sound," said the Partial. "There's a—"

A wide crack spiderwebbed out across his faceplate, centered around a small hole that seemed to appear out of nowhere; half a second later the soft puff of a suppressed gunshot wafted past them. The Partial crumpled to the ground, and Kira stared in shock. Jayden grabbed his semiautomatic. They heard running footsteps, and Kira managed to turn herself around to see Scruffy running toward them, his rifle in his hands.

"That takes care of the sniper," Scruffy called out, "but there are more coming. We've got to move fast."

"You're the one who warned us," said Kira.

"You can act surprised later," said Scruffy, dropping to one knee by the dead Partial. He slung his rifle over his back, picked up the fallen Partial's automatic, and turned to Jayden. "I'm serious—there's at least ten more behind us. We have to blaze."

Jayden paused a moment, then stood and started jogging up the hill. "Come on, Kira. This is a long damn bridge." They ran upright, not bothering to stay below the barrier, trusting speed and distance to keep them clear of the bullets. They caught up with Haru somewhere in the maze of stopped cars.

"Good to see you, Nick." Haru dropped the Partial prisoner with a painful grunt. "My arm's broken and Jayden's is shot; take a turn with the mutt." Scruffy looked behind, shrugged, and handed Haru his weapon. Before he could even pick up the prisoner, Haru shot him in the head. Kira yelped, Scruffy toppled to the ground, and Haru shot him again.

"What the hell are you doing?" Jayden shouted.

"I told you," said Haru, "as far as I'm concerned, they're both guilty. I'm not taking any more Partials home than I have to."

"He saved us!" Jayden shouted. "He killed a Partial soldier!"

"That doesn't mean anything," said Haru, checking the assault rifle. "Now shut up and carry the prisoner."

"He was also telling the truth about the group behind us," said Kira, looking back. "I can see at least one soldier already. We're not going to reach the other side in time."

Jayden frowned. "If the cat's out of the bag, we might as well catch some mice with it." He clicked on his radio and started shouting as he shouldered the Partial. "Calling all personnel, repeat all personnel, there is a Defense Grid strike team crossing the Manhattan Bridge. Partials in pursuit, we are taking fire, repeat, human soldiers taking enemy fire. Request all possible assistance." They were running now, Kira taking the lead and Haru following behind, turning and firing periodically to slow the Partials down. "Kira," said Jayden, "switch my channel." Kira clicked the knob on Jayden's belt, and he repeated the message. "Calling all personnel, there is a human strike team taking enemy fire on the Manhattan Bridge. Request all possible assistance. Change my channel again." Shots were coming toward them now, close enough to scare them into cover. They wove between the stopped cars, watching the ground for trip wires and other triggers, hoping desperately that Yoon had managed to find and mark them all. Haru fired back at the Partials, doing his best to keep them at bay; Kira chanced a look behind her and saw at least seven Partials in pursuit, and gaining quickly. Jayden ran out of breath, straining under the heavy prisoner, and Kira took over, repeating his message again and again in the hope that someone was listening. They caught up to Yoon far too quickly, and she shook her head grimly. "There's no way we can keep ahead of them and still avoid the explosives. This bridge is a death trap."

"I'm out," called Haru, dropping the assault rifle and taking Jayden's sidearm as they ran. "They're getting closer." A bullet glanced off the car in front of them, shattering the side mirror. "We're not going to last much longer."

"Calling all personnel," Kira said again, barely keeping her breath as she clutched the radio, "there is a human strike force on the Manhattan Bridge taking—"

"I've got you in my sights, strike force," the radio crackled back. "Please identify."

"We don't have time to identify," shouted Kira. "We've got a Partial army behind us."

"Jayden Van Rijn," said Jayden, "sergeant second class."

"There's a large pylon tower about twenty yards ahead of you," the voice crackled.

Kira looked up. "We see it."

"Proceed straight forward on the outside lane, pass the purple car on the left, and go past that pylon. Take shelter behind the big red delivery truck."

"Shelter from what?" asked Kira. The group jogged as fast as they could down the path they'd been given, each step lancing Kira's exhausted muscles. "What are you going to do?"

"What do you think he's going to do?" asked Yoon, pulling them down behind the Coke truck. "From what I've seen so far, this bridge has more C4 than steel."

"You don't mean—"

The bridge behind them exploded in a giant fireball, bright enough to sear Kira's eyes even in the cover of the truck. The bridge lurched, cars flew into the air, and the force of the blast shifted the Coke truck ten feet forward, pushing the fugitives across the asphalt. Kira dropped the radio, covering her ears, and when the shock wave subsided, she staggered out to look.

Twenty yards behind them, beyond the nearest pylon, the bridge was gone. Chunks of steel and concrete dangled from support cables. The river beneath was a churning sea of fallen scrap. The Partials pursuing them had been vaporized.

"Maintain position," squawked the radio. "We're sending a team to pick you up, and you'd better have one hell of a good explanation for this."

CHAPTER SIXTEEN

"**W**ell," said Mkele. "It looks like we have another chance to chat."

"Always a pleasure," said Kira.

They were camped for the night in the lee of a freeway junction. After verifying that no more Partials were going to try to pursue over the remaining bridge, the Grid had reset the watch and Kira and her companions had been taken inland, as far as they could make it before nightfall. They were unchained, but a large group of Defense Grid soldiers were keeping a very close watch. The Partial was still unconscious, secured firmly to a heavy roadside barrier.

"Last time we spoke, Ms. Walker, we discussed a number of very important issues." Mkele had arrived moments earlier on horseback, with a team of mounted rangers who quickly dispersed to strengthen the perimeter. He pulled her away from the others. "I apologize that I apparently did not make those issues sufficiently clear. Let's start with the most obvious: It is considered very suspicious, and in fact highly treasonous, to enter

Partial territory, consort with them directly, and bring one back into human territory."

"I think you and I might have different definitions of 'consort.'"

"What were you doing in Manhattan?"

"I'm a medic at the Nassau hospital in East Meadow," said Kira. "I'm trying to cure RM, and my best chance of doing that was to obtain a Partial."

"So you decided to just . . . go and get one."

"I made the request through proper channels first," said Kira. "You have no idea how medically valuable that thing could be."

"I find it hard to believe that I need to spell out for you how dangerous this is," said Mkele. "How idiotic it is. The bridge you blew up—do you honestly think that will keep them out? That any of our elaborate defenses are in any way deterring them from attacking us should they decide to launch an assault? There are a million of them, Walker, all better trained, better armed, and physically stronger than we are. We are only alive because the Partials have chosen not to kill us. And you may have just changed their minds, for all we know?" His voice was a furious roar. "And even if they don't attack, do you have any idea how much of a threat this one Partial represents, all on its own? Our intel from the Partial War suggests that it was the Partials themselves who released RM—not technologically but physically, using their own bodies as living incubators. If that is true, every single one of them is potentially a doomsday weapon. Who knows what kind of biological weapons they could have cooked up in the last eleven years? Their mere existence is a threat to our species."

"That's all the more reason we should be studying them," said

Kira. "There could be a wealth of information in just a drop of their blood, and with a full complement of organs and tissues to study, who knows what we could learn? If they created RM, and especially if you're right and they preserve or synthesize it in their bodies, they may very well hold the secret to curing it. You have to see that."

"Your job is mankind's future," said Mkele. "My job is its present, and without the present there is, as I'm sure you'll agree, no future at all. If your job ever comes into conflict with mine, mine takes priority."

"That's idiocy," said Kira.

"It's the truth," said Mkele. "As a medic, you're familiar with the Hippocratic oath: First, do no harm. First. There are approximately thirty-six thousand human beings left alive on the entire planet, and our first responsibility is to keep them alive. First. After that is taken care of—and only after that is taken care of—our job then becomes to ensure that we can produce more human beings to strengthen our position."

"You almost sound sweet when you say it like that."

"You risked the lives of five soldiers, a technical specialist, and a medic. Three of those soldiers didn't return. And now I'm going to destroy this Partial anyway."

"You can't," said Kira quickly. "We need it." *After everything we've been through to get this thing, I'm not letting you throw it away for nothing.*

"I will allow you to take a blood sample," said Mkele, "for the sole purpose of testing, in a controlled location far from any population center, should the Senate deem it allowable."

"That's not good enough," said Kira. "We need the medical

tests now—there are newborns dying every week—"

"I am tired of explaining why that is impossible."

"Then interrogate it," said Kira, trying to think of anything that would convince him to at least wait. "It was part of a larger unit, in a place where no Partials should be operating, and with some kind of contact inside our own military."

"I've heard the report."

"We need to find out why," Kira insisted. "One of our scouts may have been a Partial—"

"Or he may simply have been interrogated in the field," said Mkele. "A tortured soldier is a simpler explanation, and therefore a more likely one, than a widespread infiltration of our entire society."

"They look exactly like us," said Kira. "If I hadn't watched two of them survive an explosion, I'd never have even known they weren't human. Given how easy it would be, and how chaotic it was when we retreated to this island in the first place, we'd be idiots to not at least entertain the theory."

"Partials don't age," said Mkele. "There's no way one could live among humans for eleven years without being noticed."

"Maybe not as a teenager," said Kira, "but what about adults? What about you?"

"I assure you that everything is under control," said Mkele, his voice more dangerous than Kira had ever heard it before. "Do not presume to tell me how to do my job, which thanks to you is now a thousand times more difficult."

Kira closed her mouth, watching him, trying to gauge the situation. He was right about some of it—this had been stupid, and dangerous—but she was right too. This had to be done.

She couldn't just let him throw it all away now that the Partial was right here in their grasp. How far could she push Mkele? How could she get more than just a blood sample before they destroyed the Partial?

"Mr. Mkele!" Mkele and Kira turned to see one of the soldiers jogging toward them, waving his arm. "Mr. Mkele, we've received a coded call from the Senate."

Mkele paused, glowering, then looked at Kira and pointed at her feet. "Don't move." He followed the soldier back to the radio, and Kira watched as he carried on an unheard conversation. At last he handed the radio back to the soldier and stormed back to Kira.

"Somehow the Senate has gotten word of what you've done," he said darkly. "They want to see the Partial for themselves."

Kira smiled briefly. "Isolde to the rescue," she whispered.

"Don't get too excited," said Mkele. "Your team and that thing are both going to be questioned and sentenced in a formal Senate hearing. You will not enjoy it."

Kira looked up, suddenly alert. Some of the soldiers were moving, grabbing their weapons while Jayden and Yoon and Haru watched warily from the side. Mkele looked around quickly, searching for what had alerted them, then stepped back with a start.

The Partial was moving.

It was leaning to the side, groaning softly. Mkele stayed back; the Partial was locked into four different sets of handcuffs, two of them chaining it tightly to a steel-and-concrete road barrier, but there was still a wide circle around it that nobody seemed willing to enter. Even at a distance Kira could tell that it was still groggy, struggling to wake up, but somehow it still seemed menacing. She felt for her rifle, remembered she'd been disarmed, and cursed softly.

The Partial drew its knees in toward its chest, then stretched out as far as its chains would let it. As soon as it reached the limit of the restraints it stiffened, and Kira saw its head jerk slightly as it fought against the sedatives.

Mkele whispered softly. "How recently did you sedate it?"

"Just a few hours."

"How big of a dose?"

"Two hundred milligrams."

Mkele stopped, staring at her. "Are you trying to kill it? It'll asphyxiate."

"It's not straight morphine," said Kira. "It's Nalox—part morphine, part nanoparticle Naloxone. If the body loses too much oxygen, it synthesizes more Naloxone to reactivate the lungs."

Mkele nodded. "You could stand to give it a little more, then. Its body can clearly take it." He turned to his team. "Weapons ready, and clear away from the sides—this isn't a mob execution."

"It isn't an execution at all," said Kira. "You have to take it to the Senate—they said so."

Mkele's face was hard. "Unless it's killed while trying to escape."

"You can't do that," said Kira, glancing at the row of armed soldiers; they were waiting for any excuse to fire, their fingers practically twitching on their triggers.

Kira thought about Madison's baby, about her haunted face.

"Aim," said Mkele. Weapons clacked into place. The Partial

moved again, coughing, its throat sounding raw and horrible.

Suddenly Haru leaped into the middle of the circle, standing at the Partial's feet, and turned to face the firing squad. "You can't kill it."

"Get out of the way," growled Mkele.

"This thing is my daughter's only hope," said Haru. "The Senate ordered you to bring it in alive."

The Partial moved again, struggling to wake up. Half the soldiers stepped back, the other half surged forward, weapons searching for a clear shot around Haru. Haru cringed, gritting his teeth and closing his eyes, but he held his ground.

"That thing is a walking bomb," said Mkele.

"Yes, it's dangerous," said Haru. "But this is the most important tool we have ever had in this war. We need time to learn everything we can."

The Partial groaned again. The soldiers kept their guns up, ready for the order to fire.

Please, thought Kira, *please don't kill it.* She summoned her courage, stepped forward, and planted herself beside Haru.

The Partial moved again, brushing against the back of Kira's leg. She flinched and closed her eyes, half expecting it to rise up and kill her, but she held her ground.

Mkele stared at her, anger seething in his eyes. "Sedate it again," he said at last. "Give it everything you've got. I don't want it waking up again until we get it in a cell. We leave for East Meadow first thing in the morning."

CHAPTER SEVENTEEN

"This hearing is now in session."

Kira sat in the front row of the small Senate chamber, Jayden and Haru and Yoon sitting quietly beside her. They'd been given a change of clothes and a chance to wash up, but they were still under heavy guard. Kira felt the eyes of the whole city on the back of her head, but it was just nerves—there were no spectators, and if Mkele had done his job right, nobody even knew they were there. The soldiers present had been sworn to secrecy, the local guards had been sent away, and even most of the Senate was absent, leaving a committee of only five stern-faced politicians. Kira was grateful that Senator Hobb was among them; he never went anywhere without his assistant, and Isolde's presence gave Kira strength.

Despite Kira's discomfort, even the few people who were in the room weren't looking at her—they were looking at the Partial, chained upright to a rolling metal rig in the center of the room. It was awake, and its eyes were watching everyone closely, studying them, waiting in silence for . . . Kira didn't know for what. It was held in place with leather straps, handcuffs, chains, and even loops of rope and wire. Nobody knew exactly how strong it was—the restraints might be overkill, or they might be laughably inadequate. The room was rimmed with armed security just in case.

"You've got an interesting jury," said Isolde, sitting by Kira's side and whispering in her ear. She nodded toward the table at the front of the room. "Senator Hobb will be fair, and Dr. Skousen you already know; he tends to stay quiet during most Senate meetings, but with this whole medical angle you've got going on, I have no idea. Next to him is Cameron Weist, who I don't know much about. He's the new representative from the Grid base in Queens. The one in the middle is Marisol Delarosa, the Senate chair, and of course the harpy next to her is Xochi's mom, the representative from the farms. I have no idea why she's here. I've softened them up as much as I can, but just . . . be careful anyway. They're not your biggest fans right now."

Kira looked at Dr. Skousen. "I know."

Senator Hobb tore his eyes away from the Partial and stood up. He was as handsome as ever, almost awkwardly so. "This hearing has been called for two reasons: the discipline of these four young adults, and the determination of what should be done with this . . . Partial. Senator Weist."

"As the military representative on this council," said Weist, "I'll start with the most clear-cut matter. Jayden Van Rijn and Yoon-Ji Bak, please stand." Jayden and Yoon rose to their feet. "You are charged with falsifying military forms, abandoning your assigned mission, disabling the defense system on the Brooklyn Bridge, entering enemy territory without leave, and engaging in unauthorized activities resulting in the deaths of three of your fellow soldiers. What do you have to say to these charges?"

"Guilty," said Jayden. His face was grim and void of emotion. He stared straight forward.

Senator Weist looked at Yoon. "Private Bak?"

Yoon was silent, but Kira could see a tear in her eye. She swallowed and raised her head, standing as straight as she could. "Guilty."

"The penalty for these crimes is harsh," said Weist, "but the Defense Grid wishes to be lenient. You're both young, and frankly, we can't spare many trained soldiers. Even criminals." Weist glanced quickly at the Partial—a split-second look from the corner of his eye—then picked up a sheet of paper. "In a private military tribunal held this morning, it was determined that Private Yoon-Ji Bak, as a subordinate in these activities, was following orders from her superior officer and is as such not culpable. Private Bak, you will return with me to Fort LaGuardia, where you will be reassigned. Please be seated."

Yoon sat, and Kira could see that she was crying more freely now. She reached over and squeezed Yoon's knee.

Weist looked at Jayden. "Lieutenant Van Rijn. Just as Private Bak's rank makes her less guilty in this matter, your rank makes you more so. You've lied to your commanding officers, put civilians in danger, and gotten three of your own men killed. That they were volunteers and coconspirators doesn't matter to us, and it shouldn't matter to you—you were their leader, and now they are dead."

"Yes, sir."

"You are hereby dishonorably discharged from military

service and remanded to the custody of the civilian court. The Defense Grid recommends a sentence of imprisonment and hard labor, but that is the court's decision, not ours. Please be seated."

Jayden sat, and Kira whispered softly from the corner of her mouth, "He's a blowhole."

"He's right," said Jayden softly, "and he was more than fair. By rights I should have been executed."

"Well, don't sound so eager."

"Thank you, Senator Weist," said Hobb. "We will now proceed with the civilian hearing. Private Bak, you're excused."

"I'll sit with my friends, thank you," said Yoon, and stayed in her chair. Senator Hobb paused, shrugged, and carried on.

"Mr. Haru Sato, will you please stand?"

Haru rose to his feet.

"That was a good move for Yoon," said Isolde softly. "She's showing solidarity with the rest of you—Senator Hobb eats that stuff up."

"Will it sway any of the others?"

"I can't be sure," said Isolde.

"Haru Sato," said Hobb, "at twenty-two years old, you are the oldest member of this group, and the only adult. What do you have to say for yourself?"

Haru's eyes were as hard as steel. "Don't patronize them, Senator."

Kira heard a low murmur ripple through the court and did her best to hide her grimace. *Haru, you moron, what are you doing? You're supposed to be winning their favor, not antagonizing them.*

"Would you like to explain that comment?" asked Senator Hobb coldly.

"You just punished Jayden for making a poor choice as a commanding officer, and yet you're not going to call him an adult? Kira and Yoon are sixteen years old, an age you yourselves are currently debating as the new pregnancy age. You're going to force them to have children, but you're not going to call them adults?" He stared at each of the senators in turn, piercing them with his gaze. "I was eleven years old in the Break—I watched my father die in a Partial attack. I watched my mom and my brothers die two weeks later in a high school gym packed so full of refugees that RM went through it like a brush fire. I was the only person left alive in the entire city—I walked twenty miles, alone, until I found another group of survivors. I haven't been a child since that day, Senators, and these three went through the same thing even younger than I was. They risk their lives for this society every day, they have jobs, and any day now you're going to demand that they have children, too, and yet somehow you have the gall not to treat them like adults? This is not the paradise you lost in the Break, and it's high time you accepted that."

Kira listened with wide eyes. *Way to go, Haru. You tell 'em.* She leaned toward Isolde. "That ought to earn some respect."

"For him, yes," Isolde whispered. "It's actually really bad for you. He's trying to set you up as equals, to make sure this looks like a joint conspiracy of adults instead of one adult leading a group of minors. He could get a harsher sentence if they think he masterminded the whole thing. He doesn't want to get slammed on your behalf like Jayden was for Yoon."

"But that's . . ." Kira frowned, looking back and forth between Haru and the senators. "But he sounded so noble."

"It was brilliant," said Isolde. "A conniving weasel like that is wasted in construction."

"Very well," said Senator Hobb. "Kira Walker, do you wish to be tried as an adult?"

Damn. Thanks a lot, Haru. She stood slowly and held her head high. "I made my own decisions, Senator. I knew the risks and I understood them."

"You seem very certain of that," said Dr. Skousen. "Tell me, Kira, what were you planning to do with this Partial once you caught it? How were you going to keep it contained? How were you going to address the threat of a new contamination?"

"I wasn't planning to bring it back at all, sir. That was your idea." She paused, watching Dr. Skousen's brow grow dark with anger, wondering if she'd pushed him too hard. She forged ahead, glancing at the Partial; it looked back darkly, and she tried not to imagine how quickly it could break out of its restraints. "I was going to cut off its hand and test it in the field," she said, "with a medicomp we brought to Brooklyn. There was never any threat to anyone until—"

"No threat to anyone?" asked Dr. Skousen. "What about the three men who died across the river? What about the two women of breeding age who almost died with them? Surely you of all people, with your job in maternity, understand the need to protect every possible pregnancy."

"If you please, Doctor," said Kira, feeling her face grow hot with anger. "We've asked to be treated like adults, not cattle."

The doctor stopped short, and Kira gritted her teeth, forcing herself to keep her face as calm as possible. *What am I doing?*

"If you wish to be treated as an adult," said Senator Delarosa,

"I encourage you to keep a civil tongue."

"Of course, Senator."

"Can you tell us, for the record, what you expect to gain from your study of Partial tissue?"

Kira glanced at Dr. Skousen, wondering how much he'd already told them. "We've studied RM for years, but we still don't know how it works. Everything that should be effective in abating it isn't; everything that should inoculate us against it doesn't. We've hit a dead end, and we need a new direction. I believe that if we study the immunity from a Partial perspective—not the chance mutation that keeps us from developing symptoms, but the engineered resistance that makes them wholly immune—we can find the cure we've been looking for."

Senator Weist narrowed his eyes. "And you thought the best way to do this was to run screaming into the middle of enemy territory with no planning and no backup?"

"I asked Dr. Skousen for backup," said Kira. "He made it clear I wouldn't get any help from the Senate."

"I made it clear that you should not attempt it under any circumstances!" roared Skousen, slamming his hand on the table.

"My friend is pregnant," said Kira. "Haru's wife; Jayden's sister. If we'd done what you said, that baby would die, just like every other child you haven't saved for eleven straight years. I didn't study medicine to watch people die."

"Your motives were admirable," said Senator Kessler, "but your actions were stupid and irresponsible. I don't think there's any argument on that point." Kira looked at her, seeing again— as she always did—a remarkable similarity between her and Xochi. Not in their appearance, of course, but in their attitudes:

Adopted or not, Xochi had managed to grow up with Senator Kessler's same stubborn, passionate zeal. "We have laws in place to deal with people who do stupid and irresponsible things," she continued, "and we have courts in place to adjudicate those laws. Frankly, I find these criminals' presence here a waste of the Senate's time: I say we send them to criminal court and be done with them. This, on the other hand . . ." She gestured at the Partial. "We are in a hearing, and this is what I'd like to hear."

"We have laws," said Senator Hobb, "but I think this is fairly obviously a special case—"

Senator Kessler glared at Kira, who did her best to meet the look with as much dignity and resolve as possible. "I move that we send this criminal hearing to the proper court," said Kessler, turning back to Senator Hobb, "and deal with the real problem instead."

"I second," said Skousen.

"And I object," said Delarosa. "The presence of a Partial on Long Island, let alone right here in East Meadow, is of the utmost secrecy—we can't allow anyone, and certainly not an investigative court, to know anything about it. We will speak to the Partial, and then we will decide what to do with the defendants."

"I second," said Weist.

"I have no objection," said Hobb. Kessler paused, her face stern, then nodded.

Senator Hobb gestured for Kira and Haru to sit, then turned to the Partial. "Well. You have the floor now. What do you want to say?"

The Partial said nothing.

"Why were you in Manhattan?" asked Delarosa. She waited,

but the Partial didn't respond. She waited a moment longer, then spoke again. "You were part of an armed strike team making a temporary camp only miles from our border. What was your mission?"

The Partial remained perfectly silent.

"Why now?" continued Delarosa. "After six months of brutal rebellion and eleven years of complete absence—why are you back again?"

"Just kill it," said Senator Weist. "We should never have brought it here to begin with."

"Study it," said Kira suddenly. She stood up, feeling all eyes on her again. This was her last chance—with the Partial refusing to talk, they'd lost what little reason they'd had to keep it alive. It would be dead in minutes. She had to make them see; she had to convince them not to throw this opportunity away. "Going out on our own was dumb, and there's a million ways it could have gone wrong, and probably a million ways it could still go wrong, but look at what we've got: a live Partial, right there, just waiting to be studied. Punish us if you want—kill us if you want us killed—but somebody, please take advantage of this opportunity and study it. If I'm wrong, I'm wrong—that's okay, the damage has already been done. But if I'm right, we can cure RM and finally start putting our society back together again. No more RM, no more Hope Act, no more Voice or armed rebellions—a unified society with a chance at a future."

The senators stared at her a moment; then Delarosa called them together and they leaned in closely, whispering softly among themselves. Kira strained to listen, but couldn't make it out. Every now and then one of them stole a glance at the Partial.

"That was good," Isolde whispered. "I just hope it works. They keep staring at you, though, and that's making me nervous."

"Wait," said Kira, "at me? I thought they were looking at the Partial."

"Now and then," said Isolde, "but mostly you. I don't know what that means."

The senators conferred a moment longer, and Kira could see that yes, their furtive glances across the room were looking past the Partial and straight at her. She swallowed nervously, wondering what punishment they were going to give her. Finally they leaned back, silent, and Senator Hobb rose.

"The Senate has reached a decision," he said. "We have become convinced of the necessity for study: The Partials are immune to RM, and if we can discover the secrets behind that immunity, we may finally be able to find a cure. This Partial's body may be the key to our survival, and it doesn't appear to present any immediate threat when restrained and sedated." He glanced at Dr. Skousen, straightened, and spoke in a loud, clear voice. "We are moving the Partial to a secure facility in the hospital, confidentially and under guard, where it may be studied and analyzed in detail. After five days, it will be dismantled and disposed of. As for the study, it will be conducted by you, Ms. Walker." He looked at Kira; she was too stunned to read his expression. "You have five days. Use them well."

Kira spluttered, still trying to process the information. "You mean I'm not arrested or . . . you're giving me the body? You're going to let me do my tests?"

"Not just the body," said Dr. Skousen. "You can conduct better tests if it's alive."

CHAPTER EIGHTEEN

"It doesn't make sense," said Xochi. "My mother hates Partials—she would have killed that thing with her bare hands if they'd let her get close to it. Why do they want it alive?"

"Keep it down," said Kira. She glanced out the window again, peering through a small gap in the shades. "If anyone hears you—if anyone even finds out that we told you—there's going to be some serious hell to pay."

"Mkele probably wants to try to interrogate it," said Jayden. He and Haru started their sentences in hard labor the next morning, but the Senate had given them the night to gather their things. Haru was at home with Madison, but Jayden had come to Nandita's place. Nandita was gone, off on another herb-collecting trip; Kira shuddered to think of the explaining she'd have to do when Nandita got back. She could take insults from people she hated, but it was the disappointment from someone she loved that always broke her down. She started tearing up just thinking about it and forced herself to think of something else.

"I think you may be forgetting a key fact here," said Isolde.

"Apparently Partials are smoking hot. If you'd have told me that before you left, I would have gone to Manhattan with you."

"Come on, Isolde, that's gross." Kira grimaced.

"You saw it, same as I did," said Isolde. "That thing is an Adonis. Do something for me: When you get to spend your five days alone with that genetic perfection, try to find time for a close physical examination. Just for me."

"It's not even human," said Jayden.

"In what sense?" asked Isolde, continuing to bait him. "It's got all the right parts in all the right places. If this is what Para-Gen was going for when they started making artificial people, now I'm even sadder that it went nuts and tried to kill us."

"The questions in this hearing were nothing," said Jayden, finally deciding to ignore her. "All slow-pitch softball. Tonight they're going to put it in a subbasement somewhere, torture it, and learn everything they can. A night with some Grid soldiers in a soundproof room will take the fight right out of it."

"Now you're really turning me on," said Isolde.

"Shut up," said Jayden, and Xochi laughed.

"But why do they want me in charge?" asked Kira. "There are researchers with more experience than me, there are more skilled lab techs, there are—"

"I know," said Xochi. "Anybody in that hospital would be better for this than you. No offense."

"None taken," said Kira. "That's what I've been saying all night."

"Right," said Xochi. "So think about it: Why put your most junior student in charge of something that important unless you want to guarantee that it'll go wrong? Or to use her as a scapegoat when the whole thing blows up in their faces?"

"I'm sure there's a better reason than that," Kira said, though at heart she wasn't sure at all. She looked out the window again, scanning the dark street. Nothing.

"I don't think he's coming," said Xochi.

Kira turned back quickly. "What? No, I was just . . . looking at the trees. At the open street that isn't teeming with panthers and poison ivy."

"The world across the line was pretty different," said Jayden, nodding. "I don't know how to describe it."

"It's because there weren't any people," said Isolde. "Manhattan's gone more primal than Long Island because there's never anyone scaring away the animals or stomping down the plants."

Jayden laughed thinly. "There are forty thousand people on Long Island," he said. "There used to be millions. Sometimes I think this island doesn't even know we're here."

"It's not just Manhattan," said Kira, "it's everywhere—we saw a panther in Brooklyn. We saw a baby antelope—a little antelope fawn, probably two months old at the most. Someday they'll wonder where all those weird, two-legged animals went, and then they'll take a drink from a river, and look up at the clouds, and then they'll forget they were ever even thinking about us at all. Life will go on. There's no point even leaving a record behind, because there will never be anyone, ever again, who can read it."

"Somebody's depressed," said Jayden.

Xochi punched him in the arm. "Does anyone want some more home fries?"

"Ooh, me," said Isolde, sitting up. "Forget extinction—I'm

dying the day all our vegetable oil finally runs out."

Xochi passed her the plate and stood up. "I'm sick of 'Antonio, on His Bar Mitzvah.' Any requests?"

"Phineas," said Kira. "No—Nissyen. He always cheers me up."

Xochi sorted through her basket of players, glancing quickly at the generator to make sure there was power. Isolde took a bite of potato and pointed at Kira with the other half, talking with her mouth full.

"I think you're just spooked," she said. "All joking aside, that thing almost killed you in the field, and now you have to work with it."

"Not with it."

"With it in the room," said Isolde. "You know what I mean. I think it's scary."

"I think you're scary," said Xochi. She plugged in a music player—TO NISSYEN FROM LISA—and bubbly techno started playing in the background. "You're the most elegant one of us," Xochi continued, sitting next to Isolde, "and here you are flinging fried potatoes around like you're an outlands street vendor."

"I may be a little drunk," said Isolde seriously, pointing at Xochi with her half-chewed fry. She raised her eyebrow. "Senator Hobb gave me some champagne."

"Ooh la la," said Xochi.

"Maybe beacuse the hearing went better than expected?" said Isolde. She shrugged. "I wasn't going to say no."

"But they didn't get anything they wanted," said Kira, sitting up straighter. "Four dumb kids forced them into . . ." She stopped. "Unless that's what they wanted all along."

"They wanted it alive?" asked Jayden. "They wanted you to study it?"

"I don't know," said Kira. "None of it makes sense." She looked out the window. Still nothing.

"Doesn't it make you a little suspicious, though?" asked Xochi. "If the Senate is running some kind of weird scheme here, how many other things are they doing that we don't know about?"

"You're being paranoid," said Jayden. "What kind of horrible conspiracies do you think they've got going?"

"They're hiding a Partial inside the city limits," said Xochi. "If they're capable of that, why not more?"

The room went quiet.

"Attacks against the farms," said Xochi. "Accused Voices disappearing in the middle of the night. We accept these things because we think we know the reasons behind them, but what if we don't? What if the reasons we've been told all along are just lies?"

"I've been Senator Hobb's assistant for nearly a year," said Isolde, "and I can guarantee you I'm not keeping any dangerous state secrets."

"You're defending the honesty of a group that you know, firsthand, is lying to the people of East Meadow," said Xochi. "And they're doing it too effectively to be first-timers. The only surprising thing about it is that any of you are surprised."

"I think Xochi's right," said Kira. She felt a pit in her stomach, slowly growing deeper and darker as she thought through Xochi's logic.

"Why are you so desperate to attack them?" asked Jayden.

"Listen, Xochi, I'm sorry your mom is a bitch, but she's not the entire Senate. And what about the Defense Grid? You're talking about people who defend us and keep us safe—people who die in the outlands so that you can sit here with your monogrammed music players and your fancy foods and whine about how oppressed you are."

"Not counting your own fiasco," said Xochi hotly, "when's the last time a soldier actually died in combat?"

"Last year, in the Voice raid on the Hampton farms."

"And how do you know that was the Voice?" Xochi demanded. "Why would they lie to us?"

"How do you know there wasn't just some disgruntled farmer," Xochi pressed, "who refused to send in his quota, so the Long Island Bloody Defense Grid went out to rough him up a little?"

"Why would they lie to us?" Jayden repeated.

"Because it keeps us in line!" Xochi shouted back. "Look at everything we go through—armed soldiers in the streets, invasive searches of everyone going in and out of the market; they've even started searching homes. The Senate says jump and we ask how high because they've convinced us the Voice will kill us if we don't. Our boys go to war, our girls get pregnant, and we always do everything they say and it never changes anything. Nothing ever gets better. You know why? Because if it gets better, we don't have to listen to them anymore."

Kira flicked her eyes from person to person, shocked by the outburst. Everyone else seemed as shocked as she was.

Jayden grumbled and stood up. "You're insane," he said, walking to the door. "I've got better things to do with my time than waste it here."

"Idiot," Xochi muttered, and stormed into the kitchen.

Kira looked at Isolde, who looked back with wide, startled eyes.

"They're not evil," said Isolde. "I work with them every day—they're just people. Hobb's really trying to do his best." She paused. "You should take your own gun tomorrow. We have no idea how strong the Partials are, or what they're capable of. Do you have a handgun?"

Kira shook her head. "I'm a rifle girl, but that's mostly just at home. It wouldn't be very useful inside the lab."

"I'll give you mine," said Isolde. "Town hall is swarming with soldiers, and you just became zookeeper to a hyperintelligent predator. You need it more than I do."

Kira looked out the window at the empty street. "I guess we may as well go get it," she said softly. "The party's dead anyway." She walked out with Isolde, paused on the porch, and waited a few long seconds before stepping down and leaving.

Marcus never came.

Dr. Skousen led Kira down a long hall. "This used to be a quarantine room," he said, pointing toward the heavy steel door at the end of the corridor. "We haven't used it for that, or for anything else, really, in years. The custodians spent all night cleaning it out. I'm afraid that the seals aren't all as tight as we'd like them to be, but we've got the salvage crews working overtime looking for new medical supply stores and new hospitals and clinics— anywhere that might have the right kind of plastic for the doors and windows. We'll be safe enough for now."

And I'll be locked inside with a Partial, thought Kira. She clutched her stack of vials and notebooks and other equipment, trying not to drop them as she matched Skousen's brisk pace.

He lowered his voice, whispering covertly as they turned the final corner. "We've spent the night searching it for anything that could be a weapon, cleaning it, weighing it—anything that required it to be unrestrained. Now it's strapped down, and it's all yours."

They reached the door, a seven-foot steel barrier flanked by two soldiers in helmets and body armor. One of them was Shaylon Brown, the private she'd met on the Asharoken salvage run, and he smiled as he turned to unlock the door. Kira looked at Skousen, keeping a tight grip on her precarious load of equipment.

"Anything else I need to know?"

"Learn everything you can," he said gravely. "I didn't want you to do this, and I still think it was idiotic to attempt, but now that we have one . . . this is a rare opportunity, and I honestly don't know how long the other senators are going to allow it, five-day promise or not. Make sure you report everything directly to me, especially if you find something . . . ominous. The last thing we want is a panic."

"Got it," said Kira. "Well then." She turned to the door, took a deep breath, and walked past the soldiers. "Thanks for keeping me safe, guys." *If you need me, I'll be locked inside here with the monster.*

The entryway was a short tube of clear, flexible plastic, with a soft electric hum from a grate on the floor—an electromagnetic grid designed to pull foreign particles from her shoes. *There's supposed to be a—* She looked around for the air jets just in time to get blasted in the face by an artificial whirlwind, sweeping her clean and pulling dust and hair and other contaminants down to the same electric grid. She managed to keep her grip on her vials and papers, and when the air stopped, she pushed forward into the room itself.

The Partial lay on an operating table in the center of the room; it was strapped down tightly with thick leather restraints, and the table was bolted to the floor. It was awake, its eyes alert, watching her as she stepped into the converted room. The walls were lined with counters and medicomps and other equipment, all clean and well-lit. She had Isolde's semiautomatic on her hip.

She'd never been more terrified in her life.

Kira stood for a moment, saying nothing, then crossed to the wall and set her things on a counter. The sample vials rolled free and she paused to gather them up, placing them one by one in a plastic rack. She swallowed, staring at the rack, willing herself to turn and face the Partial. It was nothing—it was one man, not even a man but a teenager, all alone and tied up. She'd faced it and others like it under far worse conditions only a few days before. And yet things felt different here; everything seemed off and out of place. A Partial in the wilds was an enemy, and she knew how to think about it, but a Partial here, in East Meadow, in the same room . . .

She saw a glint of light in the corner of her eye, and turned to see the lens of a small camera mounted in the corner. It was obviously new and out of place, mounted blockily on the wood of the counter with thick screws. She turned to scan the room and saw five more: one in each corner, and two higher up to get specific angles on both the Partial's table and her own workstation.

Mkele's work, she assumed, and she felt some of her nervousness lift at the thought that he and his soldiers were watching her so closely. If the Partial tried anything, they'd see it and respond.

Kira let out a breath she didn't realize she was holding. She couldn't decide if knowing Mkele was watching made her feel more safe, or less. She walked past the bound Partial to the window.

She was on the second floor, looking out through a strip of tall trees to a wide parking lot full of sagging cars. Many of the parking lots in town were empty—not much business at the local restaurants while civilization was collapsing around you—but the hospital had been packed and overflowing eleven years ago, and their cars remained like ghostly reminders.

I need to take a blood sample, Kira told herself, forcing herself back to the task at hand. *I need blood and tissue. I went all the way to a war zone to cut the hand off an enemy soldier, I can take a biopsy from the thing lying tied up fifteen feet away.*

She walked back to the sample vials she'd brought with her—blood samples she'd taken from Marcus. Relics of her first attempt at studying RM, before Manhattan and the Partial and everything else. Before Marcus didn't come. She still had all the notes she'd taken from the blood, full descriptions of platelet counts and white cell counts and glucose and electrolytes and calcium levels and the vast, terrifying mass of viral structures. Every human being was a carrier, poisoning their own children long after the Partials had disappeared. Were the Partials carriers as well? Was this whole catastrophe useless?

She breathed deeply, wiped her face, and turned to look at the Partial—not a faceless thing in a black visor but a man, a boy barely older than she was, tied to a table and stripped almost to nothing. With his shirt off, she could see his body was toned and muscular, not bulging like a bodybuilder but simply fit: strong and lean and capable. Genetic perfection, as Isolde had put it. Kira tried to summon her zeal from the fight in Manhattan, tried to imagine herself cutting off its hand for study. It had brown eyes, like hers. It looked back calmly.

Dr. Skousen had said that they'd washed the Partial, but Kira looked again and saw there were flecks of something around its face and head. She stepped closer, trying to get a better look, then closer again, peering at its face. It was flecks of blood, dried and black, ringing its mouth and eye and dotting its ear on the other side. She reached out to brush away its hair, paused with her hand halfway, and dropped it back to her side.

"I take it they beat you?"

The Partial said nothing, simply watching her through dark eyes. She could feel its anger like the heat from an iron stove, radiating out in waves. She steeled herself and reached out again, and this time the Partial turned on her suddenly, jerking its head and straining at its bonds. Kira jumped back involuntarily, her heart racing, and reached for her gun. She didn't pull it out, merely felt it, solid and reassuring in her hand. She forced herself to calm down and stepped forward again, standing straight. After a moment she pulled out the gun anyway and held it up for the Partial to see.

"I was part of the group that captured you," she said. "I'm not trying to threaten you, I'm just telling you how serious I am. We've got five days together, and if you want to spend them fighting, I am more than ready."

It watched her, eyes cold and hard, as if studying her for any break it could use, any hole in her defenses it could slip through—

—and yet behind the cold eyes it was terrified. She could tell, just by looking at it, that it had never been this scared in its life. She took a step back, looking at the situation from its perspective: It was alone, a prisoner of war, beaten and chained and strapped down to an operating table, and now she was holding a gun on it.

Kira looked down at the gun in her hand and put it away. "In case you couldn't tell, everyone here is pretty much terrified of you. We don't know what you can do or how you work. For all we know, you're a biological weapon with legs."

She paused, waiting, but he stayed silent. She prompted him with her hand, but still nothing. She sighed. She wasn't sure what she was waiting for from him.

He watched her closely, and she felt uncomfortably like a bug in a jar. Who was really studying who?

"Fine, then," she said. "If you don't want to talk, that's fine. I don't think I would in your situation either, frankly, but then again I don't know if I could help myself. Humans are very social creatures; we like to communicate in order to feel—"

"You talk too much."

Kira stopped, eyes wide. His voice was dry and hoarse from days of disuse—as far as she knew, it hadn't said a word since they'd captured it, now more than fifty hours ago. She almost wasn't sure she'd heard him right. *The first human to communicate with another species in eleven years,* she thought, *and he tells me to shut up.* When the initial shock wore off, she almost started laughing.

"Point taken," she said, nodding. "But first let me explain what I'm going to do. Most of our tests here are going to be sensor-based, noninvasive stuff, looking at your organs, that sort of . . ." It closed its eyes, pointedly ignoring her, and she trailed off. "All right then, no medical explanations." Kira walked to a side counter, rooted through the drawers, and came back with a sterilized glass tube and a handful of little instruments. "Let me at least warn you, though, this finger poker is going to hurt a bit—it's nothing horrible, just a spring-loaded pin about two millimeters long. Are you going to let me use your finger, or are we going to fight again?"

He opened his eyes, saw the finger poker, and looked up at Kira's face. After a long moment, he unrolled his fist and laid out his fingers.

"Thank you." She shook a few drops of ethanol onto a ball of cotton and swabbed his index finger. His hands were firm and warm. The poker was about the size and shape of a dental floss container, and she pressed it against his fingertip. "Brace yourself."

He barely flinched. The pin jabbed into its fingertip, and she pulled it away quickly, pressing a skinny glass tube against the wound. It slowly filled with blood, more slowly than usual, and she squeezed its finger, pressing out more. The flow stopped before she could even fill the tube.

"Your blood pressure might be low," she commented, sealing up the tube with a frown. "Usually I can fill two vials on one finger. Unless . . ." She peered in closer, watching the blood in the tube as it started to congeal. She looked at its finger, prodding the hole gently. It had already sealed itself closed. "That's amazing," she whispered. She held the glass tube up to her eye; the blood was turning a rusty brown, firming up until it was capped on both ends by a small, solid scab.

She looked back at the Partial. It said nothing.

Kira's first impulse was to poke it again, deeper this time, but she recoiled from the idea almost as quickly as she had it. She wasn't here to torture it, and fast healing or not, it could still feel pain. Its flinch at the finger poker had been proof enough of that. She didn't have the stomach to wound it just to watch how it reacted.

And yet . . . wasn't that what the Senate wanted? Wasn't that what she was here to do? She wouldn't just go cutting him with knives, but they had told her to study him, and if the Partial resistance to RM was based on a powerful self-regenerative system, then she would have to test the limits of his healing power and determine how, if at all, they could use it for themselves. If she couldn't find the answer elsewhere, she would have to look there.

Could it take a gunshot? What would happen to the bullet? Her gut warred with her scientific curiosity. She shook her head and set down the scabbed-over tube.

"I'm not going to torture you," she said, going back to the drawers and retrieving a small plastic syringe and a short, sharp needle. "But I do have to get another blood sample. The medicomp needs liquid blood to give me a good picture of what's going on in there, so if you scab over on instant contact with air, we'll have to keep air out of the equation for as long as possible." She fitted the syringe with the needle, found a tube of saline solution, and drew it in and out of the needle until she was fairly certain all the internal space had been filled with liquid. She swabbed the vein on the Partial's inner elbow and held the needle above it. "Get ready for another poke."

This time it didn't flinch at all. She drew a cubic centimeter of blood and started to tape a cotton ball to the hole in its arm, but quickly realized that it was, of course, already healing over. She felt a little foolish and turned away, putting the entire syringe, needle and all, into the medicomp. The blood was still liquid. She stripped off her gloves and started tapping the screen, calling up blood tests and liver screens and everything else she could think of, triggering the "comprehensive scan" message that had identified the virus last time. With Marcus. She tapped yes and waited, practically holding her breath, while the medicomp catalogued the blood.

She hadn't allowed herself to think about Marcus yet; she hadn't ever really had time. Less than twenty-four hours ago she was still in the back of a Defense Grid truck, pulling into East Meadow for her secret hearing with the Senate. Marcus hadn't come to Xochi's last night—and she hadn't gone to look for him—and then in the morning she'd come straight here. Was he still mad at her? Was she even still mad at him? Yes, she was—of course she was—but at the same time she could see his side. She knew now that he had been . . . what? Trying to protect her? She didn't need to be protected, not when she was the only one trying to do something here. But was he right about RM—that it couldn't be cured, and they were ruining their lives by trying? She couldn't believe that, couldn't even allow herself to think it. She was going to cure the damned thing, and that was all there was to it. But then what did she think she understood about Marcus?

That he was scared, and thought he was going to lose her. She could understand that. She'd been half convinced she was going to die herself.

The medicomp chirped, and Kira looked back at the screen. It had higher-than-average electrolytes in its blood, a glucose level that looked borderline diabetic, and a white cell count so high she couldn't help but take its temperature, fearing an infection. It was 98.6 degrees exactly, just as she was. Maybe its physiology had a slightly different baseline of normal? The results that would indicate illness in a normal human patient, but as far as she knew, they were normal for a Partial. She copied the details down in her notebook, marking the anomalies she wanted to go back and study later.

But the most important part of the scan was what was missing after she'd gone through it all. It had no trace of RM whatsoever.

No RM. She looked up, ecstatic; the Partial was still lying on the table, staring silently at the ceiling, and somehow still managing to look dangerous. Anyone else in that position would look like they'd given up, but there was something about it—the tension in its muscles, the alert flicker of its eyes—that told Kira its mind was racing.

In that moment it didn't matter. Kira felt like laughing—the Partial had no trace of RM in its blood, just like she'd predicted. Its body could destroy or expel the virus completely. All she had to do was figure out how.

She tapped the screen quickly, fingers dancing across the surface as she pulled up the files on the virus. Now that she knew the Partials didn't carry it, she had to figure out how, exactly, the humans did—what was the infection process? It wasn't enough to just say, "They got sick"; she needed to know how the virus traveled from person to person, and what happened when it got there, in precise microbial detail. She needed to watch the process in a human and in a Partial, to see how they differed. She pulled up the image of the virus again, the yellow-tinged blob that lived in the blood. *You look like a balloon,* she thought, *but you killed 99.996 percent of the human race.*

She needed to focus. What information did the file already have? Size, for one thing: four hundred nanometers. That was huge for this scale—definitely big enough to be stopped by a good air filter. She glanced across the room to the plastic tunnel by the door, wondering what kind of filter it used. *A system like that should be able to stop a four-hundred-nanometer virus,* she thought. *Four hundred nanometers should keep it away from a fetus, as well; nothing that big should be able to cross the placental barrier. That could explain why the babies don't get sick until after they're born.*

Kira paused, caught by a sudden thought. *If the virus is big enough to be contained, why can't we deliver infants in a contained environment?* They scrubbed the room, they sterilized their tools, they wore gas masks—they did everything they could think of, yet the virus still got through.

I'm not the first person to ask that question, she thought. *Marcus and Dr. Skousen both said that people have been researching this since the Break. That means there'll be records somewhere of their findings.* She called up the database files in the microscope, searching for studies of all their clean-room births, and found several. None had been successful, obviously; the rate of sickness and the onset of RM was virtually identical to that of normal births, as if the clean room had shown no effect at all. Attached to the records was another set of studies, this time focusing on the existence of an RM variant found only in the air. Kira opened this with interest—she knew that RM was airborne, of course, but the actual structure of the airborne virus was not exactly entry-level medicine, and they hadn't talked about it yet in any of her classes. The report contained more images, similar to those in her blood sample but much smaller: between twenty-three and thirty-one nanometers. Kira frowned. Something that small would be almost impossible to catch, even with a clean room. She looked at the Partial, feeling a surge of her old anger.

"You made pretty damn sure we couldn't get away from this thing, didn't you?"

The Partial turned its head to look at her, and Kira felt like she could almost see the thoughts whirring through its mind. When it spoke, its eyes seemed almost . . . curious. "You can't reproduce."

"What?"

"That's why you're trying to cure RM. We don't have children, so their absence didn't seem odd at first, but you don't have any, do you? You're trying to cure RM because your children don't survive it."

Kira wanted to scream at it, to force it to acknowledge its own hand in their extinction, to attack it for daring to speak so matter-of-factly about something so terrible, and yet she stopped, one thought catching in her mind.

Did it not know the virus was still killing them? She knew she shouldn't trust it, but it seemed like something it was just now understanding. It really hadn't known. But if it hadn't known, that suggested two very important things: first, that the Partials weren't spying on them. The theories cropped up now and then, that Partials were hiding among them, infiltrating the island with deep cover spies. But if that were true, this one would already have known that human infants were dying. Its surprise meant they weren't being watched.

Or if they are watching, she thought, *they aren't telling each other what they see.*

The second thing it suggested was that the Partials—or at least this Partial in particular—did not know how RM worked. It hadn't expected the virus to stick around, and presumably most of the Partials it interacted with thought the same. Were the Partial leaders hiding the information from their own soldiers, or did they not know either? And how could they not know the function of a virus they'd created? It was possible the virus had mutated; Kira shuddered at the thought of it. If something as deadly as RM was mutating, acting beyond its original parameters, who knew what it was capable of?

She supposed there was one way to find out how much he knew. "You," she said, "Partial. What do you know about RM?"

It didn't answer.

"Oh, come on," said Kira, rolling her head back in frustration. "Are we going to go through this again? Can't you at least say something?"

"Well, human," he said, "you're going to kill me in five days. I don't see much of an incentive to say anything."

Kira stormed back to the medicomp and threw herself into the chair, so angry she could hardly think. It was going to be killed because it had killed Gabe, and Skinny, and six billion other people. After everything it had done, every atrocity it had been a part of, how dare it have the temerity to imply that it was a victim?

The images on the screen seemed to swirl and blur; how could she concentrate with that thing lying twenty feet away? It was times like this when she needed Marcus to make a joke, to defuse the situation and help her realize what mattered and what didn't. She looked at the door, but of course he wasn't there. He didn't even know where she was.

The Partial was right about one thing: She only had five days. She needed to work. She pushed the Partials out of her mind and forced herself to focus on the task at hand: a screen full of viral images, a series of reports on the viral structure. It had two forms, one for blood and one for air; the Blob and the Spore, the yellow and the blue. *Concentrate!* The Spore was tiny, perfect for traveling through the air. That must be how the virus passed from host to host. But then what was the Blob for?

None of the studies had the answer; they knew both forms of the virus existed, but not how they worked together. Kira turned back to the sample report from Marcus's blood, combing through the results for any sign of the Spore. If it *could* get into the body, it *would*; there should be some sign of it in Marcus's sample, but there was nothing. That meant that whatever happened to the Spore when it got into the body was happening very quickly, and leaving no trace.

That is, the Blob *was* the trace. Kira ran through the possibilities in her head: The virus obviously reacted to human blood and tissue—that was how it worked, using the host body's own material to replicate itself—so maybe there was an extra layer of interaction. Maybe the Spore wasn't designed to replicate itself at all, just to convert itself into the Blob and let that one replicate. It was weird, but it was possible. *Whatever it does,* thought Kira, *it has to do it quickly: By the time we get a chance to test the blood, any samples of the Spore have all been converted.* Kira ran her fingers through her hair, trying to figure out how to see the transformation in action. If she could get a sample of uninfected blood, and get it into the medicomp fast enough, she'd be able to study the actual process of infection. But where could she find uninfected human blood?

In the newborns. There were four pregnant women in the city due to deliver in the next week, and several samples beyond that if one of the other mothers delivered early.

She would put a request in to Dr. Skousen, just to see what he said. They always took blood samples at birth, but they usually didn't test those samples for several minutes while they dealt with other problems—most blood samples aren't this time-sensitive. If Kira's theory was correct, they'd have to test the blood immediately if they wanted to see this specific reaction.

The next question was the more difficult one: If the Blob came from transformed Spores, where did the Spores come from? Did the Blob create them, or did it transform back? Observing that change would be difficult, because she had no idea how it worked, and thus how to re-create it. Obviously the transformation couldn't happen in the blood, because it would reverse itself instantly. The lack of any Spore samples in Marcus's blood attested to that. *In the lungs, then? Does the Blob react to oxygen the same way the Spore reacts to tissue?* It was the simplest answer, which made it the best place to start. But how could she test it?

I need to isolate the virus first, she thought. She looked around the room for something that could trap the tiny virus, and her eyes fell on a box of latex gloves. She remembered how she and Marcus used to inflate them in school, pinching them almost closed and blowing them full of air. If the virus transformation really did happen in the lungs, her breath would be full of it. *And if a rubber glove will hold oxygen, it'll contain the virus too, at least long enough to take a look at in the medicomp.* She walked to the rubber gloves, held one to her mouth, and blew it up like a balloon. *Now what?* She stood in the middle of the room uncertainly. Would the medicomp be able to read anything through the rubber? Probably, even if she felt stupid shoving an inflated rubber glove into the sensor bay. But there was another problem, which was that whatever she did with her own breath, she'd have to do the same with the Partial's breath as well. Both tests needed to be the same, or the results wouldn't mean anything, and she was pretty sure the Partial wouldn't blow up a rubber glove. She let the glove deflate. She'd have to think of something else.

"We were winning the war," said the Partial softly. Kira still started when it spoke, not expecting to hear anything from it.

"What?" Kira stared at it, then shoved the glove into her pocket. "Why the hell are you bringing that up?"

"Because you think we created the virus; that's why you're studying me as part of your mission to cure it. You think we engineered it." It shook its head. "We didn't."

"Obviously I expect you to lie to me," said Kira, "but I was hoping you'd be a little more creative."

"It's the truth."

"It is not true!" she shouted. The Partial didn't respond, simply watched her from the table. Its eyes were dark and serious. "You attacked us, you killed us, and you released that virus to finish the job."

"We were winning the war," it said again. "We were the largest branch of your military, so there was no effective way for you to fight back; we struck quickly, we took out your communications, we crippled your counterattack. You had no way of stopping us. In another few weeks, maybe as few as two, we would have taken full control of the government, and we would have done it without losing the infrastructure your society had created—electricity, natural gas, shipping and industry and food production—"

"Was that your plan?" asked Kira bitterly. "To use us as slaves? As labor to maintain your infrastructure?"

"You mean the same thing you had done to us?"

Kira stared at it, anger rising up by the second, hot as a welding torch burning through her from inside. She pulled the glove back out of her pocket, stalked to the medicomp, and threw the glove into the hazmat can.

"We didn't want to enslave you," said the Partial. "Even if we did, we didn't want or need to kill you to do it. There was no purpose, tactical or political or otherwise, in releasing a killer virus."

"You expect me to believe that a perfect supervirus, which destroyed humans and left you unscathed, was coincidentally released in the middle of your attack—and that you had nothing at all to do with it?"

"I admit that it seems far-fetched."

"Far-fetched is an understatement."

"We've been searching for an explanation ever since," it said, "but we still don't know where it came from."

"I don't know why I am even talking to you," said Kira. It was crazy to think she was putting any credence in anything it said—and she was crazy to be listening to it at all. She turned back to the medicomp, staring angrily at the images and data, but she couldn't stop herself from glancing at the Partial, first once, then again. It knew something. If she could see through its lies, perhaps there was something useful in what it was saying. Everything it said was flat and emotionless, almost as if it didn't, or couldn't, care. She swiveled fully toward it, leaning forward in her chair. "All right," she said, "since you're in such a talkative mood: Why were you in Manhattan?"

It said nothing. She waited, staring at him, and asked again in frustration, "What was your mission? Why were you so close to our border?"

"I can't tell you."

"Why not?"

The Partial stared at the ceiling. "Because I don't want them to kill me."

CHAPTER NINETEEN

It was nearly midnight when Kira left the hospital, and she shivered slightly in the cool air—summer or not, night on Long Island could still get chilly. The Partial had refused to say any more, and Kira was half grateful: As desperate as she was to know what he was talking about, she was also scared. If what it knew was so dangerous that even talking about it would get it killed . . . she shivered again, just thinking about it.

Instead, she'd spent the day buried in the medicomp files, studying the virus: its specific structure, the proteins that made up the walls and receptor nodes, the genetic payload it carried inside. The hospital had some incredibly advanced genetic equipment, some of the same old devices they had once used for genetic modification—everything from curing diseases to changing eye color—but all the people who knew how to use them had died in the Break. It was ironic, in a way, that they had such incredible technology, from a time so recent, that no living person could understand. Sometimes Kira almost thought of them as magic: mystic artifacts from some forgotten civilization. Dr. Skousen and his researchers studied them in darkened rooms, surrounded by the ancient tomes of their craft, but the magic was gone. They could find the genetic coding in RM, but they couldn't change it or even read it. All they could do was watch, and guess, and hope for a breakthrough.

Kira had found no breakthroughs. There were four days left.

She walked slowly through the city, eager to go home and collapse into sleep but still aimless, in a way, as if her brain were too tired of focusing, and wanted simply to meander. She followed it through the darkened city, passing quiet houses and cracked sidewalks and dirty roads beaten smooth by traffic. At night East Meadow seemed almost as empty as the outside world—the omnipresent plant growth was kept in check by the sheer mass of people and animals, but the houses were just as dark, the streets just as empty, the world just as quiet. In the daytime the city was populated but sparse; in the night, it was just another part of the ruin that covered the world.

Kira rounded a corner and realized where she was—where she'd been walking, subconsciously, since the moment she left the hospital. Marcus's street. She stood on the corner, unmoving, counting down the houses *five, four, three, two, one* and then his on the right. He'd lived with an older man for several years, then moved in with another foster parent when the first man died, and when he turned sixteen he moved out into his own place. It was no big deal, moving; all you had to do was find a house in good condition, clean it up, and there you were. The owners were all dead, the banks were all defunct, there were more than enough for everyone to have two, five, even ten houses if you wanted them. Long Island had been home to millions of people. The old world had been consumed with the search for More Stuff. Now there was more stuff than anyone could ever use, and little or none of anything else.

Kira saw a gleam of yellow light, faint and distant. She paused, squinting, and saw it again. It was definitely Marcus's house. Why was he up this late? She walked forward, stepping carefully over the tree-root cracks in the buckled sidewalk, keeping her eyes on the flickering light. It was a candle, shining softly through the window. She stopped on the lawn in front, peering in at the room beyond: a candle, a chair, and Marcus, asleep sitting up. The walls were bare, marked with the nails of somebody else's photos, now pulled down or stored or thrown away. She watched Marcus for an endless moment, and then suddenly he was watching her, his head raised, his eyes open.

He sat still, watching with wide eyes, waiting for her to move. She stood still and watched back.

The candle flickered.

Marcus stood up and disappeared behind the frame of the window, and then the front door opened. Kira was running up the porch steps before she even knew what was happening, and when Marcus appeared in the doorway, she threw her arms around him, sinking her face into his chest. He caught her tightly, holding her close, and she closed her eyes and soaked him in: his strength, his smell, his presence, as recognizable to her as her own. He'd been a part of her life for as long as she could remember; he was more real than anything in the old world. That was the life she'd been born in, but this—East Meadow,

Marcus, even RM—was the life she lived. She held him close, raising her face and finding his. Their lips met in a long, fierce, desperate kiss.

"I'm sorry I didn't go with you," Marcus whispered. "I regretted it every day you were gone."

"You could have died," said Kira, shaking her head and then kissing him again.

"But I should have been with you," he said, his voice hard. "I should have been there to protect you. I love you, Kira."

"I love you too," she said softly, but a voice in the back of her head said, *You didn't need to be protected.*

She ignored the voice, shoving it away. Right now, all she wanted in the entire world was to be in his arms.

"You got one, didn't you?"

Kira paused, not wanting to talk or even think about the Partial, then nodded. "Yeah."

"The rumors are going around. Everybody knows the Grid brought something back from the west end of the island, but nobody knows what. It wasn't hard for me to put two and two together."

Kira felt a wave of tension creep back through her body, remembering how tense the city had been before she'd left it. How close the people were to civil war. "You think anyone else has figured it out?"

"I doubt it," said Marcus. "Bringing a Partial into the middle of East Meadow is not exactly the first thing that's going to leap into anyone's mind."

"Maybe not the first," said Kira, "but the second, or the fifth, or the twentieth. Someone might figure it out." She felt suddenly cold, pulling away from Marcus to rub her arms. He put a hand on her back and led her gently inside.

"We have plenty of other things to worry about," he said, uncharacteristically somber. "There was another Voice attack while you were gone, a big one. They raided the kennels and killed or kidnapped almost every trained dog the Grid had. Now we can't—"

Kira stopped and grabbed him by the arm, her heart pounding. "The kennels? Isn't that where Saladin worked?"

"The boy wonder," Marcus nodded, "the youngest human on the planet. They took him when they took the dogs, and half the people working with him. It was a pretty big blow, psychologically. Without the dogs we can't track the Voice through the wilderness anymore, but without Saladin . . . it's like they came in, kicked a puppy, and stole a baby. A lot of people are calling for an all-out war."

"Why would they do that?" asked Kira. "Obviously it was going to make people mad—it's almost like they went out of their way to piss us off. It's certainly not going to win them any new supporters. Maybe they're trying to start a war?"

"They might be holding him for ransom," said Marcus. "He's a pretty big bargaining chip, and they left a note."

"A note?"

"Well, technically they tagged the kennel with twenty feet of graffiti, but still. The message was clear, the same as it's always been: 'Repeal the Hope Act.'"

Kira pushed her way through the plastic tunnel. "Good morning." She said it without thinking, then paused, wondering why. When had she started to think of it as a person?

The Partial, of course, said nothing. It didn't even seem to react when it heard her, and Kira wondered if it was asleep. She crept closer, trying to stay as quiet as she could, but the Partial groaned and coughed, rolling his head to the side and spitting.

"What are you—" She froze.

The spit was red with blood.

Kira dropped her files and rushed to his side, gently lifting his head. His face was black with bruises and crusted blood.

"Holy crap, what happened to you?"

He groaned again, slowly blinking his eyes open. "Blood."

"Yeah," said Kira, running to the cupboards to look for towels, "I can see you're bleeding, but why? What happened?"

He didn't say anything. He tilted his head, popping the joints in his neck, then held up his right arm; it moved about three inches before the restraint jerked it to a stop. He had been given a change of clothes, and Kira pulled back his sleeve to reveal an arm covered with thin lacerations, tender and pink. "They cut me."

Kira's mouth dropped open in horror. "Who?" The horror turned to anger almost instantly. "Who was it? The guards? Doctors?"

He nodded slightly, and probed his mouth with his tongue, making sure all the teeth were still in place.

"That's ridiculous," said Kira, fuming. She stomped to the microscope, snarled, and stomped back. Everything she'd thought about doing, and rejected for being inhumane, someone else had come in and done. She shot a long, cold glance at one of the cameras, an unblinking eye that stared back without emotion. She wanted to smash it, but took a breath and forced herself to calm down. Getting angry wasn't going to solve anything. *I'm trying to be the good guy here, but . . . is coddling the Partial really "good"? Would I be serving humanity better by testing his limits?* She walked to her desk and sat down, still staring straight ahead. *I don't even know what to do.*

She hung her head, and while looking down she saw the crumpled rubber glove in the garbage can. The breath test—she still needed to find a way to isolate the Partial's breath so she could search it for samples of the airborne RM. The Spore. She still hadn't found a good way to do it. The rubber gloves would work, she was pretty sure, but only if the subject was willing. She glanced at the Partial, grim and silent on the table.

She stood, pulled out another rubber glove, and walked slowly to the table.

"Do you have a name?"

The Partial eyed her carefully, that slow, studying look that made her feel like he was calculating everything about her.

"Why do you want to know?"

"Because I'm tired of calling you 'Partial.'"

He studied her a moment longer, then smiled, slowly and warily. "Samm."

"Samm," said Kira. "I have to admit, I was expecting something more unusual."

"It has two *M*s."

"Why two *M*s?"

"Because that's what it said on my rucksack," said Samm. "'Sam M.' I didn't realize the *M* was for a last name: I was two days old; I'd never met anyone with a last name. I was just . . .

Samm. I spelled it that way on a report, and it stuck."

Kira nodded and crouched down next to him. "Samm," she said, "I know you have no reason to help me, no reason to do anything I say, but I want you to understand that this is very important. You guessed yesterday that RM is still a big concern for us, and you were right. Everything I'm doing here—everything we're all doing—is to find a way to cure it. That's why we were in Manhattan, because nothing we have left here on the island was giving us any answers. I don't know if that's important to you in any way, but it's incredibly important to me. I'd give up my life to find a cure. Now I know this sounds weird, but I'm going to ask you a favor." She paused, almost talking herself out of it, then held up the rubber glove. "Will you breathe into this?"

His eyebrow went up.

"I need you to inflate it," she explained. "That will allow me to isolate your breath sample and study it in the medicomp."

He hesitated. "Tell me your name."

"Why?"

"Because I'm tired of calling you 'human.'"

She cocked her head, looking at him. Was that a joke? His voice was still as flat and unemotional as ever but there was something almost playful behind it. Was he reaching out to her? Testing her? Behind it all, that calm, calculating look never left his eyes. Whatever he was doing, he must have more than one reason for doing it. She pursed her lips, thinking, and decided to go along with it. "My name is Kira."

"Then yes, Kira, I will inflate your rubber glove."

She held it to his lips, feeling his breath on her hand, then clamped it down tight while he blew strongly into the glove. It took a couple of tries to get the seal right, but soon she had a small breath sample and pinched the glove off tightly. "Thank you." She put the glove in the medicomp sample bay, feeling only slightly ridiculous, then closed the chamber and started flicking through the screens. The scope began the long process of finding as many structures as it could, saving them for Kira to look at.

Almost immediately, a small message popped up in the corner of the screen—the scope had found a "partial match" to something in its database. Kira shook her head. *No pun intended, right, microscope?* A moment later another one popped up, then two more, then four more, partial match after partial match. Kira pulled up the image and found a bizarre protein construct, completely new and yet, like the scope said, very familiar. She peered closer. There were dozens of matches now, climbing swiftly toward the hundreds. Something in Samm's breath looked very similar to—but not exactly like—the RM Blob. Kira's fingers flew across the screen, magnifying the image, rotating it, pulling it apart. It was remarkably close to the blood-borne version of RM—a similar size, a similar shape, even some of the same nodes and receptors on the surface. It wasn't exactly RM, but it was close enough to make Kira shiver. The few small differences were the most terrifying part, because they meant it was new. A new strain of the virus, perhaps.

And Samm was breathing it out.

Kira looked up at the ceiling, moving her eyes from corner to corner. She thought about calling out, or just running out of the room, but she paused. *I need to think this through.* First of all, she wasn't sick; she had no symptoms, no discomfort, no signs of any pathogenic attack. She peered closer at the screen, studying the object: It looked like RM, but it didn't look like a virus. A virus would have a core particle in its center, a little packet of genetic information that entered a host cell and corrupted it, but the thing in Samm's breath didn't have one. She searched it carefully, using her fingers to peel back the layers of the image, examining the structure in detail. As nearly as she could tell, this new particle didn't have any way of reproducing itself. It was like a nonvirus version of the virus.

Whatever it was, the thing had given Kira something to concentrate on. She cross-referenced the image with the others in the database, searching for any sign of its purpose or function. Two possibilities immediately suggested themselves, and she jotted them down on her notepad: first, that Samm's body could, at one time, produce the Blob, and that somehow that ability had been removed or reduced, leaving only this inert, nonviral structure. It was a vestigial particle, like the human appendix: the evidence of a previous function. Kira thought about that, staring at her notepad. Is this how the Partials spread RM? Did they just breathe it out and kill everyone? But then how did that function go away—what flipped the switch and made the deadly virus turn inert? *The Partials are engineered,* she thought. *A switch like that, and the power to flip it on and off, could have been built right into them. But who holds the key to flipping it?*

Kira shuddered, the ramifications twisting her stomach into queasy knots. And yet her second guess about the particle seemed even worse: that the particle in Samm's breath was a precursor to the active virus, designed to transform on contact with human blood and become the deadly Blob. Was that the secret of Partial immunity? A virus that couldn't even arm itself until it found a human target? That was the worst possible situation for Kira, because it meant there might be nothing she could use—no defensive mechanism she could copy from the Partials to help fight off the virus. If RM targeted humans, specifically and directly, then the only defense against it was to not be human anymore.

Maybe the only way to survive was to be a Partial.

Kira shook her head, throwing down her notepad and shoving the thought from her mind. She couldn't think like this—she *wouldn't* think like this. There had to be something in the Partial genetic code that rendered RM inert, and there had to be a way to copy it and apply it to the human genetic code. And she was going to find it. The only thing this proved for certain was that what Samm had said yesterday was true: The Partials did have a connection to RM, at a very basic level. But what was it?

She tapped on the screen, opening the particle's profile information to give it a name. The blood-borne form was the Blob, because it was fat; the airborne was the Spore, because it was, presumably, how the virus spread. This new one she labeled the Lurker, because it didn't have any obvious function at all. It simply sat and waited, presumably, for the right time to strike.

"You're not going to find what you're looking for."

Kira started again; Samm had a funny sense of timing. But she was curious. "And how do you know what I'm looking for?"

"You're looking for a solution."

"I'm looking for a cure."

"The cure is only part of it," said Samm. "You're looking for a solution to your problems: rebels, plagues, political unrest, civil war. You're scared of everything, and to be fair, everything in your lives is pretty scary. You're looking for a way to move past it, to bring your lives back together. But you're not going to find the answers simply by curing RM. And you know it."

He's been listening to us, thought Kira. *A lot of that he could have picked up from the hearing, but not all of it. Not the Voice, certainly. But he's been paying attention, and he's figured it out.* Her first thought was to stop talking, to make sure the Partial couldn't glean any more info. And yet, he was tied up and had four days to live. How could deducing an impending civil war possibly help him to escape?

She felt trapped in the room and marched past Samm to open the window for air. It wouldn't budge. She strained against it as hard as she could, muttering curses at the Senate for locking her in, then remembered that this was ostensibly a sealed room, and felt stupid for even trying to open the window, which only made her curse more harshly.

"We don't want you to die," said Samm.

"Then why did you kill us?" Kira whirled to face him, feeling her face grow hot and red.

"I told you, we didn't create RM."

"What I found in your breath suggests otherwise."

If that was news to Samm, he didn't show it. "If we wanted you dead, you would be dead," said Samm. "That's not a threat, it's a fact."

"Then what do you want from us?" Kira demanded. "Why did you keep us alive? What are you planning? Is this why you were in Manhattan?"

He hesitated for a moment. "You seem like you'd do anything

to ensure humanity's survival. How far are you willing to go?"

"What are you talking about?" she asked. "What are you suggesting?"

He glanced at the corner, to a camera she knew was watching and listening to everything they said. He closed his mouth and looked at the ceiling.

"No," said Kira, leaning over him, "you can't just say something like that and then clam up again. Why did you even start talking if you're not going to finish?"

He didn't answer; he didn't even look at her.

"Is this what you were talking about yesterday? That you can't tell us because you don't want to die? I've got news for you, Samm: You're going to die anyway. If you've got something to say, say it. You were in Manhattan for a reason; are you saying it had something to do with RM?"

She waited there for a full minute, but he stayed silent, and she turned angrily back to the window, slamming the pane with her hand. The sound of the slam echoed back, but distantly. *That was weird.* She frowned, peering at the window, and hit it again, wondering what had caused the sound. Nothing happened. She leaned in closer, and suddenly a loud string of rapid pops drifted in from the city beyond. She looked out, trying to see what the noise could possibly be, and saw a plume of smoke rise up from somewhere beyond the trees. It couldn't have been more than a few blocks away. The popping continued, short bursts of rapid, rhythmic noise, but it wasn't until she saw people running that she realized what it was.

Automatic gunfire. The city was under attack.

CHAPTER TWENTY

"The Voice," said Senator Weist. Kira was packed into a hospital conference room with Mkele and the same five senators she'd met at her hearing, and the atmosphere was more tense than she'd ever felt it. "They hit the Senate building. It was the biggest strike team yet—at least forty insurgents, maybe more—and we didn't take a single one of them alive."

"What if we'd been there?" demanded Hobb. His wavy hair was limp and sweaty, and his face was pale as he paced restlessly through the room. "We don't have enough guards for this—"

"The Senate was not their target," said Mkele. "With no meetings in session, and no senators on site, they attacked during the lightest possible guard rotation. Their purpose was obviously to get inside with as little resistance as possible."

"So it was a robbery?" asked Delarosa. "It still doesn't make sense. Everything we store in the Senate building they can get more easily just scavenging the outlands."

"They were looking for the Partial," said Mkele. The room

went quiet. "Rumors are already going around. That's why I've invited Ms. Walker to join us."

"One of the soldiers talked," said Senator Kessler, "or Kira did. We never should have trusted her."

Kira started to protest, lining up her best and most horrible insults for Kessler's smug face, but Mkele cut her off.

"If Kira had talked," he said, "they would have known to attack the hospital. I think it's more likely that the Voice didn't know what we had, just that we probably had something; they obviously didn't know where it was. Even the message they spray-painted on the building was vague: 'The Senate is lying to you. What are they hiding?' If they'd known what we were hiding, don't you think they would have said it?"

"Only if they wanted to start a riot," said Weist. "News of the Partial would incite nothing less."

"A riot might be their only plausible goal at this point," said Delarosa. "The only way for them to create enough unrest to stage a coup."

"Given how little we actually lost," said Mkele, "this attack helped us more than it hurt us. The information they apparently had, combined with the information they obviously didn't have, gives me a valuable estimate of their intelligence network."

"That's great now," Hobb sneered, "but what about before the attack? How did our secret get out? If you're so brilliant, why didn't you stop any of this from happening?"

"If you had any delusions that this was going to stay a complete secret in a community this small, you were fooling yourself," said Mkele. "I advised against the Partial's presence from the beginning."

"We made our decision based on your assurances," said Kessler. "If there's a leak in the Defense Grid, you need to find it—"

"We knew exactly what we were getting into," said Delarosa. "If our plan with Ms. Walker carries through, every attack will have been worth it. The potential benefits outweigh the obstacles."

"*If* it works," said Kessler, throwing a sharp glance at Kira, "and *if* the Voice don't launch a consummate attack before we're done. That's a lot of ifs."

They're talking about my work as if they're the ones doing it, thought Kira. Her first impulse was to protest, but she held back. *No. If they think we're working on this together, that means they're invested in the outcome. They're supporting the project. It doesn't matter who gets the credit as long as somebody finds a cure.*

"A lot of ifs," Hobb continued, "and all it takes is one of them to go wrong and suddenly we're traitors and war criminals. Weist is right about the riot: If word gets out that we've got a Partial in custody, no one's going to wait for an explanation. They're going to smash everything in sight until they find it, and then they're going to destroy the Partial, too."

"Then we have to move it," said Skousen. "The attack on the town hall was highly destructive; if they do the same at the hospital, it puts too much at risk—the patients, the facilities, even the structure itself."

"But we can't move him," Kira insisted. "The Nassau hospital is the only facility on the island with the resources we need for the study. Nowhere else even has the equipment."

"The best scenario is to say nothing at all," said Mkele. "Senator Weist's initial reaction was correct, according to my simulations: If word gets out that we're hiding a Partial in the middle of East Meadow, the public outcry will be passionate and violent. People will riot, or defect to the Voice en masse. I recommend we double the police patrols and triple the guard at the Senate."

"Why complicate things?" asked Kessler. "We should just execute the thing and be done with it."

"There's still a lot we can learn—" said Kira, but froze when Kessler shot her a furious glance. *What is that woman's problem?*

"I agree," said Mkele. "What we need to decide is whether or not the things we stand to learn warrant the risk of this secret getting out. Ms. Walker, can you give us a report of your progress?"

Kira glanced at him, then back at the panel of senators. "We finish the five days," she said quickly.

"We want a report," said Delarosa, "not an opinion."

"The tests have already revealed priceless medical data," said Kira. "Even the first blood test alone told us more about Partial physiology than we've ever known before. He has an advanced platelet system—"

"It," said Dr. Skousen.

Kira frowned. "I'm sorry?"

"'It' has an advanced platelet system," said Skousen. "You are talking about a machine, Kira, not a person."

Kira scanned the room, seeing the senators' eyes filled with a mixture of distrust and anger, all aimed at her because she was speaking on behalf of their enemy. She couldn't afford that attitude, not while they were deciding how quickly to kill him. When had she started calling it "him" anyway? She nodded obediently and looked at the floor, trying to appear as unthreatening as possible. "Sorry, just a slip of the tongue. It has an advanced platelet system that allows it to heal cuts and other wounds at an exponential rate—several times faster than a healthy human."

Weist shifted in his seat. "And you think its . . . advanced healing abilities might hold the secret to curing RM?"

"Possibly," said Kira, though in her mind it seemed unlikely; she had to make this sound as positive as possible. "Even more likely is something I found this morning." She was exaggerating this part as well, but she needed to buy more time. "The Partial's breath contains traces of neutralized RM."

The senators made a chorus of surprised noises; Hobb even smiled. Kira could tell they were happy, and plunged ahead. "I was analyzing the Partial's breath to see if I could find evidence of the airborne virus, what I've labeled the Spore, but instead I found an inert, nonviral form of the blood-borne virus. It literally looks exactly like someone took an RM sample and stripped all the functional viral portions of it away—it can't reproduce, it can't spread, it can't do anything. It's the surest evidence we've seen so far that Partial biology holds some promise of helping us combat RM."

"I'm impressed," said Delarosa, nodding. She glanced at Skousen. "Were you aware of this?"

"She found it this morning," said Skousen. "I haven't had time to review her records yet." The old doctor turned heavily toward Kira. "Are you certain this is a neutralized RM, and not an RM waiting to be activated?"

I knew he'd call me on that. "I'm still researching it."

"It seems premature to present it so definitively when you

don't even know what it is."

"What little evidence there is points toward a promising conclusion," said Kira. "If it were a new virus, we'd see signs of it somewhere—new symptoms, new patients, probably an epidemic. He—it—has been in human custody for a few days, and no one's getting sick. I've been around it longer and more consistently than anyone, and I'm fine."

"What if it's not a new virus?" asked Skousen. "What if it's the same old RM, which all of us are immune to, so the sample is remaining dormant?"

"That's definitely possible," said Kira, "but my point is that so is the other theory. This could be a good sign, and either way it's the strongest, most promising lead yet. A more promising lead than I expected to find after just a day and a half, frankly."

"There might actually be something to this," said Weist. He leaned forward, looking at the other senators. "What if there really is a cure?"

"We proceed as planned," said Delarosa, and shot Weist a look that seemed, to Kira, surprisingly harsh. "Ms. Walker, I agree with your assessment: Positive or not, these findings are worth following up on. Learn everything you can, and don't hesitate to ask for anything you need."

"I need newborn blood," said Kira quickly. She grimaced at the gruesome nature of the request, wishing she'd phrased it less grotesquely. "The next time a baby is born, the instant it crowns, I need a blood sample. I'm trying to study the process of infection, so speed is paramount."

Delarosa looked at Skousen, who sighed and nodded. She looked back at Kira. "We'll do what we can."

"But what are we going to do about security?" Skousen demanded. "A Voice attack on the hospital would be devastating."

Delarosa stared at the same fixed point on the table again, deep in thought. "Mr. Mkele, this is your arena."

"More soldiers," said Mkele, "though we need to be careful with the hospital. If the Voice realize we've increased security here, they're sure to make it their next target."

"So let's move the Senate here," said Hobb. "They'll think the increased security is for us."

Mkele shook his head. "That only makes the problem worse. The Senate will continue to meet in the town hall—"

"Are you crazy?" said Hobb.

"The Voice have already searched the town hall," said Mkele, drowning him out, "and they didn't find what they were looking for. They won't attack there again. Our goal now is to confuse them with too many targets, not to lead them to the next obvious choice. We'll increase guard patrols around the city, we'll pull soldiers from LaGuardia, and we'll add armed, visible police presence to every major landmark in East Meadow. Nothing we do will give them any hints about what we're hiding or where, and they'll have to rely on their own, obviously poor, intelligence gatherers. It will buy us time, if nothing else."

"How much time?" asked Senator Weist.

Mkele looked at Kira. "All we need is three and a half more days, right? Then we destroy it and be done."

Hobb shook his head. "It's not enough to just destroy it, like we've said before. Word will get out, and we need to appear blameless. It's the only way to maintain control."

"Control?" asked Kira. She remembered the way she'd snapped at Isolde for using that word. Was that really how the Senate thought of them?

Delarosa turned to face her, her eyes cold and penetrating. "Yes, control. Perhaps you're aware of the growing unrest on this island?"

"Well of course, but—"

"The Voice?" she continued. "The terrorist attacks on innocent people? The very real possibility of a civil war tearing the tattered remnants of humanity to pieces? What do you propose we do with this situation if not wrest it back under control?"

"That's not what I'm saying," said Kira.

"But it's what you're implying," said Delarosa. "You are implying that control is bad, and that people, left to their own devices, will sort this problem out on their own without any help from us. You can't look at the state of the world and honestly suggest that it could sort itself out."

Kira saw Kessler leer in the corner of her eye, but pressed forward anyway. "What I am saying is that maybe you're squeezing too hard. The Voice's main complaint is the Hope Act—they think you're exerting too much control over common human rights."

"And what is our alternative?" asked Delarosa. "To back down? To give up on our goals for successful, immune childbirth? The future of the human race is, as you so frequently remind us, the vital heart of everything we do. We established the Hope Act to maximize our chances for reproduction—it's the simplest and best method of doing so, and yes, a lot of people complained, but there comes a point in the life of a species when complaints and civil rights take a backseat to pure, unmitigated survival." She put her pencil down and clasped her hands. "Do you know what I did before the Break, Ms. Walker?"

Kira shook her head.

"I was a zoologist. I worked to save endangered species. At one point I was in charge of the world's entire population of white rhinos—all ten of them. Two males. Do you have any idea what happened to them when the world collapsed around them?"

"No, ma'am."

"I opened the gates and let them go free. I relinquished control." She paused. "One of them was attacked by a mountain lion the same night. I passed its corpse the next morning on my way to the nearest shelter."

"So that's it, huh," said Kira, trying to ignore the chill that swept over her. "We're just another endangered species in your zoo."

"Do you deny it?" asked Delarosa.

Kira clenched her jaw, struggling to think of any response that didn't play right into the senator's hand. "There's more than ten of us."

"Thank God."

Kira looked at the row of senators, at Mkele standing stoically behind them. She couldn't think of anything to say.

"The world is in shambles," said Hobb. "We know this. What you need to understand is that we are trying to save it the best way we know how. Look around this room: Skousen is the top medical mind in the world, Delarosa is the best long-term administrator I've ever met, and Kessler is the reason you have fresh food to eat—she literally created our farm and market program. They work night and day to solve the problems you're just beginning to understand, and they've been doing it since before you knew how to read. There are plans and contingency plans you couldn't even guess at. Please trust us."

Kira nodded slowly, parsing their arguments. "You're right," she said. "I said the same thing when we planned our mission to Manhattan: Nothing is more important than making sure we have a future. I was willing to sacrifice anything."

"Exactly," said Delarosa.

"So then . . ." Kira paused. "So your plan for the future is the Hope Act, and your plan for control is to kill the Partial, like Senator Hobb said, in a way that makes you look good."

"In a way that maintains order," said Hobb.

Kessler huffed. "You don't need to spell everything out for her."

"Then what about my work?" asked Kira. "What about everything I'm doing to find a cure—how does that fit in?" She frowned. "Is it even a priority?"

"Plans within plans," said Hobb. "If you can find something, we'll jump on it, but if you can't . . . we have to be ready."

"Just remember," said Delarosa. "Absolutely no one can know of this. We brought you into our confidence first because you forced our hand, and again because you've proven yourself intelligent and capable. But you must have known this the moment you set foot back on this island: If anyone finds out about what we're doing, we won't just have a riot. We'll have a revolution."

247

CHAPTER TWENTY-ONE

Kira went to the cafeteria instead of going straight up to the lab. She needed time to think.

What was the Senate planning? Part of her knew they were right, but there was still a voice in the back of her head telling her she needed to be alert. They saw the same problems she did, but their solutions were so different: Kira wanted to cure RM, but they seemed to take it as a means of maintaining control. And yes, they had very good reasons for maintaining control—the society in East Meadow was anything but solid, and the societies beyond, in the outlands, were even worse. They needed strong leadership, a strong hand to guide them.

And yet.

She closed her eyes, breathing deeply and switching gears. *No more Senate—I need to get back to work.*

Kira walked quickly through the halls, ignoring the bustle around her. She nodded to Shaylon, standing watch by the door, and went inside the lab. The blower hissed, the decontamination circuits buzzed in the floor, and there he was, still strapped to the table, arms extended, face to the sky, eyes dark and solemn. He glanced at her as she came in, then turned back to the ceiling.

She tapped the medicomp screen to wake it up and found the breath analysis still open; the scanner had finished its task, cataloguing thousands of different particles. Many of them it recognized, both organic and inorganic: the unusual gasses present in exhalation, fragments of shed skin cells, microscopic flecks of dirt, trace amounts of minerals, and a handful of common bacteria. Nothing special. The list of particles it didn't recognize, on the other hand, was a dozen times longer. She expanded it, scrolling through with a tap of her finger: image after image of bizarre little chemical compounds, some big, some small, all oddly shaped and incredibly strange. She'd never seen anything like them before. As she flipped through them, she noticed that many of the images were similar, and the compounds seemed to break down into several major categories, repeated over and over. She started marking the images, studying the molecules and flagging what looked like key identifiers, separating them into subgroups, teaching the medicomp how to recognize the different pieces. Soon it was flying through the list on its own, dividing the compounds into nine major types with a tenth group of unconnected outliers. It still offered no hint as to their function, and Kira couldn't discern one by looking at them. Whatever they were, Samm's body was full of them.

None of the compounds were remotely as complex as the Lurker, but they still didn't match with any substance Kira was familiar with—not fabric, not food, obviously not mineral or plastic. She looked over at him, then back at the screen, then pursed her lips and stood up. They were too common and consistent to be accidental, so they obviously had a purpose, and his body would need creation or receptor sites to take advantage of that purpose. Perhaps this had something to do with their resistance? There was only one way to find out. She walked to the table, unlocked the wheels, and started pushing it across the room. She expected Samm to ask what she was doing, but he stayed perfectly quiet.

She pulled him to a stop at the DORD scanner, a heavy machine nearly as big as some of the cars out rusting in the parking lot. This was the big gun in her laboratory arsenal: a medical scanner that could catalog an entire body, layer by layer and piece by piece. She hit a switch to turn it on, then crossed back to the medicomp while it booted up. The definitions she'd created for the categories of compounds were still there, along with several of the clearest images, and she froze them to the screen before sliding the screen out, disconnecting it from the medicomp, and carrying it carefully to the DORD. The screen had an impressive amount of computing power all on its own, but it was nothing compared to the sensor systems it could attach to. She slid it into the DORD, hearing the click as it locked into place, and a few quick finger taps later the machine was ready to go. The DORD would scan Samm's lungs, throat, and nasal passages for anything resembling the mysterious compounds, which would give her a good idea of where they came from and where they went. She'd have to intuit the rest from there. Kira raised the sensor array, swung it out, and centered Samm beneath it; it was a thick, heavy piece of equipment in a white plastic shell, easily the heaviest thing in the room, but it held its own weight perfectly. She tapped start, and the DORD whirred to life.

Kira watched the screen closely, eager to see what the scan turned up. It was not a quick scan. She drummed her fingers nervously on the DORD housing, then turned and walked to the window; she wanted to ask Samm if he knew what the particles were, despite his refusal to talk, but now that the scan had started, any significant motion would upset it. She turned again and watched him, steady as a rock, almost as if he were holding still on purpose.

She saw motion on the screen and ran to check it; the DORD was already displaying and categorizing some preliminary images. She flipped through the list and opened one for the compound labeled M, a funny little horseshoe-shaped particle. The DORD had found several structures in Samm's body that it thought might be related to it: one in the nasal cavity and the rest in the lungs. Kira pulled them up, side by side on the screen, and studied them; they looked almost like glands, though not any glands Kira was familiar with. The one in his sinuses was significantly larger, and the DORD had cross-linked it to several other files. Kira opened the list and flipped through it quickly, mildly surprised at what she saw; the DORD had linked that image to every compound it had scanned for thus far. They each had a little gland of their own in the lungs, but they were all connected to the big one in his head.

Kira studied the gland closer while the DORD kept working. What did it do? She couldn't just ask the computer to guess, but she could ask it to search its database for partial matches. She started the search and looked back at the image again, buckling down for another long wait, but the results were almost instantaneous: no match. She frowned and ran the test again. No match.

Guess I'm going to have to do this manually. Given that each particle had two related structures, the obvious first guess was that one structure created the particle and the other one caught it: a writer and a reader. Which implied that they carried information. She ran another search, this time looking for anything in the database that wasn't human. The DORD found an old file, pre-Break, where somebody had scanned a dog, and she asked the computer to look for partial matches in there. One popped up almost immediately, displaying a structure remarkably similar, though far simpler, than the one in Samm. It was a vomeronasal organ.

Samm had an incredibly sophisticated pheromonal system.

Kira pulled up more files, reading what she could on pheromones: They were a system of simple chemical communication, like a form of smell but far, far more specialized. Insects used them for simple things like marking trails or warning one another of danger; dogs used them to claim territory and to signal breeding times. What did the Partials use them for?

I may as well try asking, she thought. "Tell me about your . . . pheromones." Predictably, Samm said nothing. "You have a highly developed system of chemical synthesizers and receptors; can you tell me about it?"

No response.

"Can't blame me for trying." She thought a moment, looking around the room, then opened the medicomp and pulled out the rubber glove Samm had breathed into. She brought it near his face, pricked it with a pin, and squeezed it as hard as she could, propelling the air directly into Samm's nose. He coughed and spluttered, jerking his head to get out of the stream of air, but Kira watched in wonder as his demeanor seemed to grow more calm—his heart rate rose as he reacted to the forced air, then fell again almost immediately as he reacted to . . . something else. The pheromones. His eyes relaxed, his expression softened, his breathing became more even.

He seemed, Kira thought suddenly, like he was making exactly the same face he'd made in the morning, when he'd agreed to blow into the glove.

"Kuso," he said. "That's not fair."

Kira put her hands on her hips. "What just happened?"

"You're using my own data against me, and now I—damn it." He closed his mouth and looked at the ceiling.

"What data?" asked Kira. "The pheromones? Is that what you call them?" She looked at the glove in her hand, now deflated and floppy. "You just told me something you didn't want to tell me, didn't you? You've never done that—this was a slip. What did the pheromones do?"

Samm said nothing, and Kira brought the glove closer to her face, examining it closely. She walked to the center of the room, envisioning the way it had been laid out that morning— the DORD over here, the table over there, and Samm on top of it. She'd asked him to breathe into the glove and they'd shared something, a moment of . . . of something. Of actual communication. She'd made a joke about his name, he'd made one back, and then he'd agreed to help her collect a breath sample. He'd trusted her.

And then just now, after she blew it back in his face and

asked him a question, he'd trusted her again—not for long, but long enough for his shield of hostile self-control to falter. He'd answered her question.

The pheromones had re-created the trust he'd felt that morning and forced him to feel it again.

"It's like a chemical empathy system," she said softly, walking back toward Samm. "Whatever you're feeling, you broadcast with these pheromones, so that other Partials can feel it too. Or, at least know that you're feeling it." She sat in the chair next to him. "It's like the social yawn: You can standardize one person's emotional state across an entire group."

"You can't use it against me anymore," said Samm. "I'm not breathing into your gloves."

"I'm not trying to use it against you, I'm trying to understand it. What does it feel like?"

Samm turned to look at her. "What does hearing feel like?"

"Okay," said Kira, nodding, "that was a stupid question, you're right. It's doesn't feel like anything, it's just part of who you are."

"I'd forgotten that humans couldn't link," said Samm. "All this time I've been so confused, trying to figure out why you were all so melodramatic about everything. It's because you can't pick up each other's emotions from the link, so you have to broadcast them through voice inflection and body language. It's helpful, I'll admit, but it's kind of . . . histrionic."

"Histrionic?" Kira asked. It was the single longest speech she'd ever heard him give. Was he talking openly, or was this more of his calculated planning? What did he have to gain by talking? She kept going, trying to draw out the conversation and see if he'd keep talking. "If you depend on chemical triggers to tell people how you're feeling," she said, "that explains a lot about you, too. You don't display nearly enough emotion for human society; if we seem melodramatic to you, you seem downright deadpan to us."

"It's not just emotions," he said, and Kira leaned forward, terrified that he would stop at any second, his openness popping like a bubble. "It lets us know if someone's in trouble, or hurt, or excited. It helps us function as a unit, all working together. The link was intended for battlefield use, obviously; if someone's on watch and sees something, a human would have to shout a warning, and then the other humans would have to wake up and figure out what the watchman was saying, and then they'd have to get ready for combat. If a Partial watchman sees something, the data goes out through the link and the other soldiers know it immediately; their adrenaline spikes, their heart rates speed up, their fight-or-flight reflex kicks in, and suddenly the entire squad is ready for battle, sometimes without even a word."

"The data," said Kira. "Links and data—very technological words."

"You called me a biological robot yesterday," said Samm. "That's not entirely inaccurate." He smiled, the first time she'd ever really seen him do that, and she did the same. "I don't know how you people even function. It's no wonder you lost the war."

The words hung in the air like a poison cloud, killing any hope that the conversation might grow friendly. Kira turned back to the screen, trying not to yell at him. His attitude had changed as well; he was more solemn, somehow. Pensive.

"I worked in a mine," he said softly. "You created us to win the Isolation War, and we did, and then we came home and the US government gave us jobs, and mine was in a mine. I wasn't a slave, everything was legal and proper and 'humane.'" He said the word as if it tasted bitter. "But I didn't like it. I tried to get a different job, but no one would hire a Partial. I tried to get an education, to qualify for something nicer, but no schools would accept my application. We couldn't move out of our government-assigned slum because our wages were barely livable, and nobody would sell to us anyway. Who wants to live next door to the artificial people?"

"So you rebelled."

"We hated you," he said. "I hated you." He turned his head to catch her eye. "But I didn't want genocide. None of us did."

"Somebody did," said Kira. Her voice was thick with held-back tears.

"And you lost every connection to the past," said Samm. "I know exactly how you feel."

"No, you don't," Kira hissed. "You say whatever you want, but don't you dare say that. We lost our world, we lost our future, we lost our families—"

"Your parents were taken from you," said Samm simply. "We killed ours when we killed you. Whatever pain you feel, you don't have that guilt stacked on top of it."

Kira bit her lip, trying to make sense of her own feelings. Samm was the enemy, and yet she felt sorry for him; his words had made her so mad, yet she felt almost guilty for feeling that way. She swallowed, forcing out a response that was part accusation, part desperate plea for understanding. "Is that why you're telling me all this? Because you feel bad about killing us?"

"I'm telling you this because you have to understand that the cure is not enough. The war was devastating, but the problems started long before that."

Kira shook her head, her words coming out harsher than even she expected. "Don't tell me what I have to understand." She left his side and went back to work.

"It's a communication system," said Kira. It was early evening, and since she'd skipped lunch she'd decided to join Marcus for an early dinner. He'd brought sushi from a street vendor, and they were eating together in an empty room on the third floor, away from all the bustle and people below. She took a bit of sushi, swallowed it, and kept talking, so eager she could barely keep up with herself. Her conversation with Samm still burned in the back of her mind, glowing banks of hot emotional coals, but she forced herself to ignore them. "A chemical communication system, like with ants, but a zillion times more complicated. Imagine being able to talk to people just by breathing—you wouldn't have to say a word, you'd just know everything—"

"I can't imagine you not saying a word," said Marcus. "I think you'd go crazy first."

"Ha-ha," said Kira, rolling her eyes.

"So, how does it work, then?"

"Well, I don't know what kinds of things they can say chemically—I catalogued at least twenty separate pheromones, but even at ten times that amount it would be an incredibly small vocabulary—but if, say, one of them was 'I'm wounded,' as soon as one soldier got wounded, all the others would instantly know about it, and they'd have a pretty good idea of where to find him.

It's a sense we don't even have, like a social sense, and to him it's constant and second nature. Can you imagine what it would be like to be cut off from that? He must feel more alone than . . ." She thought again about what he had said, calling humanity his parents; what was it like out there, the vast expanse of America lying empty and silent? "They're alone, Marcus. That's kind of tragic, don't you think?"

"Good thing he has you to look out for him, then," said Marcus. "I'd hate for the poor Partial to feel lonely."

"That's not what I meant," said Kira. "This is what I love to do, Marcus—you're a medic too, I thought you'd understand why this is so cool. It's not about Samm, it's about—"

"Ah, so now you guys are on a first name basis, huh?" He tried to play it off like he was joking, but Kira could feel real emotion beneath it. She knew him too well. "I'm kidding, Kira. But seriously, he's a Partial. Mankind's greatest enemy, remember?"

"That's what I've been trying to tell you. I don't know that they are anymore."

"Is that what it's trying to tell you?" He looked at Kira the way the Senators had. Like she was an idiot. "He's alone and he's chained up and that makes you feel sorry for him, but he tried to kill you—not just in the Break, but last week, in Manhattan, with a gun. He is an enemy soldier, and a prisoner of war, and if he got out of his chains who knows what he'd do, to you and to the entire city."

"I know," said Kira, "I know. But you haven't talked to him—he doesn't talk like a monster. He doesn't . . . feel like a monster."

"Two days ago he was your subject," said Marcus, "an

experiment. Two days before that he was some faceless enemy you were ready to kill and dismember for study. In two more days who knows what he'll be? A friend?"

"I'm not saying that."

"In three days he'll be dead. I've known you forever, Kira, and I can see exactly where this is going: First you'll feel sorry for it, and then you'll get attached to it, and then when he dies it's going to tear you apart because you think you have to save everybody. It's like with the newborns—you feel personally responsible for every one that dies. The Partial is just a test subject, made worse because it's smart enough to tell you exactly what you want to hear. All I'm saying is I just don't think you should get too attached."

"Too attached?" asked Kira. She felt her anger rising again. "How attached do you think we are?"

"Hold on," said Marcus. "That is not what I meant at all."

"It's not?" asked Kira hotly. "Because it sure sounded like you were accusing me of something."

"I'm not accusing you of anything," said Marcus. "I'm just warning you—"

"Warning me?"

"That came out wrong."

"Warning me about what?" demanded Kira. "Warning me not to make any friends you don't approve of?"

"I'm warning you about yourself," said Marcus. "You know you have a tendency to get caught up in these enormous dreams and then be crushed underneath when they fall down on you. You're not satisfied with helping babies, you want to cure RM; you can't just study a Partial, you have to, what? Make peace with them? Is that what Samm's saying?"

"No, of course not," said Kira. But even as she said it, she wasn't sure. "I'm just saying that, whether or not I believe Samm, there's more to them than anyone around here thinks. They rebelled because humans had oppressed them, so if we play nice with each other maybe . . . it'll work this time. I don't know." She tried to sort out her thoughts. "I'm not saying we need to drop our defenses and forget everything that's happened, just that they might not mean us harm anymore. And if they hold the key to curing RM, maybe peace is our only chance." She looked at Marcus nervously, praying that he understood her.

"They rebelled and killed us," Marcus repeated.

"The American colonies rebelled against England almost three hundred years ago today," said Kira. "They got over it, and eventually they were best friends."

"America didn't release a virus that destroyed the world."

"And maybe the Partials didn't either," said Kira. "Maybe there are a lot of things about the war we don't know. All we talk about is what they did to us, but it can't be that simple. If Samm's telling the truth—"

"It all comes back to Samm, doesn't it?" asked Marcus, shaking his head.

"What is this about, Marcus?" She turned to face him directly. "Are you jealous? I love you." She held him with her eyes. "Please, try to understand what I'm saying."

"You really love me?"

"Of course I do."

"Then marry me."

Kira's eyes went wide. It was the last thing she expected him to say, now, here, in this situation. "I . . ."

"We're young," he said, "but not too young. You can live with me. I found that big house for you. For us. We can grow old there, and when you cure RM we can have a family there. But we don't have to wait. We can be together right now."

Kira looked at him, imagining his face beside her—in the evening when she went to sleep, in the morning when she woke up, always with her through anything and everything. It was what she had always wanted, ever since she and Marcus were children together watching stars on the roof of the school.

But it wasn't that simple anymore.

She shook her head slowly, so slowly she could barely feel it, hoping maybe if it was slow enough Marcus wouldn't see her saying no. "I'm sorry, Marcus. I can't."

Marcus kept his face straight, hiding his emotions almost, but not quite, perfectly. "Not now, or not ever?"

She thought about the newborns, and RM, and the war and the Partials and her work in the lab and everything Samm had told her. Curing RM wasn't enough, he'd said. Was peace the next step? Was it even a possibility? There were too many questions, too many shadows for her to see clearly. She shook her head. "Not now. I won't know about ever until I get there."

"Okay." He paused, nodded, and shrugged. "Okay." He was taking it too well, like he'd been expecting it.

That was the hardest part of all.

CHAPTER TWENTY-TWO

Kira was only two-thirds of the way through the DORD images when they all started bleeding together. She wanted to know how the pheromone system worked, but she was starting to realize that she wasn't going to make any progress on RM there. When she hit the point where she could barely keep her eyes open, she decided it was best to call it quits for the night. *I don't want to walk home,* she thought. *I need a mattress here I can crash on.* She needed more help—there was no way one person could parse all the data it would take to study Samm's biology and find what she needed to find. Samm was still awake—she wasn't certain he ever slept at all—but since she returned from dinner he had been silent. She wanted to say something to him, but didn't know what.

The nighttime guards looked rougher than the day shift; Shaylon and his companion were gone, replaced by a pair of older soldiers, weathered and grim. She paused as she passed them, wondering if they were going to "interrogate" Samm again tonight, beat him or stab him or whatever sick tortures they could think of. She wanted to tell them not to, but what good would it do? The thought made her sad, and she shot one last glance at the soldiers, before hanging her head and walking away down the hall.

On the street outside she paused, taking a slow, deep breath of the night air. It was warmer than before. She started to walk and saw a movement in the moonlight; she froze, fearing the worst—a Voice attack, storming the hospital to find Samm—but then she heard a voice, Haru's voice, slicing desperately through the darkness.

"It's okay," he was saying. "We're almost there, it's okay."

Kira jogged forward a few steps, straining her ears to hear it more surely. Was it Haru? The shadow grew larger, and the voice clearer: It was Haru, and Madison was with him, breathing in short, painful bursts.

Kira's heart sank, just for a moment, and she exploded into action. "Mads!"

Madison gritted her teeth in pain, clutching Haru's hand in a white-knuckled death grip. He urged her forward gently but firmly, almost in the hospital parking lot by the time Kira reached them.

"She's bleeding," he said quickly, "and the pain is like nothing she's felt before."

Kira looked back at the hospital, taking Madison's other arm and helping her forward as gingerly as she could. "You shouldn't have brought her here," she said tersely. "You should have had her driven, or come for a wheelchair and an EMT so we could pick her up ourselves."

"I'm not going to leave her home alone!"

"She shouldn't have walked here, no matter how close you live."

"Just . . ." He hesitated. "Just help her."

"Come with me," said Kira. "There's always a full staff in maternity, even at night." She prayed silently as they brought Madison in through the doors, begging anyone who was listening to please, please spare Madison's baby. It was too early; it might die of poor development or breathing before it even had a chance to die of RM. She helped Madison around the corner toward maternity and stopped short, nearly colliding with a nurse running desperately down the hall.

"Sandy!" shouted Kira, recognizing the woman from her time as an intern. "She needs attention!"

"The Barnes baby is flatlining," said Sandy, shouting over her shoulder as she ran. "Tell her to hang on!"

"They're not going to help?" asked Haru.

"Everyone's busy," said Kira. "Come with me." She led them to an open door and flicked on the light, helping Madison settle into a large, soft chair.

"There goes another one," said Madison, clenching her jaw and whistling. "Oh please no."

Kira pointed Haru at a medicomp cart in the corner of the room. "Fire up the ultrasound machine," she said. "The outlets marked in red have power." She crouched down by Madison's side, brushing her hair from her face. "Hey, Mads, you want to tell me what's going on?"

"I think it's contractions."

"You're still two months early," said Kira. "Your pregnancy

has been perfectly healthy so far, there's no reason for you to be having contractions."

"These aren't just cramps, Kira." Madison winced again, squeezing her eyes closed and clutching Kira's arm so tightly Kira had to bite her tongue to keep from screaming. The pain subsided and Madison collapsed back into the chair, panting.

"Is the pain rhythmic?" asked Kira. Madison shook her head. "Can you point to it?" Madison traced an area across her belly and side, and Kira nodded. "I don't think that's your uterus, Mads, that's your stomach. I'm going to do an ultrasound."

"She's bleeding," said Haru again. "Aren't you going to do something about the bleeding?"

"I'm doing everything I can, Haru, just bring the machine."

He dragged the cart over, parking it next to Madison's chair with a terrified expression. Kira pulled on a pair of sterilized gloves and pulled up Madison's shirt to expose her belly. "Hold still," she said, placing the ultrasound probe against Madison's skin. "Screen up." The screen flickered on, a black-and-white grid with a wedge-shaped image in the center. The image flashed and moved: a sonographic re-creation of the organs in Madison's abdomen. Kira had been completely lost the first several times she'd seen an ultrasound, but after weeks of practice the fuzzy pictures seemed crystal clear. "That's your bladder," she said, moving the probe with one hand and touching the screen with her other, defining labels and boundaries that the computer then remembered and kept track of in real time. "That's your stomach, that's the baby's foot. There we go, the baby's body." She worked quickly, her fingers scurrying over the screen, lighting up measurements and calling up archived statistics from Madison's previous visits. "Head development good, chest development good, inner organs all look good. Heartbeat strong. Bladder filling and emptying. Spine looks good."

Madison grimaced again, gritting her teeth and clutching the arms of her chair. Two nurses rushed in behind them, Sandy and Nurse Hardy. "We're here, Walker, thanks for getting her started." Hardy pulled on a pair of gloves and took the probe; Kira gave it up nervously, stepping back as Nurse Hardy's more practiced hands took over the ultrasound. "Describe the pain," asked Hardy.

"Strong but inconsistent," said Kira, "localized toward the side with the stomach. She's also bleeding—I think it's an abruption."

"What's that?" asked Haru. "Is it bad? Is she okay?"

"We're doing our best, sir," said Hardy. "We just need room to work."

"What about the baby, is the baby okay?"

The image on the screen flopped in and out of view as her abdomen flexed, and Kira pointed at the screen.

"There was a shadow."

"I saw it," said Nurse Hardy, moving the probe farther down to the side and altering the angle. When Madison stopped squirming, the image stabilized on a large black oval, the stomach, and behind it a fuzzy black triangle. The computer identified it almost immediately, marking it in red. "The placenta's separating from the wall," said Nurse Hardy. "It's a partial abruption, just like you said." She stared closely at the screen, at the deep red slash across the center. "Good work, Walker."

Kira felt the wave of tension begin to seep out of her, down through her feet and into the floor, leaving her drained.

"What does it mean?" asked Madison.

"It means you're going to be okay," said Kira. "It means the placenta is pulling away from the uterus, which isn't good but isn't really threatening to you or to the baby if we stay on top of it. They're going to put you on bed rest, so you can't move around much, and they're going to do it here in the hospital so we can keep an eye on you twenty-four-seven."

"I can't stay here," Madison protested.

Kira put a hand on her shoulder. "Think of it as a resort vacation. Breakfast in bed, servants ready at all times . . . Nothing will happen to you or to your baby without us being right here to solve it."

"You're sure it's not dangerous?" asked Madison. "I mean, if you have to bring me into full-time care—"

"Twelve years ago I would have sent you home with tampons and Tylenol," said Nurse Hardy, "but these days we don't mess around."

"Okay," said Madison, "but bed rest? Like, I can't get up at all?"

"As little as possible," said Nurse Hardy. "Placental abruption is rare, but in a case like yours, it's almost certainly caused by overexertion. We need to stop that immediately."

"No more housecleaning," said Kira. "I'll talk to Xochi, we'll figure out how to take care of it for you."

Madison smiled guiltily, sucking in a breath. "I shouldn't have walked here."

"And I'm going to beat Haru with a bike chain because of it," said Kira. She shot him a dark look. "But for now, just relax."

"We need to do a blood test," said Nurse Hardy, "and then we'll give you some painkillers, and then you can take a nap."

Kira squeezed Madison's hand and stepped back as the other nurses pressed in to take care of her. The adrenaline rush was still wearing off, and Kira walked into the hall and collapsed into a chair. *That was too close.* She blew out a long, slow breath, thinking about all the things it could have been—all the ways it could have been worse. *I can't bear to see Madison like Ariel, pounding helplessly on a window just for the chance to hold her dead baby.*

But I still don't know how to save it.

She stared at the floor, too tired to think.

"Hey."

Kira looked up to see Xochi standing beside her. Her face was drawn and tired.

"Hey," said Kira. "You heard about Madison?"

"Yeah," she said, "but that's not why I'm here."

Kira frowned. *Please, no more disasters.* She sat up straight, forcing herself upright. "What is it?" Her voice sounded stronger than she felt.

"Isolde just got back from the Senate," said Xochi. "They're going to make an announcement tomorrow. The Hope Act has been amended. The age is sixteen now, Kira."

CHAPTER TWENTY-THREE

"It's official," said Isolde. She was lying down on their couch, holding a bottle of some kind of liquor. It was half-empty. "It passed this afternoon. Or yesterday afternoon, I guess—it's past midnight, isn't it?"

"I can't believe this," said Xochi. She stared at the floor. "I can't believe this."

Isolde took a swig. "It doesn't matter if you believe it or not. Your government just gave you two months to get knocked up." She held up the bottle, her face dull and red. "Cheers."

"You better get your fill of the booze now, then," said Xochi. "You'll be drinking for two pretty soon."

Kira sat on the couch in silence, watching the other girls complain and thinking about the Senate's motives. On the surface, this was likely due to the Voice's ultimatums. Anything less would be seen as a concession, and they were making a statement in direct opposition to them. But in her heart, she knew it had to be because of Samm. The "contingency plans" Hobb had hinted at. She had warned them to ease up, but instead they were tightening their grip, exerting more control. For the people who believed in the Hope Act, sure, this might be seen as a sign of strength and solidarity, but to everyone else? It was practically a declaration of war.

The worst part was keeping the secret. She knew that Mkele was right—if the truth about Samm got out now, with tensions so high, the riot would be terrifying, and she'd be right in the middle of it. She didn't dare say any more about Samm, or the tests, or anything else. Better to work as hard as she could, and cure the virus before anyone else had to die.

And yet even after two full days, she wasn't any closer. She knew how Samm thought, how he communicated, how he breathed and ate and moved, but she still didn't know how his immunity worked. She was confused. And because she couldn't tell anyone, she was confused alone.

She felt like she was drowning.

Isolde took a swig from her bottle. "Drinking while pregnant is punishable by incarceration and full-time monitoring," she said. "I have to enjoy this now."

"Your baby is more important than your rights," said Xochi. "As far as the Senate is concerned, you're just a uterus with legs."

"Grow up," said Kira sullenly. As soon as she said it, she felt guilty—she agreed with Xochi, so why was she attacking her? The Hope Act wasn't working, and the Senate was strengthening it for the wrong reasons. Maybe it was the way she said it, the focus on personal rights over everything else. Kira had believed that too, but things were different now. She'd seen the Senate debate this—she'd seen the fear in their eyes. This was about extinction, like Delarosa had said. The other girls turned to her, and their surprised looks only made her angrier. "Did it ever occur to you that maybe something *is* more important than your rights? That maybe the survival of your entire species is more important than your right to whine about it?"

Xochi raised her eyebrows. "Someone's feeling bitchy."

"I'm just sick of hearing about everyone's civil rights and everyone's privacy and everyone's inviolable power of choice. We either solve our problems or we go extinct—there is nothing in between. And if we're going to go extinct, I don't want it to be because Xochi Kessler was too worried about her rights to pitch in and save us."

Xochi bristled. "We're not talking about pitching in," she said, "we're talking about institutionalized rape. We're talking about the government taking full control over your body—what it's for, what you do with it, and what other people can do to it. I'm not letting some horny old dude screw me just because the law says I have to."

"Then pick a horny young dude," said Kira, "or get inseminated artificially—those are all options, and you know it. This isn't about sex, it's about survival."

"Mass pregnancy is the worst possible solution to that problem," said Xochi.

"Okay now," said Isolde, her voice slurring, "let's all calm down for a minute. Nobody's happy about this—"

"Sounds like Kira is," said Xochi. "Of course she's the one with a boyfriend, so I guess that makes sense—she's probably doing him anyway—"

Kira jumped across the room with a scream, blind with fury,

clawing for Xochi's neck, but Isolde leaped up to block her, tripping drunkenly over her own feet. She lost her balance, but clung to Kira so strongly Kira couldn't get past her to Xochi; Kira tried to fight past her, shoving Isolde away, gouging her forehead with her fingernail. Isolde yelped in pain, and Kira's struggling devolved into tears.

"Damn," gasped Xochi.

"Just sit down," said Isolde, easing Kira onto the sofa beside her. Kira sobbed, and Isolde held her gently. She shot Xochi a cold glance. "That was over the line."

"I'm sorry." Xochi settled herself back into her seat. "I'm sorry, Kira, you know I didn't mean it. I'm just going crazy— this whole damn thing is over the line."

"What's done is done," said Isolde. "The law is passed. Now we can complain about it, or we can get drunk enough to not care."

"You've had too much of that as it is," said Xochi, standing up and ripping the bottle from Isolde's hands. Isolde's grip was loose, her strength used up in the struggle with Kira, and Xochi took it easily, opening the window and throwing the bottle outside.

"Hey, Xochi!" It was a voice from the street, one of the local boys—Kira didn't recognize it exactly. "Crazy stuff with the Hope Act, right? You guys wanna talk? Can we come in?"

"Go to hell," said Xochi, and slammed the window closed.

"That was my bottle," said Isolde, her voice slurring. Nobody paid her attention.

"I'm sorry, Xochi," said Kira, sitting up straighter. She rubbed her eyes with the back of her hand. "I'm not mad at you, I'm mad at . . . pretty much everything else in the world. But the world doesn't have a face, so I was going to take it out on yours."

Xochi smirked, but her expression fell again just as quickly. "I'm not ready," she said softly. "None of us are ready."

Isolde traced a pattern on the couch with her finger. "Haru was right, you know. What he said in the Senate hearing. We don't have any children left, just adults who don't know what they're doing."

The girls sat quietly, lost in their thoughts. Kira thought about Marcus—she'd rejected his advances, and now the government had changed everything. A two-month grace period to get things going, and then she could get arrested just for not being something she'd never been before. If she had to have children, she wanted them to be Marcus's, she guessed; she'd never thought about anyone else, not seriously. But if she told him now, he'd know it was for the law, and not for him. She couldn't do that to him. And yet she couldn't go to anyone else without hurting him even worse.

Besides, she didn't want to be pregnant. Not like this. If she was going to create a new life, she wanted to do it because it meant something, not because she'd been forced to.

And yet she'd just yelled at Xochi for proposing the same idea. She didn't even know what to think anymore.

For just a second—just the briefest fraction of a moment—she thought about Samm, and wondered if a half-Partial child would be immune.

"Do any of you remember your mother?" asked Isolde. "Not your new one, Xochi, your old one. Your real mother from before the Release."

"A little," said Xochi. "She was tall."

"That's it?"

"Like seriously tall," said Xochi. "In every image I have of her, she's towering over me, and not just because I was little—she towered over everyone. Six-four, maybe six-six." Her voice softened, and Kira could tell she was drifting into memory: Her eyes were wet and unfocused, staring blindly into space. She grabbed a lock of her coal-black hair. "She had black hair, like mine, and she was always wearing jewelry. Silver, I think. She had a big fat ring on her hand like a flower, and I used to play with it. We lived in Philadelphia—I used to think that was the name of the state, but it's a city. Philadelphia. Someday I want to go back and find that ring." She rolled her eyes. "You know. Someday."

"My mom sold airplanes," said Isolde. "I don't know how, or to who, but I remember that's what she told me, and I thought it was so amazing, and now I look back and I think: We don't even have airplanes anymore. We don't have gas to put in them, I don't know if we even have anyone left who could fly them if we did, but my mom used to sell them like they were nothing, like they were fish rolls in the market."

"I don't think I had a mother," said Kira. "I mean, obviously I had one at some point, but I don't remember her, just my dad. I don't even remember him talking about her, but I'm sure he did. I guess they were divorced, or she was dead. Probably divorced: We didn't have any pictures of her."

"So imagine something awesome," said Xochi. "If you don't remember your mom, that means she can be anyone you want— she can be an actress, or a model, or the president of some giant company, or . . . anything you want."

"If you can't know the truth," said Isolde, "live the most awesome lie you can think of."

"All right then," said Kira. "She was a doctor, like me—a brilliant scientist renowned for her work with children. She invented . . . gene sequencing. And nanosurgery." Kira smiled. "And normal surgery, and penicillin, and she cured cancer."

"That is a pretty awesome dream," said Xochi.

"Yeah," said Kira. "I guess awesome dreams are all we have left."

CHAPTER TWENTY-FOUR

"**S**tay alert today," said Shaylon.

Kira eyed the young soldier warily, her eyes still red from tears and fatigue. "More so than normal? What's going on?"

"Mr. Mkele thinks someone's planning an attack," he said, gripping his rifle more tightly. "The Voice hiding in town, still looking for whatever they didn't find at the town hall. The new amendment to the Hope Act probably didn't help matters, either. He's sending more patrols outside, but he told us to be careful here anyway, just in case."

Kira nodded. "I'll keep my eyes open." She pushed her way through the door into the decontamination tunnel, rubbing her face with her palms as the air blasted around her. *I should be using Shaylon a lot more than I am. If I can find a way to talk to him alone, maybe after hours, I can probably learn a lot more about what the Grid is doing.*

Kira sighed. *Like I have time for another project.*

She set down her stack of notebooks and crouched by Samm's

table, checking his face and arm—a ritual that had become standard now.

"They beat you again."

Samm, of course, said nothing.

Kira watched him a moment, then glanced nervously into the corners. "They shouldn't be doing this to you. It's inhumane."

"I'm not sure that statement has any bearing on me."

"It doesn't matter if you're human or not," said Kira, probing the Partial's shins through the fabric of his pants, searching for more wounds. "They're human, and that means they need to act like it." She pulled up his pant legs. "You've got a few new cuts on here, but they're not bleeding, obviously, and you should be okay." She rolled them back down. "None of these wounds has ever gotten infected." She wondered if Samm's body produced some kind of natural antiseptic or antibiotic, and made a mental note to check it out later—through some means other than just stabbing him with a dirty knife. "You should be fine," she said, and walked to the computer.

Kira noticed immediately that the files had been read: her DORD images, her preliminary notes on the pheromones, even her handwritten notes in her notebook. Someone had moved them, sorted them, paged through them. *Is Skousen checking my work?* she wondered. *Is he duplicating it?* Some of the files were new; he'd done studies of his own while she was away. She didn't know if she should be grateful someone was watching, or indignant that they didn't trust her results. She was nearly too tired to care.

I only have three days left, she told herself. *Stop whining and work.* She struggled to concentrate on the DORD images, looking for any discrepancy between Samm's physiology and that of a human, but she kept thinking about what he said yesterday. The sincerity in his voice. What if he was telling the truth—what then? If the Partials had never created the virus in the first place, then who did? The Lurker in his breath, whatever it was, proved that he had some relationship to RM, but that didn't mean he made it. The Partials were soldiers, not geneticists; they had doctors, but they weren't necessarily capable of this level of engineering. What if the similarity meant something else entirely?

What if it was a sign of common ancestry? What if RM and the Partials were both created by the same third party?

Kira closed her eyes, trying to remember what she'd learned in school. *What was the name of the company? Para-something?* It was so hard to remember the details of the old world—names and places and technologies that simply had no meaning in modern life. Food companies were easy, because the ruins were all around her: Starbucks and Panda Garcia and a dozen more like them. She could even remember eating at some of them as a child, before the Break. Genetics companies, on the other hand, were completely outside the realm of her experience. She'd learned the name in her history class, but they hadn't made a big deal about it. It was the government who'd commissioned the Partials, Para-something was just the contractor.

Para-Genetics, she remembered. *They were called ParaGen. Haru had mentioned them the other day. But what could they have to do with RM? Certainly they hadn't created it—they were human too. It doesn't make sense.*

"Did you have a mother?" asked Samm. The question broke

Kira's train of thought in an instant, and she looked at him quizzically.

"What?"

"Did you have a mother?"

"I . . . of course I had a mother, everyone has a mother."

"We don't."

Kira frowned. "You know you're the second person in the last twelve hours to ask me about my mother?"

"I was only curious."

"It's okay," said Kira. "I never really knew my mother. I guess that makes us more alike than we thought."

"Your father, then," said Samm.

"Why do you want to know about him? I was five when he died, I can barely remember him."

"I've never had a father either."

Kira scooted her chair closer, coming around the edge of the desk. "Why are you so curious?" she asked. "You never talk, for two solid days, and now this morning all of a sudden you're obsessed with families. What's going on?"

"I've been doing some thinking," he said. "A lot of thinking. You're aware that we can't reproduce?"

She nodded warily. "You were built that way. You were . . . well, you were intended to be weapons, not people. They didn't want self-replicating weapons."

"Yes," he said. "The Partials were never intended to exist outside the infrastructure that created us, but we do, and now all those old design parameters are—" He stopped suddenly, glancing at the cameras. "Listen, do you trust me?"

She hesitated, but not for long. "No."

"I suppose not. Do you think you ever could?"

"Ever?"

"If we worked together—if we ever offered a truce. Peace. Could you learn to trust us?"

This is where he'd been angling since day one—since she'd asked him what he was doing in Manhattan. He was finally willing to discuss it, but could she trust him? What was he trying to get from her?

"I could trust you if you proved yourselves trustworthy," said Kira. "I don't . . . I don't know that I distrust you on principle, if that's what you're asking. Not anymore. But a lot of people do."

"And what would it take to earn their trust?"

"Not having destroyed our world eleven years ago," said Kira. "Short of that . . . I don't know. Putting it back together."

He paused, thinking, and she watched him carefully—the way his eyes twitched, as if examining two different objects in front of him. Every now and then they flicked toward one of the cameras, just a fleeting glance. *What is he planning?*

She looked him in the eyes. *When in doubt, don't hold back.* "Why are you telling me this?"

"Because the only hope, for either of us, is to help each other. To work together."

"You've said that before."

"You've asked about our mission. That was it, Kira—we were coming here to try to make peace. To see if we could work together. You need our help to cure RM, but we need you just as much."

"Why?"

He glanced at the camera again. "I can't tell you yet."

"But you have to tell me—isn't that why you're here? If you came on a mission of peace, what were you going to say? 'We need your help, but we can't say why'?"

"We didn't know how much you still hated us," said Samm. "We thought perhaps we could persuade you with an offer to work together. When I was captured and brought here, when I saw what's going on here . . . there was no way. But you, Kira, you listen. More than that, you understand what's at stake. That no price is too high to pay when it means the survival of your species."

"So just tell me," she pleaded. "Forget the cameras, forget whoever's listening on the other side, and tell me what's going on."

Samm shook his head. "It's not just a matter of them not believing me," he said. "If they find out why I'm here—the instant they know the reason—I'm a dead man."

It was Kira who glanced at the camera this time, suddenly filled with unease, but Samm shook his head and glanced at his wounds. "It's okay, they know I have a secret."

She folded her arms and sat back in her chair. What could be so dangerous he'd be killed just for saying it? Something they didn't want to hear—or something they did? She racked her brain, searching for a theory that made sense. Was he really a bomb, like they'd initially feared, and Samm thought the Senate would kill him to get rid of him? But what did that have to do with peace?

Peace. It was exactly what she had hoped for when she was talking with Marcus the day before. She wanted to reach out and touch it, to taste it, to know what it felt like not to live in constant fear. They hadn't known true peace since the Hope Act was established, and the Voice rebelled and the island started its slow spiral into chaos. They hadn't even known it in the years before that—the desperate rebuilding after the Break, the Break itself and the Partial rebellion, even the Isolation War that sparked the creation of the Partials in the first place. She had lived in a world of discord since the moment she was born, and the world before had been no better. They were on the brink of destruction, and everyone had their own solution, but Kira had been the only one to suggest that they might need the Partials. That they might need to work together.

That is, she'd been the only one until now. Now a Partial was suggesting the same thing.

"No," she said slowly, suspicion creeping through her like a spider. "It's too perfect. It's like you're saying exactly what I want to hear." She shook her head. "I don't believe you."

"Why would we want anything else?" asked Samm. "It's the most basic instinct of life—to outlive yourself. To build another generation that's going to see tomorrow."

"But you've never even known family," said Kira. "You didn't have families, you didn't grow up, you have no idea what it's even like. What if creation is just a phantom instinct, held over from some lost shred of DNA?"

Like a flash, Kira remembered a dog—it was giant in her memory, a growling mass of muscle and teeth. It chased her through a park or a garden, something green with grass and flowers, and she was terrified, and the dog was almost on her, and suddenly her father was there. He was not a strong man, he wasn't big or powerful, but he put himself between her and the dog. He was bitten, and she thought it was very bad. He did it to save her. That's what fathers did.

"What do you think it says about us that we don't have any parents?" She looked up and caught Samm's eye. "I don't mean us, I don't mean kids, I mean no fathers at all—a whole society, two whole societies, with no parents at all. What do you think that's done to us?"

Samm said nothing, but he held her gaze. There was a tear in his eye—the first time she'd ever seen him cry. The scientist in her wanted to study it, to take a sample, to find out how and why and what he was crying. The girl in her simply thought of the Hope Act and wondered if a law like that could ever pass if a voter knew it would be forced upon his own daughter.

Kira looked at the screen, seeing not the image but her memory of Manhattan: of the Partial attack; of Gabe's body lying slumped in the hall where the Partials had shot him. *If they were on a mission of peace, why did they shoot him?* She frowned, trying to reconcile that event with Samm's protestation of innocence. *They didn't even try to talk to us first. It doesn't make sense.*

She racked her brain for more memories, trying to call up anything that would support what she desperately wanted to be true. *What was it the Partials said right before we blew up the apartment?* She struggled to remember. *"Which group is this?"* She'd heard it clearly—at least she thought she had. *Which group of what? Had they been expecting someone else, maybe a group of bandits or the Voice? Was it pure luck that they'd found Kira instead, the one human who seemed willing to listen?*

Or was Samm simply telling her exactly what she wanted to hear?

The doors opened with a sudden buzz, and the decontamination blowers roared to life. Shaylon came through the tunnel, clutching a plastic syringe full of blood, and ran to her in a rush.

"The nurse said to give you this," he said quickly, holding out the syringe. "She said you'd know what to do with it."

"You're not allowed in here," said Kira.

"She said it was an emergency," said Shaylon, then stopped and looked at Samm. "So that's him?"

She took the syringe gingerly; the tube was still warm from the blood inside. "What is it?"

"She said you'd know," said Shaylon. "It's from the maternity ward."

Realization dawned, and Kira's eyes went wide. "It's from a newborn! One of the mothers had her baby!" She rushed to the counter, pulling out slides and vials and pipettes in a flurry. "Do you know which one?"

"She said you'd know what to do with it!"

"I do know," said Kira. "Calm down." *Please, God, don't let it be Madison.* She piped a drop onto a slide as quickly as she dared and dashed to the medicomp. "This is uninfected blood, do you understand? The babies are born healthy and then the virus hits them, and we have only minutes, maybe less, before the virus morphs and attacks." She punched in the commands and raced back to the counter, preparing another slide. "There's an airborne virus and a blood-borne virus, and I'm trying to catch them as they transform from one to the other. Turn on the microscope."

"Which one's the microscope?"

"This one." She flew across the room with the slide in hand, opening the viewing chamber and slamming the slide home. She flicked on all the switches, drumming on the scope anxiously while it slowly hummed to life, and when the screen flickered on she started the viewer, telling the computer to search for viruses. A small *ping* told her it had already found one of the airborne forms, and she called up the image immediately. The tiny virus appeared on the screen, a red highlight in a sea of gray. It was already beginning to change, but it was a still image, trapped partway from one form to the next; the scope was advanced, but nothing could take moving video at this level of magnification. More pings sounded as the medicomp found more viruses. "If we get enough good pictures," said Kira, "at different stages of the transformation, we can probably reconstruct the entire process." She told the medicomp to take another image of the same area, to see if the airborne virus had completely converted to its larger form.

The computer popped up a small notice: *Partial match.*

Shaylon pointed at it, his voice terrified. "The baby's a Partial?"

"No, it means the object it found only partially matches the records in the database." *Just like the Lurker,* she thought. "We've got something that's kind of RM-ish, but isn't a virus." She pulled up the image and stared in shock: She didn't recognize it. "That's not good."

"What is it?"

"It's a new form of the virus," said Kira, turning it on the screen to get the best possible view. "The airborne Spore is supposed to turn into the blood-borne Blob—they're the only two variations of RM in our entire database." She looked desperately for anything she could understand. "This is new."

She ticked her fingers across the screen, dissecting the image as best she could, pulling it apart to see what made it work. The computer was right—it was a partial match for the Blob, bearing many of the same protein structures in the same basic arrangement, but beyond that it was completely new—and unlike the Lurker, it was definitely viral. *Is this because of Samm? Is this new virus a result of the Lurker?* Kira tagged the image and told the computer to search its database again, looking for anything that matched it more closely. There were five hits, all in the archive of newborn blood tests: mostly premature babies, plus one still-birth, all more than eight years ago. *It didn't show up enough to stand out, but it did show up, and years before Samm got here. That means it's not Samm's fault. But then where did it come from?*

Kira tapped back into the main medicomp imager. *If it's not that common,* she thought, *then maybe it's just a mutation. Maybe this is the only instance of it in the sample, and I just happened to pick exactly the wrong spot to start looking.* She told the scope to find more of it in the blood samples, and it pinged almost immediately, then pinged again, then again and again and again, even more pings now than when it was searching for the airborne Spore. *It's everywhere.* Kira called up image after image, the new virus filling every screen, multiplying like mad. Frantically she called up a new search, looking for the Spore again, but there was nothing. The computer had saved the original images, but the structure itself had disappeared from the blood. Every instance of the Spore had morphed into this one—this Predator—and they were still replicating.

Shaylon spoke slowly, his voice thin and nervous as he looked at Samm. "What is that?"

"I have no idea." Kira gritted her teeth and dove into the growing pile of reports and scans and images, determined to find what she was looking for: the process of evolution from Spore to Blob, the details that would tell her how the virus functioned—the individual chemical steps behind every process. It was like trying to drink from a waterfall.

Shaylon froze, his finger on his earpiece, then dropped into a crouch. "Get down."

"Why? What's going on—"

"Get down!" said Shaylon fiercely, pulling her to the floor behind the metal bulk of the microscope. "There's someone here, someone sneaking around. They think it might be a jailbreak."

Kira glanced around the edge of the computer; Samm was watching them with interest. *Is someone really coming for you?* Her gun was on the counter, tucked safely in its holster, far out of reach from where she was hiding; if somebody came now, she wouldn't be able to get it in time.

She glanced back to see Shaylon listening intently to his earpiece. "They think it's outside," he said softly. "You stay here, I'm going to look out the window." He rose to a crouch and ran to the far wall, his body low, his rifle at the ready. Kira glanced at Samm, then at the door, then ran to the counter and grabbed the pistol, pulling it with her to the floor. She had cover from the window, but not from the door. Was the second soldier still out there? She drew the gun and tossed the leather holster into the corner, checking the clip and chamber to make sure she was ready.

"I can't see it," Shaylon was saying. He stood carefully, looking out the window at the tightest possible angle. He had his hand to his ear, talking anxiously with Mkele. "I don't see—wait, out in the cars. Are they still that far away?"

It doesn't make sense to attack the hospital in daylight, thought Kira. *The cars are good cover, and there are trees at the base of the building, but it's hardly ideal. If they're coming in through the wall, why not do it at night? Why not wait until they would have cover right up to the building?*

Wait, she thought suddenly, *if they're coming in through the wall—*

She jumped to her feet and ran toward Shaylon. "Get back! You're too close to the—" and then the wall exploded, brick and metal and plaster caving inward like a giant bubble, the shock wave catching Kira and throwing her backward like an invisible hand. Shaylon flew to the side, hitting the wall and flopping down like a rag doll. Even Samm was blown clear, the force of the explosion tossing his operating table like a leaf. It slammed into Kira's desk and toppled to the ground.

Kira hit the back wall with tremendous force, knocking the wind from her lungs and wrenching the gun out of her hand. She fell behind the massive DORD machine, already wobbling on its edge, and it crashed down with her, pinning her painfully to the floor. She screamed in agony, certain that her leg was broken, but forced herself to calm down.

Deep breaths, Kira, deep breaths. Get yourself under control. Slowly the world came back into focus; the pain in her leg coming clearer as she breathed. *It's not broken, it's just pinned. I can push it off.* She heard movement in the room, rubble falling and scattering. She looked around anxiously, but the DORD blocked her view of everything but the door. The plastic tunnel hung from the ceiling in tatters; a wave of rubble from the wall had shredded it and slammed into the door, blocking it shut. She felt a small electric shock in her pinned leg and saw that the plastic housing around the DORD machine had fractured. *The machine is shorting out. I've got to get away from it.* She heard more noises, definitely movement this time. *Is it Shaylon or Samm?* She pressed her arms and back against the wall, braced her legs against the machine, and pushed with all her strength.

She moved it an inch, then another, each one slow and agonizing, when suddenly she heard an audible snap in the bowels of the machine, and a surge of electricity racked her body.

The pain was excruciating. Every muscle in her body clenched at once, flexed tighter than she ever knew was possible, and suddenly the pain was gone, and she was gasping for air. Her head felt fuzzy, and she struggled to think; she felt like she'd been beaten with a metal bat but couldn't tell where. She croaked, trying to speak.

"Help."

The surge came again, a raging maelstrom of electric current coursing through her body. Her eyes rolled back and the world went dark. Her entire world was formless, placeless pain, and suddenly the shock was gone again. Her heart was fluttering erratically, and she felt her head grow light. She fought to stay awake.

"Help me," she whispered. Her voice was feeble and hoarse. "The scanner is . . . electrocuting—"

Another burst of electricity cut her off, drowning her in pain, and when it stopped her lungs took five full seconds to start working again, her heart run ragged by the extra current, her body too confused to know what to do. When she finally breathed again, desperately sucking in air, she smelled the acrid stench of her own charred flesh. Her eyes focused slowly, and she saw that the door was open now, just a few inches, and an eye was peeking through—two eyes, one white and one black.

Not an eye, she thought, her brain like mush. *It's the barrel of a gun.*

The door rocked slightly, shoved uselessly against the pile of rubble by the soldiers beyond. It didn't budge. "It's the girl. Is anyone else alive in there?"

"You have to help me," she croaked. "My heart is stopping."

"Can you see the prisoner? Has he already escaped?"

"The beats are . . . too erratic," she said, feeling her body start to shut down—her muscles, her heart, her lungs slowly fading into nothing. "You have to help me. One more shock . . . and I'm . . . ."

She heard voices—shouting and screaming that seemed a hundred miles away. A warm breeze blew softly across her face, and she opened her eyes. The world was a formless blur, and yet something was there, moving, and suddenly the pressure on her legs was gone. The massive DORD machine flew across the room; the world rang in her ears. Strong arms pulled her clear of the wreckage, and she tried to focus. Someone was holding her, carrying her, checking her for wounds.

"Thank you," she coughed. Her voice was so quiet she could barely hear it herself. She clung to her rescuer tightly. "I think . . . he got away."

"I'm right here, Kira."

I know that voice.

She struggled to think, straining her eyes, and slowly the world came into focus: Samm was holding her, his clothes still smoking from the explosion, the tattered restraints hanging useless from his arms. Around them the room was destroyed, the floor covered with rubble, the wall a gaping hole. The trees swayed in the wind. The crumpled mass of the DORD machine lay discarded in the corner; Shaylon lay in the other corner, bloody and still.

She looked up at Samm. "You saved me."

The door finally wrenched open, and soldiers poured in like a flood. "Put her down!"

"He saved me."

"Put her down now!"

Samm knelt, laying Kira gently on the floor. As soon as she was clear, the soldiers sprang forward and knocked him down with the butts of their rifles. Kira tried to speak, struggling to protest, but she was too weak. All she could do was watch.

CHAPTER TWENTY-FIVE

The room was dark. Hospital equipment beeped softly, tiny lights blinking on and off in the shadows. Kira opened her eyes, then closed them, gasping, her mind still full of pain and light, as if she were still in the midst of the explosion.

Samm saved me.

The soldiers had beaten Samm for almost a full minute before chaining him back up, kicking him in the stomach and hammering him with their rifles. He never fought back—he didn't run when he had the chance, and then he didn't fight back, he just let them hit him, over and over, an agonizing string of thuds and cracks and grunts of pain.

He's a Partial, she told herself. She had told herself the same thing a hundred times over the past three days. *He's not even human. We don't know what he's doing here, what he's thinking, what he's plotting.* And yet even as she said it, she knew she didn't believe it. He wanted the same thing she did: to solve their problems instead of just working around them. On the entire island he was the only one she'd found who agreed with her.

But he was a Partial.

Kira tried to sit up, but a pain in her leg knocked her breath away. The same leg she'd had burned by the DORD machine. She moved the blanket for a better look, but was bandaged and she couldn't see it well. She could recognize the itchy burn of her muscle fibers knitting back together, and knew she'd been treated with a regen box. It would be a while before she was well enough to sit up, let alone stand or walk.

She heard a soft sigh and looked across the room at another hospital bed. There were more than enough rooms in the hospital, but only enough juice to power a few floors, so most patients were doubled up. She peered closer at the shape in the bed, nearly faceless in the dim light, and realized with a start that it was Shaylon. He must have been shattered by the explosion—the way he was bandaged, he must have had dozens of broken bones, and hundreds of cuts and abrasions from the shrapnel.

His breaths were small and feeble, but he was breathing on his own, and he appeared stable. It looked like he was going to pull through.

He'd seen the Predator in the blood, and he'd heard her speculations on its nature. Had she given too much away? Had she exposed too many secrets? The island was ready to burst into flames at the slightest spark; when he wakes up, please let him keep quiet.

Kira heard footsteps in the hallway and looked at the door just in time to see it open.

"You're awake," said Nurse Hardy.

"What happened?" Kira demanded. "How long was I out?"

She stopped short when she saw the nurse wheel another bed into the room. It was Madison. Kira sat up quickly, gasping at the stab of pain in her leg.

"Madison, are you all right?"

"She went into early labor," said Nurse Hardy. "We managed to stop it, but I don't know if she's going to make it much further."

"I'll be fine," said Madison. She looked over at Kira. "They won't even let me sit up anymore, let alone walk. Let alone use the bathroom."

"Just stay calm and rest," said Nurse Hardy. "We'll keep you in here for a few hours while you recover, and then we'll see if we can take you back to your regular room. You have to relax."

"I'll relax," said Madison dutifully. "I'll stare at the ceiling and won't move a muscle."

"You should sleep," said Nurse Hardy. She glanced over at Kira. "And you should too. You were only asleep for a few hours, and your body needs rest. Let's have a look at your leg." She pulled back the sheet over Kira's legs and lifted up the edge of the bandage; Kira held her breath, trying not to react to the pain as the moving bandage tugged at her burn. Nurse Hardy tutted disapprovingly at the palm-size patch of blackened skin, gooey with burn cream and antiseptic. "It's healing, but it's a nasty burn. We've already used a regen box on it just a few hours ago, so we'll have to wait awhile before another treatment."

"Thanks," said Kira, gasping softly as the nurse gently laid the bandage back down.

"Go to sleep," said Nurse Hardy, "both of you." She left the room, quietly closing the door behind her. Kira looked at

Madison's outline in the darkness.

"Mads, do you know what happened up there? Was it the Voice?"

"It must have been, but I don't know much more than you do. There was an explosion. Someone got through the security perimeter."

Kira hesitated. "And Samm?"

"Samm?"

"The Partial."

Madison gave her an odd look. "I'm sorry, Kira, I don't know. I had more problems with the abruption, and I was getting examined when the explosion hit. I haven't been able to move, much less talk to anyone who has any idea what's going on."

Kira fell back into her pillow, grunting at the release of tension in her burned leg. "I can't be here. I have to find out what's happening."

"You and me both."

Kira laughed dryly. "Sounds like you're just as bad off as I am."

"Oh, you know. Sunshine and rainbows." Madison shifted on the bed, trying to find a comfortable position. "I've got ten weeks left, and I'll be lucky to make it four." Her voice grew soft and sad. "I'm going to lose her, Kira."

"You're not going to lose her."

"Even if she's born on time—even if she's born late, with plenty of time to develop—I'm going to lose her to RM."

"I'm not going to let that happen."

"You can't stop it," said Madison. "I know you're trying, I know you've done everything you can possibly do to help, but it's not enough. Maybe someday, but not for me." Her voice broke. "Not for Arwen."

Kira cocked her head to the side. "Who's Arwen?" She thought she knew all the pregnant mothers. *Maybe Arwen's a new one? I've only been working with Samm for three days, but that's plenty of time for a new mother to get on the list.*

Madison started to speak, hesitated, then whispered softly. "Arwen is my baby. I named her."

The thought hit Kira like a punch in the gut.

"Mads—"

"I know I shouldn't have," said Madison. "I know. But I love this baby, Kira. I love her more than I can even describe to you. It's like I know her already—she's so independent, and so strong, and so . . . funny. I know it sounds ridiculous, but she makes me laugh every day. It's like we're sharing a joke no one else can hear. I couldn't *not* name her, Kira. She's a real person."

"I'm so sorry, Mads." Kira wiped her eyes. "I can't imagine what it must be like for you to have Samm here in the same building—"

"Haru doesn't know I've named her," said Madison. "And no, I don't hate the Partial." Kira thought she saw her shrug in the darkness. "Whatever the Partials did, they did it eleven years ago: If I held a grudge that long, I'd be just as dead as everyone we left behind. I don't want to live in a world full of dead people." She paused, breathing deeply. "And anyway, even if she dies, at least I got to meet my daughter. At least I got to laugh with her jokes."

The door opened again, and Nurse Hardy returned with a syringe. Kira wiped her eyes.

"Just a little something to help you sleep," said the nurse.

"I don't need it," said Madison.

"You don't want it," Nurse Hardy corrected, prepping the needle. "I'm the one who decides what you need. Some sleep will do you good." She pulled the cap from Madison's IV tube, inserted the needle, and pressed the plunger. "All done. It should only take a few minutes to kick in, and you'll finally get some rest. I'll see you again in the morning."

Madison sighed. "Fine."

"I want to see Mkele," said Kira. "Now."

"And what do you expect me to do about it?" asked Nurse Hardy. "There's been an attack on the hospital; Mkele's busy."

"Can you find him?"

Hardy gestured at Madison and shrugged helplessly. "She's one of seven mothers on the floor right now. I'm pretty busy myself." She sighed. "If I see him, I'll let him know you're looking for him."

"Thanks."

Nurse Hardy left, and the room returned to darkness.

Kira wiped her eyes again. "Arwen Sato," she said. "It's a beautiful name."

"It's my grandmother's," said Madison. "I know Haru wants a Japanese name, but I think he'll like this one."

"I think he'll like it a lot," said Kira.

"Then I'll see you . . . in the morning." Madison yawned again. Kira watched as her friend slowly calmed, stilled, and fell asleep. Her breathing was deep and rhythmic.

I'm not going to let her child die, thought Kira. *I don't care what it takes. That baby is going to live.*

But how? She shook her head, completely overwhelmed. *The civil war may have already started, and I can barely walk. And that last blood sample—it was exactly what I never expected it to be. A new strain of the virus that no one's ever seen? It doesn't make sense. I thought I knew how RM worked, but now . . . everything I thought I knew was wrong. And I'm out of time to find the answers.*

Kira drummed her fingers nervously on the rails of her hospital bed. *I need to put all the pieces together.* She thought back over the things she'd learned, trying to see them in a new way. RM had four forms, or at least four that she'd found thus far: the airborne Spore, the blood-borne Blob, the Lurker from Samm's breath, and the Predator from the newborn's sample. *I thought the Spore would turn into the Blob, but it didn't. It turned into the Predator. And according to the older records, it had done the same thing in the past, so it wasn't an anomaly. Does it happen every time? What if the Predator is an intermediate step between the Spore and the Blob?*

She mentally reordered the versions of the virus, naming the airborne Spore Stage 1, the Predator Stage 2, and the Blob Stage 3. No one had ever actually seen the Blob virus kill anyone—it was in everyone's blood, so they made the natural assumption, but it had always been in the *survivors'* blood. What if it wasn't actually deadly? *What if the killer is the Predator, and then by the time we run a test it's changed into the Blob?*

Kira shook her head, cursing the explosion. *If I could test another sample, without an explosion interrupting me, I could know for sure what's going on here. Maybe. But I don't have time for more tests—I don't even have a lab anymore.* She shifted again, trying to move, and gasped at the pain in her leg. She cried out in frustration. *How can I fix this when I can't even move?*

The door opened again, and Kira looked up to see Dr. Skousen, and after him Mr. Mkele. Skousen walked to Shaylon's unconscious body.

Mkele locked the door.

"You're awake," said Mkele, studying Kira carefully. She smoothed the sheets on her legs and stared back defiantly. "I'm glad. This concerns you."

"What happened?" she asked. "And where's Samm?"

Dr. Skousen walked to Madison's bed, probing her head and face carefully with his fingers. "She's asleep."

"Good," said Mkele. "Let's get started."

"What the hell is going on?" Kira repeated, trying to sound as firm and commanding as possible. Instead she felt weak and vulnerable—wounded and tired, half-naked in a hospital bed. She pulled the sheet tighter around her thighs and back. "That was a Voice attack, right? Have they attacked other sites—has the civil war already started? And someone tell me what's happened to Samm!"

Dr. Skousen pulled a small bottle from the pocket of his lab coat, followed by a small syringe and a tiny needle. The needle seemed to fill Kira's vision, glinting softly in the faint light.

"Samm is contained," said Mkele. His eyes looked tired, his face gaunt. "We're here to contain the other loose end."

Kira tensed, eyes shooting around the room to look for exits—the door was locked, the window was locked, and her leg screamed in pain even just thinking about running. She looked at Dr. Skousen, slowly filling the syringe, then at Mkele. "You're going to kill me?"

"No," said Mkele, walking toward her, "though we do ask that you refrain from shouting."

Dr. Skousen held up the syringe, and flicked it with his finger. Kira's eyes grew wide, she opened her mouth to scream, and Mkele clamped a hand over her mouth, grabbing her shoulder and holding her still. Dr. Skousen stepped not toward her, but back toward Shaylon. He inserted the needle in the young soldier's IV tube and pushed in the entire dose.

"We did not want this," said Mkele, practically whispering in her ear. His voice was thick and heavy. "Whatever else you think of us, know this: Our hand has been forced."

Kira watched in horror as the chemical from the shot swirled through his IV tube and into his body. *No*, she thought. *No, no, no.*

"I'm going to let go of you now," said Mkele, hands still clamped tight around her face. "I'm going to uncover your mouth. You are not going to scream." He waited until Kira nodded, still wide-eyed with terror, then lifted his hands and stepped away. "There. It's done."

"What did you do?"

"We gave him medicine," said Mkele, "but I fear that even with it, he won't pull through."

"You killed him," said Kira. She looked at Dr. Skousen. "You killed him."

"No," said Skousen. He sighed. "He died tragically from injuries caused by the explosion."

"But why?" she pleaded.

"He saw too much," said Mkele. "Far more than he was intended to see. He would have told others, and we cannot have that."

"We could have stopped him first," said Kira. "We could have isolated him, and explained what we needed, and—"

"You've met the boy," said Mkele. "I trust him to go where I tell him, and to shoot where I aim him, but I do not trust him to keep this secret. Not after what's happened."

"Then what about me?" Kira demanded. "Obviously I can't keep a secret either, so why not kill me too?"

"Shaylon was a liability. You are an asset."

Kira felt a chill run down her spine.

"It won't be long now," said Dr. Skousen, dropping the implements back into his pocket and glancing a final time at Shaylon. He looked at Kira, said nothing, and turned away.

"As for the Partial," said Mkele, "we're meeting as soon as we can to decide how best to dispose of him."

Kira's heart stopped in her chest. "But I have two more days."

"You have no lab, and you can't even sit up. East Meadow is turning into a war zone, and we do not have time for anything that will jeopardize our ability to win that war. Harboring a live Partial is too great of a risk, but a dead one . . ." Mkele sighed and rubbed his eyes. When he spoke again his voice was soft, almost sad. "I had hoped you could do it, Kira, truly I did. Perhaps someday we can try again."

"We don't have to give up."

"You're no closer to a cure now than when you started three days ago—you're further, in fact; your records were destroyed in the explosion, along with all of the equipment you were using, most of it irreplaceable. If not for the Voice, we might have been able to salvage something—anything—but there's simply no time left. We had to act." He straightened, and the old, cold demeanor crept back into his face and stance. "It's time for us to step in and put this society back together, one way or another. Good night, Kira."

They opened the door and walked away.

Kira looked at Shaylon, her heart pounding in her chest. He lay quietly; she watched the lights blink on the wall behind him. *I've got to do something.* She threw back the sheet and tried to move her legs, biting back the scream as her burn shifted and stretched. If the drug they gave him was a poison, there might be an antidote; there had to be something she could do to save him. She took a deep breath, screwed up her courage, and threw her legs over the side, clutching the bed rail and groaning loudly as another wave of pain tore through her. The lights behind Shaylon began to blink more rapidly; the soft beeps became more strident. She put her legs on the floor, cold and bracing against her feet, and limped to a stand, being careful not to put any weight on her ruined leg. Even with that, the change of position was more painful than she'd expected, and her legs gave way, dumping her on the ground. She screamed in agony, her hands curled into claws, her legs flailing in the air, and in that moment the alarms went off over Shaylon's bed. His body began to buck and writhe, broken bones grinding together. Feet pounded down the hall, nurses bursting into the room and throwing on the lights. Kira clamped down on her pain, struggling to sit up.

"It's a heart attack," said a nurse.

"Get the crash cart," said a doctor. They ignored Kira on

the floor, trying desperately to save Shaylon's life while his broken body flailed and twisted. They drugged him, they shocked him, they bound him and hit him and did everything they could think of, and all the while Kira watched from the floor, oozing new blood and sobbing uncontrollably.

CHAPTER TWENTY-SIX

"**Y**ou shouldn't be out of bed."

Kira winced, leaning heavily on the IV stand for support. "I'm fine." She wasn't, but she didn't have time to lie around. Her time was up: Samm would be killed, the cure would be lost, Arwen would die, the entire island seemed ready to collapse in a cloud of rubble. Kira had a plan, and she wasn't going to let a charred leg keep her from carrying it out.

The nurse shook his head. "You have a third-degree burn the size of a tennis ball. Let me help you back to your bed."

Kira held out her hand, favoring her burned leg as well as she could. "I'm fine, really. The regen box has already knit most of the skin back together, and there was barely any muscle damage. Just let me walk."

"Are you sure?" the nurse asked. "You look like you're hurting pretty bad."

"I'm sure." Kira took another step, using the IV stand as a cane and dragging her burned leg gingerly behind her. The nurse watched her, and she did her best to smile and look normal. In truth she felt horrible—she'd given herself a second treatment with the regen box, despite the risk of overdose, and the burned cells were only just starting to grow back. But she had to get up. She had to reach the Senate.

They were nearby, she knew it. They were likely still using the town hall, as Mkele had suggested, but for a secret meeting of their Machiavellian subcommittee she knew they'd be here, in the hospital, hidden from the world and surrounded by guards.

She just had to find out where in the hospital they were.

The IV stand was on wheels, which squeaked softly as she limped down the long, white hallway. Every step was agony. She stopped at a nurses' station, panting with exertion.

"Are you okay, Kira?" It was Sandy, the maternity nurse.

"I'm okay. Do you know where Dr. Skousen is?"

Sandy shook her head. "He's asked not to be disturbed."

"Sandy, I know he's in a meeting with the other senators," Kira whispered. She watched Sandy's face for a flash of recognition, saw it, and smiled inwardly. "It's related to the secret project they've had me working on. I need to be there."

Sandy leaned toward her. "Look, I don't want any part of this. They're in the smaller conference room on four. Do what you need to do."

"Thanks, Sandy." She headed for the stairs as quickly as she could. *The fourth floor: ten steps up, turn a corner, ten more steps. Repeat twice more.* Kira gasped. *I'm never going to make it.* She shook her head, remembering Shaylon's dying body, remembering Samm. *I have to find them. I don't have any choice.* She gripped the handrail tightly, planted the IV stand on the first step, and slowly raised herself up. The wheeled stand wiggled slightly on the stair, but she held it in place. Every step hurt her leg, and soon her arms were exhausted from supporting so much of her weight. At the first landing she collapsed against the wall, her head resting on the plaster while she sucked in huge gulps of air. Her leg hurt more than she'd ever imagined anything could hurt, but she couldn't stop. *They're going to kill Samm.* She clenched her jaw and kept going, forcing herself to take the next step, then the next, then the next. Landing after landing. Floor after floor. When she reached the fourth floor she fell to the tile and crawled, until a soldier guarding the conference room ran to her side. It was the same guard from the last meeting, which meant he'd recognize her. Kira said a silent prayer of gratitude and hoped they hadn't thought to tell him she wasn't allowed in this time—why would they? They thought she was still bedridden.

"Are you okay?" He lifted her to her feet. "They didn't tell me you were coming."

Thank you. She struggled to her feet, holding on to the soldier with one hand and her IV stand with the other. "I wouldn't miss it. Help me in there." She leaned on his arm and limped to the door, throwing it open with all the force she could muster.

Mkele and the senators were clustered around a table, Samm bound with chains in the corner. Everyone looked up at her in shock, and Kira could feel the hate in Kessler's eyes like a laser. Delarosa merely raised her eyebrow.

Hobb turned to Skousen. "You told us she was too injured to move."

"Turns out he's not actually a very good doctor," said Kira, wincing and dragging her leg into the room. The soldier grabbed her shoulder, stopping her short.

"I'm sorry, senators," he said. "I didn't realize. I'll take her back."

"No," said Delarosa. "She made it up here, the least we can do is listen to whatever she has to say."

"We know exactly what she'll say," said Kessler.

Delarosa turned to the soldier with a stern glare. "Thank you; please wait outside. And if anyone else shows up, announce them before you let them in."

"Of course, ma'am." The red-faced soldier closed the door, and Kira glanced at Samm. He hadn't been cleaned up since the explosion, and his clothes hung in filthy tatters. What skin she could see was riddled with scrapes and gashes, already healing but still obviously painful. He said nothing, but nodded curtly in acknowledgment.

She turned back to the senators, still panting from her exertion, and collapsed into a chair. "Sorry I'm late."

"This meeting does not concern you," said Weist. "Your project has been terminated, we're going to get rid of this . . . thing, and if we're lucky, we might be able to clean up the mess."

"But the project is working," said Kira. "I'm almost done mapping the development of the virus, and if I could just have a bit more time—"

"You've accomplished nothing," said Skousen. "We risked the security of our city and the integrity of this council so that you could study a Partial, and when we need to see results all you can do is ask for more time?"

"But now we understand—" said Kira, but Skousen was too furious to be stopped.

"You understand nothing! You say the virus has multiple forms: What triggers the change from one to another? Can we stop it? Can we bypass it? Can any of the forms be attacked or negated? Science is about specifics, Ms. Walker, not grand, helpless gestures of defiance. If you can give us a mechanism of change or a specific means of defense, then do so, but if not—"

"Please, I just need more time."

"We don't have any more time!" shouted Delarosa. It was the first time she had ever raised her voice, and Kira quailed at the force of it. "Our city is falling apart—our entire island is falling apart. Voice attacks in the streets, bombs going off in the hospital, rebels fleeing the city and infiltrating our defenses and killing our citizens. We need to save some semblance of this civilization."

"You're not listening to me!" said Kira, and the sound of her own words shocked her. "If Samm dies we all die, not today but inevitably, and there will be nothing we can do to stop it."

"This is an obsession," said Delarosa. "A noble one, but still an obsession and still dangerous. We will not let it destroy the human race."

"You're the ones who are going to destroy it," said Kira, tears beginning to creep into her eyes.

"I told you," said Senator Kessler, "the same canned message every time." She looked Kira over. "You sound exactly like Xochi, like the Voice, spouting this groundless, incendiary tripe."

Kira struggled for words, but they caught in her throat.

"Your job is the future," said Mkele softly. "Ours is the present. I told you before: If our goals ever conflict, ours takes priority. An organized Voice attack on East Meadow is imminent and there are only so many battles we can fight at one time. Before we do anything else, the Partial must be destroyed."

Kira glanced at Samm. As always, he was expressionless, but she could tell that he knew this was coming. She turned back to the senators. "Just like that? Not even a trial or a hearing or—"

"The hearing was four days ago," said Weist. "You were there, and you heard the decision."

"You gave us five days of research," said Kira. "We've only had three."

"The laboratory is destroyed," said Skousen, "along with most of your work. You're in no condition to continue, and there's not enough data left for anyone else to finish what you started. Not in time."

"Then move us to another laboratory," said Kira. "Surely somewhere we have the equipment—all we need is the time. The five days was an arbitrary timeline in the first place."

"And risk further attacks?" asked Delarosa. "Absolutely not."

Hobb leaned forward. "The plan we're considering will still allow for—"

"Then let him go free," said Kira suddenly. She swallowed, nervous, watching as their eyes grew dark and narrow. She plunged forward before they could protest. "He's done nothing to hurt us, he's even helped with the research. There's no reason why we shouldn't let him live."

"Is this a joke?" hissed Kessler.

"It serves your purpose," said Kira. "You want him gone: He'll be gone. If nothing else, it will help alleviate the possibility of a Partial retaliation."

Skousen and Kessler scowled, and Weist shook his head. "Do

you honestly think that will do any good?"

"Of course she does," said Mkele. "She's an idealist."

"She's a plague baby," said Kessler. "She's developed an attachment to this thing, but she has no idea what the Partials are really like."

"And you do?" asked Kira. She tried to stand, gasped at the shock of pain, then rested back and turned in her chair. "You fought them eleven years ago—eleven years. Is it impossible to consider that something may have changed?"

"You can't believe anything it tells you," said Mkele.

"He's a soldier, not a spy," said Kira. She turned to look at him; struggling, in this last moment, to decide once and for all if she could trust him. If he had been honest the last few days, or if he was really the monster the senators made him out to be.

He watched her, outwardly calm and yet not quite concealing his nervousness, his determination. His hope. She looked back at the senators and spoke strongly. "Samm has faced captivity and torture by people who want to see his entire race destroyed, and he's done it without crying, without complaining, without begging, without anything but strength and determination. If the other Partials are half as understanding as he is, we might just stand a chance—"

"I'm on a mission of peace," said Samm. His voice was firm and confident; Kira turned to him, tears forming again in her eyes as he stepped forward to the full reach of his manacles. The senators were silent. "My squad was in Manhattan because we were coming here, to talk to you. We came to offer a truce."

"Lies," snarled Kessler.

"It's the truth," said Samm. "We need your help."

But why? thought Kira. *We can't trust you if you don't tell us why.*

He looked at Kira for a moment, fixing her with his eyes, then turned to the senators and drew himself up, standing as tall and proud as he could. "We're dying."

Kira's eyes went wide; the entire room was shocked into silence.

"Like you, we can't reproduce, though ours is an engineered sterility built into our DNA—a fail-safe to keep us from getting out of hand. That never bothered us before because we don't age, either, so there was never any danger of us disappearing. But apparently there's a fail-safe for that, too."

Dr. Skousen regained his voice first. "You're . . . dying? All of you?"

"We discovered ParaGen designed us with an expiration date," said Samm. "At twenty years, the process that halts our aging reverses, and we shrivel and die within weeks, sometimes days. It's not accelerated aging. It's decay. We rot alive."

Kira's mind reeled. This was the great secret he'd never dared tell—that the Partials had a ticking clock, just like the humans did. That's why they wanted a truce. She was too shocked to move, but looked at the senators, trying to guess what they were thinking. Kessler was smiling, but Hobb and Weist were staring at Samm with shocked eyes and open mouths. Delarosa looked like she was trying not to cry, though Kira couldn't tell if they were tears of joy or sorrow. Weist was mumbling under his breath, his mouth moving almost as if he didn't realize it. Mkele was stone faced and silent.

"They're dying," said Kessler, and Kira nearly recoiled from the vicious glee in the woman's voice. "Do you realize what this means? The first Partials were created in the third year of the Isolation War, which was . . . ten years before the Partial War. Twenty-one years ago. The first wave of them would have started dying last winter, and the youngest have what, two years left? Three at the most? And then they'll be gone forever."

"Everyone will be gone forever," said Samm, and Kira felt more emotion in his voice, more earnestness, than she'd ever felt before. "Both of our species are going extinct—every sapient life form on the planet is going to die."

"Our shelf life is longer than yours," said Delarosa. "I think we'll take our chances on our own."

"That's what I've been trying to tell you," said Kira, finally finding her voice. "Without them there is no cure." She looked at Samm, finally understanding his pleas. "We have to work together."

Samm nodded. "You can have babies, but they die of RM; we're completely immune, but we can't reproduce. Don't you see? We need each other. Neither species can beat this alone."

"Think what this will do for morale," said Hobb. "Once the people hear this, they'll . . . they'll declare it a holiday. A new Rebuilding Day."

"What is wrong with you people?" Kira demanded, struggling to stand before collapsing heavily back into her chair. "He thought you'd kill him when you heard his secret, but it's worse."

"We were always going to destroy it," said Mkele. "That was never in question."

"What this means now," said Delarosa, "is that we're going to do it in public, where this news can get out and do its job:

unifying the human race."

"Try to see the larger picture," Hobb said to Kira. "You're trying to save a group of people who are actively killing one another in the streets. Do you think a treaty with the enemy is going to change that? If they won't even listen to us, what makes you think they'll do anything for a Partial?" Hobb leaned forward, earnest and intense. "The Voice were calling for our heads long before the Partial showed up, and if word gets out that we're hiding one, it will only get worse. The people are going to want answers; they're going to *need* answers. And they need *us* to provide those answers, because when we provide them we'll win the people back. We'll have control of the island again; we'll have peace again. We know you want peace."

"Of course," said Kira, "but—"

"Be careful," murmured Delarosa, looking not at Kira but at Senator Hobb. "What are you telling her?"

"She can help," said Hobb. He fixed Kira with eyes so deep and blue she felt herself caught by them, drawn in like water in a glass. "You're an idealist," he said. "You want to save people; we want to give you that opportunity. You're also intelligent, so you tell me: What do the people want?"

"They want peace," said Kira.

"Nobody blows up a building because they want peace," said Hobb. "Try again."

"They want . . ." Kira watched Hobb's face, wondering where he was going with this. *What do the people want?* "They want a cure."

"Too specific."

"They want a future."

"They want a purpose." Hobb spread his hands, gesturing grandly as he spoke. "They want to wake up in the morning knowing what they're supposed to do, and how they're supposed to do it. A future will give them purpose, and a cure will give them a future, but down at the core, the purpose is all they really want. They want a destination—they want a goal they can reach for. When we established East Meadow, we thought that the goal of curing RM would be enough. But it's not a goal we've been able to reach, and over eleven years of fruitless nothing the people have fallen apart. Their purpose has withered and died. We need to give them something attainable—do you see where I'm going with this? We need to give them Samm."

"No!" shouted Kira.

"Nobody knows who caused that explosion," said Senator Delarosa. "It was probably the Voice, yes, but what if it was a Partial?"

Kira felt the room grow cold. "It wasn't."

"But what would it mean for humanity if it was?" Hobb licked his lips, gesturing with his hands as he spoke. "Humanity needs a purpose, and now this Partial has blown up our hospital." He snapped his fingers. "There's their purpose: an enemy! The people grow enraged—not against us, but with us. The island unites against a common foe. It might even sway the Voice—can you imagine what a coup that would be? All the rebels back on our team again, all this anger and violence directed out instead of in. The human race is tearing one another apart, Kira, but this will save it. Surely you can see that."

"But it's a lie," said Kira.

"Because only a lie will save us in time," said Delarosa. "I want a cure more than anyone, and yes, a real cure might unite us, but the clock has run out. The Voice have issued an ultimatum of civil war; the devil is at the gates. If we don't do something now, tomorrow, we lose our chance to do anything at all."

There was something wrong with their story—even beyond the obvious deception, there was something deeper and darker lurking somewhere inside. It made Kira queasy. "Why are you telling me this?"

"This plan will work without you," said Hobb, "but think how much better it will be with you. You're young and pretty, you're capable and idealistic, and you've been at the heart of everything we've done—you went to Manhattan and brought back the secret, you searched for the cure, and you were injured in the line of duty by the first Partial attack in eleven years." He gestured at her leg. "If *we* tell this story, people will believe it; if *you* tell this story, people will die for it. You can make it personal and meaningful—you can be the hero who unites the world again. You'll be the face of peace."

"This is evil," said Kira. "You're asking me to lie to everyone I know." She pointed at Samm. "You're asking me to be a part of his murder."

"The wolves are hungry," said Delarosa. "We can kill ourselves fighting them, or we can throw them a body. The death of one Partial is the cheapest price for peace we could ever hope to pay."

And then all at once, like a thunderbolt in her brain, Kira saw it—the deeper secret she couldn't see before. The senators wanted to use this explosion to win back the Voice, but that would never work if the Voice had been the ones to set the bomb:

They would know the Senate was lying. The only way to blame Samm was to use an event that no one knew the truth about, and that meant the Voice didn't set that bomb.

For the Senate's plan to work, the bomb had to be set by . . . the Senate.

She almost shouted it out right there, accusing them without thinking, but for once in her life she managed to hold her tongue, biting down on the truth that she knew would get her killed where she stood. The Senate had set the bomb—the Senate had masterminded this entire thing from the beginning. They wanted to solve the Voice problem by creating a common enemy, and she had given them one; she'd dropped Samm right in their laps with her idiotic trip to Manhattan. That was why they'd brought him back, and that was why they'd put her in charge of the project—so that one day they could blow it all up without losing anyone important, and they could pose with the rubble and bring everyone together against the big, bad enemy they could never let go of. It was the same general plan they'd just explained to her, but deeper and older and far more sinister. They wouldn't back out of it now, no matter how much she talked.

Kira looked at Samm—not just looked at him but stared at him, thought at him, *willed* him to understand her, wishing with all her being that she could link with him and breathe her thoughts straight into his brain. *I'm sorry,* she thought. *I can't stop them. Please . . . I'm sorry.*

"It's time for you to choose," said Delarosa. "Join us, bring peace to the island, put an end to the Voice threat . . . or stay a rebel, and live your days as an exile. You could live comfortably on one of the farms." She leaned forward. "You are a firebrand, Ms. Walker—people follow you, and if you join our cause, they will follow you into the brightest future we've seen in decades. A new dawn for humanity. The choice is yours."

I'm sorry, she thought again. She gripped the IV stand, gritted her teeth, and dragged her charred leg one step back toward the senators. "There's nothing I can do to stop you."

She could feel Samm's shock like a wave of betrayal, slamming her in the back and washing up and over her head. *Just trust me,* she thought.

Hobb narrowed his eyes. "You'll do it?"

"No, I won't." She half turned, not daring to look Samm in the face again. "I can't keep fighting you—look at me, I can barely stand up—but that doesn't mean I'm going to sell him out to help you and lie to my friends." A tear rolled down her cheek, but she kept her gaze firm, desperate for them to believe her. "Do whatever you have to do and be done with it. I won't stop you." She turned to the door, took a painful step, then paused, gasping for air. "And get one of your goons out there to carry me back downstairs. I can barely move anymore."

"Of course," said Hobb. "Take your time. Recuperate. This will take us a few hours to set up anyway."

Kira nodded. *That's exactly what I'm counting on.*

CHAPTER TWENTY-SEVEN

The guard laid her gently in her hospital bed, cringing as she groaned in pain. It wasn't fake—her leg seemed to hurt more now than it had climbing the stairs. She tried to arrange the blanket over her legs, but even that much motion brought tears to her eyes. The guard moved her legs for her, then turned off the lights and left. Kira closed her eyes, clenched her teeth, and forced herself to sit up.

Never underestimate me.

The regen box was still in the room, and Kira gave herself another treatment—a third in less than eight hours, accelerating her cell growth far past the point of safety. It would cause long-term damage, but in the short term it would let her walk. She peeked out the door and smiled grimly. Her wound was so bad, and her walking so debilitated, that the guard hadn't even stayed to watch her.

She found Marcus in the cafeteria, staring silently at a tray of untouched rice. *Will he even help? He has to.* She inched slowly toward him across the empty floor. "Hey."

He looked up, eyes wide with shock, and leaped to his feet. "Where have you been? I came in as soon as they reopened the building, and you weren't in your room—I tore the building upside down until they finally made me come in here and wait." He looked her up and down, frowning in renewed concern. "How on earth did you get in here? You can barely walk."

"Magic," she said coolly. "Can you do me a favor?"

"Of course."

"I need an MRI."

He frowned again. "They won't give you one?"

"I want you to do it."

"Why?"

"I want you to hold my hand while it runs."

"I . . . okay." He grimaced, obviously confused. "Wouldn't you rather have a DORD, they're so much better—"

"I need an MRI."

"Then let me find someone to run the scan while I—"

"Just you," she said firmly. "Just you and me."

Marcus nodded, his face worn and worried, but there was a look in his eye—he was starting to pick up on what she was doing. "Okay, sure." He offered his arm and she took it gratefully, staggering alongside him back into the main hallway.

"What's really going on?" he whispered.

"Call it a medical hunch. I want to see something." She hesitated for a moment, trying to figure out what to say to him. They hadn't spoken since his proposal.

He walked in silence, and she did the same. *After everything I've done to him, will he even trust me anymore?*

They made their way down the hall to the radiology center and found a private room. Marcus eased her onto the exam table, and she let out a gasp as the weight came off her leg. She felt like she'd been running a marathon through a sea of broken glass. The MRI machine was smaller than the DORD in her lab—just a doughnut instead of a full-body box, and not nearly as powerful—but its electromagnetic field was exactly what she needed.

"I need to go turn it on," said Marcus. He ran to the viewing room, fiddled with the controls, and Kira took a deep breath. *This is it. This is either the beginning, or the end.* The machine hummed to life, the powerful magnetic field washing over her, and she reached out her hand as Marcus came back.

"We don't have much time, so just listen," said Kira, leaning back while the MRI ran its sequence. "Mkele has me under heavy surveillance, and I am almost certainly wearing some kind of listening device. The field from this machine will disrupt it, but I don't know how much time we'll have before his goons get suspicious." She glanced over at him, and then faced forward again. "Do you trust me?"

"What?"

"Do you trust me?" She felt him staring at her, but she kept her eyes forward.

"Yes. Of course I trust you. What's going on?"

"The Senate set the bomb that blew up my lab. They killed Shaylon and threatened me. This entire thing—Samm, the studies, the bomb—has all been a ploy to generate enough fear, aimed in a precise direction, to cement their power over the island. Now they're using this scenario in order to—" She

320

dropped her eyes, then found her courage and finally looked at him. "Marcus, they're going to kill Samm."

She saw something play across his face. Whether it was horror or shock or jealousy, she couldn't tell. His eyes flicked up toward the ceiling, then slowly turned back to her.

"Kira," he said, "they were always going to kill it. To kill . . . Samm. You know this." His voice was even and controlled, enough that she knew he must have been repressing something powerful. "Besides, why would they blow up their own people? Their own hospital?"

"Because it's part of their plans," said Kira. "I could never figure out why I got the assignment to study Samm, but this must have been it. I'm just a plague baby to them, the least experienced medic and the most expendable. If the bomb had killed me, they could have used me as a martyr, but since I lived, they offered me a role as their figurehead; the brave young scientist who survived the Partial attack."

"The Partials set the bomb?"

"The Senate set the bomb, I told you that. But they're going to blame Samm, they're going to kill him, and they're going to use his death to rally support." She begged him with her eyes, willing him to believe. "They told Shaylon to go to the window, Marcus. They told him to stand right next to the wall before they blew it up."

"No," said Marcus, shaking his head. "It was the Voice— they've been attacking East Meadow for weeks, there's probably at least one cell of them here in the city." But as he was speaking, she could hear the doubt creeping into his voice.

"Did anyone actually see them?" asked Kira. "Did anyone

actually attack the hospital, or did the military just say they did to cover their own tracks?"

Marcus stared at her, saying nothing.

"I know it sounds crazy," said Kira, but Marcus cut her off.

"No, it's not crazy. Coming from Xochi it would sound crazy, but from you . . ." He took her hand. "I trust you, Kira. If you say that they're trying to kill you, then I believe that they're trying to kill you."

Kira closed her eyes, praying to anyone who would listen. *Thank you, thank you, thank you.* She looked at Marcus and spoke quickly. "I don't know how much longer we have before someone comes to see why the listening bug isn't working." She took a deep breath. "We need to break him out—I'll explain everything later, but that's our goal: We get him out, we take him north, and we follow him home. They're dying, just like we are, and they've offered a truce. We're going to take them up on it."

Marcus stuttered, searching for words. "Are you nuts?"

"He saved me, Marcus. Samm had the chance to run when the bomb hit: He was free from his bonds, and no one was watching, and there was a giant hole in the wall. He could have run and been free, but he picked up the DORD that was electrocuting me and saved my life."

Marcus froze, looking her straight in the eyes—in her eyes and past them, to something she could only imagine. The pain in his face nearly broke her heart.

"I should have . . . ," he said. his gaze still lost. "I tried to . . ."

"You tried to save me and I wouldn't listen." Kira choked back a sob. "I've been reckless and stupid and I know it, and now

I'm in too deep, and I know you want to pull me out and make me safe but we can't do it—not yet. I need you to come with me. I know it's dangerous, and I know you don't want to do it, but I need you, Marcus. I need you to believe me; I need you to trust me. I need to hear you say you'll come with me."

Marcus stayed silent. He rubbed his eyes, pulled on his face, gritted his teeth. Kira covered her mouth with her hands, blowing out a long breath, never taking her eyes off him. *Please, Marcus. Please say yes.*

Marcus stood, turning to the side. Kira closed her eyes, crying silently.

"I'll do it," he said. Kira's eyes flew open.

"You will?"

He stepped back to the table. "I'll help you break him out, I'll help you take him home, I'll do anything for you. For you."

"Oh, Marcus . . ."

"Last time you left, it killed me. I'm not going to let you do this on your own." He stared at her, loving and longing, then turned and threw his hands helplessly in the air. "Now, how the hell are we going to do it?"

Her mouth opened and closed. She had no idea. "Whatever it is, we have to do it tonight."

"We'll need Xochi's help," said Marcus. "Xochi and Isolde at the very least. Jayden and Haru if we can convince them to help."

Kira shook her head. "They're never going to trust a Partial. We have to do this without them."

Marcus whistled low. "This is crazy." He shrugged. "Get Xochi and Isolde together, and give me some time to gather a few things. We'll meet at your place in two hours."

"Perfect," said Kira. "Now get back over there and run some kind of analysis on the images this thing just took—anything at all, it doesn't matter, we just need this to look like a real MRI."

Marcus nodded and ran to the computer, sitting down and typing something out. Barely a minute later a soldier poked his head in the door: Kira was lying quietly on the table, and Marcus was in the viewing room, watching the screen. The soldier looked around, nodded, and went back outside.

Marcus waited until the door was shut, then met her gaze and stared. Kira stared back.

They had two hours.

Kira flexed her leg. She'd been tempted to use the regen box again, but it seemed to be healing just fine, it was the pain that was the problem; she'd split the difference and given herself a prodigious shot of painkillers. She checked the wrapping on her burn a final time, making sure it was tight, and pulled on her pants. She walked with a limp, and she was more than a little dizzy, but at least she could walk.

She peeked out of her room; she was still unguarded. Either the senators believed her willingness to go along with their plan, or they thought Mkele's surveillance was enough to keep tabs on her. Which wasn't to say that the hall was clear of guards: There were at least ten, maybe more, armed to the teeth and clustered around a door at the far end. *At least we know where they're keeping Samm,* Kira thought. She slipped into the hall and limped briskly in the other direction. Sandy wasn't at her desk. Kira still had a little luck left.

It was nearly dusk now, a familiar half-light she recognized from so many long days at work, but tonight the familiarity made her heart catch in her throat. She couldn't help but wonder if this would be her last time in East Meadow—her last time crossing the turnpike, her last time passing the big blue house on the corner, her last time watching the sushi vendors amble slowly down the sidewalks. She turned on her street, let herself into her house, and quietly packed her backpack with everything it would hold: extra lights and batteries, several pairs of dry socks, a knife and a set of tools. She broke down her rifle and stowed that as well, concealing it in the backpack as best she could—it wouldn't be a military operation this time, so all they'd have were the weapons they brought with them. She still had Isolde's pistol strapped to her hip—hardly an uncommon accessory these days—and made sure to pack plenty of ammunition for both weapons. Last of all she grabbed her medkit, sealed her bags tightly, and set them by the front door, waiting for the others to arrive. She sat down, frowned, and realized that Nandita still hadn't come back from her trip.

Nandita had been gone longer now than she ever had before, and Kira wandered into the kitchen, suddenly anxious. Everything looked normal enough. She walked to the back of the house, and when she found no one she sped up, taking a full inventory of the house. Nandita wasn't anywhere.

Did the police take her? Was she attacked while collecting herbs? It was possible she'd simply left, like Kira was doing now, packing her essentials and heading out to a farm or another outlying community, but she never would have left without saying something. *This doesn't feel right.*

Marcus came first, nodding to Kira in silence and slowly sweeping her with a digital stethoscope; she looked at it quizzically, but he motioned for her to be patient. Xochi and Isolde came a few minutes later, and Kira kept them silent while they watched Marcus search the rest of the room. The scope beeped softly as he ran it past the speaker hub, and he spoke loudly and clearly.

"Hey, Xochi, is it okay if I listen to some music?"

"Sure," said Xochi, just as clearly. She glanced at Kira, and Kira could see from the gleam in her eyes that she'd figured out what Marcus was doing. They turned to watch him work.

Marcus went to the hub, pulled out a monogrammed pod— KAYLEIGH, 2052—scanned it fruitlessly, then unplugged the hub unit itself and pulled it from the shelf, turning it over and around and examining it from every angle. He paused, looking at the back of it and motioned for the girls to come and see. He pointed through the black metal grille to a small object hidden inside, and they nodded and stepped back.

"Be careful with that drink," said Xochi. "Last time you almost ruined my player."

Kira filled a bucket of water in the kitchen and set it in front of Marcus. He crouched over it with the stereo.

"Thanks. Oh, crap—!" He plunged the stereo into the bucket, bugged speaker first, and held it under for a few seconds. He tried the scope again, found no signal, and smiled. He ran a quick scan of both Xochi and Isolde, found nothing, and nodded to Kira. She connected KAYLEIGH, 2052 to a smaller speaker, cranked it as loud as it would go, and set it in the center of the room.

Marcus held up the digital scope. "I was one of the on-call medics when the bomb went off this morning, and I happened to get this thing a little too close to one of Mkele's listening devices in your lab. Looks like it makes a pretty good detector." He dropped it on the couch. "The room's clear, and anyone listening from outside will have a hard time hearing over this."

Kira looked at each of her friends in turn. "We're about to commit treason, so if anyone wants to back out, now's a really good time to do it."

Xochi looked at Kira. "Is this what I think it is?"

Kira shrugged. "Do you think it's a plan to attack the hospital, free the Partial, take him home, and conspire with his people to save the world?"

Xochi's eyes went wide. "Actually no, I wasn't really thinking that at all." She shook her head, a quick jerk as if she was shaking water from her face. "Rescue the Partial? Are you serious?"

"They've offered a truce, and the Senate has rejected it." Kira took a deep breath. "If I can work with them I can cure RM—I know I can. But you've got to trust me."

Xochi's jaw worked up and down, lost for words. Finally she nodded. "I trust you, Kira. Let's commit some treason."

"Rock on," said Marcus. Isolde nodded as well, but looked pale and nervous.

Kira sat down, speaking softly even with the music blaring, just in case. "The Senate has lost it. They blew up the hospital so they could frame Samm, and now they're going to kill him in a political power play. Madison's baby is coming any day now, and we still don't have a cure, and the Voice is practically champing at the bit to stage a coup."

Xochi grimaced. "What's the plan?"

"We've got to get Samm out of the hospital and off the island," said Kira. "Start by packing clothes, camping gear, and weapons, and meet me at the corner of Turnpike and Prospect in an hour. Isolde," she said, unbuckling the pistol holster, "I've still got your gun—"

"I can't go with you."

"You said you were in," said Xochi.

"I'll do everything I can from here," said Isolde. "I just can't leave."

"We'll need everyone we can get if things go bad out there," said Kira.

"I can't go," Isolde insisted. "If it were just me, I'd be with you, but I'm . . ." She paused. "I'm pregnant."

Kira's jaw fell open. "You're what?"

"I'm pregnant," said Isolde. "I found out this morning. You know I'll help you, but I . . . I can't risk it." She looked Kira in the eyes. "I'm sorry."

Kira shook her head, still trying to parse the information. She looked at Isolde's belly, still supermodel flat, then up at her face. "Was it . . . artificial?"

Isolde shook her head. "Senator Hobb."

Kira gasped.

"Was it consensual?" snarled Xochi. "Because if it wasn't, I'm going to take a detour to the Senate chambers on my way out of town, and I'm going to shoot him first."

"No," said Isolde quickly, "there was nothing improper— well, I guess he's my boss, which is improper, but he didn't force me. I wanted him to. We were working late, and I—"

328

"Were you drunk?" asked Marcus.

"That's Isolde's business," said Kira. "She said it was her choice." She flashed Xochi a hard look. "We can shoot him when we get back. Isolde will stay behind and cover our trail. She did it perfectly last time."

"What is our trail?" asked Marcus. "Even if we can get him out of the hospital, what then? Down through Brooklyn, like you did before?"

Kira shook her head. "They'll be watching that route as soon as they figure out what we're doing. We need to head north, and cross the sound."

The room fell silent; the very idea was terrifying. None of them knew how to pilot a boat, and Xochi was the only strong swimmer in the group. Plus, the land between here and there was riddled with the Voice.

"She's right," said Xochi slowly. "There's too much Defense Grid between us and Manhattan; north is the best way." She drummed her fingers on the table. "How helpful is this Partial going to be? Does he know where to find a boat?"

"There are boats all along the North Shore," said Kira. "We see them all the time on salvage runs. All we have to do is find one with a full tank of gas—the gas'll be old, so it'll destroy the engine, but it should get us across before the engine dies."

"If we can make it there," said Marcus. "The way things are these days, the Voice are more likely than ever to attack a group from East Meadow."

"They're not going to go after a bunch of unarmed kids," said Xochi.

Kira shook her head. "Oh, we'll be armed."

"Still," said Xochi, "they're revolutionaries, not murderers."

"You're planning too far in advance," said Isolde. "None of this will matter if you can't get Samm out of the hospital. Or if you can't even get into the hospital."

"That's the hard part," Kira admitted. "They're holding him in a reinforced room on the first floor—I saw it on my way out. It's swarming with guards. If we can find a way to surprise them—"

"He's actually not there," said Marcus. Kira raised her eyebrows, and Marcus leaned forward to whisper. "Mkele's set up the first-floor room as a decoy. Samm's being held upstairs in the conference room, with just two guards on the door."

"How do you know?" asked Xochi.

Marcus smiled and looked at Kira. "You know that new fish guy who works the hospital parking lot? I got one of the guards hooked on his oysters, and he asked me to bring him some for dinner tonight. There's just two of them up there." He grinned. "It pays to be nice."

"That'll help us get in," said Xochi, "but as soon as we hit that room they'll call for backup, and we'll never get out again."

"How about a diversion?" asked Isolde. "I won't be with you, so what if I do something to pull all the soldiers' attention somewhere else?"

"A diversion might work," said Marcus, "but it's going to have to be huge—we can't just distract the guards, we have to put them onto something else and hope to get out in the commotion. But it has to be epic."

Kira nodded, staring coldly at the floor. If she was in, she needed to be all in.

She spoke slowly. "How about a citywide riot?"

CHAPTER TWENTY-EIGHT

Kira stood on the corner of Turnpike and Prospect—a block from the hospital, in the shadow of an old ruined restaurant. Aladdin's. A kebab place, by the looks of it, but all fallen and overgrown. The coating of kudzu helped her peek around the corner without being seen, watching the hospital. A crowd was already starting to form. Word was spreading.

"Isolde's doing well," Kira murmured. "I guess when a known Senate aide starts spreading rumors, people listen."

"The Senate will know it was her," said Xochi. "They'll kill her for this."

"Even if they trace it back to her, she'll be fine," said Kira. "She's pregnant now. Not even Mkele would risk hurting her."

"So he can preserve his image?" asked Xochi. "He won't even have one after this. Killing a baby will be the nicest thing he's done all week."

"Isolde will be fine," Kira insisted. She paced a few steps, test-ing her leg; it still hurt terribly, and she grimaced at the thought of the grueling workout she was about to give it. She paused, thinking, then pulled off her backpack and opened the medkit.

Xochi watched with a frown as Kira pulled out a syringe and a bottle of Nalox. "Drugs?"

"I can barely walk," said Kira, prepping the needle. "If I'm going to spend my night running from Grid gunmen, I want some more painkillers."

Xochi smirked. "Did you bring enough for everybody?"

"Shut up." Kira pricked her leg, drove in the injection, and slapped a Band-Aid on the tiny bubble of blood that welled up from the hole. Almost immediately she felt the reaction, more in her head than her leg: a buzz in her perception, a slight delay in her movements. The morphine was strong. *Did I give myself too much?*

"Better?" asked Xochi. Kira nodded, and Xochi shook her head. "Just stay in front of me if we start shooting. I don't want your drug-addled reflexes getting me shot in the butt."

"There's Marcus," said Kira, and pointed at a large group coming down the street. Marcus's tall frame walked at the center of it. The crowd was shouting and mumbling and arguing loudly. Kira caught snatches of conversation: ". . . said a Partial . . . why wouldn't they tell . . . new kind of RM . . . the Senate knew . . ."

"If it wasn't before, the secret's definitely out now," said Kira. "It's going to ruin the Senate's plan either way."

The crowd passed by, angrily calling for Kira and the others to join them. Kira picked up her bags and fell in with the back of the group; Xochi followed her, and Marcus hung back to join them.

"Nice night for a vigilante execution," Marcus whispered.

The crowd in front of the hospital was enormous, shouting and chanting. The front doors were blocked by a wall of armed soldiers, and the crowd moved loosely before them, forward and back like an uncertain tide. Kira felt a surge of doubt: What if the riot led to more deaths? Madison and the other mothers, at least, should be safe—the maternity center was the best-defended spot in the city. It was too late to back out now. She said a silent prayer and kept walking.

"We're going to have to be very careful getting him out of there," said Marcus. "If this group finds him, they'll tear him limb from limb."

"They don't know what he looks like," said Xochi. "We can sneak him out like one of us."

"They're just as likely to mistake a human for a Partial as the other way around," said Kira, scanning the mob nervously. "We may have overdone this a little."

"We haven't done anything yet," said Xochi, pressing forward. "This mob doesn't do us any good until it gets inside and starts breaking things." She charged into the crowd, pushing toward the front, shouting loudly as she went. "They've been in league with the Partials all along! This is how they do it—new diseases, new deaths, new oppressions. This isn't the first time!"

Kira and Marcus followed as best they could, jostling violently through the heart of the throbbing crowd. The drug haze in Kira's head made the crush surreal and terrifying, loud and angry and larger than life. She shook her head, trying to concentrate.

Xochi reached the front and turned around, climbing on the hood of an old, discarded car. "Do you know why they're doing this? Because they want to control us! Because if we're terrified, we'll do anything they tell us to." The crowd roared in agreement, and Xochi continued. "'Inform on your friends!' 'Don't leave the city!' 'Get pregnant before RM kills us!'" The crowd was louder now, more agitated, roiling around Kira in fierce Brownian motion.

Someone threw a rock at the soldiers, missing the men but cracking loudly against the glass door behind them. More rocks followed, a vicious hail, and Xochi kept shouting as loudly as she could.

"We're sick of secrets! If the Senate has a Partial in there, bring it out where we can see it!"

The crowd surged forward, a flood of fists and anger. The soldiers fired into the air and the crowd pulled back, but not as far as before; the gap was smaller now than ever.

"They didn't shoot anyone," said Kira. "They're probably under orders not to. We have to rush the doors now, before they're cleared to use lethal force."

"They're firing on their own people!" shouted Xochi, reaching for her own pistol. Kira and Marcus shoved forward in alarm, struggling to reach her before she turned this into a shoot-out.

"They have automatic rifles!" Kira shouted, her voice drowned by the crowd. "Xochi, don't!"

Xochi turned, pistol in hand, and Marcus grabbed her leg and yanked her down. She fell with a thud on the hood of the car, pistol up, and Kira grabbed it, keeping it pointed at the sky. Xochi choked, fighting for breath, then groaned and coughed when it finally returned.

"Ow," she gasped.

"You can't shoot yet," Kira hissed. "The soldiers will turn this into a massacre."

"Then we need to make this happen now," said Marcus, and jumped on the car beside Xochi with a rock in each fist. "Storm the doors!" he shouted, throwing his first rock. It hit a soldier in the arm and he whipped up his rifle, pointing it at the crowd; the officer next to him pulled the soldier's arm back down, shouting something Kira couldn't hear. Marcus threw his second rock and hit one of the doors squarely in the center, shattering the safety glass into a pile of tiny cubes. It was like a signal to the crowd, and they surged forward again. Xochi shoved her pistol back into her hip holster, and the trio ran forward with the crowd, slamming to a halt as the front line impacted with the soldiers. Kira felt herself being smashed from both sides, felt her feet being stepped on, felt a painful kick against her burn that almost brought her to her knees. *If I go down, I'll be trampled to death.* She fought for air, pushing forward with all her strength.

"The crowd will turn to the right when we break through the doors," said Marcus, grunting with the exertion. "Go left and head for the stairs."

The crowd behind was pushing forward too strongly, but there was nowhere to go; Kira's chest compacted under the pressure, the air slowly squeezed out of her lungs. She saw spots, felt her head go light, and suddenly the dam broke. Rioters surged ahead through the doors, pressing the soldiers back or simply swarming around them. Kira ran forward blindly, carried by the crowd, trying simply to stay upright. She passed through the doors and into the wide foyer, picking up speed as the crowd spread out beyond the bottleneck. She shook her head, trying to clear it, then remembered the stairs and cut left, weaving through the angry mob, keeping her eyes on the unmarked door to the stairwell. Marcus reached it just as she did, and Xochi just after; they pulled it open and dove through into blessed empty silence.

Kira panted, slowly getting her breath back. Her leg throbbed dully. "Anyone following us?"

"Doesn't look like it," said Xochi. "Let's blaze—we have to go now, before the soldiers regain control."

"Assuming they even can," said Marcus, leaping up the stairs two at a time. He turned the corner, and his voice echoed down. "We'll be lucky if we have an island left to save after this."

Kira pulled out her pistol and moved up after him, Xochi close behind. *Fourth floor,* thought Kira, counting each flight of stairs as they passed it. *Will the Grid pull guards away from Samm to help downstairs, or will they see what's happening and add even more?*

They reached the fourth floor, and Kira crouched by the door, bracing herself.

"Give me a minute to get out my shotgun," she said, reaching for her bag. "If we're starting a firefight with armed soldiers, I don't want to be stuck with this peashooter—"

She was interrupted by the loud crack of a gunshot on the other side of the door. She looked up in alarm.

"They're already firing?"

"That wasn't toward us," said Xochi. "Somebody's beat us to the Partial's room."

"The other stairwell," said Kira, and threw open the door. Halfway down the corridor the soldiers were crouched low, facing the other direction, guns trained on the far end of the hall. She gasped: Haru was there, and Jayden, and three other armed rioters, though Kira couldn't tell who was with who. She dropped to the floor and brought her pistol forward, though at this range it would barely do anything.

"Behind us!" shouted one of the soldiers, turning toward Kira, and in that instant one of the rioters landed a lucky shot on the man's shoulder. The soldier cried out and fell prone, and Haru swung his rifle around and shot the rioter. The lone remaining soldier pressed himself even farther into the doorway.

"We're surrounded!" he shouted, thumbing his radio. "We need backup on the fourth floor ASAP!"

"They're going to kill Samm," Kira growled, racing forward. "Haru! Jayden!"

The second soldier was down, and at least one of the rioters lay sprawled on the floor several yards behind the rest. The group swung up their rifles, but Haru and Jayden recognized Kira and ordered everyone to lower them again.

"Kira," said Haru, "can't say it's a surprise to see you here." He checked his chamber and racked the slide, pointing back the way they had come. "Barricade those doors. Most of the mob hasn't figured out he's up here yet, but they're going to eventually."

"We're not here to guard him," said Kira. "We're here to break him out."

Haru stared, then laughed and shook his head. "Are you serious? Are you crazy? We brought that thing here so we could interrogate and dissect it, and now you want to make a deal with it? I was with you before, Kira, but this has gone too far." He pointed his rifle at her chest. Xochi and Marcus pointed their guns at him, and Jayden and the other three pointed their guns back. Kira stood in the middle, breathing slowly, trying desperately to stay calm. Her head swam with the morphine.

"Samm is innocent," said Kira. "The group we met on the island was coming to East Meadow to offer us a truce. Peace, Haru."

"How do you know this?"

"He told us."

Haru looked around, as if to ask if he was the only one who hadn't lost his mind.

"It's true," said Marcus.

"He tried to kill us," said Haru, turning his gun on Marcus. "They took our scout, shot Gabe in the face, and chased us off the island with a squad full of rifles, and all of a sudden that means they wanted peace? That's not the kind of peace I want any part of."

"He's an ally," Kira insisted. "He can help us rebuild."

Haru shook his head, as if the world had gone mad. "Damn plague babies—do you have any idea what we lost the last time we trusted the Partials?" He gestured angrily toward the city. "Every one of the houses out there used to be filled. Every building was still standing—every school was full of children. Ninety-nine point nine percent of the population died, Kira: If that happened again, we'd have two people left. Two, on the entire island. We will never rebuild anything."

"They're dying," Kira insisted, "just like we are. If we work together, we can save us both—"

"I don't want to save us both!" Haru shouted. "I want to save my child and murder every Partial on Earth!"

"Saving your child is why we're here!" Kira said, raising her voice. "You can guard him all night if you want but the Senate is going to kill him in the morning, and we don't have a cure yet. If I go with him, we can find one."

Haru stared at her, rage and confusion warring in his eyes. "I'm not letting you take it."

"She named her, Haru." Kira felt her voice crack and forced herself to stay firm. "Your baby has a name: Arwen Sato. Your daughter is Arwen Sato." She glanced at Jayden. "Your niece is Arwen Sato." She looked back at Haru, drilling into him with her eyes. "We can save her."

"Not in time," said Haru. His eyes were wet, his face red, his teeth bared.

"No." It was Jayden. He moved his arm, swinging his rifle around from Marcus to Haru. "Kira's right. Put down your gun."

"Are you crazy?"

"I hate the Partials as much as you do," said Jayden, "but Maddy is relying on us. If there's any chance we can save my sister's baby, I'm willing to take it."

"So you're going to kill her husband instead?"

"Not if he puts down his gun." Jayden's eyes were cold. "The rest of you too, put them all on the floor."

Slowly Haru complied, and the other three men behind him. Xochi gathered their weapons while Jayden kept them covered with his rifle. Kira tried the door, rattling the locked knob, then dug through the pockets of the dead soldier until she found a ring of keys.

"This one's still alive," said Marcus, examining the other downed soldier.

"Stable?" asked Kira.

"If we stop the bleeding."

"Wrap it," said Kira, standing up. "We'll lock him in with the others and they can help him after the riot."

"Speaking of which," said Xochi, "we need to get out of here. These guys called for backup, and the instant this riot comes even partly under control they're going to send every soldier they have up here."

Kira nodded. "See if you can see how they're doing." Xochi ran back to the stairs. Kira turned to the door, trying several keys before finding the right one. The room beyond was dark, and Samm was chained to a chair in the middle of it, speckled with cuts and scabs and bruises.

"You look like hell," said Kira.

"It's okay," said Samm, grunting in pain, but Kira could have sworn she saw the hint of a smile. "I have a very advanced platelet system."

Kira ran forward painfully and searched through her key ring for something to unlock the chains. There were two pairs of manacles and three different padlocks, and she opened each one with a turn and a click.

"You didn't have to save me," said Samm.

"You didn't have to save me." She opened the last lock, pulled away the chains, and paused there, crouching beside him. He turned his eyes from the door and looked at her for a split second, their eyes only centimeters apart, his breath on her cheek. When she spoke again, it was a whisper. "Thank you."

Samm stood and followed her into the hallway, squinting at the light and rolling his head back and forth to work out the kinks.

Jayden led Haru and the others into the room as they left it; Haru spit on Samm as they passed, but Samm didn't respond. Marcus finished binding the soldier's wound and put him into the dark room with the others, and Kira locked the door tightly.

The door at the end of the hall swung open, and Jayden and Kira spun to face it, guns ready, but it was only Xochi; she ran toward them anxiously.

"We have to get out of here *now*. The soldiers gave up on the decoy room and fell back to guard the maternity ward, so the mob's searching the whole building for this thing." She motioned to Samm with her chin. "It's only a matter of time before they make it up here."

"Give me one of their guns," said Samm.

"Do we trust him with a gun?" asked Jayden.

"We're a long way past that," said Xochi, handing over Haru's rifle. Kira unconsciously tensed as Samm took the weapon, but if Samm noticed he didn't show it. He checked the gun expertly, then squatted down and quickly gathered the remaining ammo from the discarded packs on the floor.

He stood calmly. "How do we get out?"

"There's a back service stairwell in the north wing," said Marcus. "It's locked on all floors, so no one will be in it, but we could shoot the lock."

"And so could the mob," said Samm and Jayden, almost in unison. They looked at each other, and Jayden raised an eyebrow.

"The elevator shaft, then," said Kira. "There's a ladder that runs down to the ground level—we used to play around in there when Marcus and I worked custodial during school. We can take that to the basement and look for the service door out the back."

Samm frowned. "That could be dangerous with a mob searching the building. The elevators will likely be running."

Marcus whistled. "Now I really want to visit Partialville. You guys have enough juice to run elevators?"

"Ah," said Samm, nodding. "Unused elevator shaft it is, then."

They ran quickly down the corridor, searching for the elevators, and found a maintenance door in a side hall. The elevator shaft was a long drop—they were on the fourth floor, plus the hospital had two basements and a sublevel filled with elevator machinery. Kira leaned over the edge, peering deep into the pit. It disappeared into blackness just a few floors below. She summoned her courage and started the climb down. Marcus followed quickly after, then the others one by one; Jayden came last, locking the door behind him. Kira's backpack seemed heavier than before, dangling over the seven-story drop, and her medkit swung wildly with each new rung of the ladder. She heard voices through the wall on the third floor, and someone on the first floor was banging loudly on the elevator doors. The entire shaft echoed with fierce, metallic clangs.

"Where do we get out?" whispered Xochi.

"At the bottom," said Kira, trying to speak softly. "If we go all the way to the basement, there's a loading dock they used to use to bring in supplies—it's all back corridors and rear exits, so we're not likely to see anybody."

"And if we do?" asked Samm.

Kira didn't have an answer for that.

The halls here were even darker than those above; there was

no power on this floor, and no windows to let in the moonlight. Distant shouts and crashes told her that the mob had already made it down here. Kira searched in her bag for a flashlight and clicked it on, shining the thin white beam against the walls. Marcus and the others joined her quietly, searching the shaft for an exit.

"You remember where that loading dock is?" whispered Marcus.

"Sort of."

"Awesome."

Kira found the door out of the shaft and turned off her light before opening it, wary of attracting unwanted attention. The hall was dark and empty, and she turned the light back on, covering it with her hand; it glowed soft and red, giving just enough light to see the walls. "This way." They crept cautiously down the hall. A string of footsteps echoed behind them, rubber shoes squeaking against the linoleum, and then they were gone. Kira held her breath and kept walking. They came to a crossroads and she uncovered her flashlight, risking the full beam: nothing to the left, but sudden faces on the right, eyes shining in the darkness.

Kira reared back, but Samm dove forward, one of the intruders falling limply to the floor before she even knew what was happening. The bright beam of the flashlight shook wildly as she staggered away, and the hallway became a staccato slide show of darkness and terror: Samm's foot in the side of a screaming man's knee, Samm's rifle butt buried in another man's face. Lances of light strobed across a Grid insignia on a flailing arm, droplets of blood hanging in the air, a man half fallen as he tried to flee. Jayden brought up his rifle at the same time Kira regained control of the flashlight, and by then it was over: Samm stood motionless, poised for a counterattack, and the floor around him was littered with fallen soldiers. Kira counted six men, all unconscious.

"Holy . . . ," muttered Jayden, staring at the scene. He pointed his rifle at Samm. "What did we let out?"

"None of them are dead," said Samm. "The blood is from the third one's nose."

Kira tried to gather her thoughts. "What just happened?"

Samm dropped to the floor to gather their guns, disassembling them with practiced efficiency. "I'm not used to humans, so I was relying too heavily on the link and they got too close. I think it worked out, though, since we didn't have to shoot anyone."

"Well, thanks for not shooting anyone, I guess," said Marcus. "My contribution was to somehow refrain from peeing myself. You can thank me later."

"We need to go," said Samm, standing up; he held the fallen soldiers' firing pins, and dropped them into his pocket. "There are at least two more groups down here, and maybe more that I can't hear."

"Okay," said Kira slowly, "just . . . don't do that to any civilians."

"Yes, ma'am."

Kira led the group to the left, then to the right, pausing here and there to read signs on the walls and to listen for more footsteps. There were at least two other groups in the basement, prowling and shouting and cackling in the darkness. She heard a crash of breaking glass. She pressed forward.

She found a wide tunnel capped by a high metal door, and broke into a jog. "This is it—there's a big ramp on the other side that leads up to the rear parking lot. We head north and we watch for patrols—the Defense Grid will be everywhere, but they'll be distracted. As long as we don't call any attention to ourselves, we should be able to slip through the gaps." She turned to Jayden. "Thanks for your help—we would never have gotten out of there without you."

"What do you mean, 'thanks'? I'm going with you."

Kira looked at him carefully, ghost white in the beam from the flashlight. "You sure?"

"You're going to need all the help you can get," he said. "Besides, I just freed a Partial and locked five pissed-off patriots in his cell. If I stay here, I'd be lucky to get arrested before they shot me."

Kira nodded and saw the others doing the same. She put her hand on the doorknob and opened it slowly. The sky was dark, but still brighter than the pitch-black tunnels of the basement. Kira jogged slowly up the ramp, listening to the sounds of a city in chaos: shouts and screams; the scuffing and pounding of running feet; the intermittent cracks of sharp, staccato gunfire. She reached the top and saw a deep orange glow through the eastern trees—a fire. A group of three or four rioters ran past her in the dark.

Xochi whispered over Kira's shoulder. "You think Isolde made it to the Senate building?"

"I hope so," said Kira. "It's going to be the only safe place in town for the next several hours."

"You think we did the right thing?" Xochi's voice was hesitant; uncertain. "You think we'll have a home to come back to?"

"I think Mkele's a lot better at his job than we give him credit for," said Kira. "It might look different by the time we get back, but it'll all still be here." She looked behind her, saw that the group was all together, and looked forward into the darkness and chaos. "Move out."

PART 3

FOUR HOURS LATER

CHAPTER TWENTY-NINE

It was nearly midnight before they got far enough from East Meadow to feel comfortable speaking freely; a wide forest beyond the highway, away from the press of ever-present houses.

"There's a cluster of farms to the north," said Jayden, hiking carefully through the underbrush, "near a pair of old country clubs. One of them has a harbor, and we're sure to find a boat there."

"On the North Shore?" asked Kira. "There's not a lot of settlements up there."

"It's tucked down into a bay," said Jayden, "and relatively close to the Grid base in Queens. Not that we should have any trouble with them," he added quickly, "but the closer to Queens we get, the shorter our distance across the sound."

"Do you know the name of the bay?" asked Samm.

Jayden shook his head. "Does it matter?"

"I want to get a sense of where we'll land on the other side."

Jayden looked at him oddly. "How well do you know our island?"

"We've sent scouts, of course," Samm answered, "but never very far inland, and obviously the maps we have from before are all uselessly out of date."

"'Never very far,'" said Xochi. "I told you no one was infiltrating the island."

"I said *we* haven't been," said Samm quickly. "That doesn't mean nobody is."

"Who else could there be?" asked Kira. "There's you and there's us, right? Everyone else is dead—you said so yourself. Unless—are there more humans alive on the mainland?" She felt her heart leap at the thought—it was stupid and impossible, but just for a second, before she could catch herself, she wished that it was true.

Samm shook his head. "There are no other humans."

"Then who?"

Samm glanced over his shoulder again. "We can talk about this later, right now we have to keep moving."

"No," said Jayden, standing in front of him and halting the group. "We just betrayed our own species to bust you out of jail, so you can cut it with the secretive crap and tell us what you know, *now*." He stared Samm firmly in the face, and Kira became acutely aware of the rifles each young man was holding at his side. Samm stared back, his dark eyes analyzing Jayden like an insect pinned to a wall. He sighed.

"There are no other humans," he said again. "But there are other groups of Partials."

"What?" cried Marcus. "I thought you couldn't make new ones?"

"Not new Partials," Samm clarified. "We're just . . . we're not exactly unified anymore."

Kira couldn't read his expression in the dark, but she could tell the admission made him profoundly uncomfortable.

"This would have been good to know before we broke our own island in half," said Marcus.

"But the link," said Kira. "You have a chemical communication system that normalizes emotion and behavior—how can anyone ever rebel from that?"

"They have a hive mind?" asked Jayden.

"It's not like that," said Samm, "it's like a . . . we don't think the same thoughts, we just share them."

"Let's walk while we talk," said Marcus. "We're still being chased, you know."

Samm nodded and started walking, and the others fell into step beside him. "The link is . . . I still don't know how to describe it to you. It's a sense. It's like describing sight to someone who was born blind."

"Is it a network device?" asked Jayden. "An implant? I thought we took everything when we bagged you in Manhattan."

"Not a device," said Samm, holding out his hands. "It's just a . . . link. We're all linked together." He nodded slightly at the houses around them. "If we were a team of Partials, walking through these ruins at night, we'd all know, intuitively, how all the others were feeling. If Kira saw something that made her wary, she'd register that chemically, and we'd all sense it, and within seconds we'd all be wary: Our adrenaline would increase, our fight-or-flight response would prime, and the entire group would be ready for something only one of us saw. If someone in our group got hurt, or captured, we'd all be able to sense what was wrong and follow that sensation to wherever that soldier was."

"Probably don't get lost very often, then," said Marcus. "If I could tell where the rest of you were, I wouldn't ever wander off."

"No," said Samm firmly, "you wouldn't."

"Sounds like it could also tell you friend from foe," said Jayden, nodding. "That would come in pretty handy."

"It doesn't work on humans," said Samm, "because you don't carry any data. But yes, it does help us identify other Partials who aren't in our unit, which makes telling my faction from the others pretty simple. It also makes it easy for other factions to find me, which might be a problem."

"But that's the part I don't get," said Kira. "The link tells you friend from foe, it tells you one unit from another—it stands to reason it would carry authority as well, right? You were created as an army, with generals and lieutenants and privates and all that: Does the link tie into that command structure?"

Samm's answer was stiff. "It does."

"Then how could you split into factions? It doesn't make sense."

Samm said nothing, stomping irately through the under-brush. After a long pause he said, "After the—" and then stopped again almost immediately, standing in the middle of the road. "This isn't easy to talk about."

"You have disagreements," said Kira simply. "Everyone has those, all the time—"

"We don't," said Samm. His voice was even, but Kira could sense an undercurrent of . . . frustration? "Is disobedience really so common among humans that you can't understand why we'd want to obey? We're an army; we obey our leaders. We follow our orders." He set off down the road again.

"Anyone who doesn't is a traitor."

"We're coming up on a bridge," said Xochi.

The group slowed, studying the terrain in the moonlight, then stopped to confer.

"A river?" asked Samm.

"Only in a really bad rainstorm," said Kira. "That bridge goes over the expressway; most of these roads pass over it."

"We want to follow it west," said Jayden, "but probably not directly. Too easy for anyone following to find us."

Kira wondered how long it would take Mkele to figure out what their plan was; as soon as he did, he'd be right on their tail. Sneaking off the island wouldn't be the first thing he'd suspect, which might buy them some time. She set down her bags and stretched her back, twisting from side to side to pop out the kinks. "Do we want to cut west now, or after we cross?"

"Definitely after," said Jayden. "It'll be the least cover we pass through until we reach the water, so let's get it out of the way."

Kira pulled on her pack and shouldered her shotgun. "No sense waiting around then."

They crept forward through the trees, eyes scanning the bridge ahead, ears alert for anything that stood out from the ambient sounds. This was beyond the reach of the old urban areas, just thick forests and old-growth trees. Lighter foliage on the right probably led to an old mansion, the grounds now overgrown with kudzu and hundreds of tiny saplings. The bridge was wide ahead, easily double the width of the back road they'd been following. They crossed another narrow road and ran through the trees to the thick cement barrier at the edge of the bridge.

"Nothing to do but do it," said Marcus. They gripped their packs and guns, took a deep breath, and ran.

The bridge was shorter than the waterways they'd crossed on their trip to Manhattan, but her fear and tension gave Kira the same feeling of dangerous exposure. The expressway stretched out for miles in either direction—anyone looking would be able to see them. *We just have to hope we made it here first.* They plunged back into the trees on the far side, panting from exertion, taking quick stock of the area.

"Clear," said Samm, lowering his rifle.

"I didn't see anyone out there," said Xochi.

"Doesn't mean they didn't see us," said Jayden. "We can't stop until we cross the sound."

The road continued just a short way before hitting a T, and here they turned west to follow the curve of the expressway.

Marcus jogged forward to walk by Kira's side. "How's your leg?"

"Hardly worth mentioning, all things considered." In truth it itched like mad, the aftereffects of the regen box, and it was all she could do not to roll up her pants and start gouging it with a stick. She couldn't help but worry whether she'd overdone the treatments and ruined the tissue, but she forced herself not to think about it; there was nothing she could do out here anyway. "How are you?"

"Out on a moonlight stroll with the girl of my dreams," he said, then added, "and Xochi, and Jayden, and an armed Partial. So pretty much my secret fantasy come true."

"Tell us more about the—" Xochi started, but then a horse whinnied, and the group stopped abruptly.

"Now I've made the horses jealous," said Marcus, but Jayden shushed him with a gesture.

"It came from over there," he whispered, pointing to the north side of the road. "One of the farms I told you about."

"So we're close?"

"Not nearly, but we're on the right track. We follow this road west until . . . until we smell seawater, I guess. If you'd told me we were coming out here tonight, I'd have brought a map."

"West, then," said Kira, "and quietly."

They followed the winding road until it reached a new stretch of buildings, though even here the road was still heavily forested, and the buildings removed from the road. They rose empty and ominous from the trees, too far from arable land to be useful as farms, yet too close to the North Shore to be useful as anything else. Even bandits stayed away from here.

They continued in silence. A mile or so later the road crossed a major street, and the old world had commemorated the occasion with a strip mall, now cracked and crumbling. They debated heading north, but Jayden insisted they stay west for another mile at least.

"If we go north too soon we could get trapped in the middle of the farms, away from the water," he said. "What was your plan, just go north until you ran out of land?"

"Pretty much," said Kira. "There are boats everywhere."

They heard a low rumble from behind them; an engine.

"They're closer than I thought," said Jayden, "and that engine sound means they're using the jeeps. They must really be serious." He paused, sucking in a breath. "They have maps and we don't, they have the advantage. I admit that. But I promise you:

If we go north now, we'll get trapped between the soldiers and the farms. Someone is bound to find us."

"This looks like it used to be a housing development behind the strip mall," said Marcus. "We can weave through there and avoid most of their patrols."

"Are you sure they're not tracking us?" asked Samm. "They should be going slower than this if they're stopping to search."

"They don't have to search for us, they know where we're going," said Xochi, echoing Kira's thoughts from earlier. "They're trying to reach the water first."

"Then we go north," said Samm. "We need to stay ahead of them."

"You're the boss," said Jayden, but she could tell he didn't like it. They stuck to the main road now, practically jogging to keep the right pace. The wide street was relatively clear, and they could move quickly even in the dim light. Xochi and Marcus were breathing heavily, struggling to keep up, and Kira was wincing with every other step, feeling lances of pain through her burned leg every time it hit the ground. Soon they heard more engines behind them, getting closer each minute, and the next time Kira turned, she saw lights behind them like glowing eyes.

"Get off the road," she grunted, and the group dove into the greenery, burying themselves behind tree trunks and kudzu. Three small jeeps roared past, engines snarling like wild animals. Kira counted four or five soldiers in each one.

"They're not even looking for us," said Kira.

Marcus leaned out to peer back down the road. "Nothing behind them. You think it's a coincidence?"

"They're trying to cut us off," said Samm. "The only good

news is that them being here means we're probably on the right path."

"Doesn't do us any good now," said Jayden. "We have to go west."

"We don't know what's west of here," said Kira. "For all we know we'd be running straight into the Grid army. These could just be outriders."

"It's smarter to stay on the path northward," Samm agreed. "At least this way we know what we're getting into."

"Okay," said Marcus, "but we stay in the trees. Now that they're ahead of us, they could be waiting somewhere and watching the road."

The trees slowed them down, and they moved almost by feel through the thick woods. Several times they had to cross side streets, and every time Kira held her breath, certain they would hear a cry of alarm, or worse yet a gunshot. Nothing came. When they reached a long stretch of ruins—old shops and offices—they crossed the main road to the far side, sticking to the cover of the woods.

Eventually even those woods thinned, and Kira looked out across a wide expanse of streets and cross streets and flat, empty parking lots. Squat buildings rose up like fat, sagging mushrooms, and the pavement was cracked and dotted with weeds and trees, but even so it was terrifyingly open.

"Another strip mall," she whispered. "We can't cross this."

"You want to go around?" asked Marcus, crouching down to catch his breath. "Or just turn west? We've been walking north for miles now, surely we're close to the bay Jayden was talking about."

"That or we've gone too far," said Jayden, "and we're about to run straight into the farms."

"I don't know how much longer I can go," said Xochi. Kira could barely see her face in the darkness, but her voice was starting to slur with exhaustion.

"We can't stop," Samm insisted.

"We don't have your endurance," said Jayden. "I've trained for this, but they could collapse at any moment. We've been running for what, nine miles? Ten?"

"Eight point four," said Samm. He didn't even seem tired.

"I'm fine," wheezed Marcus, but Kira thought he looked ready to fall over. Xochi could barely even talk.

"We go west," said Kira. "The sooner we get into a boat, the sooner we can rest."

Xochi nodded and lurched forward, pained but determined. Samm jogged forward to take the lead, and the rest fell into a slow, limping line behind him.

The side road slanted west around the strip mall, then slowly curved south again. Samm gave another signal and then dropped into the bushes, waiting in tense, rasping silence as a pair of horses clopped past them. They waited longer, giving the horses time to get far ahead, then crawled to their feet and pressed forward, shambling painfully on legs too tired to move any faster. Kira's burn was agonizing now, an unrelenting fire deep inside her leg. She curled her hands into tight fists, taking short breaths and trying not to think about it. *I just need to make it to that tree. Just that one tree, and then I'll be fine. Just a few more steps. Now that tree, just beyond. That's all I have to do. One tree at a time.*

"I can smell the ocean," said Samm, and soon Kira could

as well—salty and heavy, cool and bracing in the night air. They redoubled their efforts, panting loudly, no longer caring about stealth but simply trying not to stop. The trees gave way to another shopping center, and another beyond that. Marcus walked closer to Kira now, shaky as well but doing his best to support her. She clung to his arm and hobbled forward.

"This way," said Samm, turning north on the next road. Moonlight glistened on a silver expanse of water, smooth as black glass, and Kira looked eagerly for a boat. There was nothing.

"It's too shallow here," she panted. "We have to keep going."

"'Boats all over the North Shore,'" Jayden muttered. Kira didn't have the breath to respond.

Samm led them through a wide courtyard, wading through waist-high saplings with buildings on every side. They heard more hoofbeats on the road behind them, and they collapsed into the underbrush with abject exhaustion. This time the riders stopped, their horses slowly turning as they examined the area.

"Think it was them?" said one.

"That or a cat," said the other. They eased their horses closer, still looking around. Moonlight glinted faintly off the long metal lines of their rifles.

"Too much noise for a cat," said the first. "Give me the light."

Kira didn't dare to move or even breathe. The second rider pulled a flashlight from his saddlebag and handed it to the first, who clicked it on and shined it at the building on their left—a church of some kind, broken and leafy. Samm moved his rifle into position, sighting carefully at the first rider, but Kira shook her head: *We can't afford the noise.*

We can't kill our own people.

There was a soft knock on a far wall, and the riders looked up in unison. They shined the light on the building, but Kira couldn't see anything. They led their horses toward it, and Xochi whispered softly.

"I threw a rock. Let's get out of here before they come back."

They crept backward through the brush, inch by inch, always keeping their eyes on the riders. Marcus stood and hurled another rock, farther this time, and the riders paused, listened, and finally followed it. Kira stood as well, leaning on Samm as she rose, and the group backed around the corner of the ruined church.

"There's more over there," Samm whispered, pointing west toward the bay. He looked at Kira, his eyes lost in shadow. "Sooner or later we're going to have to shoot someone."

Kira closed her eyes, trying to clear her head. "I know this is dangerous, and I know it might come to guns—that's why we have them. But I don't want to shoot anybody if we can get away with it."

"We might not have a choice," said Samm.

The bushes rustled behind them, and Kira heard the stamp and snort of the horses. Samm raised his rifle, but Kira stopped him again.

They waited, holding their breath, praying for the soldiers to move on. An eternity later, they did.

"They're moving south," Samm whispered. "Don't waste it— move."

The group was practically running now, watching the ground in front of their feet because they couldn't see any farther. The road plunged into forest, and soon the dark shape of a massive house rose out of the trees beside them.

"There," said Kira. "A lot of these mansions have private docks."

They swerved to the left, through the grounds and around the house to the harbor. The yard behind was a maze of exotic plants and flowers that must have once been a giant garden. They followed a winding, overgrown path to the edge of the sound, black water lapping softly against the shore, but there was no dock and no boat. The ground was soft and marshy, and they slogged north to the next mansion, their heavy shoes becoming even heavier with mud. The next house had a narrow wooden walkway that turned into a dock, and their feet clumped loudly as they ran out over the water to a large white boat.

"Hallelujah," Kira whispered, but Samm shook his head.

"The water level's dropped, or the shore's been packed with sediment. It's sitting up on mud."

Kira looked again and saw that the boat was listing slightly to the side, pushed up out of the water and tilted over toward one edge. "What do we do?"

"The marsh goes on forever," said Samm, looking north. "It's this or nothing."

"Then we push it out," said Jayden. He stowed his rifle over his shoulder and jumped into the water with a splash. It reached almost to his waist. He put a hand on the boat and rocked it; it didn't move easily, but it moved. "Everybody get in here."

Kira glanced over her shoulder nervously before jumping into the sound, gasping in shock at the cold water. The others followed, bracing their shoulders against the hull and heaving in unison. It tilted but didn't move; Kira slipped in the mud, barely catching herself before falling face-first in the icy water.

"Again," said Samm, setting himself firmly against the side. Everyone got into position. "One, two, three, push." They strained against the slick side of the boat, pushing with all their strength. It moved a few inches. "Again," said Samm. "One, two, three, push." They shoved against the boat with everything they had, moving it another few inches—farther this time, but not far enough. "Again," said Samm. "One, two—"

A light clicked on, blinding them—a bright white beam from a flashlight on the dock, shining against the white boat and lighting up the entire group. They froze, blinking, too shocked to move. The holder of the flashlight said nothing, simply staring, twenty yards away.

I have my gun, thought Kira, feeling its weight on her back. *I can pull it around in seconds. But will it do any good? We can't push this out before backup comes looking—we can't get away even if we fight back.*

Nobody moved.

The light clicked off.

"Clear!" the silhouette shouted. It was a girl's voice. *Yoon.* "There's nothing here. I checked out the sound; just an old boat shifting in the waves." The silhouette waited, watching, then turned and walked away. Kira realized she'd been holding her breath, and let it out softly.

"Was that the girl who went to Manhattan with you?" asked Marcus. "I think we owe her a cookie."

"I think we owe her a whole damn bakery," said Xochi. "If I wasn't hip deep in mud, I would kiss her on the mouth."

"Shut up," said Jayden. "They heard us before, they'll hear us again." He braced himself against the boat one more time and mouthed, *One, two, three.* They pushed, moving the boat nearly a foot this time. They pushed again, then again, over and over, dragging the boat nearly twenty feet through the shallow marsh. Forty feet. Eighty feet. They could see more lights on the shore, more searchers. They pushed the boat again, forcing it through the mud, praying the soldiers wouldn't hear them.

The water got deeper as the harbor opened up, and soon the boat was floating freely, they pushed it even farther, toward water deep enough to take their added weight. Samm helped them into the boat, then climbed in himself. Marcus and Jayden found oars, and they pushed north toward open water.

" "We're safe," Kira sighed. Xochi was already asleep.

"Safe from your people," said Samm, looking north toward the mainland. "Now we have to face mine."

CHAPTER THIRTY

"**W**e're going to land near Mamaroneck," said Samm. He squinted at the sky, then back at the distant shore. "I think."

The bay they had left was long and thin, and they didn't dare to try the boat's motor until the shores on either side fell away and the dark blue sound opened up around them. It worked fitfully, but it worked, and they headed north as straight as they could until the sky began to lighten and the featureless horizon became tinged with the green and brown of the mainland. They angled toward it, curving west. Kira hoped the motor would last until they got there; she was far too tired to row.

"Mamaroneck?" asked Jayden. "That might actually be a sillier name than Asharoken."

"Mamaroneck is a good spot," said Samm. "It's a little farther south than I'd like to be, but nobody's stationed there. We should be able to land without being seen."

"How important is it that we aren't seen?" asked Marcus.

"These different factions—are we talking about differing movie opinions or full-scale holy war opinions?"

"If they see us, they'll attack us," said Samm. "I'll be imprisoned and used for leverage in one dispute or another, and I don't know what they'll do to you."

Kira looked up at the stars. "I take it not all the factions are as friendly as yours."

"Mine isn't especially friendly either," he said quickly. "Just because they sent a peace proposal doesn't mean they'll open their arms to any human that walks in. Our disagreements with the other factions are . . . heated, and that's made us cautious, and over time that's made us suspicious. We still have to approach carefully."

"How can we tell the factions apart?" asked Xochi. "Do you have different uniforms, or . . . I don't know, different-colored hats?"

"I don't know if you can without the link," said Samm. "My faction is called D Company, and most of us still wear that insignia, but honestly by the time you're that close it's probably too late. We're talking about a war zone."

The motor cut out again, sputtering to a stop. Jayden stood up, yanking on the pull cord a few useless times, then hit it with a wrench and yanked again. The motor came back on with a sound even feebler than before.

"Old gas," said Jayden, throwing the wrench back into the bottom of the boat. "It's either killing the engine or running out. Either way we're going to end up rowing the last mile or two."

"Who are we going to run into?" asked Kira, looking at Samm. "How much of a war zone are we talking about?"

"The main group of rebels is north," said Samm, "in a place called White Plains, and beyond that in Indian Point. They're the ones who run the reactor."

"Whoa," said Xochi, "a nuclear reactor?"

"Of course," said Samm. "How else would we get our energy?"

"Solar panels," said Xochi simply. "That's what we use."

"And it's probably sufficient for your needs," said Samm. "The nuclear plant in Indian Point used to power hundreds of millions of homes before the war—now that there's not much more than a million of us left, it generates more than enough for anything we could ever need. The rebels maintain it. D Company found a way to tap into it a few years ago, and they still haven't noticed."

"But nuclear power is dangerous," said Xochi. "What if something happens? What if it leaks or melts down or whatever?"

"A lot of them did," said Samm. "When RM hit and the humans started dying—when you really started to disappear, and we knew there was nothing we could do to stop it—we found as many nuclear plants as we could and then shut them down safely. There's another one in Connecticut, just sixty miles away from you guys across the sound." He pointed to the northeast. "If that had gone into meltdown, you'd probably all be dead."

"Right," said Jayden derisively. "The noble Partials trying to save mankind."

Samm nodded. "Haven't you ever wondered why the world isn't more messed up than it is? Why the cities aren't burning, why the air isn't black with nuclear fallout? You died too quickly—some of you had time to shut off the power plants and the factories before you disappeared, but not everyone, and all it takes is one unattended reactor to cause a lethal meltdown. Even when we realized what was happening, we couldn't shut them all down; we lost one in New Jersey, and another in Philadelphia, and more and more as you move west across the continent. That's why we tend to stay east of the Hudson. Other parts of the world had even more reactors than we did, but without an army of Partials to step in and stop them, we think a lot more of them may have gone critical. Maybe as many as half."

Nobody spoke. The coughing buzz of the motor filled the boat. *We always wondered if there were more survivors,* thought Kira. *The RM immunity would have left the same percentage alive in other countries that it left in ours.*

Is it really possible that everyone else is dead?

"The question about what to do with you is what eventually split us apart," Samm continued softly. "Some wanted to just finish you off, but most of us, like I said, wanted to save you. Even then, we couldn't agree on the best way to do it. The arguments grew . . . heated. To say the least. And then the first wave of our leaders started dying, and it all fell apart. D Company is practically all that's left of the truly obedient Partials—the only ones with a direct link to the Trust."

"And what's the Trust?" asked Kira.

"The senior command," said Samm, "the generals of the Partial army, and probably from advanced genetic templates, because none of them have died. Well—none of them have died from an inherent expiration date. There were eight of them, men and women, but I think the rebels may have killed two, or at least captured them." His voice changed as he said this, and his expression grew dark. "It was the Trust that told D Company where to make our base, and when to approach the humans."

"I'm getting the impression that D Company is relatively small," said Marcus. "That's wonderful—we finally form an alliance, and it's with a persecuted splinter group just as messed up as we are. This'll make the rest of the Partials even more determined to kill us."

The engine died again, and this time no amount of yanking and beating and swearing could get it running again. Samm and Marcus took the first turn at the oars, pulling hard toward the shore, and soon the green line became dotted with white: a wide harbor filled with boats. They reached the first line in just half an hour: large yachts anchored far from shore, covered stem to stern with seagull droppings. Kira wrinkled her nose in disgust.

"I was hoping to trade up for a new boat, but these are unusable."

"They're too big anyway," said Samm, stowing his oars as their boat bumped gently against the stained hull of another. "We can't row them, and I assume none of us knows how to sail." They shook their heads. "At the very least we can stop and look for supplies."

"Okay," said Kira, "but not this one. I don't want us getting . . . bird flu, or bird diarrhea, or whatever that stuff will give you."

Samm nodded.

They rowed to the next boat, then the next, working their way farther into the harbor until finally finding a yacht that looked clean enough to board—still filthy, but not as bad, and their options were running out. They maneuvered around to the back, where the name *Show Me the Money III* was emblazoned across it in faded letters. Marcus gripped the stern while Samm climbed aboard.

"The rest of you wait here," said Samm. He climbed over and descended into the depths of the yacht, and Marcus leaned close to Kira.

"What do you think?" he whispered. "Do you still trust him?"

"He hasn't done anything to change my mind," said Kira.

"Not directly, no," said Marcus, "but that story was . . . I don't know. It's a lot to take in."

"At least it's plausible," said Jayden. "We've always wondered why the Partials turned around and left eleven years ago, and why they've never attacked us since. If they're too busy fighting one another to bother with us, that makes a little more sense."

"I'm still suspicious," said Marcus. "Something about this place doesn't feel right."

Samm emerged with an armload of objects from the yacht. "Bad news," he said. "According to the boat's harbor papers, we're in Echo Bay, not Mamaroneck, which means we've gone a lot farther west than I thought. There's a map here that should help us get back on track." He handed the items down to Kira, who took them carefully into their boat: a map, a pair of binoculars, a deck of cards, and a pile of clothes and blankets. "I haven't had a change of clothes since you captured me," said Samm, stripping off his rumpled uniform. "Plus this yacht is filthy." Kira couldn't help but stare at his chest and arms, more chiseled than she would have expected after two weeks of being tied to a chair. She looked away after a second, feeling foolish, while Samm stripped down to his underwear and dove into the water. Marcus glanced at Kira, giving her his *You can't be serious*

look, but Xochi watched the athletic Partial surface with obvious appreciation. He climbed back into their boat, dried himself
as best he could with a blanket, and slipped into a new set of
clothes.

Kira unfolded the map, searching the sound for Echo Bay.
"You're right," she said. "This is a lot farther west than I thought.
Where is D Company?"

Samm looked over her shoulder, pointing at a spot along the
coast. "Greenwich; like you, we built our city around a hospital.
Looks like it's about twelve, thirteen miles away."

"That's not bad," said Jayden.

"It's not," said Samm, "but that route goes through rebel territory, here." He pointed at a spot about halfway along. "We
could search for another boat and try to skirt the coast, but I
don't recommend it. Our engine barely made it here, and I think
there's a storm coming."

"I don't exactly want to travel through enemy territory,
though," said Kira. "We won't be able to hide, thanks to your
link—as soon as they get close, they'll know exactly where you
are."

"Also true." Samm nodded.

"We've still got gas," said Jayden, checking the engine. "That
means the problem's with the motor itself."

"Then let's find a new boat," said Kira. "The longer we can
go before walking, the better. Our nine-mile run last night
almost killed us."

They rowed through the harbor, searching for a boat they
could handle, and finally found one docked on the side of a
much larger yacht—a lifeboat, maybe, or a backup designed for

emergencies. Samm climbed aboard, peeled off the cracking canvas cover, and fired up the motor. It started on the fourth try and purred much more evenly than their first boat. He and Marcus and Jayden managed to unhook it from the yacht and dump it into the water, and then the five travelers transferred their gear from one boat to the next. It was much smaller—a rowboat with a motor, not the fancy motorboat they'd been riding in thus far—but it held them, and the engine worked, and Marcus steered them back out of the harbor and north toward D Company.

"Farther out from the shore," said Samm. Marcus steered away from land, deeper into the sound, and Samm watched the shore with nervous eyes. "Farther."

"Too much farther and we can't see the shore at all anymore," said Marcus. "We'll get lost again."

"I can see the shore just fine," said Samm. "Which means anyone on the shore can see us. Go farther."

Marcus frowned and glanced at Kira, but steered farther out into the water. The mainland was a distant line on the horizon now, barely even visible. Samm watched it intently, giving Marcus minor course corrections when necessary. Kira and Xochi and Jayden lay in the bow, draped uncomfortably over the fiberglass benches, trying to get some sleep.

It was Marcus who first spotted the storm.

"How long have we been out here?" he asked, his hand still guiding the rudder. "Is the sky supposed to be that dark this early in the morning?"

"Wind's picked up as well," said Samm. "It's cooler than it was a few minutes ago."

"I've seen a few of these sound storms from the shore," said Jayden, sitting up. He looked worried. "They get pretty heavy out here, or at least it always looks that way."

"I'll turn toward shore," said Marcus, but Samm stopped him.

"We're passing rebel territory right now," he said, looking at the map and then peering back out to the north. "It's not safe."

"Have you seen the sky?" asked Marcus, pointing to the thick gray clouds. "That's not exactly safe either."

"This boat barely fits us," said Kira. The water was choppy now, bucking the boat gently as they plowed forward through the waves. "If it gets too rough out here, we'll flip right over."

"We can't go in," Samm insisted. "It's too dangerous."

"Then everybody hold on," said Marcus. "This is about to get a lot more exciting than we'd planned for."

The storm raced toward them, and they to it; Kira felt fat drops of rain on her face, mingling with the salty spray of the sea. They pulled out their blankets and cowered under them for shelter, but the rain seemed to be coming almost horizontally with the wind. The sky grew dark above them, an eerie half-light, and the small boat started rolling with the waves.

"I'm going closer to shore," said Marcus, turning the rudder before Samm could protest. "It's impossible to see in this storm anyway—no one's going to spot us."

The storm grew worse, the drops giving way to thin, slashing knives of rain. Kira gripped the side of the boat tightly, holding on to Xochi with her other hand, certain that each new wave would be the one to dump them over the side. She was soaked to the bone. It was nearly as dark now as it had been last night.

"Get us closer to shore," she shouted to Marcus, grabbing Xochi's arm even tighter as another wave lurched the ship up and sideways.

"I'm going straight toward it already," shouted Marcus. "Or at least I was last time I could see it. I'm just afraid the ocean's trying to turn us around."

"We're too heavy," shouted Jayden. "We have to lighten the load."

Kira tossed her backpack over the side, keeping her guns and strapping her medkit tight around her shoulders. Xochi dug through her bag and Marcus's, salvaging what ammunition she could, then threw the rest over after Kira's. The boat rocked violently until it seemed to Kira that they were being tossed around almost at random. She had no idea what direction they were pointing, or where they were going, when suddenly a giant rock appeared through the rain ahead of them. Marcus swore and turned to the side, trying to miss it, but another wave of rain slashed down and covered it again, plunging them back into the same gray chaos as before. She thought she saw a tree to her left—a tree, in the middle of the ocean—but it disappeared so quickly she couldn't be sure. *We must be near the shore,* Kira thought, *it's the only explan*— and then a giant white shape loomed out of the water beside them, slamming into them with a boom that nearly tipped the boat. It was another yacht, straining against its anchor before being pulled back under the waves. A surge of water picked them up, nearly throwing them through the air, and Kira heard herself screaming, felt herself choking on rain and seawater splashing up from over the side. Water sloshed madly in the bottom of the boat, but they were still upright.

"Hold on!" she shouted, useless and obvious, but she felt powerless and had to say something. The wind roared in her ears and blew mad shapes through the rain around them. Another yacht reared up, missing them by half an arm's length, and then they were once again lost in the roiling limbo of the open sea.

Marcus was shouting, but she couldn't hear the words. He pointed, and she turned to look; the rain was so fierce she could barely see, squinting her eyes almost shut to keep out the rock-hard pellets of rain. She saw it too late, but doubted there would be anything she could have done anyway—a massive black wave, as high as building, crashing toward them from the side. She had just enough presence of mind to take a breath and hold it, and then the wave struck and the world went away.

Space became meaningless—there was no up or down, no left or right, just force and pressure and acceleration, ripping her through a cold, seething nothingness. She lost her grip on Xochi's arm, then found it again, clinging desperately to the only solid thing in the universe. The wave carried her farther, dragging her through the formless void until she thought her lungs would burst, and suddenly she was in the air, tumbling. She took a breath just in time to hit a wall of water and have it knocked out of her again. She held fiercely to the arm, never letting go, irrationally certain that it was the only thing keeping her alive. The second wave passed and she bobbed up from the water, sucking in a long, desperate breath half mixed with seawater. She choked and breathed again. Another wave crashed down, and she was gone.

❧ ❧ ❧

Rocks. Heat. Kira woke with a start, trying to get her bearings, disoriented by the sudden change from angry ocean to solid ground. She coughed, spitting up slick, salty water.

"You're alive," said a voice. Samm. She looked around, finding herself in some kind of marsh next to a low rock wall. Samm knelt against it, looking out with the binoculars. Beyond the wall, the sea lay still and placid.

"We're on land," said Kira, still trying to process the situation. "What happened?" She looked around in sudden panic. "Where are the others?"

"Over there," said Samm, pointing across the water. Kira crawled toward him, her legs too weak to stand, and clambered up to lean against the wall. "The big building, just to the right," he said. He handed her the binoculars. "I wasn't sure it was them at first, but it is."

Kira searched for the big building he'd pointed to, then looked to the right, probing slowly across the landscape. She saw movement and snapped onto it, looking carefully: three people. She couldn't see them clearly, but she was fairly certain she recognized their clothes.

"We're all alive, then," she said, staring at the one she thought was Marcus. "I grabbed someone underwater. I thought it was Xochi."

"It was me," said Samm simply, still scanning the horizon.

Kira crouched next to him. "What is that, an island?"

"The other side of the bay," said Samm. "It looks like the storm dropped us right where we needed to go—though obviously in two separate groups. I guess we can't complain too much."

"This is Greenwich?"

"Close enough," said Samm. "If I've got our location right, your friends are actually closer than we are."

"We need to signal them," said Kira. "They keep looking out to sea—they don't know we're over here."

"Too dangerous," said Samm. "Even if you could shout that far, any Partials in the area would hear you first and get to us first as well."

"We can't just let them wonder."

"If they're smart, they'll head inland, looking for anything that can tell them where they are. We can go up around the bay and find them."

"We can find another boat and row over there—"

"No we can't," said Samm firmly. "This is close to Green-wich, but it's south, and that means rebel territory. They watch these waters, looking for D Company—the only reason they didn't see us come in was the storm concealing us. If we row out across the bay, we'll be spotted for sure."

"Then won't they be spotted as well?"

"Not if they wise up and get out of the open," said Samm. "They're actually safer here than we are—I'll automatically link to any other Partials in range, but you humans are effectively invisible. No one expects to find humans on the mainland, so we don't look for them; we rely too heavily on the link. If those three stay smart, they can move through the entire area without being caught."

"Great for them," said Kira, still watching her friends through the binoculars. "How are we going to get past the rebels?"

Samm held up a waterlogged blanket, one of the ones they'd found in the old yacht, and started ripping it into strips. "The link data is transmitted primarily through our breath. If I cover

my mouth and nose tight enough, I should be able to mask my presence. A little." He frowned.

"Are you going to be able to breathe?"

"That's why this isn't a perfect solution," he said. "A gas mask isn't perfect, but it's much better. I don't know how much the rebels know about the mission we launched in Manhattan, but it's conceivable that things have escalated, and if so, that's what their scouts will be wearing. They're the ones we'll have to be careful of, because I won't know they're coming until it's too late." He wrapped the wet black cloth around his face, covering his mouth and nose and tying the ripped blanket tightly behind his head. He took a deep breath, trying it out, then tied another strip over the first to give it more grip.

"This should work for a while." His words were muffled, only barely discernible. Kira nodded and followed him back through the grounds of an old manor house, wishing she'd managed to keep hold of her guns in the shipwreck. She didn't like the prospect of meeting other Partials without them.

The manor house turned out to be on a small, rounded promontory, connected back to land by a series of narrow asphalt lanes. They crossed each one at a run, crouching low and then ducking behind the nearest spray of foliage, looking for signs that they'd been spotted. If there were other Partials watching, they kept themselves hidden. Kira looked back across the harbor whenever she could, hoping to catch a glimpse of her lost friends, but they were hidden as well. She doubled her pace, desperate to round the harbor and find them before they wandered too far away.

Samm led her through a small shipyard, full of dry, cracking boats and rusted tracks leading down into the water. Beyond that was an old park, overgrown with trees and kudzu, yet originally big enough, Kira estimated, to have made for a series of good-size cornfields. It surprised her that the Partials hadn't planted it, but she supposed a war zone wasn't the best place, and this was, as she understood it, the outskirts of the Partial civilization. Perhaps all their farms were farther north? Or did they get food by some other means she couldn't guess at? It bothered her, suddenly, how little she really knew about the Partials: Here she was, in unknown territory, trusting the enemy she'd been raised to hate. The reason she was an orphan. The reason she'd learned to fire a gun at eight years old.

Do I really know what I'm doing?

Samm led her away from the water's edge, into the wooded park where they'd be harder to see. He moved quickly but carefully, his eyes darting back and forth, examining not only their flanks but the ground and the trees above them. Kira fell into rhythm beside him, watching for ambush, avoiding fallen branches. They passed a funeral home, and she studied it solemnly. Death seemed to hover in the air.

Beyond the trees they came to a highway, flanked on the far side by another row of thick trees. It cut through the forest like a hallway, and Samm peered down it in both directions—flat to the west, and climbing a small hill to the east. "We'll make better time on this than next to it," he said. "It doesn't take us through the town, just around the edge, so there might not be anybody watching."

"Will it take us to Marcus and the others?"

"They'll have to cross it, too." Samm nodded. He pointed toward a curve in the road, far to the east. "That's the end of the peninsula, if I'm remembering correctly. If they haven't already crossed, we can catch them there."

They ran quickly, making up for lost time; the highway was raised, with extra layers of asphalt between it and the dirt below, and nothing had managed to grow through. No one crossed their path, ahead or behind them. Soon the road began to rise, and Kira realized with shock that the rest of the country wasn't rising with it—it wasn't a hill, just an elevated road. Smaller roads began passing underneath it.

"Stop," she said. "We may have already missed them."

"I was thinking the same thing."

"We need to find them."

"We're almost to the base now," said Samm, shaking his head. "We should go straight there and then send out a search party—they'll find your friends better than we can."

"Unless someone else finds them first," said Kira. She looked out from the elevated road, trying to see through the gaps in the trees below. "We can't just leave them out here for the rebels to find."

"I don't think they will," said Samm, tapping his face mask. *The link.*

"Then you go," said Kira, "and I'll look for Marcus. Your search-and-rescue team can find me just as easily as they can find them."

"We can't split up again," Samm insisted. His voice was low, barely audible through his makeshift mask. He seemed jumpy for the first time, and Kira felt herself grow nervous at the sight of it.

"What's wrong?"

She heard the roar of an engine, a distant echo through the trees, and she went pale.

"You use cars, too?"

"Electric, mostly, but yes. There's an oil refinery farther north."

Kira glanced up and down the highway, trying to pinpoint the sound. "Behind us?"

"I think so." He started jogging forward. "We have to run."

"We don't have time," said Kira, peering over the edge of the sidewall. It was at least twenty feet down, but the trees were crowded close, and she thought she could reach one. "We need to climb down."

"We can't go down," said Samm fiercely, rushing back to grab her arm. "We have to move forward."

"The engines are getting closer, we don't have time to—"

"There are rebels down there," he whispered urgently.

Kira dropped to her knees, crouching behind the wall. "You're linking with them?"

"I can't help it."

Which means they know we're here. Kira stared at him, studying his eyes. *We don't have weapons. We can't fight. The enemy already knows we're here.*

Do they know my friends are here as well?

"How close?" Kira whispered.

Samm grimaced. "It's not that precise when it's muffled like this, but I can tell they're close. Seventy, eighty yards."

"That's pretty precise," said Kira. "You think they heard us talking?"

Sam shook his head. "They're on alert, but it might not be for us. We have no way of knowing until they're closer, and then if we're wrong, it's too late."

Kira punched the concrete with the side of her hand, swearing under her breath. *I'm not going to let them get captured.* She took a deep breath, shaking her head at her own stupidity, and stood up. "We're going down."

"We can't go down."

She jogged to the spot with the closest tree, looked at the underbrush two stories below, and clambered onto the sidewall. Samm pulled her back, and she shook him off. "I'm not leaving my friends," she said firmly. "You can either come with me or go for help." She climbed back up, balancing carefully, and tried to gauge the distance. *Seven feet. Maybe ten. That's long for a standing jump, but I'll get extra distance as I fall.*

Which is not very encouraging.

"Don't do it, Kira."

She jumped.

She kept her hands wide and wrapped her arms around the biggest branch she could, catching it with her elbows and swinging wildly beneath it. The tree caught her as she caught it, and the rough branches dug sharply into her skin and clothes. The tree shook with a second shudder, and she saw that Samm had followed her. She smiled. "Thanks."

"You're crazy," he muttered.

"That's what everyone keeps saying."

They climbed down quickly, hearing the roar of the engine grow louder and louder. The sound split as it neared, becoming two engines, then three, then four. Kira dropped the last few feet to the ground and raced into the underpass, crouching in the shadow of a thick concrete pillar. Samm threw himself down beside her, and they listened as the cars rumbled overhead, streaking away to the east and slowly fading into the distance.

Kira whistled. "That was close."

"Not as close as it's going to be," said Samm. His voice was stiff and strained.

"Are you hurt?"

"No," he grunted, "just . . . what's your plan?"

"They can't sense me coming, right? So I'm going to jump one from behind and take his gun."

"They can't sense you on the link, Kira, but that doesn't mean you're invisible."

"How much can they sense from you?" she asked. "Thoughts? Motive?"

"Not exactly," he said, "more like health, proximity, emotional state. Things like that. I won't be able to glean anything from them that would help you grab one."

"I don't want you to read their minds," said Kira, looking out at the wide, tangled lawn. "I want you to be bait."

"Whoa." He held up his hand. "Are you serious?"

"It's okay," she said. "I'll stop them before they hurt you." She grinned. "You said they rely too much on the link, right? So if the link tells them there's a Partial hiding around one corner, they won't even bother to look around the other."

He shook his head. Kira could see that his breathing was accelerated; his face twitched and scowled. "As soon as you jump one, the link will tell the others he's in trouble."

"Then we hit fast and be gone before they show up." She pulled him farther behind the pillar. "I know it's dangerous, but my friends are in the same danger—worse, even, because they don't have you." Her voice softened. "We can do this."

"That's great," said Samm, "but you're talking about finding a scout trained and equipped to avoid being found. It's not going to happen."

"Keep your voice down," Kira whispered. "It already has." She gestured around the edge of the pillar, and Samm carefully peeked out. He ducked back and pressed his mouth to her ear.

"Forty yards out."

"He probably heard us fall out of the tree," Kira whispered. "I don't think he's seen us yet—he's not trying to hide, just checking something out." She pointed to the far side of the underpass. "You crawl over there. He'll see you and walk right past me." Samm seemed nearly rigid with tension, like he was clenching every muscle in his body; he'd been like that for a while. *The other Partial's too close,* she thought. *I don't have time to see if he's injured.* "Are you sure you're all right?"

"Fine," he grunted. He turned and crawled through the underbrush, working his way to the far pillar, then across to the next in line. Kira nodded, impressed at the tactic. *This way the rebel scout won't pass as close to my pillar,* she thought, *so he'll be less likely to look behind it.* Samm moved stiffly, almost painfully, and she wondered again if he'd hurt himself in the jump to the tree. *But no—he was already acting strange on the road above. What's going on?*

"Hold it," said a voice, and Kira was shocked to hear that it was female. She froze in place, hoping her plan had worked and the Partial wouldn't notice her. Samm stopped as well, pausing on his hands and knees in the thin weeds below the bridge. He didn't speak. Kira heard footsteps behind her, to the side, then held her breath as the Partial walked past in a straight line toward Samm. Seen up close she was obviously female: thin in the waist, round in the hips and chest, a bun of jet-black hair done up behind the strap of her gas mask. Her eyes had a marked epicanthic fold, like she was Chinese, which Kira couldn't puzzle out—the Chinese were the enemy in the Isolation War. Why make a Partial the other soldiers might mistake for an enemy? She held a menacing rifle trained on Samm's back, the muzzle tipped with the fat black cylinder of a suppressor. Kira recognized it as a sniper rifle.

The girl stopped just a few yards away, maybe two good strides if Kira sprinted—probably not enough time for the girl to react. Kira nodded, gearing herself up for the attack. She'd learned a little hand-to-hand in school, though not much; the Defense Grid figured if a Partial got that close you were screwed anyway, since they were so much stronger. Kira hoped it wasn't true, and rose to the balls of her feet.

"Don't say anything," said Samm. His voice was strained, like he was speaking through teeth clenched as tight as he could make them. "Don't speak." He put his hand to his face, covering his mouth and nose. Kira stood, placing her feet carefully, coiling her muscles for a charging tackle.

Small of the back, she told herself. *Hit low and hard. Pin her arms. Strike at the base of the skull to knock her—*

"Samm," said the girl, and Kira froze.

She knows his name? Is that part of the link?

Or is she part of his company?

"Don't speak," Samm growled, but already Kira's thoughts were flying, connections snapping together in her mind. If this girl knew Samm, that meant they were part of the same faction, which meant the nearby soldiers were Samm's own comrades. Samm's own officers. He'd said the link was also used to enforce the chain of command: They could sense Samm was here, and they were ordering him to respond. That's why he was moving so stiffly—it was taking every ounce of his strength to resist them.

But why is he hiding from his own people?

"Talk to me, Samm." The woman stepped forward, keeping the rifle aimed squarely at his back. "We thought you'd been captured."

Samm lowered his head, nearly collapsing into the dirt. *He won't hold on much longer,* Kira thought. *Go!* She pelted forward, arms spread wide, shoulder down to nail the Partial in the small of the back.

And then the Partial whirled around.

Kira was already inside the range where the long rifle would be useless as a gun. Instead the Partial brought it down like a club, slamming the heavy stock into the side of Kira's face just as Kira wrapped her arms around the girl's waist and knocked her solidly to the ground. Both girls gasped in pain at the impact, but Kira's head was still ringing from the rifle blow, and the other girl recovered first. She dropped her gun and grappled Kira with cold efficiency, twisting one arm behind her back and kneeing her painfully in the stomach. Kira fought wildly, clawing at the Partial's face and neck and very nearly escaping from her grip, twisting just enough to keep it from becoming a true submission hold. Suddenly Kira felt the cold metal edge of a knife on her throat, and the girl spoke calmly in her ear.

"Stop moving now."

Kira froze; there was nothing she could do. If she'd had just two more seconds to work with, maybe, but somehow the Partial had known that Kira was there.

"Let go of her, Heron, she's with me."

"She doesn't link."

"She's human."

Heron's voice was surprised, but she didn't loosen her grip. "You captured one? The mission was a success? Where's the rest of your team?"

You captured one? thought Kira. She loosened the girl's grip on her throat and shouted loudly at both of them. "What the hell is going on?"

"They're dead," said Samm, stepping closer to Heron, "but it's not what you think. You can let her go—she's not a threat. She's on our side."

Kira couldn't believe what she was hearing. "Were you planning this all along?" she asked. "Was this whole thing just a trick to get me back here?"

"It's more complicated than that," said Samm quickly. He was in front of her now, the mask ripped off. "Kuso, Heron, let her go, she came willingly!"

"So there was no peace proposal?" Kira demanded. She felt herself grow hot, felt her eyes begin to tear, felt a rush of shame and anger that she had ever trusted this thing. "No truce?"

Heron smiled. "A truce? I'm impressed, Samm; you may have a future in espionage."

Kira saw a flash in the corner of her eye, the glint of light on a hypodermic needle. She screamed and felt it prick into her neck. The effect was almost instant: Her eyes grew heavy, her mind seemed to warp and bend. The world grew dark and thick, and Kira had time for one last thought before she fell unconscious.

I'm going to die.

CHAPTER THIRTY-ONE

*B*eep. *Psssssssh.*
  Beep. Psssssssh.

Kira was heavy—before she perceived anything else, she could feel her own weight, her body too weak for her muscles to move. She was lying down.

Beep. Psssssssh.

There was a noise, rhythmic and soft, somewhere near her head. Near? Yes, she was sure of it. Wherever she was, the noise was nearby. She tried to roll her head, but her neck wouldn't turn; tried to open her eyes, but her lids were too leaden to move.

Beep. Psssssssh.

There was another noise, a white-noise buzz in the background of her perception. She focused on it, tried to parse it, to understand it. Voices. A low murmur.

"... the subject ..."

"... burn mark ..."

"... tests positive ..."

They were talking about her. Where was she?

Beep. Pssssssssh.

She was in a hospital. She remembered being under the bridge, Samm betraying her, the girl, Heron, injecting her with something. Was she being healed? Or studied?

". . . all normal except . . ."

". . . ready to proceed . . ."

". . . preparing first incision . . ."

Kira moved her hand, a herculean effort, dragging ten tons of flesh and bone across three inches of table. The voices stopped. Her hand hit a barrier, a leather restraint; she could feel one on her other hand as well. She was tied down.

"She moved. Didn't you sedate her?"

Kira opened one eye, then squinted it shut again at the brutal shock of bright lights. She heard a rustle and a sharp metal crash.

"Get those out of her face, she's waking up." Samm's voice. She opened her mouth, suddenly aware of a plastic tube stretching past her tongue and down her throat. She gagged, coughing, trying not to retch, and the tube slid out like a long, slick snake. She coughed again, swallowed, cracked one eye the tiniest fraction.

Samm was standing over her.

"You," she coughed, "bloody bastard."

"We have to begin," said a voice.

"Stop," said Samm. "She's awake!"

"Then we sedate her again. With a bigger dose this time."

"You bloody"—she coughed again—"bastard."

She could see better now, her eyes adjusting to the light. She was surrounded by women in hospital robes and surgical masks.

She was in some kind of operating room, but it wasn't like any operating room she'd ever seen. Metal arms hung from the ceiling like the limbs of a giant insect, scalpels and syringes and a dozen other instruments poised mere inches from Kira's face. The walls were glowing with a muted, multicolored light—computer screens, the walls were computer screens, alive with graphs and charts and scrolling numbers. She saw her heartbeat, the thin line spiking in perfect unison with the pounding in her chest; she saw her temperature, her blood oxygen level, her height and weight in precise thousandths of a measurement. She turned her head again and saw her own face, scrubbed and topped with a plastic hat, her body stripped and bare, strapped down to the flat metal table. Her eyes were wide with terror. She gasped and the image gasped with her, the wall-size face twisting into a rictus of fear, a live camera feed of her dying moments filling the room like a horror show. She panicked; her breathing accelerated; her heart pumped; the graphs scrawled mad, thumping lines three feet high across the walls.

"I'm sorry," said Samm. "I tried to tell them you came willingly—"

"You were not asked to bring a volunteer," said a stern voice. A woman stepped forward. Her blue mask hid her face, but her eyes were the color of polished gunmetal, cold and unfeeling. "You have succeeded where your entire squadron failed. Do not risk your commendation now by interfering."

Samm turned back to Kira. "They've asked me to be here, to talk to you, so you'd have someone you trusted—"

"I don't trust you!" she shouted. Her voice echoed through the operating room, raw and ragged. "I helped you! I rescued you! I believed everything you said! Every word about surviving together or not surviving at all—and it was all a lie?"

"I was telling the truth," said Samm. "When we reached the mainland, I was trying to keep you away from them until I could explain things—that you'd come to try to help us."

"Then let me go!" Kira sobbed. The face on the wall sobbed with her, a mockery of her despair. She moved her legs, struggling against the restraints; she pulled on her arms, vainly trying to cover her chest and groin. She felt exposed and vulnerable and helpless. "Get me out of here."

"I . . ." Samm's face went rigid again, the same concentration he'd shown before—she could almost see his body seize up as the link took hold, forcing him to obey his superior officers. "I can't." He let out a breath, the tension gone, his muscles relaxing. "I can't," he repeated. "I obey my orders." His expression darkened.

"Very good," said the woman. She stepped forward, and one of the metal arms swung around with her, shining a light in Kira's face, blinding her again. "Samm says you came willingly?"

"I did," said Kira. "I came to help you."

"And you think your dark-age technology is of any value to us? You barely understand how your own genetics work, let alone ours."

"It doesn't matter anymore, it was all lies."

"Some of it was," the woman agreed, "some of it was not. I am surprised Samm told you about our plight, our 'expiration date,' but that much, at least, was true. That's why you're here."

"I'm a medic," said Kira. "I've focused my studies on pathology and reproduction, trying to find a cure for RM. I can use that knowledge to help you."

"Your human studies are worthless," said the woman. "I assure you our needs lie in a completely different area."

"I've studied Samm, too," said Kira, "not like this—" She paused suddenly, thinking how much of Samm's experience *had* been like this. How much of it had been worse. "My people did not treat him well," she said slowly, "and I'm sorry for that, but I helped him. I studied him noninvasively. I was humane."

The woman smirked. "Humane? Even the word is an insult."

"You have a genetic deficiency that we don't," said Kira. "You're immune to RM and our babies are not." She pleaded with the woman. "We need each other."

"The last time Partials and humans tried to work together, it didn't work out so well," said the woman. "I think we'll take our chances on our own."

Another metal arm swung into place, a bright hypodermic needle gleaming at its tip. Kira started to protest, but the needle darted forward like the tail of a scorpion.

CHAPTER THIRTY-TWO

The needle pierced Kira's chest, a sharp sting almost instantly dulled by the slow, spreading numbness of a topical anesthetic.

"You can't put me under again," Kira insisted, trying to sound stronger than she felt. The steel-eyed doctor shook her head.

"We're not putting you under, girl, we're prepping you for this." She held up a syringe in her white-gloved hand, much bigger than the other, with a thick needle nearly four inches long. Kira shuddered at the sight of it, inching away as far as she could in her restraints. "Don't worry," said the doctor, though her voice carried no hint of compassion. "That anesthetic is excellent; you won't feel a thing. It's important that you be awake for this test so we can observe your responses—we were going to wait, and perform a different experiment first, but since you've woken up early, we may as well get started." The doctor turned away, and another arm of the spiderlike medical robot swung down and pricked Kira's thigh, drawing a vial of blood into a clear glass syringe.

Kira's heart was racing. "What was that?"

The doctor spoke idly over her shoulder as she studied one of the wall screens. "Since you've proven somewhat resistant to our sedatives, we're going to analyze your blood and mix one custom. We need you awake for now, but it wouldn't be good for anyone if you wake up during the next test."

Kira fought against her tears, irrationally determined not to let these monsters see her cry. *I am stronger than my trials.* She saw movement from the corner of her eye and cringed as a sudden fluid shape blotted out the light. She bit back a scream, but the shadow moved past her face and settled over her body; it was Samm, spreading a blanket to cover her.

"We need her chest exposed for the injection," the doctor snapped.

"Then you can move it," said Samm. "If she's going to be awake, at least give her some dignity."

The doctor paused, studying Samm with narrowed eyes, then nodded. "Fine."

Samm leaned in close to Kira's face. "I tried the captain on a radio, but Dr. Morgan is outside the command structure—she's on special assignment from the Trust. She'll be hard to stop."

"Go to hell," said Kira.

Samm looked down, no longer meeting her eyes, and walked away silently.

Kira could hear the other doctors discussing in low tones, manipulating one of the wall panels with their fingertips.

". . . other subjects . . . pheromone . . . RM. . . ."

Kira's ears snapped to attention, all her energy focused on trying to hear exactly what the doctors were saying. She couldn't see past them to the image they were looking at, but as she concentrated, their words became clearer.

". . . so we'll inject her, and see how she reacts. We're looking for the time it takes the particle to be absorbed, the range and coverage it achieves, and any hint of necrotic activity."

It's their last-minute prep, thought Kira.

But what are they going to inject me with?

Dr. Morgan hefted the big syringe and turned toward Kira; the others moved with her, spreading out around the table. The medical spider spun into place, grippers and pincers and lights and scalpels all hovering above her like a spiky metal nightmare. As the doctors left the wall panel, Kira saw the images they'd been looking at—recognized them immediately from her own study of Samm: a magnified picture of the Predator, the stage of RM that appeared in the newborn's blood, and beside it the Lurker, the one she'd found in Samm that shared so much of the Predator's structure.

Dr. Morgan pulled back the sheet, exposing the top of Kira's chest. "We have reason to believe that this is going to make you very sick, very quickly." She held the syringe over Kira's heart. "We'll be monitoring your vital signs, of course, but we need you to tell us anything else you may experience: pain in your joints, shortness of breath, loss of vision or hearing. Sensory details our instruments can't detect or interpret."

"You're injecting me with the Lurker," said Kira, already feeling her body starting to panic, and struggling to keep her breathing even and calm. "The particle you produce, the inert version of RM. What are you expecting it to do?"

"A version of RM? I told you your knowledge was useless

to us." She plunged the needle into Kira's chest—she could feel it sliding in, pain and pressure and a horrifying sense of invasion. *The anesthetic isn't working!* Dr. Morgan pressed down on the plunger, and Kira gasped at the sudden flood of fire in her chest, pumping directly to her heart and from there to the rest of her body, filling her in seconds. Her breath caught; her hands grasped involuntarily at the edge of the table, scrabbling for anything solid to hold on to. The injection seemed to take ages, and when Dr. Morgan finally pulled out the needle, Kira whimpered, imagining she could still feel the fluid as it coursed through her.

"No reaction yet," said a masked doctor, her eyes fixed firmly on the wall. Another shined a light in Kira's eyes, checking her dilation with one hand and her pulse with the other.

"Everything normal."

"We're not sure how quickly this works," said Dr. Morgan, watching Kira closely. "We haven't experimented on humans since just after the Partial War."

Kira breathed deeply, summoning her control after the violation of the injection. The particle still rotated slowly on one of the screens. *Am I going to die? She said the Lurker's not a new version of RM—then what is it? And what are they expecting to see?*

She remembered one of their snatches of overheard whispering and looked back at the images on the wall: the virus and the Lurker, so similar and yet so unlike a virus. It had always confused her, dealing only with her own incomplete information, but here with the Partials she knew more. She had heard them talking about it.

"You called it a pheromone," said Kira.

Dr. Morgan paused suddenly, looking at Kira quizzically. She followed Kira's eyes to the images on the wall, then looked back at Kira. "You know this particle?"

"We thought it was a new stage of RM, because it looked so much like the other, but you called it a pheromone. That's why Samm was producing it—it's part of your link data."

Dr. Morgan glanced to the side of the room, beyond Kira's field of vision, and Kira could tell from her eyes that she was frowning. She looked back at Kira. "Your knowledge is more extensive than I expected. I confess that when you—a human, of all things—told me you were a medic, I didn't really take you seriously."

Kira fought down a wave of nausea, still reeling from the pain of the injection. She composed herself again and looked at Dr. Morgan. "What does it do?"

"That's what we're trying to find out."

"Is it part of the link?" asked Kira. "Is the whole RM virus just a side effect of your abilities?"

"Over the past twelve years I've catalogued every pheromone the Partials produce," said Dr. Morgan. "I've isolated every particle, I've tracked them back to the organ that produces them and the stimulus that triggers their production, and I've determined their precise purpose and function. Every one of them." She nodded at the image on the wall. "Except that one."

Kira shook her head. "Why would you have a pheromone with no purpose? Everything about you was built with a purpose."

"Oh, there's a purpose," said Dr. Morgan. "Everything at ParaGen had a purpose, as you say. One of those purposes was a fixed time of death, and it is our suspicion that this pheromone might somehow be related to it. If we can study certain reactions, we might be able to combat it." She gestured at the images behind her. "As you can see from the wall screen, the pheromone doesn't react with other Partials, and it doesn't react with humans. It reacts with RM."

Suddenly Kira saw the two images in a new light: not as versions of each other, but as a combination. The Predator didn't just look like the Partial pheromone, it was the Partial pheromone, with an airborne RM Spore wrapped around it. That was how the Spore became the Predator—not on contact with blood, but on contact with the pheromone. *On contact with blood, the Spore turns into the Blob.* Kira's mind filled with the image of the newborn baby's blood, the bizarre Predator virus multiplying like mad and yet not causing any damage to the cells. *Samm was right there: he'd been breathing the Lurker into the air for days. It got into the sample, attached itself to the Spore, and rendered the virus inert.*

That was the secret of RM. That was the cure. A tiny little particle inside their greatest enemies.

"When the humans fell, we began to research the question of Partial sterility, to see if we could undo it." Dr. Morgan seemed oblivious to Kira's shock—or was interpreting it as uneducated bewilderment. Kira struggled to hide her emotions as the doctor kept talking, suddenly terrified at the prospect of this cold, calculating woman in possession of so powerful a secret. If Dr. Morgan was concerned about Kira's reaction, she didn't show it. She walked to the wall, tapped the screen, and called up a series of other files—other faces, other human girls, as pale and wide-eyed as Kira, strapped to the same table and subjected to the same experiments. "We needed a nonsterile control for our experiments, and naturally this led us to the study of humans. It was only after the last girl died that we noticed the link between our pheromone and RM: Somehow the virus is absorbing the pheromone into itself, though how and why we have no idea. Eventually we were caught up in . . . other concerns, but when the crisis of the expiration date began to surface, we realized we needed to take up the studies again." She turned back to Kira, idly playing with the empty syringe in her hands. "And here you are."

Kira nodded, bursting with her secret, trying not to give it away. *I need to get out of here. I need to get home.*

I can save Madison's baby. I can save them all.

"Still no change," said another doctor, monitoring Kira's vital signs. "If the reaction is occurring, it's not having any measurable effect."

"It's not occurring," said another doctor in a completely different tone. "And it's not going to." Everyone in the room looked toward her, even Kira. The doctor tapped a panel, and it expanded to fill the whole wall, showing lists of acronyms and abbreviations that Kira immediately recognized as a blood test. "She doesn't have any of the virus in her blood."

"That's impossible. Even humans immune to the symptoms carry the virus."

"You're right." The doctor paused. "She has the coding."

The room went silent. Kira looked at the doctors' faces, registering their shock. In the space behind her she heard Samm's voice dripping with confusion. "What?"

"Let me see that," said Dr. Morgan, stalking across the room to the wall screen. She tapped it furiously, dragging charts across the wall and zooming in and out on a rapid flurry of images. She stopped on a strand of DNA, not a scoped image but a graphical re-creation, and stared at it with enough intensity to burn a hole through the plating. "Who performed the scan?"

"The computer did it on its own," said the other doctor. "We asked for a full analysis, and it's part of the package."

"She's not on the link," said Samm. Kira's heart flipped in her chest, the implications of their words starting to come clear.

"What are you talking about?" she asked. She tried to sound strong, but her voice cracked.

Dr. Morgan turned to face her, ripping off her mask and looming over Kira's bed like a tower of seething stone. "Who sent you?"

"What?"

Morgan screamed it again. "Who sent you?" Kira didn't answer, and Dr. Morgan threw the empty syringe across the room, shattering it against the picture of the DNA. "Who's trying to infiltrate my plans now—Cronus? Prometheus? What are they planning? Or maybe it's not me they're after," she said, turning away with wild eyes. "Maybe they're planning something else, and now that I've stumbled onto it I can use it against them."

"I don't know what you're talking about," Kira protested.

"You were with the humans until Samm brought you here," said Dr. Morgan, crouching over Kira with her eyes wide and her teeth bared. "Tell me what you were doing there. What was your mission?"

"I don't know what you're talking about!"

"You're a Partial!" Dr. Morgan shouted. "It's all right there on the wall! You have no RM in your bloodstream, you have bionanites sweeping your blood clean of our sedatives, you have the damn ParaGen product tags coded into your damn DNA. You are a Partial." She stopped suddenly, staring down at Kira; on the wall screen behind her Kira saw her own face twisted in shock and confusion. The doctor's expression changed slowly from anger to fascination, and her voice dropped to a whisper. "But you didn't know that, did you?"

Kira opened her mouth, but no words came out. A chaos of protests and realizations and questions ran madly through her head, starting and stopping and derailing one another uselessly until her mind was a white noise of abject terror. She heard a loud boom, saw Dr. Morgan shouting at her through a haze of confusion, heard another boom, then Samm's voice cut through the chaos.

"Explosions. We're under attack."

CHAPTER THIRTY-THREE

Dr. Morgan looked up wildly, screams and gunshots echoing from beyond the closed door. The doctors scrambled; the medical insect reared up, knives and other lethal attachments clicking and rotating and locking into place. Samm rushed to the door, securing it tightly, then stood back.

"They're here for Kira," he said.

"Of course they're here for her," Dr. Morgan snapped, "but who are they? Which faction?"

"We need to get out of here," said one of the other doctors.

"We're not armed," said Samm, shaking his head. "We're not prepared for an attack. Our best plan is to stay here and hope the other soldiers repel it."

"This room doesn't seal," said one of the doctors, nodding at the heavy door. "Anyone who passes will link us."

"They'll know we're here," said Dr. Morgan, "but not her. That could buy us precious time."

"That's what doesn't make sense," said Samm. "How can she

be a Partial if she doesn't link?"

"Only the military models link," said Dr. Morgan. "At least, the way we're used to. It was part of the soldier enhancement package. But ParaGen made other Partials for other purposes."

Kira was shaking her head, only dimly aware of what anyone was saying. *I'm not a Partial.* Once again, faced with a problem, her mind seemed to split in two: on one side a scientist, counting all the reasons she could never be a Partial. *I age, and they don't. I don't link, and they do. I don't have their strength or reflexes, and I definitely don't have their miraculous healing.* But even there she had to stop herself, suddenly unsure. *My leg recovered abnormally quickly from the burn, without any of the expected side effects from the regen box.*

She shook her head. *More than anything else, I don't remember being a Partial—I grew up in a human house, I have a human father. I went to school in East Meadow for years. I've never been contacted by Partials, approached by Partials, nothing. It makes no sense at all.*

And yet even as she analyzed her life, behind it all was the other side of her, the emotional side, the lost child crying in the darkness: *Does this mean I never had a mommy?*

The sounds of battle were getting closer.

"It's ridiculous," said one of the doctors. "Why bury a Partial agent in the human population? One who doesn't even know what she is? What possible reason could there be?"

"Maybe it was an accident," said one of the doctors. "Maybe she got lost in the chaos, fell in with the refugees, and ended up on the island without knowing why she was there?"

"Everything had a purpose at ParaGen," said Dr. Morgan.

"Everything. She isn't an accident." She looked up. "If we can fig-ure out what she's supposed to do, we can use her against them."

The room shook with the sound of a gunshot against the door; doctors yelped and jumped back; Samm and Dr. Morgan stayed as firm as iron.

"They're here," one of the doctors said, panicked. "What do we do?"

"Get me down from here," said Kira, still strapped to a table in what was about to become a battlefield. "Untie me!"

"Get behind the spider," another doctor hissed, moving to the far corner of the room. The others followed, eyeing the spiky arms warily, slinking around the outside of the room.

"There's no one in the hall," said Samm, confused.

"Yes there is," said Dr. Morgan. "Humans."

Another gunshot rocked the door, blowing it off its hinges. Marcus appeared in the doorway with a shotgun, and Kira called out, "Get down!" just as the medical spider swung a vicious sur-gical razor at his neck. Marcus dropped, rolling under the blade, then raised his gun and blasted the spider at close range. Kira shrieked, feeling the heat from the gunpowder, the rain of shrap-nel cascading down from the damaged robot. The sound of the blast nearly deafened her.

"She's in here!" shouted Marcus, calling over his shoulder, then turned and nodded at her. "Hi, Kira."

Xochi stepped in behind Marcus, already crouched low, training a pair of semiautomatics on the doctors in the corner. "I just reloaded," she said, "so feel free to make any sudden moves."

"Get them," snarled Dr. Morgan, but Samm seemed frozen in place.

Jayden came last, dodging another scalpel from the spider and crouching inside the door. Marcus fired again at the spider, disabling it, then rushed to Kira's side and began untying the restraints.

"You're a hard girl to find," said Marcus, forcing a smile.

"They're close behind us," said Jayden. "Don't take any longer than you have to."

"Can I shoot the doctors?" asked Xochi, running her pistols back and forth across the line of them.

Jayden fired into the hallway. "And now they're here; I told you to hurry. We're pinned down."

"Samm, stop them," said Dr. Morgan, but still Samm didn't move, his body tensed, his face frozen with some intense, invisible effort.

"How did you get in here?" asked Kira. Marcus finished her first arm, and she instantly used it to work on her other arm while Marcus moved down to her legs.

"We saw you get captured," said Marcus, shooting a venomous glance at Samm. "We followed you here, ran out of ideas, and then another group of Partials attacked the hospital. When the outer defenses fell, we just kind of . . . slipped in the back."

"We heard them talking," said Xochi, "and Samm was lying: All D Company does is crazy research, like this, on humans and Partials alike. The other group follows something called the Trust."

"*We* follow the Trust," said one of the doctors. Kira shot a glance at Dr. Morgan, but the cold woman stayed silent, her face revealing nothing.

Marcus finished untying Kira's feet while Kira finished her

second hand, and when she was free she clutched the sheet to her chest and sat up. Jayden fired again into the hallway.

"Do you have a plan to get back out?" asked Kira.

"Honestly, I'm kind of shocked we made it this far," said Marcus. "Are you okay?" He noticed her bare shoulders and frowned. "Are you . . ."

"Yes," said Kira, looking around for her clothes. There was nothing in the room but a tray of syringes and some debris from the broken spider. She pointed at one of the doctors. "You, give me your lab coat."

"They're getting closer!" shouted Jayden.

The doctor didn't move, but a grim gesture of Xochi's pistol encouraged her to take off her surgical smock. Dr. Morgan shouted with rage.

"Damn it, Samm, stop them!"

Samm's hand came down on Marcus's shotgun, discarded on the table where he'd left it to help with Kira's ties. Kira swore, diving away from Samm off the far side of the table, but the Partial soldier simply stood there, staring straight ahead.

"Samm," Dr. Morgan began, and suddenly Samm brought up the shotgun and fired—not at Kira or her friends, but at Morgan. She dodged, shockingly nimble, and the wall screen behind her exploded in sparks and shards of glass. Xochi began firing as well, but Morgan was too quick; round after round tore into the wall screens while the doctors screamed and cowered on the floor. Dr. Morgan danced ahead of the bullets, all too quickly working her way toward the door. Samm leaped across the room, fired and missed again, and the third time the shotgun clicked on an empty chamber. He spun it around, gripping the barrel with a roar, and drove it into the back of Morgan's skull as she made a final dive for the hallway. The doctor slumped to the floor, and Xochi pumped a round into her thigh.

"And stay down!"

"She was too strong," said Samm, and grabbed the ammo belt from Marcus's shoulder. "I'm sorry that it took me so long. How many are outside?" He slid a shell into the chamber, then another and another, quickly and methodically.

Kira rose to a crouch, watching Samm in wonder. *Is he really on our side?* Jayden turned warily, sizing him up, then looked back at the open door.

"Just four," he said, "around that near corner. The main body of their force is tied up with the rival Partials."

Samm checked his gun quickly, making sure the safety was off. "Cover me."

Jayden fired out with his rifle, clearing the hall, and Samm dove past him in a blur, rolling to the far wall and then dashing down the corridor toward the enemy position. Jayden stopped firing, and the Partials peeked out just in time for Samm to come barreling into them, shotgun blasting.

Kira took the doctor's offered surgical smock and pulled it on, wrapping the back all the way closed with a pair of ties around her waist. For good measure she took the doctor's mask and hairnet as well, and finally her shoes.

Samm came back, his face and shoulder bleeding. "Hallway's clear. I think we can make it to the jeeps, but we have to go now."

"I'm getting really sick of trusting this guy," said Xochi.

"He's coming with us," said Kira. *There's something I have to talk about, that I can't talk about with anyone else.* She gave him a long glance, wondering what it meant now—if she was really a Partial, if she was really an agent, if she was really everything they thought she was.

"We have to go," urged Marcus.

"One thing first," said Kira. She scooped up the last syringe from the tray in the corner: a sample of the Partial pheromone.

The cure for RM.

CHAPTER THIRTY-FOUR

Samm drove, the only one of the five who really knew how. Marcus examined Kira's wounds in the backseat: It seemed the Partials had done little more than give her a few shots, draw some blood, and prep her for a surgery that never happened. The burn on her leg was almost fully healed, but the sight of her own shin, nearly scarless, seemed suddenly strange and alien; a sign not that the regen box had worked better than normal, but that her own body was healing well beyond the human standard. Just like Samm.

She looked at him, saw him looking back at her in the rearview mirror. Their eyes locked for a moment, silent. The others didn't know, and Kira and Samm had said nothing.

Am I really a Partial? How could I not have known? Partials heal quickly, but this is the first major injury I've ever really had, so I've never had a chance to see my own healing abilities in action. I've never really been sick, either—does that mean anything? She racked her brain for anything else she knew about them. *Partials are sterile, and that's never come up. Partials are fast and strong and agile, but is that only the soldiers?* She remembered Dr. Morgan, screaming frantically about secret Partial designs and some kind of inter-faction war. *If I'm not a soldier, what am I? How many groups are out there, and what do they want? And why would any of them plant a Partial agent in a group of human refugees?*

"You've been quiet," said Marcus.

"I'm sorry," said Kira. "I've had a lot to think about."

This time it was Marcus who glanced at Samm, studying him silently, thinking. He looked back at Kira, then down at her leg. "Looks like you're doing great. You're sure they didn't do . . . anything else?"

Kira felt caught; she felt claustrophobic in the back of the car, even with the windows down and the wind gusting wildly. "What do you mean?"

Xochi raised an eyebrow. "We find you buck naked, strapped down to a table. What do you think he means?"

"Nothing like that," said Kira quickly.

"You said they knocked you out, how do you know they didn't do something while you were—"

"Nothing happened," said Samm. His jaw was hard, his eyes cold. "I never left her side for a second. They didn't do anything to hurt her."

"But they were going to," said Marcus, "and you didn't really do a whole hell of a lot about it until we showed up."

"I did everything I could!"

"Stop arguing," said Kira. "It's the link—he couldn't disobey them."

"That's not making me any happier about having him here,"

said Jayden. He was in the other front seat, watching the passing ruins with the shotgun ready for action.

"I helped you this time," said Samm. "I helped you get away. What more do you want from me?"

"Everybody just calm down," said Kira. "I'm pretty sure we have more important things to worry about right now."

"More important than whether we can trust the enemy soldier taking us who knows where?" asked Xochi.

"I'm driving east," said Samm, "away from the controlled zones."

"And into the uncontrolled zones," said Marcus. "That sounds safe."

"Our people aren't like yours," said Samm. "We don't have the Voice and bandits and all these little outlying . . . nonconformists. If there's no faction of the army out here, there's nothing out here. Everything west of here is full of people trying to find us, so we're heading east until we think we've lost them. Then we'll . . . I don't know what we'll do then. Hide."

"We'll find a boat and go back to East Meadow," said Kira. Marcus looked at her in surprise.

"Are you serious? After what we did when we left?" He shook his head. "They'll kill us."

"Not when they find out what I'm bringing back." Kira glanced down at the syringe in her lap, and Marcus's eyes followed. He frowned at it, then looked back at her in shock.

"You don't mean . . ."

Kira nodded. "I'm ninety-nine percent certain."

"What?" asked Xochi.

"The cure for RM," said Kira. Jayden turned around, eyes

wide, and even Samm lost control of the car for just a split second, swerving and regaining direction. Kira held up the syringe. "I found a particle in Samm's breath that bore a resemblance to RM, though it wasn't a virus. It turns out it's one of their pheromones that they don't have any use for—all it does, literally its only function, is to bond with RM. The RM particles I saw in the newborn's blood is really an inert form of RM created through interaction with the pheromone."

Marcus furrowed his brow. "So the infants die because we don't have any Partials around?"

"Exactly. But if we can get this into their system early enough—right at birth, maybe even before birth through some kind of intrauterine injection—they'll resist the virus and we can save them." She gripped the syringe tightly. "Madison was close to delivering when we left East Meadow, and Arwen might already be dying. But we can save her."

Marcus nodded, and Kira could see the wheels turning in his head, parsing all the data to the best of his ability. After a moment he looked up. "This might be true." He nodded again. "Based on what I've seen of your work, which is admittedly little, it does sound . . . possible. But are you willing to stake your life on it?"

"Are you willing to stake our species against it?"

Marcus looked down. Xochi caught Kira's eye but said nothing.

The trees broke, and the road rose up to a bridge across a narrow inlet from the sound. "There are boats down there," said Jayden, but Samm shook his head.

"We need to keep going. They're going to send someone after

us as soon as they finish with the other group of Partials; for all I know both groups are going to come after us. We need to put as much distance behind us as possible before they get organized enough to follow."

"What we need is to get out of this car," said Jayden. "Make some distance first, yes, but then we hide this thing and never look back. It's too loud—they'll be able to hear us halfway across the continent."

"She'll still be able to find us," said Samm.

Marcus looked up. "Who?"

"Heron. Special Ops. No matter what we do to cover our tracks, she'll find us."

The car made good time—not too speedy, because the roads were buckled and treacherous, but still faster than they could have gone on foot. Across the bridge they joined a major highway, taking the time to glance back for pursuers, but there was nothing they could see. Several miles later the road turned sharply north, and they left it to drive south through a rural, wooded suburb. The roads were narrow and twisty, curving back on themselves in unpredictable patterns, and soon they gave up on the car and left it on a side street nearly buried in overhanging foliage. Kira stopped to scour the closest house for clothing, but the area was thick with humidity, and everything inside was rotted and unusable.

Samm could smell the ocean, but none of the humans could; Kira swore she could smell it too, a salty bite on the edge of her perception. She didn't tell anyone. They cut a path south and west, winding carefully through already sparse neighborhoods now almost fully reclaimed by nature. Saplings grew up not just around but in the houses, kudzu and mold and moisture breaking them down until their roofs were caved in and their walls were sagging with untended life. Flowers sprouted from porches; weeds sprang up from furniture half glimpsed through shattered windows. When they reached the harbor, Kira breathed deeply, as if freed from an airless cavern.

"We're on the wrong side," said Marcus, pointing. "Houses over here, wharf over there."

"Looks like bigger houses to the south," said Jayden. "One of them's bound to have a private dock." They skirted the waterfront, half searching for a boat and half watching behind for an ambush. Kira had seen Heron in action; she'd lost a fight to her in seconds. She didn't want to have to fight her again.

"There," said Xochi, and they broke into a run. A long white dock stretched out from the shore, beaten by the elements until it was practically driftwood, and at the end bobbed a wide motorboat with a tattered canvas awning. Jayden leaped in, looking in the dashboard compartments for a set of keys, while Samm searched the dock itself for extra tanks of gas. Neither found anything, and they cursed and ran to the next house along the shore. This one had a small sailboat, which none of them could pilot, but it had a small motor, and the keys were in the ignition. The engine turned over on the seventh try. Samm found gas cans, but they were empty.

"You'll need extra just in case," he said. "We're much farther east than our last crossing, and the sound here is two or three times as wide."

He took the cans toward the house, ready to take gas from the cars, but Kira stopped him. "What do you mean, *you'll* need gas?" she asked. "You're not coming?"

Samm shook his head, looking out at the water, up at the house, anywhere but at Kira. "Your people will kill me."

"The Partials will kill you, too," said Kira. "You're a traitor now. At least with us you'll have . . . something, friends, I don't know. We can help each other."

"You're a wanted terrorist," he said. "Lot of good we'd do each other." He began moving toward the house.

She watched him, then looked back at the others. "I'm going to help him with the gas." Marcus glowered at the dock but said nothing.

Samm and Kira trudged up the short hill to the house, which turned out to be some kind of beachhead resort. The parking lot was filled with cars, one of them even sporting a skeleton, and Samm got to work crawling underneath and puncturing their gas tanks with his knife, letting the degraded, sludgy fuel drip down into the cans. Kira wanted to talk to him, to ask him about what she was—just to say it aloud, *I am a Partial*, but she didn't dare. She paced uselessly, hemming and hawing, starting and stopping, so afraid to talk that she could barely even think. Finally she gave up, and she let the old habits take over, eyeing the old cars for anything she could salvage. Most of the cars were packed with luggage—people fleeing the virus? Fleeing the country?—and the tightly sealed suitcases revealed clothes in much better condition than the rags she'd found before. She found clean underwear, rugged jeans that mostly fit, and an armful of shirts and socks that she brought with her just in case.

"So," said Samm. He was sitting on the ground, the gas cans scattered around him.

Kira paused, holding the clothes. "So."

Kira looked at him, at his face, at his eyes. She'd felt so close to him, and now . . . Was it the link? Maybe she really could do it, in some smaller way, and that's what she'd been feeling. She shook her head, lost in conflicting emotions. Had their connection been nothing but some kind of Partial biological quirk, or had it been real?

If it was only the link, did that make it less real? And if she could connect that deeply with someone, did it really matter how?

"You really didn't know?" He squinted at her in the fading sunlight. "You really thought you were . . ." He trailed off, and Kira felt grateful he hadn't said it out loud.

"I had no idea. I'm still not convinced."

"You're definitely not like me," he said, "but you're"—he nodded at her friends—"not like them either. You can't link, and yet I almost feel like you can, like there's something between us that . . . I don't know. I don't know what you are."

Kira opened her mouth to respond, but she didn't know either. "I'm Kira Walker," she said finally. "What else is there to know?"

Samm said nothing, merely gathered the gas cans.

"You can come with us," she said. "We can hide you somewhere, in the farms or some little community. You'll be safe there."

Samm looked at her now, brown eyes as deep as wells. "Is that really what you want? To hide and be safe?"

Kira sighed. "I know even less about what I want right now than about who I am. I want to be safe. I want to know what's going on." She felt her resolve stiffen. "I want to find who did this, and why."

"ParaGen," said Samm. "They made us, they made you, and if your theory's right about the pheromone, they made RM too."

Kira smirked. "You always said you didn't do it."

The corner of Samm's mouth turned up, just a bit, in the tiniest hint of a smile. "When did you start to believe me?"

Kira looked at the ground, kicking at a rock with the toe of her shoe. "I said what I want." She looked up. "What about you?"

"What do I want?" Samm paused, considering the question with his typical solemnity. "The same thing as you, I guess. I want to know what's going on, and why. And I want to fix it. After everything that's happened, I'm more convinced than ever that peace—"

"Isn't possible?"

"I was going to say that it's the only chance we have."

Kira laughed dryly. "You really do have an amazing knack for saying exactly what I want to hear."

"You learn what you can," said Samm, "and I'll do the same. If we ever see each other again, we'll share."

"We'll share what we've learned."

"Yeah."

They waited a moment longer, watching each other, remembering each other, and Kira thought for a moment she could even feel the link tying them together like an invisible wire. They walked back below, lugging the clothes and gas. Samm set them heavily in the boat.

"This should get you across," he said, "assuming the motor holds."

Jayden fired it up again, and the boat roared to life. He shook Samm's hand. "Thanks for your help. I'm sorry for the way I treated you before."

"Not necessary, but thanks."

Xochi shook his hand as well, and then Marcus, though he never met his eyes. Kira climbed into the boat and offered around the shirts and socks to anyone who wanted a change. Marcus stepped in last, untying the ropes as he came.

"Where are you going from here?" he asked.

"I thought I'd try to hide," said Samm, "but I figure it's too late for that now." He glanced back at the trees. "Heron's right there." Kira and her friends started, reaching for their weapons, but Samm shrugged. "She hasn't attacked, so I don't know what her game is."

"You're sure you'll be okay?" asked Kira.

"If she wanted me dead, she'd have done it by now."

Jayden gunned the motor and pulled away from the dock.

Kira watched Samm as he slipped into the distance and slowly disappeared from view.

CHAPTER THIRTY-FIVE

Their motor gave out more quickly now than on the first crossing, and despite their extra gas, they found themselves rowing most of the way across. The currents carried them east, and they saw the island long before they managed to pull in close and land the boat. Night had fallen, and they took shelter in an old beach house, grabbing a few hours of sleep before moving on. At first light Kira scoured the place for food, but the cans in the pantry were bloated, and the food inside smelled rank when they opened them up. They set them aside and searched instead for a map, eventually finding an atlas near a collapsed bookshelf. There was no detailed section for Long Island, just a larger map of New York in general, but it was better than nothing—she recognized enough of the names to know where they were going, and hoped that some of the road signs outside would help them discover where they were.

They parceled out the guns they had left—a rifle, a shotgun, and two pistols—and traveled quietly, wary of the Voice and Defense Grid patrols. Kira cradled the syringe as carefully as she could, wrapping it in a ball of extra shirts and strapping it around her waist for protection. She said a silent prayer that there would still be time to save Arwen, and watched the shadows for danger.

After barely an hour of walking, Kira began to recognize the terrain—so much of the island looked alike, crumbling houses buried in kudzu and surrounded by trees, but something about the road itself seemed familiar. The way it curved, or rose, or fell; she couldn't place it. After a moment she stopped scanning the forested road with a frown.

"We've been here before."

"We haven't even turned," said Jayden. "How could we have been here before?"

"Not this morning," said Kira. "I just . . . there." She pointed to a house set back from the road. "Do you recognize it?"

The others peered at it, and Marcus's eyes went wide with surprise when the realization hit him. "Is that the drifter's hideout? Tovar?"

"I'm pretty sure," said Kira. "Maybe he has some food stashed in there."

As they approached, it became more obvious—they'd only seen the front at night, in the rain, but they'd seen the back more clearly, and they recognized it immediately. Kira tried the doors, trying to remember which one the old drifter had left unblocked, but froze in place when she heard the click of a gun hammer.

"Just stop right there," said a voice. It was definitely him. Kira took her hands from the doorknob and held them up to show they were empty.

"Owen Tovar," said Kira. The others were standing silently, guns raised, searching for wherever the voice could be coming from. The drifter had a knack for staying hidden. "It's me, Kira Walker. Do you recognize us?"

"The four most wanted criminals in Long Island?" he said. "Yeah, I'm pretty sure we recognize you."

We, thought Kira. *Who else is in there?*

"'Most wanted,' huh?" asked Marcus. "My mother always said I'd be famous one day. Or at least I assume she did."

"I'm going to ask you to set your weapons down now," said Tovar. "Nice and easy, right at your feet."

"We came here because we thought you were a friend," said Kira. "We need food—we're not here to rob you."

Tovar's voice was lean and cold. "Is that why you drew your weapons and tried the door without knocking?"

"We didn't want to wake Dolly," said Marcus. There was a pause, and Tovar laughed; Kira thought it was coming from a vent near the top of the wall, but she couldn't be sure.

"I forgot how much I liked you," he said. "Looks like you're not being followed, so go ahead and put down those guns, and you can come on in for a chat."

Kira looked at Jayden, who shrugged and set down his rifle carefully by his feet. Marcus and Xochi followed, and Kira did the same. *If we're about to get robbed . . . ,* she thought, then shook her head. *We have nothing—surely he can see that. The only valuable we have is the cure, and nobody knows about it.*

"There you go," said Tovar. "Now, say hello to my friends." A bush moved to the left and Kira flinched, and then another bush moved, and a boarded-up window swung open, and suddenly the backyard was filled with men and women in various forms of camouflage and homemade armor, all of them armed.

"Easy," said the woman in front, and Kira thought she recognized the voice. "Keep your hands in the air and step away from the guns."

"Gianna," said Kira, realization dawning. "You were with us last time we came here—you were on the salvage run that found the bomb."

"Kira Walker," said Gianna with a smile. She glanced at Jayden, and her expression soured. "And the fascist plague baby. Keep those hands where I can see them."

"What is this?" demanded Kira. "Are you . . . the Voice?"

"The very same," said Tovar, stepping out of the back door with his fat black shotgun on his hip. "The new regime is out in force, rounding up refugees and runaways. I don't know if it's good luck or bad that we found you first."

"You're the Voice," said Marcus, as if still trying to get his head around it. He laughed. "That might be the weirdest thing I've ever heard—and you," he said, turning to Gianna. "Were you the Voice back then, too?"

"Not until after," she said. "I get testy when I'm detained without cause."

"Still, though," said Jayden, "you were a sympathizer. I was right not to trust you."

"Even a paranoid clock is being followed twice a day," said Tovar. He gestured to the open door. "Come inside so we can reset our trap. If the Grid does drop by, I don't want to be caught in the open flapping my gums."

They filed inside while the Voice went back into hiding.

Tovar led them down one hall while Gianna locked the door and took their guns down another. Inside, the house was more or less as Kira remembered it, including the laconic camel in the living room.

"Hello, Dolly," said Marcus. "Long time no see."

Xochi offered her hand to Tovar. "Looks like you know everyone else. I'm Xochi."

"Xochi Kessler," said Tovar, ignoring her hand as he searched in his wagon for food. "Or should I say 'the infamous Xochi Kessler.' Your poor mother is worried sick."

"My poor mother can go and hang herself."

"She'd much rather hang you," said Tovar, handing her a can of ravioli. "I'm still looking for the can opener." He turned back to the wagon. "I did mention that you're wanted criminals, yes? Bounties on your heads, posters in the town square, the whole bit. Here it is." He turned back to them, pointing at Kira with a rubber-handled can opener. "She's the great betrayer, the Partial-lover, the ringleader of the whole thing. These two are the dupes who went along with it." He pointed back at Xochi. "You're the ungrateful daughter: the symbol of how anyone can believe the Voice lies and go traitor." He handed her the can opener. "I'll look for spoons."

"Who's in charge now?" asked Kira. "What happened after we left?"

"After you personally threw the island into anarchy, you mean," said Tovar, handing her a set of mismatched silverware.

"How much did they say about us?" asked Kira.

"That you were in league with the Voice, who are in turn in league with the Partials. That you broke into the hospital and broke a Partial agent out of Grid imprisonment, and are currently either hiding in the wild or escaping to the mainland to aid in a Partial invasion. How much of it should I believe?"

Kira spoke carefully. "I guess that depends on how you feel about Partials."

Tovar sat on the couch across from her, watching Kira carefully. "Aside from murdering everyone I know, the Partials haven't really been a big part of my life. Consider my opinion 'generally very poor.' That said, I figure if they wanted us dead, we'd be dead, so if you have another perspective, I'm listening."

Kira nodded. "Do you consider yourself an open-minded man, Mr. Tovar?"

"I'd like to think so."

"It's going to have to open really wide to swallow what we've got to tell you," said Marcus. "Number one: The Partials didn't create RM."

"And they're not looking to destroy us. At least not all of them," said Kira. "At least not yet. Which leads us to number two: Yes, we were in league with a Partial. We broke him out and took him off the island, and then he helped us get back here."

"Mother of mercy," said Tovar. "And that caused the riot?"

"It's the other way around," said Kira sheepishly. "We started the riot as a distraction for the jailbreak."

Tovar whistled. "You don't mess around."

"No, we don't."

"Is that everything?" he asked.

"For now," said Jayden. "Now it's your turn."

"Where to start," Tovar mused. "Two nights ago you spread your rumor, started your riot, and left right when it was getting interesting. The coliseum burned, though not to the ground; the town hall also burned, with more than a handful of senators inside it."

Kira went white, thinking of Isolde. *We thought it would be safe there. Did she die inside it?* "What about the hospital?"

"The hospital was never set on fire, though I can't say as much for the houses across the turnpike. The hospital was, on the other hand, the home of the biggest riot of the night, and the body count was, shall we say, high."

"Are the mothers okay? How many people died?"

"Maternity was untouched," said Torvar. "And I'm afraid I don't have exact numbers—probably less than the Senate is reporting, probably more than you'd expect."

"What is the Senate reporting?" asked Kira.

"Two hundred." Tovar's voice was as hard as flint. "A very high price for a Partial life."

It was worth it, Kira swore, though it broke her heart to think it. *Two hundred.* She looked up at Tovar, still not sure she trusted him enough to explain why they'd be willing to go to such an extreme. They were still prisoners, after all; he'd offered them nothing but information, and promised them nothing at all.

"Who's left of the senators?" asked Xochi. "Apparently my mother, but who else?"

"It might be more accurate to ask what's left of the *Senate*," said Tovar. "The few senators who lived through the night declared a state of emergency, declared martial law, and filled the city and the countryside with soldiers from the Grid. Elections to replace the fallen have been postponed until 'a state of peace and equilibrium is reached,' which is an awful lot of syllables for 'never.' It's totalitarianism in all but name."

"Yes," said Kira, "but who are we talking about specifically? Which senators?"

"Oh, you know," said Tovar with a shrug, "the real hardliners, like Kessler and Delarosa. Hobb's a weasel, so of course he's in there as well, and the one from the Grid—Senator Weist. That's how they got the military's support so quickly."

"The same ones who've been running this from the beginning," said Kira. Her skin went cold, and she gripped Xochi's hand for support. "They planned this entire thing—Samm, and the explosion, and even the riot. This isn't a provisional government in the wake of a national disaster, this was a planned and calculated coup."

"They couldn't have planned Samm," said Marcus. "They had no idea you were going to go out and get him."

"Who is Samm?" asked Tovar.

"The Partial," said Kira. "And they didn't have to plan his capture, just what to do with him afterward. They'd probably been planning some kind of power grab for a while, and then when we showed up with Samm, we gave them the means to pull it off."

"They're only in charge until the city gets back on its feet," said Jayden, "and they're only doing it because of the riot we caused. What else were they supposed to do?"

"Do you actually believe that?" asked Xochi.

"They responded too quickly," Kira protested, feeling the rage build up inside of her. It was so familiar now, so much a part of her, that it filled her easily. "They had to have a plan already in place, to deal with exactly the kind of situation we forced them into—we started a riot, and they went to Plan F or whatever and seized the whole island. Even when we thought we were stopping them, they were still ready for us."

"They're trying to save the species," said Jayden. "Yes, they're being extreme about it, but maybe that's the only way to make it work—a solid grip on the island, with a single vision to lead it and army to enforce it."

"Remember where you are," said Tovar.

"I don't like it any more than you do," said Jayden, "but they don't have the—" He stopped, glanced at Kira, and started again. "For all they know this is the only way to save us from RM: to take the Hope Act to its natural extreme and ranch us like cattle until someone's born immune."

"Delarosa used to be a zookeeper," said Kira softly, thinking of all her friends still trapped inside the city.

Tovar snorted. "No kidding?"

She nodded. "She saved endangered species. I guess we're just another bunch of rare white rhinos." Kira swallowed her rage and took a long, deep breath. "Mr. Tovar," she said, looking up to meet his eyes. "We need to get back to East Meadow."

"Then you're crazy," he said.

"Crazy or not," she said, "we need to go. And you need to take us there."

"Then you're crazy and stupid," said Tovar. "In three days, when all my forces are gathered, we're going to launch our biggest offensive yet. It's like your friend said—when the entire species is at stake, people are willing to go to extremes. We're going to take that government down and you do not want to be anywhere near it when we do."

"Three days?" Kira's mind raced. "That might be all we need. If you can get us there without being seen, actually inside the city, we might not need a war at all."

Tovar frowned. "I'm not an assassin, Kira, if that's what you're thinking."

"Of course not."

"And I'm not a martyr either. Getting you or anyone else into East Meadow would be extremely dangerous. When I die it's going to be for a pretty damn good reason."

"A good reason is not the problem," said Kira, and held up the syringe. "We have the cure for RM."

Tovar stared at it, his mouth open, then laughed out loud. "And you expect me to believe that?"

"You believed all the crazy bad stuff," said Xochi, "why not the crazy good stuff, too?"

"Because crazy bad stuff is well within the realm of my experience," said Tovar. "Curing RM is in the realm of magical pixies and talking dogs that piss whiskey. It's impossible."

"It's real," said Marcus, and looked at Kira. "We'll stake our lives on it."

"Suppose it is," said Tovar. "What do we do with it? Walk into town, hold it in the air, and wait for the magical pixies to make everything right again?"

"If the Senate taught me one thing," said Kira, "it's that power comes through the people—the only reason they have control is because the people have given it to them."

"Also because they have guns," said Marcus.

"They don't have guns," said Xochi, "they have the allegiance of people with guns."

"Exactly," said Kira. "If we can change that allegiance, we can free everyone in the city—everyone on the island. If we show them a live human baby, the purest, simplest proof that our way works and the Hope Act doesn't, the people will rise up so fast your head will spin. We can restore freedom and unite the island, all without firing a single shot."

"Say your cure works," said Tovar, "and we can actually show them, as you say, a live human baby." Tovar's voice nearly broke, and Kira could practically see the emotion running through him as he said the words. "You've already been in league with the Partials—you've crossed the sound and met them in person. Won't people just assume it's a Partial trick of some kind? A baby Partial, or an engineered . . . doppelganger or something?"

"The mother will have to be an East Meadow regular," said Marcus, "someone people will recognize as one of their own." He glanced at Jayden. "His sister is about to deliver—she may already have."

Kira nodded. "It's not enough to just show up with a baby: we have to go in, grab Madison, and get her out. Right under the Grid's noses."

Tovar looked at Kira. "I get the distinct impression that nothing is ever easy where you're involved."

"Welcome to my life," said Kira. "How many soldiers do you have?"

"Ten."

Kira raised an eyebrow. "I saw a lot more than ten in the backyard alone."

Tovar's voice hardened. "Are you asking about soldiers, or armed civilians with more guts than training?"

"Point taken," said Kira.

Tovar studied them carefully, his eyes flicking from one face to the next as he thought. "We may—may—have a way to get you inside. Are you sure you can do it?"

Kira grinned. "Haven't you heard? I'm the most wanted criminal on the island. I think it's about time I start living up to my reputation."

"Hell, yes," said Xochi.

Tovar paused, studying her, his brow furrowed. Finally he broke into a smile. "When you put it that way," he said, "I'm pretty sure I heard a talking dog just last week. Didn't drink its piss, though." He stood up. "It's still midmorning, and the weather's with us; if we start now, we can get you beaten and in police custody before dinner. I have a few tricks up my sleeve, though. I'll round up the troops."

CHAPTER THIRTY-SIX

One of the tricks up Tovar's sleeve turned out to be uniforms: dozens of Defense Grid uniforms stolen from the depot they'd raided in the old East Meadow High School. "We stole a mountain of ammunition and trail rations, too," he said slyly, "just to make it look like we were after their supplies, but this was the real prize. Worth a thousand bullets each if you use them right." Kira nodded and shrugged one on over her normal clothes.

The living room, already cramped, was now packed with an assortment of Voice leaders. Kira studied them as they talked, poring over makeshift maps of the island; they were determined, at the very least, and appeared capable enough, but they lacked the smoothness she had seen with the Defense Grid. The Grid was better organized, even for something as simple as a salvage run. One person laid out the plan, while the others listened attentively. The Voice could not have been more different.

"This is Farad," said Tovar, pointing to a stern man with a

fiery shock of red hair. "The uniforms are nice, but he's our real secret weapon: a Grid soldier, so newly defected to our cause that the Grid leaders, we hope, don't even know he's left."

Farad glanced around the room nervously, visibly uncomfortable in a room full of people who were so recently his enemies. "I tried to hang on after the riot," he said softly, "and the new rules, but . . . I just can't anymore. They've taken this too far."

"Farad was a driver," Tovar continued, "and it just so happens that we've recently, ah, liberated a jeep from a Grid outrider." He turned to Kira. "Probably one of the same ones that tried to chase you down after the riot. It's in good condition, has a covered back with the official Grid logo, and Farad knows the passwords to get it through the border."

"He knew the passwords," said a large man by the wall; he was old, with gray hair and a beard, but his arms were thickly muscled. "They might have changed them—they will have changed them if they're smart."

"But they don't know I've left," said Farad. His voice was thin and cracking. "I mean, they can't know, right? Not this quickly?"

"As far as they know you're still on a scouting mission," said Gianna. "Of course, if you run into anyone who knows you're supposed to be on a scouting mission, it won't matter how many passwords you have."

"Even in these uniforms they're going to recognize us," said Jayden. "Kira and Marcus at the very least once we get to the hospital—everyone there knows them."

"And they're the ones who know the hospital," said Tovar. "None of us do, at least not well enough. Here's the plan: Farad drives you back and gets you through the border, while the more notorious members of your band stay in the back and keep your eyes down. It's risky, but if you're careful you can make it work. You drive to the hospital, to that rear service door you were telling me about."

"The same one we slipped out of the night of the riot," said Kira. "There's a big ramp leading down to it, which will make us hard to see—any guard around the building will know we're there, obviously, but they won't have a good look at anyone who gets in or out of the jeep."

Tovar nodded. "Make your way through the lower levels, up to maternity, and grab your friend. This is the trickiest part."

"Which is why I'm going," said Gianna. "Once you guide us through the back hallways, I can get in and out of maternity without raising eyebrows—nobody knows me, and with this uniform I'll look official."

"You hope," said the bearded man.

"Seriously, Rowan," said Tovar, "is this really the time? Do we have to argue with every little step of the plan?"

"Your so-called plan is just 'good luck and don't act suspicious,'" said the bearded man. "You're sending them into the heart of enemy territory, I'd like to think you'd have something a little more workable."

"I don't even want them to go," said Tovar, throwing up his hands. "I'm trying to plan a full-scale assault of this city, and this is the best I could come up with given my time and resources."

The bearded Rowan turned to Gianna. "Are you willing to risk your life for 'the best he could come up with'?"

"We're willing to risk it for this," said Kira, and held up the syringe. "This is not an abstract concept, this is an actual cure—an actual injection that will save a child's life. Can you even imagine that? A living, breathing child that lives for a week, a month, a year; a child that laughs and crawls and learns to talk." Her voice cracked. "I would die for that in a heartbeat."

The room was silent.

Rowan stirred first. "Being worth the risk doesn't justify a risky plan."

"This plan will work," said Tovar fervently. "Farad has the codes, and our informants in the city have fed us the full rundown of hospital security. We can get them in, and we can get Madison Sato out. We'll take her to the eastern farms, she can deliver there, and the baby will live."

"I'm going to split the cure into three separate doses," said Kira. "One stays with Tovar, here in the back lines, to be used on Madison's baby Arwen. The second goes with us, just in case Arwen has already been born; depending on how advanced the virus is, we have to inject her on-site."

Tovar pointed at Rowan. "The third goes with you, east to Flanders or Riverhead or somewhere the Grid presence is weakest. Inject every newborn you can find." He looked at the syringe in Kira's hands. "The cure is too important to risk on a single mission."

Kira nodded, but a niggling voice in the back of her mind posed the question: *Do I have the pheromone? If I'm really a Partial, can I cure RM too?* She almost didn't dare to consider it—didn't dare to hope—it would be too easy, and nothing so far had been easy. *As soon as I get the chance—as soon as I have the right equipment—I have to test myself.*

Gianna whispered reverently. "We're pinning an awful lot of hope on this."

"I know," said Kira.

"So that's the team," said Rowan, "Gianna, the new guy, and these two medics."

"And us," said Jayden. "Madison's my sister."

Xochi nodded. "And Kira's mine."

Kira felt a pang of conscience, as stark as if she'd willfully betrayed them all. *What would they do if they knew what I really am?*

The car died two miles northeast of East Meadow. Gianna and Farad spent nearly an hour under the hood, cursing and banging and trying to get it started; Kira and Marcus sat by the curb and planned their route through the hospital: where to go, how to get there, and what specific medical phrases to teach Gianna to help get Madison out of the nurses' sight. Kira had kept the syringe in her own gear, carefully wrapped and cushioned and strapped to her waist. She touched it reflexively, making sure it was safe. Farad walked over tiredly and dropped a chunk of oily black metal on the road beside her.

Marcus looked at it. "Bad gas?"

"The gas is the cleanest I've seen in a while," said Farad. "This is the starter—it's not cracked or bent or gummed up, it's just . . . old." He flopped down on the curb beside them. "Of all the things that could have gone wrong, I never would have guessed this."

"But you can still get us in," said Kira, "right?"

"I could get me in," said Farad, shaking his head. "You're

too famous, and without the jeep to hide in I just don't see it working. And even if I could get in, one guy wandering home alone is going to raise a lot more eyebrows than a full squad with a vehicle. I'd certainly be questioned, probably detained, and in any case would never be able to get to your friend in time. I definitely couldn't get her out."

"Let's look at our options," said Jayden. "We can't just give up, and we don't have time to go back."

"We could find another Grid patrol and steal their jeep," said Xochi.

"I meant realistic options."

"We could probably get one of these other cars running," said Gianna, but Farad shook his head.

"They'll know the difference between a fleet vehicle and a salvage," he said. "With enough time and the right equipment, maybe, but we have to do this now if we want to stop Tovar from a frontal assault. He hasn't given us much leeway."

"We'll have to cross on foot," said Kira. "That's never been hard before—the border's too big to patrol the entire thing."

"East Meadow's never been under martial lockdown before," said Gianna. "We have informers on the inside, and we've scouted the perimeter. It's as tight as a drum."

Kira looked at the sky, guessing at the time of day—late afternoon. "We'll try to slip through in the dark. Does your radio pick up the Grid channels?"

"Of course," said Gianna, "just like their radios pick up ours. Anything important will be in code."

"And I don't know them all," said Farad.

"Then we'll have to make do," said Kira, standing up. "Let's find a weak spot in the border."

They struck south on what a battered street sign eventually identified as Walt Whitman Road. They passed a long shopping mall on one side, and a few hours later a deeply wooded park on the other. Once, across a wide parking lot, they saw a group of Grid soldiers investigating a tall, shattered-glass office building. The soldiers waved and shouted a greeting, the noise echoing emptily across the expanse, and Farad waved and shouted back. The soldiers turned and went back to their work. Kira kept a steady pace until they got out of view, then hurried the group along to put as much distance between them as she could. They saw more border patrols as they drew closer to the eastern edge of the city, security getting tighter and tighter, until finally they saw in the distance a road completely blocked by cars—more than just the detritus of eleven-year-old traffic, these cars had been hauled into place and braced with sheets of wood and metal. Kira shook her head, muttering lowly.

"They've barricaded the city."

CHAPTER THIRTY-SEVEN

"That's Gardiners Avenue," said Jayden. "We're very close." He paused. "How far do you think the wall goes around?"

"It doesn't make sense to build it here and nowhere else," said Gianna. "Otherwise they'd just build a fort and guard the intersection."

"Either way," said Xochi, "we can sneak past them mid-block somewhere. They can't have guards along the whole length of it."

The others agreed, and they picked their way through the overgrown yards of a sprawling residential neighborhood. They worked their way down to a spot halfway between cross streets, and when Kira peeked out through the kudzu-covered fence, she saw that the barricade was lower here—just cars in a line, with no reinforcing boards or boxes. *They haven't had time to finish the whole thing.* As if to balance it out, the far side of the street was not a row of houses but a strip mall with a wide parking lot—anyone watching from a post at either intersection would have that much more time to see them as they pelted across the extra open space.

"Curse this wretched island and its strip malls," said Kira. "Everything on this island is covered with trees—how can there be this much open ground?"

"There's some underbrush," said Xochi, "but probably not enough to hide us all the way across."

"Look down there," said Gianna, pointing south. "That next clump of soldiers is at least two blocks away. The gap between guards is actually pretty big—when it gets dark, we'll have a pretty good chance."

Kira looked south, then north again, gauging the distance. "Flip around the radio and see if you can find what channel that checkpoint is using."

Gianna started clicking the knob, *tic*, pause, *tic*, pause, *tic*, pause, searching for an active frequency. Each time she heard voices she stopped, listening for street names, and Kira felt a surge of relief when they heard a man mention Gardiners Avenue.

"That's us," said Kira, tapping her fingers on the wall. "Keep monitoring all three channels; we'll set a watch, lie low, and wait for dark." She peeked back through the fence, sizing up the distances to either guard post. *At night, if we stay down, they shouldn't see us at all.*

Each hour that passed, Kira felt her stomach twist further into knots. *What am I? Why am I here—and who put me here? Do I have* the pheromone? *Do I have something worse?* A hundred thousand questions swirled madly through her head, and she was desperate for answers. She forced herself to forget them, to think about the task at hand, but that was even worse. When she thought about Madison and Arwen, it was all she could do not to run straight to the hospital. She patted the wrapped syringe on her waist, and forced herself to be patient.

When darkness finally fell, Farad pulled more planks from the fence and pushed a small hole through the kudzu. They shouldered their gear, strapped it on tightly, and poised on the brink in a thin line: Farad, Xochi, Jayden, Gianna, Kira, and Marcus. Kira gripped her rifle and took a deep, slow breath.

"Keep the radio on," said Kira, "as quiet as you can make it. If the Grid sees us crossing, I want to know about it."

Gianna smiled thinly. "Already done."

"Then we go," said Kira. "Stay down, stay silent, but if they spot us just run for it."

Farad bounced loosely on the balls of his feet. "Ready . . . set-y . . . spaghetti." He dropped to his stomach and slipped out, pushing silently through the weeds toward the makeshift wall of cars. The others followed, trying not to rustle as they went. There were a few long seconds of desperate silence, and suddenly the radio burst into cries and shouts and static.

"There! There! South of Twenty-Three!"

A bullet slammed into the asphalt barely ten inches from Kira's hand.

"Stealth is over," she said. "Just run." They leaped to their feet and charged across the street, vaulting the wall of cars; Kira planted her right hand on a broad metal hood for leverage; it scalded her skin, still hot from a day in the sun, but she jumped up and tromped across it, two quick, clanging steps before leaping back down to the ground beyond. The radio was screaming alarms, and she heard warped, echoing gunfire—first over the radio, then in real life as the sharp reports finally reached her ears. Farad was across now, sprinting through the parking lot toward a gap in the strip mall buildings, when suddenly Gianna dropped like a stone, a puff of thick mist hanging in the air above her.

"No!" Kira screamed, following so close behind Gianna that she tripped over her body and crashed to the broken asphalt. She found her feet and tried to rise, turning to help Gianna, but Marcus grabbed her as he passed and pulled her to her feet, dragging her forward.

"Keep going!"

"We have to help her."

"She's dead, keep going!"

Kira wrenched her arm from his grip and turned back, hearing a bullet slam into the ground somewhere dangerously close. Gianna lay facedown in a puddle of blood. "Forgive me," Kira whispered, and grabbed not the girl but her radio. *This is too important to leave behind.*

Kira felt her body twist with an impact, but she kept her feet and ran again toward Marcus and the others. *Where was I hit?* She catalogued every limb as she ran, trying to identify the pain, but felt none. *Too much adrenaline,* said the scientist in her head, strangely calm and analytical. *You're going to bleed out and die without ever feeling the bullet.* She reached the shelter of the alley and ran on while Marcus cursed her wildly from behind.

"Are you trying to get killed?"

"Shut up and run," said Xochi, pulling them through a broken gate that listed sadly on one rusty hinge. The space beyond was a backyard, dense with weeds, and they fought through them to the shattered back door of a sagging house, the paint peeling off in long, faded strips. This close to the edge of the city the houses were still uninhabited, and they dropped to the floor in a skeleton's living room. Jayden turned back with his rifle to cover the door.

"I've been hit," Kira said, dropping the radio to pat herself, looking for blood. Farad snatched up the radio, thumbed the switch, and barked into it, "Checkpoint Twenty-Three, this is Patrol Forty. We're right here, but the Voice have not come through the houses. Repeat, they have not come through the houses. Do you have visual contact? Over."

"Negative, Forty," squawked the radio. "Still searching. Over."

"Understood, we'll keep searching as well. Over and out." He clicked off the radio and threw it back to her. "You risked your idiot life for that thing, we may as well use it."

"What's Patrol Forty?" asked Xochi.

"They're stationed on the north side," said Farad, "which is a different radio channel. That gives us maybe ten minutes before they figure it out. Now we've got to get out of this house before a real patrol comes chasing us in here."

Before he even finished whispering, they heard footsteps and voices in the yard behind them. Jayden grabbed his gun and ran to the back door, crouching behind the sagging wall.

"This is the Long Island Defense Grid," Jayden shouted, glancing back at the others and gesturing for them to pick up their guns. "You are ordered to drop your weapons and surrender immediately."

There was a small pause, and Jayden listened with his head

cocked. After a moment a voice shouted back, "Is that you, Patrol Forty?"

Jayden smiled wickedly. "Yes, it is. Is that Checkpoint Twenty-Three?"

Kira heard the men outside cursing. "Don't tell me we lost them!"

Farad pulled on his uniform cap and stepped carefully out of the back door. Kira watched through a tiny gap in the crumbling wall.

"We checked this whole area," he said. "They haven't come through."

"What do you mean they haven't come through?" asked the soldier. "We chased them right down this alley."

"I've got men in half of these houses," said Farad, gesturing around him, "and none of them have seen anything."

"How could you let them get past you?"

"Listen, soldier," said Farad, "you're the ones who let them get past the border—we're trying to clean up your mess here, not ours. Now spread out. We'll check these houses, you check those, and don't forget to leave someone here to guard this alley. The last thing we need is more of them crossing your checkpoint."

The other soldiers muttered a bit, and Kira heard them tromp away to the next house. She exhaled, then continued checking herself for a bullet hole. Finally finding it—in her backpack. She hadn't been hurt, but her equipment was destroyed.

Farad stepped back inside, whistling lowly in relief. "Let's get out of here."

"I can't believe that worked," said Xochi.

"It won't work for very long," said Jayden. "They're going to search Gianna eventually, and they're going to see she's wearing a Grid uniform. We've got about sixty seconds to disappear."

They worked their way to the front of the house and slipped from there into the next yard, then the next, moving deeper into East Meadow and as far from the infiltration site as they could. As they walked, the city became more populated, the houses better tended, and at last Kira saw the glint of window glass. *I'm home.* And yet even as the city looked familiar, it looked wrong; the houses were occupied, but the doors were all closed and the glassed-in windows were all curtained or even boarded up. On a nice summer night like this, even after sunset, the streets should be full of people talking, chatting, enjoying themselves, but now the few people who walked the streets did so quickly, eager to get back inside again, avoiding eye contact with everyone else. Groups of Grid soldiers and Mkele's special police patrolled the city at regular intervals, and Kira saw more than one of the scared, furtive citizens stopped and questioned in the streets. *They're looking for us,* she thought, *but they're punishing the wrong people.*

They reached the Turnpike and took shelter in a ruined storefront, looking across at the hospital that had practically become a fortress. There were guards on the doors, but more important there was a perimeter of guards all around the grounds. The rear door they'd been planning to use was probably still available, but without their Grid jeep they couldn't get to it safely, let alone get out again with Madison.

"This is going to be interesting," said Xochi.

"No kidding," said Jayden. Farad merely shook his head.

"Bad news," said Marcus, and motioned them over to the radio. They clustered around him, and Kira heard a staticky voice shouting an urgent warning: ". . . I repeat, the Voice has Defense Grid uniforms. They are already inside the city, and there may be more coming. Full identification checks are now mandatory for all encounters, code protocol Sigma." The message repeated, and Marcus shook his head. "This just keeps getting better and better."

"I don't know code protocol Sigma," said Farad, pacing nervously in the ruined building. "Some of it, maybe, but not enough. We won't get past anyone now."

Kira stared at the hospital, willing herself to find something, anything, that she could use to get in. *I'm a wanted criminal with a face well-known by every single person in that building. If I get in, it will be because I'm in chains.* She shook her head, forcing herself to think it through. *I am stronger than my trials,* she thought. *I can use my trials to help me; I can make them serve my own ends. Don't say, "I'll never do it," say, "How can I turn this situation in my favor?"* She studied the building more closely, counting the guards she could see, estimating the number of guards she couldn't, drawing a detailed mental picture of the inner hallways to guess where each soldier would be stationed. She counted the windows, determining the exact location of every good entrance point, and found to her dismay that each one had been blocked by cars or reinforced with sheets of metal and planks of wood. *It's too well defended. They've thought of everything—they've anticipated every plan we could use.*

She glanced up at the snipers on the roof, commanding a matchless view of the land around the hospital. *Partial or not, they could still shoot me down no matter how fast I try to run—*

She paused, her eyes caught by a gleam of light from a window. *That's the fourth floor—the only people who use that floor are the Senators. Are they meeting right now? Is there any way* that *could help me?*

"Even if we get in," said Jayden, "I don't know how we'd ever get out again—not with Madison. They barely let her out of her bed, they'd never let her out of the hospital, and we don't even have the jeep to hide her in."

"You are just a little ray of sunshine," said Marcus. He stood up. "This is fantastic—we can't get to the hospital, we can't get out, we probably can't even get out of East Meadow. Our uniforms don't even help us anymore—we have literally nothing."

"That's not true," said Kira, looking back at the hospital. There was definitely light on the fourth floor. "You have me."

"You'll excuse me for not jumping with joy," said Farad.

"See that light?" she asked, pointing at the lit upper windows. "That's the Senate, and you're going to bring them the one thing they want more than anything in the entire world: me."

"No, we're not," said Marcus hotly, echoed by all three of the others.

"Yes, you are," said Kira. "Our plan is destroyed, we can't get Madison out, but we can still give her the shot—if we can get inside. You don't need me to be there when you do it, and I was serious about giving my life for this. If Arwen lives, I don't care what the Senate does to me."

"We're not going to give you up," said Xochi.

"Yes, you will," said Kira. "You pull down your hat brims, march up to the door, and tell them you caught me trying to sneak across the border. It's the most believable story we could possibly come up with, because any soldier smart enough to be listening to his radio will know people have been hitting the border all day. They won't even ask for ID, because why would Voice spies turn in one of their own?"

"Good question," said Xochi. "Why would we? That doesn't gain us anything."

"It gets you inside the hospital," said Kira. "Just hand me off to the guards inside, they'll take me up to the Senate, and you head to maternity."

"We don't have to hand you off," said Marcus, "once we're in we could just . . . make a break for it."

"And set off every alarm in the building," said Kira. "If you turn me over, you can work in peace." She took Marcus's hand. "If this cure works, humanity has a future; that's the only thing we've ever wanted."

Marcus's voice cracked when he spoke. "I wanted it with you."

"They might not kill me outright," said Kira, smiling weakly. "Maybe we'll get lucky."

Marcus laughed, his eyes wet with tears. "Yeah, our luck's been awesome so far."

"We'll need to call ahead," said Farad, hefting the radio, "just like we did with the checkpoint. If they hear us before they see us, we stand a much better chance of making this work."

"We can't risk the same trick twice," said Jayden. "Someone who knows exactly how many patrols there are, and where they've been assigned, is going to be listening. It won't take long to figure out we're lying."

"We can't just show up without calling in first," said Farad.

"How suspicious would that look?"

Xochi drew her pistol, screwed on a silencer, and shot the radio squarely in the center; Kira and the others leaped back with a chorus of startled yelps. "Problem solved," said Xochi, holstering her weapon again. "The evil terrorist Kira Walker shot our radio during the fight. Now: Kira is my best friend in the world, but she's right. Her plan is the best, fastest way to get us inside that hospital, so take her weapons away and let's do this."

Kira pulled out her weapons and other gear, stripping herself of almost every piece of equipment she had; the men in the group eventually started helping, resigned to the fact that the decision had been made. Marcus wasn't happy about it, but he wasn't doing anything to stop it, either. The last piece of equipment was the syringe, wrapped tightly and padded with old shirts, tied firmly to an extra belt inside every other layer of clothing. She took it off, held it a moment, and handed it to Marcus.

"Take care of this," she whispered.

"I don't want you to do this."

"I don't either," she said, "but it has to be done."

Marcus stared into her eyes, saying nothing, then took the belt and tied it carefully under his shirt. He made sure his clothes covered it, then smeared his face with dirt, altering his complexion enough that the nurses at the hospital might not recognize him. *Might*. Jayden and Xochi did the same, and Kira hoped it would be enough. *I just have to make sure everyone is looking at me.*

CHAPTER THIRTY-EIGHT

Kira twisted and pulled, screaming as they carried her toward the first row of guards. "You have to let me go! I'm trying to help you, you idiots, can't you see that?" The time for stealth was long past: Her job now was to be as visible as possible so that no one looked closely at her friends. She ripped her arm loose from Farad's grip and attacked Jayden with it, trying to make it look as convincing as she could; he responded in kind by slugging her in the side of the head, then curling her arm behind her in a sudden choke hold that held her completely immobile. "Oof," she grunted, "nice one."

"Shut up, Voice." He dragged her around and cursed at Farad. "That's how you hold a prisoner, blowhole. Now don't let go again."

"I think you're breaking my arm," said Kira.

"Good," said Xochi, loud enough for the nearest group of soldiers to hear it. The group called out, but Xochi stepped up before they could say any more. "We caught her!" she said, waving the broken radio like a trophy. "Hurry, clear us a path to the Senate—I don't want any civilians getting close enough to try anything."

The sergeant of the other group hesitated. "Who do you have?"

"Kira Walker," said Xochi. "In the flesh—she was part of that group that tried to jump the border. See for yourself." She gestured to Kira, who stared back proudly.

"Holy crap," said the sergeant, coming closer and peering at her carefully. It wasn't anyone Kira knew, but he nodded. "That's definitely her." He paused a moment, then spit in her face. "My best friend was killed by the Voice, bitch."

Marcus stepped up quickly to stop him. "Stand down, soldier. This is a prisoner, not a dog."

"She attacked the hospital," said the soldier. "What are you defending her for?"

"We're taking her to the Senate," said Marcus. "They'll decide how to punish her, not us. Now you heard her—clear the way!"

The other squad glared at him angrily, and Kira held her breath, praying they didn't ask for identification. She kicked Jayden in the shin, trying to look as dangerous as she could, and he swore and twisted her arm again—painfully enough that she didn't have to fake her reaction. Apparently the show was enough.

"Let's get her up there, then," said the sergeant, and led them toward the hospital, clearing a path through the crowd of soldiers.

"We're getting into the real danger zone now," Jayden murmured. "I used to work with some of these guys."

"Me too," said Marcus, scanning the gathering crowd with

his gun at the ready. He nodded faintly to the left. "That one, for instance."

"Then we steer right," said Jayden, and angled just slightly away.

I need them to look at me, not my escort, thought Kira, and launched into another tirade. "The Senate is lying to you! They're the ones who brought the Partial here, and they told me to study it and I found a cure! I found a cure for RM, and the Senate tried to destroy it! Your children don't have to die!" It was working: More and more soldiers were watching her now, every eye fixed on her face. They were almost at the front doors. *Just a few more steps,* Kira thought, *just a few more.*

The soldier leading them stopped, staring at the door, then turned toward Kira. His eyes were dark and clear. "Do you really have a cure for RM?"

Kira paused in surprise, not knowing what to think. Was he just curious? Did he really care? The question seemed loaded with extra meanings, little hints and messages and signs she couldn't hope to interpret because she didn't know anything about the man giving them. Was he on her side? Did he support the Senate? She looked past him to the front lobby of the hospital, open and ready; all her friends had to do was get inside, turn right, and follow the hall. They could save Arwen. They could do it.

But the people have the real power, she thought, remembering her conversation with Torvar. *These are the people we're trying to reach, the people who will follow us or stay with the Senate. How many of them are like Jayden, like Farad, wanting to rebel and just needing that final push?*

Can I give them that push?

She turned back to the soldier and looked him straight in the eye. "Yes, I do," she said. "I have a cure for RM. But the Senate would rather kill me than let you have it."

"Give it to me," the soldier whispered, leaning in close. "I can use it—I can't save you, but I can use the cure and save the children."

Was he telling the truth? Was he bluffing? Was he trying to trick her? She couldn't give it to him without blowing Marcus's cover, and the entire group's, but what if she could—what then? Who in the crowd would attack her, and who would leap to her defense? Who would believe her, and would they believe her enough to let her into the maternity wing? It wasn't enough for the soldier to promise to help—she had to see it, right here, or she couldn't take the risk.

She whispered back, searching his eyes for some hint of understanding. "You can't be half a hero."

"ID challenge," said another soldier to the side. He took a step closer, and Kira's heart sank. "We're supposed to ask everybody, even soldiers, and you're not getting into this hospital unless I know exactly who you are."

The crowd of soldiers stood breathless, watching the exchange, straining to hear. In the background Kira could see soldiers gripping their weapons, shifting their weight, getting ready for a firefight. *I don't know who to trust,* she thought wildly. *If people start shooting, I don't know who to hide from, who to attack, I don't know anything. I don't even know what this soldier wants.* Jayden reached down with his free hand and undid the snap on his holster, freeing the pistol for an easy draw. The soldier in front of her did the same—

—and turned to the side, putting the ready pistol just inches from Kira's fingers.

"Hey, Woolf," he called, addressing the soldier who'd challenged them. "Do you have a pair of handcuffs? There are a lot of sympathizers in this crowd, and I want to make sure she's bound before we take her upstairs."

A lot of sympathizers, thought Kira, staring at the gun in front of her. *That might be a message for me—he's ignoring the ID challenge and offering me a gun. He has to be on our side. But what is he doing? If he's going to fight for us, why not just fight? What does he expect me to do?* The crowd of soldiers watched carefully, poised on the brink of whatever her decision would be. *Who's with us? What am I supposed to do?* She looked at the soldier in front of her, quickly running out of a good reason to be standing sideways. *He's giving me the choice,* she realized. *He's not fighting yet because he wants to know if I'm serious or not—if I'm really ready to die for this, or just full of hot air. Anything we start here is going to be bloody. A lot of us are going to die.*

He's waiting for me to make the first move.

"I said 'ID challenge,'" said the other soldier, stepping in closer. His rifle was ready in his hands; if he got too suspicious, he could kill them all in seconds. Kira made her decision and looked sharply to the left, past Farad and out into the crowd. The soldier followed her eye line, and she grabbed the waiting pistol in a single motion, pulling it around, flicking off the safety, and firing at the suspicious soldier's head. He dropped like a sack of fish, and she shouted at the top of her lungs.

"Fight for your future!"

The crowd erupted in screams. Kira ducked, and Marcus

452

pulled her heavily to the ground. "You're going to get shot up there!"

"I'm going to get shot everywhere!" she shouted, and turned back toward the hospital doors. The soldier who'd given her the pistol went down, and Kira quickly traced the path backward and shot the man who'd fired the bullet, firing twice. The ground before them began to clear, and Kira jumped up, dragging Marcus with her as she dashed ahead to the doors; Jayden and Xochi followed close behind. Almost as soon as they entered the building, Kira heard a burst of gunfire echoing down the corridor and dove to the floor behind a tall information desk.

"This is plywood," said Jayden. "It's not going to stop any bullets."

"And the crowd outside is not entirely in our favor," said Xochi. "I don't like lying on the floor in full view of a revolution. We need a strategy."

Jayden laughed grimly. "Press the attack and hope for the best."

"Hope is not a strategy," said Kira.

"It's not plan A," said Jayden, "and it shouldn't be plan B, but it is every plan C that has ever been made."

Kira nodded and took her shotgun back from Farad. "Then I'll cover you—somebody with an effective range take out those shooters." Before she had time to think better of it, Kira leaped to her feet and started firing down the hall, blast after blast from the shotgun. It was a long-barreled, single-shot weapon, useless in close quarters, but at medium range like this it laid down a devastating hail of buckshot that sent the loyalist soldiers ducking for cover. Jayden popped up beside her with his rifle, sighting carefully and taking quick, precise shots every time an enemy raised his head or stuck out his gun. Marcus and the others used the time to run ahead, staying well out of Kira's line of fire, and when her trigger clicked on an empty chamber, she called out to Xochi, who took up position in a doorway and continued the barrage on her own. Kira and Jayden ran forward to join the others, and Kira threw herself into the room next to Marcus.

"Are you okay?" she asked.

"Same old, same old," he said, clenching his teeth at the thundering booms that shook the walls and ceiling. "How about you?"

Kira nodded. "The cure's okay?" She felt for it on Marcus's waist, brushing his fingers briefly as he did the same. The syringe was intact and the padding was dry; nothing had broken or leaked out. She left her hand there for a moment longer, looking into Marcus's eyes.

"I'm sorry," she said softly. Xochi screamed defiantly behind them, ducking back to reload while Farad took up the fight.

"What, this?" asked Marcus, gesturing around. "Don't worry about it—happens all the time."

"You wanted to live in peace," said Kira, loading fresh shells into her shotgun. "That's all you've ever wanted, just the two of us together, and I wanted it too, but I—"

"I know," said Marcus, all joking gone from his voice. "I wanted everything to stay the same, but you wanted things to be better. And you were right, and it's going to be better, it's just . . . going to be a whole lot worse for a while first. And I think I knew that, and I was scared of it."

Farad grunted behind them, not a scream but a soft, guttural moan, and his body fell to the ground. Xochi cried out, and Kira turned pale at the sight, dragging him back out of the line of fire. Marcus felt his neck for a pulse, bending close to listen for breathing, but there was too much blood—there was no way he was still alive. Marcus shook his head, confirming her fears. "He's gone."

"What now?" asked Jayden. The hallways was eerily quiet now that no one was shooting, though faint sounds drifted in from the distance: muted screams and pops of gunfire from the outer grounds; wails of patients trapped and helpless in the hospital; desperate screams of tiny infants, burning alive as the fever ate their bodies. The four friends crouched in the room, trembling and terrified. Kira looked through the door, but all she could see were a few narrow feet of the opposite wall. Not knowing what was out there made her feel blind and deaf. Jayden reloaded his gun quickly and efficiently, though Kira could see his fingers shaking with fatigue and adrenaline. "One more on our list of failed plans," he said. "We couldn't sneak in, we're sure as hell not sneaking back out again, and there's no point dragging you up to the Senate. Straight to maternity?"

"Straight to maternity," said Marcus. He grimaced, shaking his head. "Kira was ready to die so that we could give Arwen the shot; I think we should be ready to die for it, too. It's only two more doors down—if we can get in and inject her, even if we never get back out, we've won. The baby will be saved, and thanks to our display outside, everyone will know who did it."

Xochi took a breath. "You think we're going to make it?"

"Only one of us has to," said Jayden.

Marcus stood up, undoing his shirt and removing the belt

with the cure. He looked at Kira, then picked up his rifle. "If only one of us lives through this, I'd kind of prefer it to be you. Are we ready for this?"

"No," said Xochi, "but that's never stopped us before." She grabbed a rolling chair and waited just inside the door, looking back. Kira and the others checked their weapons and nodded, and Xochi pushed the chair out into the hallway.

A burst of gunfire filled the hall, and the four friends leaped out after it, firing wildly at the surprised gunmen who were aiming at the wrong moving object. Xochi led the way, stumbling as a round took her in the arm, but she was already to the maternity room and slammed into the door; it didn't budge, so she stepped back, shot the lock, and fell through as the door swung open. Marcus followed more slowly, either aiming very poorly or missing on purpose, trying not to kill the enemy soldiers but to scare them into cover. It seemed to be working, and Kira and Jayden did their best to keep up a steady barrage as they jogged forward. Suddenly Xochi screamed, and Kira heard a gunshot. Marcus sprinted through the maternity door a moment later and Kira heard more shots, and then suddenly she was down, a sharp pain in her leg like nothing she'd ever experienced.

"Get up," growled Jayden, firing wild bursts into the end of the hall. "I'm almost out—I can't keep them down forever."

Kira struggled to stand, but her leg felt limp and useless; blood soaked her pant leg and pooled around her on the floor. "I've been shot."

"I know you've been shot, just get out of the hallway!"

Kira lunged forward, crawling on her hands, dragging her leg behind her. The pain was growing now, and she could feel her own consciousness fading as her blood pumped eagerly onto the floor. Jayden cursed and fired more carefully, saving his shots, trying to keep the soldiers at bay one bullet at a time. Kira pulled the cure from her shoulder and held it up.

"Take it and run," she said. "Leave me here and save Arwen."

"You know, Kira," said Jayden, firing his last bullet and throwing down the rifle, "I don't think you know me very well at all." He stooped, grabbed her by the shoulder and waist, and heaved her up to her feet, surging backward toward the maternity door, keeping himself between Kira and the enemy. The soldiers fired, and Kira felt his body shake with one impact, then another; his breathing grew ragged, his pace slowed, but he never stopped. Kira clung to him, calling his name desperately as he groaned and cursed and wheezed. At last he tumbled sideways into the maternity door, and they collapsed to the floor.

"Jayden!" screamed a voice. Kira turned to see Madison crouching protectively over an intensive care incubator, and her heart sank. *She's already born. Are we too late?*

Beside her was Haru, wild-eyed and disheveled, clutching a gun. He aimed it at Kira. "Drop your weapons."

"Jayden!" Madison screamed again and tried to rush forward, but Haru stopped her with an iron grip on her arm.

"Stay here."

"He's hurt!"

"I said stay here!" Haru's voice was like thunder, and Madison pulled back in fear. "We are not letting them near our baby."

"Jayden," Kira whispered, "stay with me." She looked around quickly, seeing Xochi and Marcus both standing straight against the wall, their guns on the floor and their arms in the air. Marcus moved to help her, but Haru roared at him to stop.

"Do not move!"

"My brother's dying!" screamed Madison. "Let them help him!"

Kira struggled to sit up, careless of her own wound, and carefully examined Jayden's back; he'd been hit by multiple rounds. A moment later Marcus joined her, carefully removing Jayden's backpack to see how much damage had been done. Kira didn't see if Haru had let him move, or if he'd just come anyway.

The soldiers from the hall were in the doorway now, guns trained on them.

"She . . . ," said Jayden, though his voice was almost too quiet to hear, "has . . . the cure."

"What did he say?" asked Madison.

"He said idiot Voice lies," said Haru. "Don't even listen to him."

"He said I have the cure," said Kira. She turned painfully, dragging her bloody leg. Was it just her imagination, or was the wound already starting to heal? She clutched the cure in her hand and held it up. "It's right here."

"You're not getting anywhere near my daughter," said Haru.

"I'm going to save her," she said again, grabbing the wall and pulling herself, inch by agonizing inch, to her feet. She rested her weight on her good leg and tried to ignore the other, willing herself to stand through sheer mental force. "I have sacrificed everything I had, and everything I am, to save your daughter. Are you really going to be the one to stop me?"

"You're a Partial agent," said Haru. "You're in league with them—God only knows what you're trying to do to my daughter, but I will die before I let you do it."

"I'm fine with that plan," said Xochi.

"He's dead," announced Marcus, falling back from Jayden's body. He looked up at Haru, gasping for breath and reeling from exhaustion. "He died for this, Haru. Don't do this."

Madison wailed in despair, and the child in the crib wailed with her, an incoherent cry against a world that brought nothing but pain. Kira stared at Haru fiercely. "You have to let me try."

"Try?" asked Haru. "You mean you're not even sure?"

Kira paled, thinking of all the ways she could be wrong, all the ways the injection could fail. *What if I've done all this for nothing? What if I've killed my friends and destroyed my world for nothing more than a sloppy experiment and some bad guesses and my own stubborn pride? The Senate warned me about this: They said I was risking thousands of lives and the future of the human race for one overriding obsession. Is it because I'm a Partial, driven to destroy everything just because that's how I'm made? Thanks to me, the entire nation is in chaos, thousands are dead, and without a cure, we may never recover. Without a cure, it won't even matter.*

But with a cure . . .

"I don't have any data for you," she said. "I don't have any facts, my studies were all lost when the lab exploded, and the cure itself has never been tested. I don't have anything that can prove to you that what I'm doing is right. But Madison," she said, looking her adopted sister straight in the eye, "if there is one thing you know about me, one thing at all, it's that I always try to do the right thing. And no matter how painful this has been, no matter how much hell we've been through and how many of us have died, this is the right thing to do."

"Shut up!" screamed Haru, shoving the pistol forward. Kira ignored him, keeping her eyes on Madison's.

"Madison," she said again, "do you trust me?"

Slowly, tearfully, Madison nodded. Kira held up the cure, still wrapped on the belt, and Madison stepped forward.

"Madison, stay back," growled Haru. "I am not letting you give our baby to that traitor."

"Then shoot me," said Madison fiercely. She planted herself squarely between Haru and the incubator; his hand quivered, faltered, and dropped to his side.

Kira collapsed to the floor, and Marcus ran to the cupboards on the wall to find a needle for the syringe. The soldiers in the doorway didn't move, watching the whole thing with their guns pointed at the floor. Xochi helped Kira to her feet and took her to the incubator; Kira could feel the heat from the tiny body's fever like a pit of dying coals. Marcus handed her a needle and swabbed the child's arm with disinfectant.

Kira prepped the injection, hesitating over the red, screaming body. Right now the Blob virus was roaring through her like a pack of wild dogs, ripping and tearing, eating her from the inside. This syringe, this pheromone, would save her.

Kira leaned forward. "Hold her still."

Madison held the baby close, Marcus and Xochi stopped moving, even Haru fell silent in the background. The entire world seemed focused on this single moment. Arwen's thin, hoarse crying filled the room like smoke, the final, desperate sparking of an engine about to fail. Kira breathed, steadied her arm, and gave the baby the shot.

CHAPTER THIRTY-NINE

"**W**e have discovered a cure for RM."

Cheers rang through the coliseum, applause and shouts and cries of joy. It wasn't news—something so world-shaking could hardly be contained, and the news of Arwen's recovery had spread like wildfire—but still the people cheered. Senator Hobb smiled at the crowd, his giant holographic head mimicking the expression in the air above him. Kira sat neatly on the stand behind him, crying again and wondering, as she had a thousand times in the last week, if it was all really true. If it was all really happening. She caught Marcus's smile from the audience, and smiled back. It was real.

Hobb raised his hands to call for order, smiling indulgently as the crowd continued to celebrate; they wanted their chance to cheer, and he seemed happy to give it to them. Kira marveled at the man's capacity for change—not two weeks ago he was helping to turn the island into a totalitarian state, and it had collapsed catastrophically around him, and yet here he stood, smiling and clapping. Kessler had managed to maintain her seat as well, and Kira stole a glance at her on the other end of the stand. The other members of the subcommittee had not been so lucky.

Hobb quieted the crowd again, and this time they followed, growing hushed as Hobb prepared to speak. "We have found a cure for RM," he said again. "We found it, of all places, in the Partials—in a chemical they excrete in their breath, which reacts with the virus to nullify it completely. We learned this thanks to a series of tests performed by our local hero, Ms. Kira Walker, under the supervision of the Senate." Scattered applause filled the hall, and Hobb waited patiently for it to die down. "These tests were performed, as the rumor mill has already told you, on a live Partial subject obtained as part of a secret mission by members of the Defense Grid. We admit, shamefaced but honest, that we were not as open with you about these tests as perhaps we should have been. We feared a violent riot, and in the end that is exactly what we got. Rest assured that in the future the Senate will be much more transparent about our goals, our plans, and our methods for carrying them out."

Kira blew out a long, nervous breath, watching the crowd for signs of unrest. Everything Hobb was saying was, technically, true, but the way he said it felt so . . . greasy, at least to Kira. He admitted just enough to seem repentant, while taking credit for much more of the process than the Senate had truly been a part of. The crowd wasn't cheering him, but they weren't booing him either.

"Arwen Sato is doing fine," said Hobb, "more fit and healthy than we had dared to hope. We didn't want to risk taking her from the hospital, where she is under the strictest care of both the doctors and her mother, but we did record this holo so that you could all see her."

Hobb sat down, and the holo-image in the center of the coliseum changed from a close-up of his head to a scene from the maternity center; Kira, even knowing exactly what the movie was, couldn't stop herself from crying as Saladin, the youngest human alive, stood beside the red-faced baby in the hospital crib to whom he was passing the honor. The sight of the child sent a gasp of awe through the audience, and Kira let herself get drawn up in it: the first human baby in eleven years that wasn't sick, wasn't screaming, wasn't dying or dead.

The holo stopped and Hobb stood up, his eyes brimming with tears. "Arwen Sato is the future," he said, echoing Kira's thoughts. "That child, that precious little girl, is the first of a new generation—the inheritors of a world that will, we hope, be better than the one we have known for the last eleven years. Our scientists are working around the clock to replicate the compounds that saved Arwen's life, so that we can begin applying them to other children, but that is not enough. If we want a brighter tomorrow, we must tear down the shadows of yesterday. That is why I am pleased to announce that the Hope Act is now and forever officially repealed."

The audience cheered again, though not as unanimously. Many of the people in East Meadow still supported the Hope Act, saying that the existence of a real cure only made it more important to have as many children as possible, but the Senate had chosen to repeal it as a peace offering to the Voice. The same peace offering had included the resignations of Alma Delarosa and Oliver Weist; between them they had managed to soak up most of the blame for the city's rapid dip into martial law. Skousen had also left, not in ignominy but to focus his time on replicating the cure. In their place the people had elected Owen Tovar, newly pardoned of his crimes with the Voice. The new Senate was a combination of East Meadow and Voice, both their ideas and their ways of thinking, and the island was finally at peace again. At least in theory. Kira looked down the row of Senators on the dais, seeing gaps and holes as each one sat closer or farther from their neighbors; this one avoided that one's eyes, and that one whispered conspiratorially in the ear of the next. The crowd in the coliseum mirrored this behavior on a larger scale: they were united, but there were still deep rifts running just below the surface.

"We have not yet decided a course of action," said Hobb, his voice rich with earnest sincerity. "Our medics and researchers are working to unlock the secrets of the cure, and once they do we will begin synthesizing more. This is our plan for the time being, but should things change, rest assured that your votes will decide what steps we take next. Our society will work together, or not at all.

"But there is one thing more." He paused, a purely theatrical moment that Kira saw worked marvelously well: The crowd hushed and leaned forward. Hobb raised his finger, tapping it gently in the air, and finally resumed his speech. "There is one thing more that we discovered in our experimentation on the Partial. Something that will change the course of our lives, and of the entire world." He took a breath. "The Partials are dying, rapidly, and there's nothing they or anyone else can do to stop it.

In a year, our greatest enemy will be gone forever."

The cheer that rose from the crowd shook the coliseum to its core.

"We can't synthesize it," said Kira. Marcus had walked her home after the town hall meeting, and they were sitting in her living room. Kira knew the truth, and it burned inside her like a white-hot coal: The cure, the Lurker, could not be replicated artificially, and her own private tests had shown that she did not produce it. If she was truly a Partial, as Dr. Morgan and the others had claimed, her purpose and her origins remained a mystery she could only guess at.

She prayed it was not sinister.

"We can't make it, we can't fake it, we simply don't have the tools," she continued. "I'm not even sure the tools exist—maybe ParaGen had something, and whoever made the virus in the first place, but they're gone now. The only way to get it is from the Partials themselves."

"Isolde says the Senate is preparing for the possibility of an attack on the mainland," said Marcus.

Kira nodded. "A contingency plan." She was the island's expert on the subject and consulted with the Senate often, but she worked more closely with Skousen; she knew they were planning something, but she didn't know the details. "Did Isolde say anything about a timeline?"

"A few months, maybe." Marcus shrugged helplessly. "It was one thing to watch the newborns die before, but now that there's a cure . . . Three more have died since we saved Arwen, and the women Tovar injected with the other two doses haven't given birth yet. We don't know what's going to happen, but regardless, the people aren't going to sit still once things go back to the way they were. And now that they know the Partials are dying, it's only a matter of time before they start calling for a new plan. There are proposals for peace talks and envoys, too, not just war, but with the state of things we saw over there . . ." He shook his head. "Any ambassadors we send are as likely to get shot as deliver a treaty."

"Just like what we did to them." She frowned. "Maybe." She still wasn't sure what to think about Samm—had he been lying the whole time? Was peace with the Partials even possible?

"Kira," said Marcus, and instantly she heard the change in his voice: a deep breath, a softer pitch, a searching tone that filled her name with a deep and portentous meaning. She knew exactly what he was going to say, and she cut him off as gently as she could.

"I can't stay with you."

Even as she said it, she saw Marcus deflate—first his eyes, the brightness bleeding out of them, his head hung low. His face fell, his shoulders drooped.

"Why?" he asked.

Not "why not," thought Kira, but "why." It's such a different question. It means he knows I have another reason—not something pushing me away from him, but something pulling me toward something else.

"Because I need to go away," said Kira. "I need to find something."

"You mean someone." His voice was rough, tears close to the surface. "You mean Samm."

"Yes," said Kira, "but not like . . . it's not what you think."

"You're trying to stop a war." He said it simply, a statement rather than a question, but Kira could sense the same question underneath it: *Why?* Why was she leaving him? Why wasn't she asking him to go? Why did she need Samm when he was right here? He didn't ask, though, and Kira wouldn't have been able to answer him anyway.

Because I'm a Partial. Because I'm a question. Because my entire life, the entire world, is so much bigger than it was a few months ago, and none of it makes sense, and everything in it is dangerous, and somehow I'm at the center of it. Because groups I didn't even know existed are using me for plans I can't possibly comprehend. Because I need to know what I am.

And who.

"Now it was her turn to cry, her voice cracking, her eyes growing wet. "I love you, Marcus, I do, and I always have, but I—I can't tell you this. Not yet."

"When?"

"Maybe soon. Maybe never. I don't even know what it is I can't tell you, I just . . . just trust me, Marcus, okay?"

He glanced at her bag, packed and ready by the inside of her door. "Are you leaving today?"

"Yes."

"Now?"

She hesitated. "Yes."

"I'll come with you," he said. "There's nothing keeping me here."

"You can't come with me," said Kira adamantly. "I need you to stay here." *I'm not ready for you to learn the things I want to learn about myself. I'm not ready for you to know what I am.*

"Fine, then," said Marcus. His words were short and clipped, trading sadness for anger and only barely concealing either. He stood slowly, walked to the door, opened it. Waited.

"Thank you," said Kira. "For everything."

"Good-bye," said Marcus.

Kira blinked back a tear. "I love you."

Marcus turned and walked away. Kira watched the empty doorway long after he was gone.

Nandita had never returned, and the house was cold and empty. Kira assembled her things: her bag of clothes, a bedroll and camping supplies, a new medkit; a rifle over her shoulder, and a semiautomatic at her hip. She looked around her house one final time, straightening the sheets on the bed, and her eye caught the gleam of a reflection on the nightstand. A framed photo. Kira frowned and walked toward it. *That's not mine.*

It was a photo of three people, standing in front of a building. It was upside down, and she turned it around slowly.

She gasped.

Standing in the middle was her, as a child, barely four years old. On her right was her father, exactly how he looked in her memory. On her left was Nandita. Behind them, on the high brick wall of the building, was a single word.

ParaGen.

In the corner of the photo someone had written a small message, the letters jagged, the handwriting hurried and desperate:

Find the Trust.

ACKNOWLEDGMENTS

The book you hold in your hands represents the collaborative effort of a great many people, in whose company I count myself lucky to be. First and foremost is my editor, Jordan Brown, who did so much, and with so much passion, that we should really be listing him as a full collaborating creator. Similar credit goes to Ruta Rimas, who contributed so much to the creation of the book and our early, formative ideas for it. She switched publishers halfway through, moving on to new projects, but her psychic fingerprints can still be seen on every page of the book.

Many friends and readers provided their own insight to the manuscript, including such personal luminaries as Steve Diamond, Ben Olsen, Danielle Olsen, Peter Ahlstrom, Karen Ahlstrom, Ethan Skarstedt, Alan Layton, Kaylynn Zobell, Brandon Sanderson, Emily Sanderson, and my brother Rob Wells. I'd further like to thank some of the artists whose work had an influence on this particular book, with special gratitude to Ursula K. Le Guin, Ronald Moore, Kevin Siembieda, and Muse.

This novel was greatly helped by the readers of my website, www.fearfulsymmetry.net, who helped name some of the key groups and concepts in the *Partials* world. The Hope Act was named by my wife, the Break came from Eric James Stone, and the Voice came from Michele Chiapetta. Thanks to them and to everyone else who gave us such amazing input; it was a fun crowdsource project and we'll definitely be doing it again.

As always, and perhaps most importantly, I couldn't have written this book, and certainly couldn't have done a very good job on it, without the invaluable assistance of the three women who make my life navigable: my agent Sara Crowe, my assistant Janella Willis, and my wonderful wife and the love of my life, Dawn.

As a final note, many thanks to Nick Dianatkhah, who is always on hand to die in whatever surprising and horrifying way a story may require.